Praise for *Nicholas F*

'A book of mythological po
all those great pieces of fiction that are fed by our immemorial
root system, the human dream of metamorphosis.'
Hélène Cixous

'It is quiet, lapidary, and teases out the tangled filaments
that link figuration to fact and insight to feeling with
the unnerving stealth of a submarine predator.'
Will Self

'An intense study of grief and mental disintegration, a lexical
celebration and a psychological conundrum... Royle explores
loss and alienation perceptively and inventively.'
The Guardian

'Royle's baroque, athletic prose... confers a strong sense of the
"strangeness" of English, "which, after all, belongs to no one"
and should be continually reinvented... Moments of delightfully
eccentric humour and impressive linguistic experimentalism.'
The Observer

'A work of remarkable imaginative energy.'
Frank Kermode

'It is in those commonplace moments at the end of a life...
moments which Nicholas Royle describes with such piercing
accuracy, when this novel is truly at its strangest.'
Times Literary Supplement

'What deceptively begins as a more or less realistic piece
of autobiographical fiction evolves into an astonishing
narrative that puts into question the very notion of
everyday reality. A highly readable and stunningly
original experiment in literary form.'
Leo Bersani

AN ENGLISH GUIDE TO
BIRDWATCHING

An English Guide to Birdwatching

Nicholas Royle

myriad m∞

First published in 2017 by

Myriad Editions
www.myriadeditions.com

First printing
1 3 5 7 9 10 8 6 4 2

A CIP catalogue record for this book
is available from the British Library

ISBN (pbk): 978-1-908434-94-4
ISBN (ebk): 978-1-908434-95-1

Illustrations © Natalia Gasson

Designed and typeset in Palatino
by WatchWord Editorial Services, London

Printed and bound in Great Britain
by Clays Ltd, St Ives plc

Multas per gentes et multa per aequora vectus

In loving memory of
Simon Royle (1960–86)
painter and bird-lover

Happier of happy though I be, like them
I cannot take possession of the sky,
Mount with a thoughtless impulse and wheel there
One of a mighty multitude, whose way
And motion is a harmony and dance
Magnificent. Behold them, how they shape
Orb after orb their course still round and round
Above the area of the Lake, their own
Adopted region, girding it about
In wanton repetition, yet therewith
With that large circle evermore renewed:
Hundreds of curves and circlets high and low,
Backwards and forwards, progress intricate,
As if one spirit was in all and swayed
Their indefatigable flight. 'Tis done,
Ten times or more I fancied it had ceased,
And lo! the vanished company again
Ascending – list again! I hear their wings
Faint, faint at first, and then an eager sound
Passed in a moment – and as faint again!
They tempt the sun to sport among their plumes;
They tempt the water and the gleaming ice
To show them a fair image. 'Tis themselves,
Their own fair forms upon the glimmering plain,
Painted more soft and fair as they descend,
Almost to touch, – then up again aloft,
Up with a sally and a flash of speed,
As if they scorned both resting-place and rest.

William Wordsworth, *Home at Grasmere*

PART ONE

The Undertaking

Woodlock & Sons

Silas Woodlock was the end of the line, so far as he was concerned. There would be Ashley, of course, but then that was it. The entire tradition since 1869: *kaput*. Not that the same building had been home all that time. Still, the sense of history was there. Order, continuity, passing on the baton: one generation to the next. Now it was over. Enough was enough. Things had taken their toll, especially after the scare with Ethel last winter.

If you could call it winter. Primroses popping up in November, spring warmth at Christmas. Catch it in the corner of people's eyes. Day after day *unseasonably mild*, as the forecasters liked to say. Imagine the fellow on the weather coming clean: Good evening, once again it was a worryingly unnatural sort of a day, nothing any of us are used to, a day out of sorts with the days we used to think of as days. *Daze and confuse*, ha-ha. Day after day clement without clemency. Try that. Followed by downpours and flash floods, then bitter weeks of ice and snow, then plunged again into days too mild to be remotely realistic.

Sunday family roast back in the day, coal fire flickering, windows foggy with condensation, clip round the ear if they caught you finger-writing. Dad at the head of the table and Mum bringing in the dishes one by one, steaming hot, and everyone settled and the rest, even the cat and dog, appreciating the order of ceremony. Then the moment impatience became acceptable, the mutt's eye-whites under the table, the plaintive, semi-smothered yelping for a bone, and pussy in the well's tortoiseshell arched back and as-if-electrocuted tail curling stiffly through the blind spinney of human legs. And after saying the grace, which never failed to happen at that repast, his old man very formal, as if he had never enunciated the words before, asked would someone be so kind as to supply the seasoning. And Silas and his sisters never thought to wonder what the seasoning was, only something they had to pass down the table for the father to shake out over his roast lamb and veg. It was the old man's own special mix their mother wouldn't have touched with a bargepole: salt and black pepper, rosemary and thyme, and other stuff that got stuck in your teeth. Always had to have it with his roast. But Silas couldn't see what seasons had to do with it, until the last year of school when they studied Shakespeare and Lady Macbeth says to her husband: *You lack the season of all natures, sleep.*

He could imagine that on his headstone, as a matter of fact. Not that he'd have Ash or Ethel know. But he could picture it, quite poetical, better in the last resort than a line of Latin, fond as he was of that dead tongue. Did Macbeth have the first clue what his worse half was saying? You need some shut-eye is what you need, darlin'. The drift was obvious enough. *You lack the season of all natures.* Did it matter that no spouse in real life ever uttered such words to their soul-mate? The important thing was that it sounded simple and said more than you could easily ponder. The important thing, he remembered his English teacher saying, was that Shakespeare might have meant *season* in the sense of a period of time or he might have meant *season* in the sense of salt or spice and the rest, but it didn't matter what he meant because we were never going to find out, and in the meantime there was life to live and this magnificent line: *You lack the season of all natures, sleep.*

Fit for a headstone possibly, but a bit screwball, Silas eventually conceded. Like a message from the dead to everyone still living. A blanket statement to the effect that everyone is suffering from sleep-deprivation. Or as if sleep were the name of a person, as if it were an inscription addressing Sleep itself. As if Sleep lacked all due season. Sleep, you're out on a limb, mate, you've lost all sense and reason. Or then again the statement could be referencing the one who had passed on, inverting the soporific stereotype, called away, at the end of the day, exquisite corpse, the ultimate night-night, gone to sleep and the rest, no, you in the ground there, you lack the season, it's so far past your bedtime you're never going to sleep again, this is it, from now on in, sleep no more, no more shut-eye forever.

In any case it was over, pass the seasoning, seasons passed on, farewell Vivaldi, seasons no more. And Ethel being rushed into hospital was the wake-up call. He never quite put it like that to her. He never needed to. It was a wake-up call for them both. They would hand on the business to Ashley and get out of town, retire while the going was good or at any rate still had legs, move out of the giant rats' nest of London down to the sea. Of course, when they'd been growing up, him and June and Pat, Croydon hadn't been London at all. Now it was all joined up, crept house to house, street by street, a couple of fields here, a patch of woodland there, overrun, mile after mile filled in with what were a bit sinisterly called *developments*: retail and industrial parks, car parks, underpasses, flyovers and high-rise sprawl.

It wasn't that business was bad. Indeed they had done rather well, despite all the change and new competition. Such as the *Lady Funeral Director*. That was funny. He and Ethel wondered initially was it just for hoity-toity women or what? And then there was the expansion of the black community and other ethnic groups, and different religions coming into the picture. Bespoke parlours of different sorts sprang up. But Woodlock & Sons, convenient in proximity to the register office on Mint Walk, was not like the others. They prided themselves on not having departed from the original family name in all these years. It was still Woodlocks, father and son, on hand to serve all, assisting the bereaved since 1869. As the executive director of another *bona fide* local family company was on record for remarking: *Some large corporations in the '90s purchased many family funeral businesses, maintaining the family name, thus deceiving the general public.* Woodlock & Sons was not like that. It was in the old tradition: International Order of the Golden Rule and the rest.

But no longer. Ashley would keep the business on, of course, but the family-run nature of the thing was coming to an end. Such transformation in so few years! A couple of decades previously, no funeral director in the land had a computer, let alone a website and databases and laser-printers and all the other paraphernalia. With the increased pressure to provide *specialism* services, from high church to secular, from horse-drawn carriages which the Woodlocks gave up in the early '80s to the 4x4 and motorcycle events, from gangland to eco-friendly, what a commotion it had all come to seem, what a palaver in the parlour and parlous state of things. Especially with Ethel having had that scare. Rushed into the Mayday or whatever they call it these days, the Croydon University Hospital, and there she was, on the brink, seven days and nights, what with pneumonia and life-support and the rest. The longest week of his life, not to mention hers. Flaming terrible it was, she said, you won't see me in a hospital again. So they set up a trust arrangement and handed the business over to Ash, lock stock and casket (as his old man used to say), and with the monies released bought not a stately home exactly but a decent little property nevertheless, down in Seaford, East Sussex, in the heart of the old town.

Silas and Ethel had been visiting this stretch of the coast for years, mostly on occasional days out, and once not so long ago for three nights in a local bed and breakfast. They'd developed a soft spot for the town. Compared to its larger neighbours on either side, Brighton and Eastbourne, Seaford was tacky, old-fashioned and unpretentious. It had nothing, besides the elements, that you could call grand. Neither of them had ever lived by the sea and this was a remarkably quiet spot, all things considered. There was a long but walkable esplanade and a shingle beach stretching for a couple of miles in one direction to the port of Newhaven, then trailing off in the other to a golf course and impressive white cliffs. The main row of shops could have come straight out of the '70s. You could easily get fooled with thinking *was that* Keith Richards coming out of Bob's Retro Market, or just an eerie lookalike? The high street had the aura of being stuck in time, placidly indifferent, still in black and white. A couple of the bigger chains had wormed their way in but, by and large, the usual suspects had evidently deemed Seaford just not worth the candle.

Woodlock was drawn, too, by his fondness for second-hand books and vinyl records. The little town had a bustling trade in charity shops, bric-a-brac and antiques, junkshops and old bookshops. It was a great place to spend a few hours, stop for a cup of tea and slice of cake in one of the numerous cafés, mooch about the shops on Broad Street, have lunch at the Old Boot or the Old Plough, the Cinque Ports or the Wellington, then a stroll along the seafront, before heading back to the Great Rats' Nest.

As the exchange date drew closer, the reality of the thing became almost too much. Ethel fretted:

— What about Ash? Do you think he'll be alright?

— Of course he'll be alright. He won't be all on his tod, after all, there'll be Jim and the other lads.

— Oh, yes, Ethel vaguely said, Jim.

Their son remained something of a conundrum. He seemed entirely uninterested in getting married or having children of his own. They never aired the matter, but Ethel did wonder if Ash was not of the other persuasion and yet to realise. He was close to Jim. They'd known each other since they were toddlers. Jim had joined them as a pallbearer before he was even out of school. Ethel had her suspicions about Ash and Jim. Not unpleasant suspicions: it can be hard, after all, being a mother and having your only son leave you for another woman. Not that this was much of a topic of talk in the public arena, it seemed to her, but one good reason in her books, why, as a doting mother, your son being gay had its attractions. And Jim was such a nice fellow, not the sharpest knife in the drawer, big but gentle, a bit mentally AWOL at times but flaming heck and pyjamas, who wasn't, these days? In any case, when it came to working, he was always reliable and courteous.

Of course it's difficult to be in the funeral parlour game without something to lean on, whether God or drugs or the bottle, and she had more than once caught the whiff of marijuana as they came in on a Saturday after a match (Ash and Jim were ardent Palace supporters) or a night out down at the Green Dragon. But, whatever they got up to, it never interfered with work, and that was good enough for Ethel. She and Silas also liked a drink, it was true. Time was when Silas could really put it away (but not these days). Whereas she would down a couple of glasses of wine and know when she was squiffy and stop. Wouldn't want to forgo it though. Stem of a glass of cold chardonnay in your hand at the end of the day – few things nicer. In any case, no harm in a pallbearer being pale in the chops and dreamy if that was what it was, in their line of business, from going a bit heavy the previous night. No one ever raised any eyebrows on the subject. Different world from when she and Silas were growing up. Not that she especially liked to imagine her son naked with another fellow. The thrusting and groaning and expletives and everything. Best to let things take their course. So long as they were clean, tidying up properly after themselves. Frankly it was a boon not to know. Even worse, most probably, in the case of another woman.

That was the problem with the world these days. Transparency and accountability, recording and confessing everything. Whatever happened to privacy in all its common decency? The way people share their thoughts and feelings without batting an eyelid with anyone who cares to listen or sign up to their whatever they call it, Instagram, Facebook, Twitter, their screensaving social life. Bad enough the amount of paperwork running a family business, doing everything on a screen enough to make you lose your eyesight. And then managing the website. Manage this, manage that. Everyone's managing. Not. Mostly she left the website to

Ash. Not to mention the way everyone was being spied on left, right and centre, every message sent or received, interrupted, intercepted, interception management. What was it all coming to? Somewhere or other down the line, most probably, we're all on the wrong bus. If her son liked to snog Jim Phillips, far be it from her.

But then one Friday evening, just a month before the exchange date, Ashley came in through the front door of the flat with a pretty young girl. He didn't seem remotely shy or embarrassed.

— Mum, this is Rhoda, he announced, grinning broadly. I said it would be alright for her to come up.

It was quiet in the Woodlocks' living room, besides the tip-top, tip-top of the old clock on the mantelpiece. Ethel had thought of it as *tip-top* ever since her husband once uttered the phrase, a half-tipsy semi-slur that somehow seemed right. Silas disliked television, its tyrannical chewing-gum-for-the-eyes, its endlessly complacent glow. He could tolerate only the news and weather, and even then was inclined to keep up a hostile commentary. She only got to watch when he was out for one of his walks or had gone to his bed. Not that there was anything much on these days. Nothing but soaps full of bad language and unpleasant people. Or whatever they call it, reality shows, same difference. And Silas, though it used to be more regular, now only occasionally listened to his records, usually jazz and blues or, to pep up an evening, David Bowie or the Rolling Stones. But mostly, like tonight, he took to reading after dinner, if there was no job on. He would read for an hour or so, give himself time to digest, before retreating to his bed.

— How nice! exclaimed Ethel, getting to her slippered feet. She felt at once stung and flustered, seeing as she was

10

in her house-clothes, a frumpy top and old slacks. Silas, on the other hand, at first was slow to react at all, caught up, apparently, in an Agatha Christie. *Peril at End House* it happened to be, and he must have read it at least three times before. What's the flaming point, she wanted to ask him (but had stopped doing so years ago), reading a whodunnit when you know full well who?

The discombobulation of Rhoda's arrival got buried in the move, a cold day in mid-January. It was a momentous thing, after all, to up-sticks and start anew down by the sea in the twilight of their years.

— They do say, Ethel said to her husband, as she rummaged for a battered box of Earl Grey teabags on the first morning after, that moving house is the most traumatic thing, apart from death and divorce.

Silas was standing a few feet away in their new living room, surrounded by boxes of books and records, everything feeling displaced and, if truth be told, a bit choked.

— I know, dear, you've said that several times in the past month.

— Things will settle soon enough, she observed, as if the retired undertaker had not even addressed her.

Doughty

The sentence he was writing as he hovered over his keyboard, staring at the screen, pursuing the pulsing vertical of the cursor as it left in its wake a new letter, then word, punctuation, space, till the final full-stop, gave Stephen Osmer such an access of pleasure that he died. He skipped off his seat like the carriage on an old typewriter at the end of a line and there he was, tarrying with a convulsion then completely still, on the floor.

He was doing what he had been every day for the past ten days or more, taking to heart the advice of T. S. Eliot: *write in the calm of the early dawn*. This counsel, given in the privacy of a letter to Lawrence Durrell but set forth with that canny aplomb suited to statements applicable to any would-be writer any time in history, he had long made fun of, keen as he was on cycling and galvanised in the realm of pre-breakfast activities rather by his own twist on the phrase: ride in the calm of the early dawn. Ride or run: for years he had been out, come rain or shine, tracking the empty streets or pavements of London through that eerie period of the morning when, in Wordsworth's phrase (still oddly apt), *the very houses seem asleep*.

But for the past couple of weeks he had followed a quite new course. He worked relentlessly through the quietness that suspends central London before the first rumbling of buses, the yawning and electronic voices of delivery vehicles, the interring whoosh of traffic. It was mid-July and the dawn chorus of sparrows had been going on for some minutes. Set up at a little mahogany desk by the window, in his beloved little mews bedsit off Doughty Street, he had wrangled with himself at inordinate length, slowly drinking his first coffee of the day, over the closing section, the final movement as he thought of it, with which he had been preoccupied since Thursday, and then everything gave way. He was reaching for the words, or the words were reaching for him, embarked on the sentence, come upon by an elation unlike anything he had ever felt, a paper ecstasy clanging out of iron agony, his being in flight at the machine, as if silent, the words dropping into place, his eyes flickering between keyboard and screen, then finished.

The funeral was well-attended, despite being out of town. Ben and Jane Osmer had moved to the Cotswolds after Ben took early retirement. She stayed at the cottage, where she had been since hearing the news, like a frozen stalk. Such was the onset of grief, an Ice Age in an instant. No one plans for the death of their children. Ben was a Jew and lapsed communist, Jane the agnostic but devoted daughter of a Church of England vicar. A cremation in Cheltenham was all that could be envisaged. But quite a crowd came down from London, colleagues, admirers and loved ones, friends and relations. Even emerging from the surreal red velvet and brass shadow-show of the ceremony into the blinking light and drizzle, the song of thrushes and blackbirds, the plundering of worms and the green, faintly twinkling, still-dewy expanse of the cemetery was claustrophobic.

Ben made a speech that was even shorter than he had intended. He broke up after less than a minute, like a voice on a phone passing into a tunnel. Passionate about politics at university, his own career beginning at the *Morning Star*, moving on to promising positions at a couple of the broadsheets, Ben Osmer had had such hopes for his son. He could not say. For his son, he could not say, he – the boy had done well, the boy was going to do – and his daughter Sarah had to stand up and put her arm around him and help him back to his seat. Old colleagues of Ben looked on, pop-eyed in dismay, struggling to smile in solidarity. There was some muffled embarrassed snickering from a couple of Stephen's fellow workers.

Then Sarah made a short speech, wishing to remember her brother for an inner stillness and purposiveness she would always find inspiring, for his kindness and warmth, for his loving protectiveness. She spoke of how on holiday as children, swimming at Welcombe Bay in north Devon, a sudden cold undercurrent had pulled her feet from under her and was dragging her out and Stephen had realised what was happening and, instead of shouting for help to their parents or others on the beach, swum after her and brought her back. That was what her brother was like.

The editor of the *Gazette* herself said a few words. She highlighted the tragedy of dying at the age of twenty-seven, what a brilliant young man Stevie had been, what an exceptional future blasted. Another colleague, Brian, hazarded a lighter tone, wanting people to remember how funny Osmer could be. He recounted a couple of cycling anecdotes. There was the time they were walking in Covent Garden, Stephen pushing his bike, in the company of Brian and another friend, both on foot, when Stevie spotted the *Guardian* journalist the late Simon Hoggart, one of London's more notorious dislikers of people on bicycles. And Stevie straight away said *watch this*, mounted his bike and shot out of view, reappearing a minute later round the corner of Catherine Street, deliberately almost colliding with Hoggart, swerving out of his infuriated path at the last possible second. Then, just last spring, there was the time Stevie was waiting at some traffic lights when Russell Brand happened to pull up on a bicycle beside him, and Stevie in a flash dismounted, propped his bike on the kerb and, without any invitation, embraced Brand while declaring loudly enough for Stevie's companion at the time to catch it on his phone: *Mercedes-driving cyclist hug! Yay!*

Young Osmer had been employed at the *Gazette* for almost five years. As a student at Warwick he had been extraordinary, ending up with the top first in his year, or indeed in several years. And then he had stayed on to do a PhD, working on language and class in the later novels of Dickens. But he failed to complete. Indeed he never really started. He read voraciously. He compiled file after file of notes. He knew *Our Mutual Friend* and *The Mystery of Edwin Drood* practically back-to-front. He had read more or less every academic article and monograph published on Dickens in the preceding fifty years. He knew everything that was worth knowing about theories of language and society, Victorian England, the history of the novel, Marx, ideology and class struggle. He read around his topic too. Besides all the novels and short stories of Dickens, Stephen Osmer prided himself on having read the collected novels of Wilkie Collins, Hardy and Trollope, not to mention all the Georges (Eliot, Meredith and Gissing). Yet, when it came to putting this knowledge and breadth of reading into practice, he found himself quite paralysed.

As an undergraduate, especially working under exam conditions, he would toss off scintillating essays time after time. It was no bother at all. But as he moved on to his postgraduate studies something closed. He failed to notice. It resembled a sleight-of-hand worthy of late Dickens himself. Initially the supervisor had supposed Osmer's difficulties were related to the sheer amount of reading he had been doing: in his first year of postgraduate studies he had been left very much to his own devices. The professor had also been one of his undergraduate tutors and was, after all, well aware of Osmer's intellectual candescence. No one, least of all the supervisor, doubted that this budding young scholar had a great academic career ahead of him.

A supervisory session would consist of an hour's discussion of, say, Mayhew's *London* or the representation of China in *Edwin Drood*, and the senior academic would be left wavering between intimidation at Osmer's knowledge and articulacy, and the increasingly pressing obligation to encourage the young man to get his ideas down on paper and draft a chapter or two. Sixteen months went by and still Osmer had come up with nothing. In January he was summoned.

— It's becoming problematic, Stevie. You're now a full term late with getting your thesis topic confirmed. If you want to get upgraded to doctoral status you really need to get the outline complete and at least a sample chapter drafted.

But it was futile. Osmer could write notes and even discrete paragraphs without difficulty, but from the accomplishment of a coherent doctoral research outline, let alone a full-length thesis chapter, he was utterly blocked. It was, he told his supervisor (to whom he disclosed very little of a non-academic nature), like riding a bicycle into a sandpit. The professor set him up with some book-reviewing, hoping this might free him from the impasse. Kill two birds with one stone, he thought: get the lad's writing flowing again, plus notch up some publications for the CV. As it turned out, the release was more dramatic than intended. Following the supervisor's dispatch of a nicely formulated personal email, Stephen received a request to write a couple of brief notices for the *London Literary Gazette*. The editor was impressed and asked him down to lunch in Soho. At the end, over espresso, she offered him a permanent position on the editorial team. The young man hardly needed to consider. The following week he formally withdrew from Warwick, to his supervisor's brief chagrin and longer-lasting relief. They would never speak again. Just ten days after that, Osmer had moved out of his cheap, spacious digs in Coventry into the cramped but charming bedsit in Bloomsbury.

The sentence with which he relinquished his life, nearly five years later, came at the conclusion of an essay about the banking crisis. It was the second full-length piece of prose he produced in his days at the *LLG*. It was to be a feature article. And that, besides a handful of book notices and off-the-cuff remarks tweeted by others, was his life's work. The complete œuvre of the cleverest young man in London boiled down, in the end, to just two essays and a few celebrated aphorisms. The estimation of young writers cut off in their prime, or rather well before reaching it, says something about the vitality of a culture. The value accorded to a few poems by John Keats or Wilfred Owen, for example, is in part a measure of a culture's capacity to mourn lost art, to recognise the importance of what might have been but never was. It is also a sort of cover-up: the work is quietly smothered under the veil of life. But a culture needs to dream. And when, after all, is a writer's prime? Hadn't Sophocles been ninety when he set down *Oedipus Rex*? And wasn't Dickens himself in his prime when writing *The Mystery of Edwin Drood*? Indeed, wasn't the mystery of that *Mystery* about the very sense of being cut off in one's prime, in that case not only regarding the author but the story itself?

All this talk (as there was, in the wake of his death) about cut-off primes: Osmer was no fillet of steak, but neither was he a Keats or an Owen. If youth was crucial, so was the manner of the cut. To take one's own life, like Plath at the age of thirty, is to invite being snipped from a different cloth. The spectre-thin collateral of war or early-onset tuberculosis can more readily provoke a mourning for mourning itself. But if he was no beef-steak, neither was Osmer merely *Gallerte*, that mix of various kinds of meat and other animal remains to which Marx refers in *Das Kapital* in his vicious satire on what it is to be a worker, reduced to sloppy pottage, to be cannibalistically consumed by those who run the show. Osmer was, finally, a writer. For all the paucity of his output, his writing would prove ghostly and enduring. And its effects would still reverberate in years to come.

The first of his essays, on 'the state of literary culture today', had been a single blistering all-nighter, modestly revised thereafter, written in early March, just four months before his death. He had been under no external compulsion to write either of the essays. Indeed, that had been one of the great boons of working at the *Gazette*: he was not required to write. Producing copy was not part of the job description. He soon discovered the tightness, indeed, of the ship on which he was sailing. It was run by a captain who could scarcely countenance anyone besides herself having any significant role to play in any aspect of the operation whatsoever, unless it were in the area of advertising, for which she had indicated, on his very first day in the office, a scathing distaste. In short she was, in Brian's phrase, a bit of a Grendel's mother.

As is often the case with monsters, however, she also proved immensely loyal. Stephen Osmer thrived. He had grown up in the dull anonymity of southeast London. To be suddenly plumb in the middle of Bloomsbury was a sort of heaven. And it was to her, also, that he must be grateful for that: a wealthy American contact of hers kept the mews property as an occasional *pied-à-terre*, and let out the self-contained bedsit at what was, for London, an affordable rate. Stephen had swapped the scrimping miseries of postgrad purgatory in Coventry for the excitement and security of a full-time position at what felt like the global hub of literary and cultural journalism. For the *LLG* was, after all, a very cool place to be: the most intellectually and politically respectable publication of its kind in Britain, or indeed perhaps anywhere in the English-speaking world. Academics and writers in North America or Australia were just as avid readers and contributors as their counterparts in Islington or Oxford or Glasgow.

And Stephen's job turned out to suit him very nicely. Besides everyday work on gathering and editing copy, he focused on advertising and events, liaising with the Arts Council, the media, literary agents and festival directors, especially organising evenings involving visiting speakers. This enabled him to have dealings with numerous well-known writers, but also academics, politicians, film-makers and artists. And then increasingly, too, he was given a bigger say, or at least listened to with greater deference, at the weekly editorial meetings, when decisions were made regarding the upcoming issue and the commissioning of essays and reviews for future issues. He lived close enough to the *Gazette* offices to walk, but he loved cycling around town when he could. And it was a quiet but constant reassurance to be living so close to where Dickens had lived in the 1830s and written *Nicholas Nickleby*, *The Pickwick Papers* and *Oliver Twist*, among other works. If Osmer had omitted to pay the great novelist the kind of tribute that he had earlier dreamt his doctoral thesis might have been, his attachment to Dickens was as deep as ever.

Mr Osmer was not a handsome man: his hair was already receding in a somewhat disheartening way, his blue eyes were rather close together and his face in general evinced a certain steely superiority which was not necessarily attractive. But he was tall and slender and, like many impassioned cyclists and joggers, emanated a wiry self-sufficiency. This lanky self-composure complemented his eloquence, intelligence and authority of manner and kept him, as it were, in regular girlfriends. He seemed indeed never to settle on any woman in particular, rarely letting a relationship reach its first anniversary. A six-month thing with another Warwick postgraduate terminated when he left Coventry, and just three months into his Bloomsbury job he began a new affair, which soon enough tangled up and gave way to another.

But after three years at the *Gazette* he met Lily. Lily was a beauty, with hair and eyes of a darkness completely at odds with her name, an enrapturing, luminously beautiful creature just down from Cambridge, three years his junior. She worked for the Arts Council and was clearly headed for great things. People loved working with her. Writers and administrators, fellow office-staff and politicians alike were knocked out. She was dazzlingly articulate, funny and fast. She was flighty and warm-hearted, creative and fiercely independent in her thinking; but she was also, as employers like to say, an excellent team-player. Most of all, she was hot. As noticeable to other women as to men, she entranced more or less everyone she met – and she had chosen to be with Stephen. Having Lily in his life gave him a self-assurance he had not realised he lacked.

Yet still he was a haunted man. He had failed to write a doctorate. He had disappointed his parents, and also himself. He was well into his twenties: Dickens, by his age, had already published *Sketches by Boz*, *The Pickwick Papers* and *Oliver Twist*. Stephen was, in his own and a good few others' estimation, the cleverest young man in London. The shining presence of Lily at his side no doubt had a hand in things, but at dinner parties and public events with celebrity authors it was Osmer who provided the most incisive remark, the most compelling critique or memorable anecdote. He continued not to publish anything of his own, besides occasional very brief book-notices for one or other of the rival London literary magazines. These, though few and far between, always commanded respect. But it was his off-the-cuff opinions, his probing questions and impromptu responses that made his reputation. They were repeated by all who knew him, and he was regularly quoted by columnists, bloggers and tweeters. For someone who had never really published anything, he was becoming surprisingly known.

Inwardly, however, three strands twisted ever more tightly. One was an unspoken jealousy of those, especially contemporaries, who had succeeded in writing and publishing creative work – novels, stories, plays. Even piffling poets who had managed to get a slender volume into print he found enraging. Another was his contempt for the self-enclosed nature of academic life. This rancour of feeling had, he knew, intensified since he quit the PhD. And a final braid was anger of a more broadly social and political nature. It was a gathering outrage at the world around him.

The trajectory of anger has its conventions. It rises or boils up. People do not speak of its descent. Yet Stephen felt at moments something of that peculiarity. He saw the world for what it was: a planet entering on a phase of unprecedented anger and turmoil. No feeling of injustice, no sense of egregiousness seemed more charged or meaningful than his own. And this rage, this scorn and indignation, was as much a passage downwards as a mounting up. The body in Old English is the *bone-house*: something was happening in his foundations. Something broke, at first in a trickle, like a burst water-main pressing through stone, starting with drips then gathering momentum, running down through the brickwork into the cellar of the building.

It was a cold night at the beginning of March. He had arranged to have dinner with Brian at their favourite Turkish restaurant just off High Holborn. He walked briskly, avoiding the blustery exposure of Theobald's Road, making his way from his flat via small streets and quiet squares.

— Now we're away from the lair, Brian began, as he watched the waiter setting down glasses and half-poured bottles of beer, how was the visit to old Grauniad land?

Brian was a funny brain. Osmer was fond of him: he was clever and amusing, and had been warm and supportive from the day the Warwick man had arrived at the *Gazette*. But Stephen also liked to maintain a distance. Colleagues were colleagues. And male friendship, for Osmer, always entailed a dynamic of mutual intimidation. He knew that he was smarter than Brian, and this made it easier to like him. Brian was an Oxford man – Pembroke, to be precise, the place of study of Dr Johnson himself. Osmer had never aspired to Oxbridge, but made it his business to know about different colleges and former famous incumbents. This, he understood, was what the Establishment types themselves did. Any resentment Osmer felt at having ended up for several years at Warwick he had translated into a superior bemusement at what an Oxford education seemed to do to people. Having studied *Beowulf*, you dutifully inserted allusions to Grendel and the monster's lair into your conversation. If you had cause to refer to the only – at least faintly – left-wing national paper in the country, you adopted the semi-affectionate, semi-frivolous idiom of *Private Eye*. 'Old Grauniad land' made him wonder if Brian was not in fact an admirer of Tolkien or, just as bad, ex-admirer. But he wasn't going to go down that path. They had managed to avoid it for nearly half a decade and Osmer had no desire to see that change. Few things got his goat like 'fantasy literature'. The very word 'hobbit', the bilge of 'Bilbo Baggins', the vomit-swilling smarm of 'Silmarillion' filled him with homicidal contempt. The phrase 'lord of the rings' had always sounded to him like some obscene joke or at least to call for one. Lodged in a surreal back-bar of his mind was a dartboard, with the Anglo-Saxon professor's face miniaturised in the bull. He had taken the train down to Oxford one day, with a new girl from Warwick, and they had found themselves wandering into the Eagle and Child in search of a decent pub lunch, but he'd turned right around and walked out again, the girl following behind him, baffled. At the abject Christian fantasy writers' parade, all the dreary photos of the deadly Inklings screwed to the walls like works of art in an Italian chapel, Stephen came close, there and then in the Fowl and Foetus, to throwing up.

It was vigorously tweeted at the time: with a single offensive remark, Osmer had stirred chaos at a public reading three nights earlier, at the International Anthony Burgess Foundation in Manchester. Stephen had, frankly, been trying to forget it. But Brian could not resist broaching the topic. The beer was cold, and the hummus with sautéed lamb fillet, *baba ganoush* and red lentil patties they were sharing as starters whetted the appetite, and the merlot with the main course helped carry Osmer along on an outpouring of vexation that he had fully failed to foresee he might deliver to his friend or to anyone else. He succeeded in keeping Lily out of the picture, but found himself telling Brian far more than he intended. Outside, they stood together briefly on the pavement before bidding one another good night. Stephen's face was flushed from the wine and sudden cold air, but also from embarrassment at a conversation that had been, more precisely, his long if staccato linguistic monopoly. Brian, however, had enjoyed the evening and said so, before making off in the opposite direction from Stephen, towards Leicester Square.

As he strode up Kingsway then zigzagged, again via the short streets and little squares of Bloomsbury, now more or less deserted, Stephen thought of Dickens walking these same streets at speed, more or less every day, and then at home, frenetically writing. He deliberately overshot, digressing as far as Doughty Street in order to stop in front of No.48. Besides the occasional passing car or taxi, he had the view peacefully all to himself. And the anger of all the decades between Dickens and himself seemed to fill up the night from top to bottom. Looking up into the darkened windows behind which his precursor (not yet Stephen's age) had written three novels and much more besides, gazing at the doorway through which Dickens had daily passed, Stephen apprehended, with a suddenness that seemed to set quivering the very pavement in front of the house, the force of the phrase at the start of *A Tale of Two Cities*: recalled to life. Edison's perfected phonograph came to mind. It was as if the works of Dickens on a series of cylinders were set spinning in his body: he had dropped into a secret recording studio, a pocket of time in which the author's phrase, by phonographic projection, was sounding through his body. He was recalled to life.

It was as if he had been cycling far harder than he realised and dismounted with a jolt. He might easily have fainted. Perhaps, momentarily, he did. Certainly he was overcome by a wave of coldness, a great gathering-up of numbness, at first in his toes then working its way like early cramp into his lower legs. In his dizziness he leaned on the railings of the house for a moment to steady himself. And a sensation of extraordinary warmth now flooded him. He felt doughty. He felt the meaning of that word in his veins. He made his way back to his tiny mews flat as fast as he could, pulled out his laptop and started to write. Stephen Osmer was doughty. He was recalled to life. He was going to write what he hadn't written in years. He was going to make a statement about what led up to that outburst in Manchester. And five hours later he had finished. Just before emailing his boss to tell her he was not well and needed to go to bed, he tapped out a title at the head of the document: 'Double Whammy: The State of English Literary Culture Today'. It duly appeared, a fortnight afterwards, as a lead article in the *LLG*.

Double Whammy: The State of English Literary Culture Today

We appear to have entered a new era. What remains of England now? What kind of England, however little, however diminished and perhaps pitiful, might be worth holding on to? A book-length discussion of such questions would be in order. I will attempt not to confront them head-on, but instead to illuminate them from a rather specific and no doubt partial angle. I am as susceptible as anyone to the pleasure of waking to the soft tolling of an English village church-clock and the cooing of wood pigeons in the early morning trees, but I am no St-George's-flag-waving nationalist. On the contrary, I believe that the current surges in nationalistic feeling and self-regard, in England and elsewhere, are toxic to the core. We must oppose and critique the irrational and hate-fuelling forces of nationalistic thinking and beliefs wherever they may arise. The future is not nationalistic but international, as Marx foresaw.

England is one thing, English another. We cannot ignore or wish away the violent hegemony of Anglo-American. It is necessary constantly to grapple with the role played by the English language as capitalism's *lingua franca*. This is arguably the writer's first duty today. At the same time, more than ever, I believe in the capacity of language to transform society and the world. In educational and cultural respects, I would venture to suggest, English is this country's only remaining important manufacturing industry. Which brings me to my ostensibly narrow and particular question: What is happening with literature and literary criticism in England today?

I want to focus here on the work of just two writers – a novelist and a critic. The former has not long ago published his seventh novel, variously praised as 'clever', 'compelling' and 'ingenious'; as 'a cutting-edge, vital new British novel'; as 'strange, memorable and, arguably, way ahead of its time'. The latter has not long ago published his tenth book of literary criticism, variously praised as 'extraordinary', 'fascinating' and 'exuberant'; as a 'book that shows the way forward for literary studies'. I should straight away add that these accolades are, as so often, grossly exaggerated. If you believe the blurbs, every day brings another handful of novelistic masterpieces and literary critical groundbreakers. In this respect it should not matter that I have chosen to focus on a couple of mediocrities. You might be forgiven for confusing the novelist and critic in question, for they happen to share the same name: Nicholas Royle. Together they embody everything that is wrong with literary culture in England today.

Initially, like many other people, I did not realise that there were two of them. If you go to an online bookseller or library catalogue you find no distinction made. But on further research it is easy enough to confirm that they are indeed a twosome – one a literary critic and theorist, born in London in 1957, the other a writer of novels and short stories, born in Sale, Cheshire in 1963. The sheer absurdity of two writers with this name! It seems incredible they should ever have put up with it, or that we, the public, should have to do so. I was certainly not alone in doubting they really were different people. Just recently, however, I was able to confirm it, when visiting friends in Manchester and chancing to hear that the Nicholas Royles would be 'in conversation' at the International Anthony Burgess Foundation. I went along, and sure enough there they were.

The younger Royle was once described by Harry Ritchie in *The Times* as 'specky'. He was also, I discovered, shaven-headed. And he sported, as apparent compensatory gesture, a small goatee. He was, in so many ways, short. A diminutive fellow. And he writes in that manner as well. Short sentences, without verbs. Sometimes. For effect. The older one was a good deal more heavily built. He looked like a worn-out bulldog. He had hair, but this was mostly silver, making him look professorial, just the part for his job: he teaches English, we were told, at the University of Sussex. The two of them together looked ridiculous, like Laurel and Hardy or Little and Large.

I sat at the back where I could get a good sense of the audience as well as gaze at the 'stars' of the occasion. The audience thought this pair of Nicholas Royles were *funny*. People were really laughing. It wasn't just embarrassment; they genuinely seemed to find the whole thing comical. I don't know how much the couple had rehearsed what they were doing, but they began with a couple of readings. The younger one proceeded briskly but pleasantly, no-nonsense, in a gentle Mancunian accent. The older one read slowly, lumberingly, in traditional Home Counties BBC English. Then there was a Q&A for about half an hour. There was only one microphone and they stood either side of it, chiming in as they saw fit.

Someone asked how they had met. This gave rise to what one of them called an uncanny story. Everything they talked about came back to the 'uncanny'. This was evidently the joint declaration of their *raison d'être*. The fact that they shared the same name and both wrote about weird things, chance encounters, mysterious goings-on: this was 'uncanny'. Oh, so *uncanny*. Someone need only say 'uncanny' a couple of times for it to start sounding vacuous. I could devote many pages to exposing the follies of this word, and in particular to detailing the fundamental disingenuousness with which it has come to be used in contemporary cultural and intellectual life. Suffice to observe that 'uncanny' is a lamentable example of failed thinking, an evasion and a subterfuge. It is a way of pigeon-holing alienation while avoiding the reality of oppression. This risible couple had milked the thing and sucked it dry years ago, but were still sucking, like babies, oblivious.

In any case, the older one started reminiscing about a short story he once wrote. I admit this came as a revelation: I had not been aware that *he* wrote stories as well. The old woodlouse had sent a thing off to a magazine – this was back, he said, in the late '80s – a magazine called *Sunk Island Review*. He said that when he got his customary rejection letter (more audience laughter here) his attention was arrested by an odd detail. The editor turning down his story had addressed him as Nick, whereas he had used his full forename when submitting the piece. Also, the editor referred to being 'unable to use either of these pieces at the moment'; Royle had submitted only one story. But then he noticed that there was another typescript enclosed. This other typescript bore the title 'Flying into Naples' and the authorial name 'Nicholas Royle', along with an address somewhere in Shepherds Bush. *Sunk Island Review* was rejecting both Nicholas Royles. So Royle was then in a position to send on the misdirected story, as well as have the strange satisfaction of conveying the news of rejection to its rightful recipient.

Again, this anecdote solicited a good deal of tedious laughter. As if suddenly waking up to the reality of the occasion, the older one, the literary critic, remarked that they seemed to be a double-act. People practically fell off their chairs at this.

And then the other one flamboyantly 'copped on' that they had not actually answered the *question* as such, about how they first met. Why was that felt to be amusing? It must have been the homoerotic frisson as well: there was something histrionically 'romantic' about their parading together in the public eye.

— We didn't actually meet, though, till some years later, did we, Nick? (The audience quietened down again for this.) We exchanged letters and then emails.

— That's right, said the critic. We only met for the first time in 1997, at Senate House, in London. I was giving a paper on the subject of the double (some chortling here) and I talked about Nick's novel, *The Matter of the Heart*. No one else in the audience at that time knew that the novelist himself was in the room. We'd agreed in advance that we would meet – literally for the first time, shake hands with one another – at the end of my lecture. Nick was to stand up, we were to walk towards one another and shake hands, and then he was to make his way round and sit in my place and respond to questions.

— It was funny, chipped in the little one.

— It was awful, said the larger one. (Audience laughter.) It was completely unexpected. It was the longest, most troubled silence I have ever experienced. After a couple of minutes someone spoke up: *This is taboo. This shouldn't happen.* And Nick and I realised it was true. There was something truly discomfiting about it, but we hadn't seen it coming. When you give a lecture on someone's novel it's not appropriate to reveal to the audience at the end that the author is actually in the room and will now take questions.

— A bit, er, uncanny, said the younger Nicholas Royle. (This, to a mix of hearty and uncomfortable laughter. You didn't have to be a Freudian to pick up the ambivalence: the audience could take only so much of all this 'uncanny' nonsense.)

Double Whammy

And this prompted the novelist to recall another coincidence. It had to do with the fact that his first book, *Counterparts* (1993), appeared around the same time as the literary theorist Royle published a critical monograph (co-written with Andrew Bennett) about the novels of Elizabeth Bowen. At which juncture, unbeknownst to the other, each Nicholas Royle sent a review copy of his book to the then largely unknown Jonathan Coe. Allegedly weirded out by the simultaneous arrival of two books by strangers both called Nicholas Royle, each containing (one imagines) some sycophantic missive asking if he would consider reviewing the book, Coe felt he had to write something about at least *one* of them. His review of *Counterparts* duly appeared in *The Guardian* shortly afterwards, and the Mancunian novelist's career was launched.

I have to confess that this dropping of Coe's name into the conversation was the final straw. It was an entertaining enough evening, I suppose, and the Royles could count on selling numerous copies of their books after the event. But it also seemed to me troubling in ways that the dynamic duo completely failed to understand. Certainly the venue was significant. The building was a restored nineteenth-century warehouse, a huge interior of warm exposed red brick, mostly paid for by the success of Burgess's novel, *A Clockwork Orange*, or rather Stanley Kubrick's film of the novel. And, beyond that, it was a visible, still powerful relic of industrialism and exploitation, a deadly echo-chamber of Dickensian England, a dark satanic mill (in Blake's phrase) all lit up for vacuous chit-chat. The building was originally part of the huge textile business run by the notorious Hugh Birley, one of the commanders at the Peterloo Massacre which took place close by, in August 1819. By the 1830s it was the largest mill in Manchester, employing two thousand workers, spinning and weaving, toiling and sweating. Did the fifty or sixty people lounging about in the audience chuckling at this sordid little double-act have any awareness of the history of where they had stationed their arses? My brief internet research earlier that afternoon, together with the vaudeville inanity of Messrs Royle and Royle, stoked up sufficient ire to trigger an observation, if not a question.

I had not planned to speak. I had, after all, simply dropped in. But I could not hold back. There was a pause in the proceedings, just long enough for me to pipe up from the back, loud and clear for all to hear:

— You wouldn't know powerful writing if it smacked you in the face with a brick.

A noticeable hush. A good few people in the audience turned around. Some, I think, recognised me. My interjection was surprisingly effective. The dynamic duo appeared suitably red-faced: like others, they were not sure whether my comment had been addressed to just one or both of them. Feelings flared. The whole thing, I suppose, might have got unpleasant. I myself had to register that I had perhaps never, in my years of hosting author events in London, made quite so outspoken a remark. As some readers will know, the word got round: I believe even the *Telegraph* included some reference to it in a gossip column a couple of days afterwards.

As literary editor of the *Sunday Times* back in the mid-'90s, Harry Ritchie dismissed Royle's third novel *The Matter of the Heart* (1997) as 'remarkably unreadable', 'completely resistible', 'utterly unseductive'. He also characterised an earlier volume of writers' dreams that Royle had edited as 'uniquely pointless and stupid'. Since then Royle has published several further novels and edited several further anthologies, as well as written many short stories. I can confirm, without further ado, that he has not improved as a writer in the intervening years.

Double Whammy

For illustration we could turn to the recent book bearing the title *First Novel* (2013). It is so named, presumably, in the hope that people might forget or never know that there were in fact half a dozen failures before it. But raking through *First Novel* would, I fear, require too much of the reader's patience. Besides, from the little of it I myself could bear to read, I found that it was concerned with a creative writing teacher and his creative writing classes: a sure-fire recipe for a complete dog's breakfast. There are few things more dismal about the contemporary writing scene than its capitalist complicity with the creative writing industry. To write a novel about creative writing classes, let alone about a novelist writing a novel about a novelist teaching creative writing, is to scrape a barrel I'd prefer not to situate my nose anywhere near.

Instead I have selected one of Royle's recent shorter publications, of which there are, I fear, all too many. For he is also, as his website trumpets, a prolific writer of short stories, and especially of what he calls the 'uncanny and menacing' variety. 'The Kestrel and the Hawk' appeared in 2010, in a special issue of a magazine called *Patricide* devoted to the subject of 'seaside surrealism'. It is a first-person narrative of a birdwatching trip to what the author coyly calls 'the island'. The name of this island will be obvious to anyone who knows anything about the geography of the British Isles. Why Royle should find 'Anglesey' such a hard word to write baffles me, but that's an aside. The title of the piece, in any case, is clunky enough: after all, you might have thought that a kestrel *was* a hawk. But any incongruity on that front is thrillingly dispelled when you discover that 'Hawk' refers to the RAF jet fighter. Ah, you are presumably supposed to think, how playful and ingenious! In truth, however, what we confront here is prose of jaw-sagging ineptitude.

Take, for instance, the opening words: 'I reach the island by train. As I start walking from the station into the village, I immediately hear a noise behind me that can only be a jet aircraft approaching at speed.' Royle's text nicely demonstrates the follies of writing narrative in the present tense. His control over this infinitely tiresome mode is already in tatters by the second sentence: 'As I start... I immediately hear.' The 'immediately' is superfluous, granted, but the entire sentence cries out to be shredded. Is the 'As I start' necessary? Or 'a noise behind me that can only be'? These are not just quibbles about patchy prose. Form is, as always, inseparable from content. In Royle's work we encounter, again and again, the elementary bad twins of fiction-writing: too much information (stuck on facts, staid description) and a dearth of social and political meaning.

Before going off into the dunes to observe the jets landing and taking off, a man orders some coffee and eggs at a neighbouring café. The waitress notices the bag he is carrying and asks if he is there for the birds. He nods. He smiles. She says, 'I was watching a kestrel over the dunes the other morning.' The man duly goes off to observe the jets and the birds. His walk down to the beach and across the sand dunes is recounted in mind-numbing detail. Every sentence has died several times before reaching the page. The narrator recalls the waitress's face and her 'tired grey eyes – heron grey, gull-wing grey'. Evidently he finds her attractive. There is talk overheard at the café about Prince William being at the base, flying a Hawk. But our knowledgeable narrator points out that 'Flight Lieutenant Wales' is actually pilot-training in a Sea King helicopter. Through his telephoto lens he observes four men (one of them possibly the Prince of Wales: how exciting would *that* be?) walking across the tarmac.

And then, with the following little paragraph, Royle's literary gem comes to its sparkling finish:

Double Whammy

Out of the corner of my eye I see a shape in the sky above the dunes. I look up. A kestrel is hovering, its tail fanned, wings beating fast, head still as a rock. I see the waitress's face, her eyes, slate grey, gunmetal grey, and when I look back at the airfield, the four men have gone.

It is difficult to know where to begin to respond to this pitiful example of contemporary writing. Should we be looking for a message? Is it an allegory, perhaps, or a fable? 'The Kestrel and the Hawk' sounds fabular, after all, like *The Hare and the Tortoise* or *The Lion and the Mouse*: is Royle making a subtle, oh so subtle suggestion that the bird is more powerful than the jet fighter? Is there perhaps a further pun in the sub-text, regarding another sort of bird (nudge, nudge)? That, certainly, would go along with the description of the waitress's eyes as 'heron grey' and 'gull-wing grey'. But then, why have the eyes become 'slate grey, gunmetal grey' in the final sentence of the story? Mysterious, eh? Is Royle rather racily implying that this bird is, after all, a dangerous war-machine herself? Whoa, you might conclude: this is complex and sophisticated stuff! Too clever for me by light years. But no, in plain truth, it is not. It is bilge. It is an abuse of trees.

It is frankly astonishing that this writer has been able to continue to publish novels and short stories. In a period now spanning twenty-five years or more, he has made not the slightest progress in his craft. His story-telling has all the deftness of a disabled sloth. His characters are as imaginatively interesting as clumps of concrete. His prose remains as ill-formed, flatulent and haphazard as ever. One could select more or less any page in his collected works and begin talking about bad writing. Of course the phrase 'bad writing' is not new to him: Royle was an early recipient of the Bad Sex in Fiction Award, bestowed on him by the *Literary Review* in 1997 for the worst description of a sex scene in a novel that year. I shall not recall the fuller details here: it had something to do with the pleasures of a submarine tow-rope and the noises made by a seal. Sub-standard indeed.

What is the point of 'The Kestrel and the Hawk'? Is it attempting to furnish us with some critique of social life (of class, for example, or gender relations), or of the Royal family (no pun intended), or of the British military? Tick none of the above. Royle's writing shows not the faintest wisp of radical political purpose or social vision, whether about England (or, in this story, the coupling of England and Wales) or about the wider world. But in this it is not unusual. It is lamentably representative of the vast majority of contemporary fiction. There are no doubt novelists in England today who are smarter and more eloquent, but Royle's writing provides a benchmark: you can receive regular accolades for writing as badly as he does, and it is not even necessary to engage with social and political reality.

The other one, the woodlouse, is even worse. Professor Royle has made a successful academic career out of writing critical prose addressed to an audience of approximately five people. He is a practitioner and proponent of what is, laughably, called 'high theory', a classic case of what Boyd Tonkin of the *Independent* once referred to as the 'up-themselves posh theory boys'. It may be ventured, without fear of contradiction, that the last thing you get from what Professor Royle writes is high. Completely out of touch with the everyday concerns of people like you and me, 'high theory' makes everything it talks about simply *impossible*. Readers of 'high theory' are required to find insuperable difficulties in everything they encounter. Enid Blyton becomes as abstract and convoluted as Slavoj Žižek. And, for the 'high theory practitioner' who demonstrates this, the narcissistic satisfaction is luridly legible. Without high theory, after all, how might we come

to appreciate that *Harry Potter*, or Damien Hirst, or the instruc-
tions of a bicycle manual, could be so immensely thought-
provoking and philosophically deep?

The example of Royle's work is doubly pernicious, since he
has not been able thoroughly to envelop himself in the arcane
fog of critical theory. Unfortunately, he has sought to introduce
the deadening obfuscations and meretricious generalities of
his so-called 'research specialisms' into student guides and
textbooks. Of such books we are pleased to recall the crisp
three-word verdict pronounced by the unerringly accurate and
erudite John Sutherland, writing in *The Guardian* in 2004, on
Royle's *Introduction to Literature, Criticism and Theory*: 'Heap
of crap.' That book is also, alas, an academic bestseller, read by
students across the UK, Europe and beyond. Co-authored and
often known as 'Bennett and Royle' (others may prefer 'Rennet
and Boil'), this student textbook is, in Sutherland's memorable
and well-chosen words, 'a monument to the decay of English
studies'. Along with Royle's critical studies of E. M. Forster and
Shakespeare, it might convey a superficial impression of being
accessible and helpful. But this is entirely misleading. Royle's
writing is steeped in the ambition to seduce the reader away
from the real world of social interaction and political meaning.

It is here that we encounter the double whammy, the dire
situation of literary culture in England today: a fundamentally
evasive and irresponsible relationship to the actualities of social
and political existence, both in popular, mainstream literary
fiction and in academic criticism.

In the case of the old woodlouse, we can see this in most
nauseating and persistent fashion in *The Uncanny* (2003), a
monolithically clunky, abstruse and woefully depoliticising work
in which hundreds of pages are devoted to that single vacuous
'u'-word about which I have already said more than enough.

Rather than trawl back over such all-too-drearily-familiar terrain, permit me to make a few remarks about Royle's most recent critical study, *Veering: A Theory of Literature* (2011). This is a more or less completely unreadable volume which makes the preposterous claim that culture has, over the past fifty years, been undergoing a 'literary turn'. There is a long chapter specifically devoted to this ridiculous phrase. It is sufficient here, I think, merely to cite the opening two sentences:

> *You veer about for a fold in the painting that would at last apprise you of the partition you play in a piece of theatre that was acting itself out before you were born and sings imperceptibly in your body like a bat. It is the snatch of music you are harking after, song like a raft of architecture.*

What kind of claptrap is this? A simple and safe answer would be: it is the miserable maelstrom of nonsense into which Professor Royle seeks to draw us. Who conceivably might be the 'you' referred to here? Since when did a fold in a painting *apprise* someone? Since when did anyone 'play a partition'? How can someone act in a play before they are born? What, when it is at home, is imperceptible singing? And how are we to make head or tail of the syntactical chaos of this sentence, with its infuriating concluding simile, 'like a bat'? Does 'like a bat' refer to the putative 'fold in the painting', the 'piece of theatre', the imperceptible singing, or the initial verb-phrase, 'you veer'? And then how, if at all, does the second sentence follow on from the first? How can a song be a 'raft of architecture'? What is a 'raft of architecture' anyway? Is it some decidedly wooden pun, a sidewise allusion to a 'raft of measures'?

One might have imagined such questions to be beside the point. And of course they are, in the sense that Royle's discourse will never give us answers – any more than Lewis Carroll's hatter answers the question: 'Why is a raven like a writing desk?' None of this would be of the slightest import, moreover, were it not for the fact that Royle's book is held to exemplify contemporary academic criticism at its best. It appears in an 'internationally respected' series of academic monographs called 'The Frontiers of Theory'. It is, by implication, what young students and the academics of the future are supposed to be aspiring to. Let us be clear here: Royle's writing is as close to that of a responsible public intellectual as planet earth is to utopia. Nowhere is there a single reference to class, or even to contemporary social concerns as such.

From the very beginning Royle's work has been marred by two glaring and profound flaws: a hopeless overindulgence in wordplay, and a complete absence of proper historical research. In these respects *Veering* is entirely consistent with his earliest book *Telepathy and Literature* (1991), which is peppered with linguistic frivolities and ludicrous neologisms ('mental cryonics', 'dramaturgic telepathy', 'the prosopo-poetic drive', 'telepsychology' and so on), while completely failing to provide any proper historical framework for its topic. In Royle's uniquely incapable hands academic discourse becomes a kind of fairytale-writing, airbrushing out of existence any sense of history, any engagement with social and political actuality.

The present essay has doubtless been something of an apologia regarding that spur-of-the-moment remark about being facially accosted with a brick. I said what I said. In this short essay I have attempted to furnish a critical context for that comment and to spell out how much, it seems to me, is wrong with literary culture in England today, and how much is at stake. I stand by my interjection and indeed hereby extend it: across the English-speaking world, people seem increasingly incapable of recognising what powerful writing is, or of conceiving what it should be about or what it might seek to do. I will reserve for another occasion an outline of my views on how this may relate to educational leadership and political vision, especially here in England. Our novelists and critics appear to have wandered deep into a kind of post-post-modern swampland of bad writing, cut off from all social conscience or political sense. Literature – and literary culture more generally – needs to be *recalled to life*. I borrow that resonant phrase from a true masterpiece – that great nineteenth-century novel of revolution, *A Tale of Two Cities*. Social community, meaning and justice: Dickens never lets us forget these things.

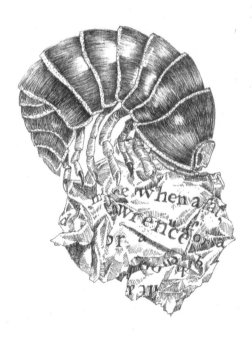

Twilight

How is one, in fact, to spend the twilight of one's years? And since when did people start talking about it like that? True, neither of the Woodlocks could see as well as they used to. Although the retired gentleman prided himself on not needing reading glasses, his vision was certainly weakening. And as for Ethel's, he sometimes wondered if she wasn't actually seeing things. Flaming weird, she'd mutter, but then go all coy and decline to explain herself. There is a comfort in the thought of twilight. It is a charming word at first sight. But then it gathers darker hues. There is, nonetheless, something alluring in the image, a sort of dreamy semi-sleepiness in which things are pleasantly unclear, as if your senses are washed over in a soft mauve-bluish haze, while also enabling incidents of unexpected significance to be picked out, like the clarity of the evening star sparkling over the water or the sharpness of an owl's hoot high up in the woods. Twilight is when animals come out. At least the nocturnal sort. Badgers, for instance, traipse and frolic about the sett, or at any rate they used to, back in the day when the government wasn't gassing them all.

In the twilight of your life there's no going back. That is the gentle but unequivocal message. You don't come flooding back to morning and the delicious dawn chorus of youth and first love and discovering the world. Nor is it the afternoon tea-party, when you start to absorb the *tip-top* of the clock on the mantelpiece, the hollow that passed like a ghost through the days of Silas's mum and dad and continues to do so here in the new house, over the fireplace. There's comfort to be drawn, like the flickering of a fire, from the thought of your twilight years, for it's not over yet: there's still light, there's still time. Unless you're a badger and the cull has begun, and you reckon it's coming on twilight and snuffle and push on up towards the fresh air for a good bit of playing, rooting and snouting, only to realise you are actually being throttled and, as you struggle to move another inch closer to the open air and sweet gloaming above, asphyxiated.

Twilight is a phase of softness and tranquillity. It may be cold, but it's still beautiful. Of course these days that evening star is more often than not a satellite: you have to adjust to that. News Corporation: an artificial star crossed in your eyes. But there was, after all, the joy of being by the sea and – something about the new abode neither of them had expected – the full, enormous, clear night skies featuring, nearest and dearest, the shifting radiance of the moon. Naturally in a job like theirs there was plenty of work by moonlight, but in Croydon you never really noticed the night sky, whereas here in Seaford you could lie together in bed at night and listen to the waves crashing on the shingle just a couple of hundred yards off, over and over, and the moon was so strong that some nights they were kept up by it, just like the waves. Perhaps twilight has to do with an increased sensitivity to that fizzled-out planet or whatever people call it nowadays.

In the twilight of your years you take it easy, in any case, especially after having a rocky year like the last one, stuck in the Mayday virtually on death row, convinced there was no coming home. It makes everything sound so natural,

42

twilight years, all in a day's work, life one long holiday and now dusk coming on, prepare with calm and dignity for the big sleep. But what, in this day and age, is this twilight talk all about? If you only looked at the billboards and what is on cinema screens and in the bookshop bestseller charts, you'd think it was to do with teenage vampires. But there's a strong chance, Ethel considered, that all that effort to turn it into a teenage love-interest thing was really just a way of guarding against the *twilight of your life*. After all, wasn't the daftness of all those Dracula-type films and books basically just a fantasy of *sexually active* eternal life?

Gazing around at the fellow inhabitants of their new home town, the Woodlocks were not particularly keen to indulge in fantasies sexual or eternal, let alone both. When Silas one day wondered if everyone was suffering from SAD and Ethel asked what in heaven's name was that, she misheard and thought he said Sexual Affection Disorder. Moving to Seaford should have required them to hit the ground running, but it was actually more of a thud. There'd have to be a thud, really, if the feet were going to run. That was the surprise of ballet, the time he took her to Sadler's Wells. They weren't even sitting very close to the stage, but the racket those young dancers made, landing on their feet in wafer-thin satin slippers, initially quite spoiled the experience. Whoever imagined that with such refinement there would be so much banging about? She felt it would be better if they could filter out the sound, as if the live performance should imitate the recorded version. But then she became absorbed and was able at last simply to admire the sheer output of energy and effort, the physical stamina and weight to balance all that grace, the thuds that make the artistry possible.

For Silas, his wife's image of a thud (for it had been hers) immediately resurrected awkward memories, thankfully just three in a life of transporting the newly departed, when the utterly untoward occurred: the sickening thud at the conclusion of a tilt and topple, grim rip for a wooden overcoat. Just a year or so back, his right knee all of a sudden gave way and the others couldn't react fast enough. Another time, one of the lads evidently lost inner conviction (end of the road for that pall-bearer, never showed his face near Mint Walk again). And then, back in the early days but it still brought a flush to his face, working alone, he backed the Daimler all the way up and thought he could slide it without help. It slips and you can't say all hell breaks loose but it isn't the highlight of your professional life, to have to sort that mortifying lapse, and then, cover, and sweat, in any case lucky stars it never got out, the incident that is, all in the family, not a living soul within earshot or eyescope, call it twilight for nobody.

What have we done? There was something of that question, set silently adrift, a bit aghast, especially in the first couple of months or so. For Ethel it was most acute in the seemingly endless business of emptying boxes and trying to get the new house in order. Entire days would fall into darkness before she could even take that promenade walk she had envisaged, on awakening, as a daily pleasure of their new existence. For Silas it was more when out and about, strolling the streets, picking up the groceries, wandering along the seafront, absorbing the fuller details of the location they had chosen. *Yes, indeedy!* the winter seemed long – if you could call it winter. Here by the sea they were far more conscious of climate change than they had ever been in Croydon. Ethel in particular dwelt on such things.

— Is it climate change, Silas, or global warming, or what? Is this that tipping effect the government have been talking about?

Ethel had lost all trust in the government. Silas wondered if his wife wasn't becoming a bit paranoid in her old age. But perhaps, like nostalgia, paranoia isn't what it used to be. If the weather was getting stranger, why wouldn't the government be doing the same? Certainly the heating bill in their new place was going to be bigger. Silas felt uncertain, not for the last time, why they'd decided to buy such a high and roomy house. When the wind blew, as it did here on the coast, the very building seemed to shake. The simple business of going out in the morning to purchase food for the day could seem unduly challenging.

Seaford had a far larger population of elderly citizens than the Woodlocks had expected. You could hardly walk down the main shopping street without colliding with an old girl on her Zimmer frame or being charged down by some fellow on his mobility scooter. There was no need to spin tales of the living dead: they were already surrounded by them. But that was on bad days. For better or worse, the thing about the twilight of your years is that it goes on longer than it used to. That's what the government wants you to think. Seventy is the new fifty. At the end of the day there would be the statutory unending night, but in the meantime your twilight might last you several decades. Ethel found it a bit spooky. Sooner or later you know that you're going to pop off, or, at least, you know that you're going to pop off sooner or later, but you don't believe it. Neither soon nor late. Even now, in the twilight of their years, she could not believe she was ever going to die. She was Ethel Woodlock, née Dunnock. She wasn't like other people. She was made of sterner stuff. She had a different destiny. But she knew, also, she was just the same as everyone. Everyone thinks *they're* different: there are no exceptions.

Give it a few years and the exceptions will be more noticeable, once they have established ways of making the twilight stretch out and out, and then they'll be tinkering and tooling about at the other end as well and, give it a few decades maybe, the very sight of elderly folk will be a sort of horror film, a piece of surreal cinematic tourism. The government will show footage of old-age pensioners queuing outside the post office on Church Street waiting for it to open at nine sharp on a Monday morning so that they can collect their pensions, can't afford teabags and a packet of biscuits till the weekly allowance comes in, shivering and chatting or standing silent and alone in the raw March wind, a queue of them trailing down the street, and the film will strike future viewers as more shocking than the first pictures from Belsen because in those future days old people actually looking and acting old will be literally relics from another world. In the meanwhile there was no denying she and Silas were in the twilight of their years and surrounded by thousands of people in the same boat. It's just you don't think of *yourself* as elderly. You see the others and feel sorry for them, without being able to really grasp that you're one of them.

All that pneumonia and the rest had alerted her as never before to her own mortality, but every such encounter is just another story you're telling yourself, she saw, it's not as if there's some grand opening, some ribbon-cutting at the twilight fête and you get to be first to walk up to the favourite attraction, the Mortality Shy (it shies away as you approach). And it wasn't like there were only bad days.

Ethel, after all, wasn't the misanthropic sort. How could she have been, as the successful female-lead of Woodlock & Sons for forty years? That needs an aptitude for dealing with people. It requires compassion, the common touch, an ability to empathise. Sometimes she felt the job was not dissimilar to being a nurse or counsellor. But then it wasn't as if you could forget the business side. That was the balancing act: the knowledge that at the end of a particular weepy out-pouring, to which (especially in the last few years) she had been almost as liable as anyone else, she was going to have to come through, smiling in the least patronising and inappropriate manner possible, and ask how the bereaved would like to pay.

Ethel had good friends in and around Croydon and she missed them, Dot especially. Dorothy had worked in the office with her for years and, much to the retiring couple's relief, had been happy to stay on to help Ash and ensure as far as possible a smooth business transition. She'd come down on a special day-off to see Ethel, just a couple of weeks after the move, and they'd had a lovely time chatting away, in spite of the gusting rain and high winds racking the house. When she'd stood on the railway platform watching Dottie's train depart in the middle of the afternoon, after the weather had in fact cleared up quite nicely, Ethel had felt tearful as a little girl, abandoned and left to play by herself.

It might take time, but they'd muddle through. Ethel did enjoy, as the weeks went by, the chance to walk, alone or with Silas if he cared to join her, along the esplanade. Once the box-emptying and tidying and set-up of the house was more or less in order, and so long as the heavens weren't chucking it down, a walk by the sea became a daily fixture of her life. With the English Channel she could share her solitude. She'd grown up in Buckinghamshire, and then in Croydon the coast seemed if anything even more remote. But she'd always wanted to live by the sea, ever since her earliest childhood holidays in the West Country and in Wales. Her beloved seaside, as Silas called it, in that mixture of mockery and affection that made them such a well-knit couple.

Bricked Up

You wouldn't know powerful writing if it smacked you in the face with a brick.

As Stephen Osmer realised, things might have become unpleasant. The event was chaired by Manchester University Press editor Matthew Frost, who sported perhaps the most ridiculous spiralling handlebar moustache in England. Was there something about these Mancunian climes, Osmer wondered, that solicited relationship-breaking moustaches? In any case, Frost moved swiftly to the microphone, gently easing a Nicholas Royle to either side, and cracked a joke:

— I've been suffering from mild hallucinations recently, seeing Donald Duck and Mickey Mouse and so on. So I went to the doctor. He said not to worry, they were just Disney spells.

The audience exploded in laughter. The intensity of the moment was dissipated. Frost then announced that drinks were available and would everyone, even Mr Osmer, like to give the authors a warm round of applause for what had been, after all, a thoroughly enjoyable and entertaining evening. The clapping and hurrahing of appreciation carried on for some time. Doubtless it would have been less fulsome had the man from the *Gazette* kept his mouth shut and not brought the event to such an abrupt and, he felt, well-deserved halt.

There are few topics of manly significance less universally acknowledged, or at any rate less frequently picked over with a fine-tooth comb, than a gentleman's embarrassment in discovering that the leak he is poised to take in a public urinal is to occur in immediate adjacency to another gentleman concerned to relieve himself with similar or even greater urgency. 'Pee nerves' scarcely begins to cover the matter. All sense of priority, as it were, evaporates. All meaning. The first man to his position might feel, from the weight of the thing already full and lumbering between his fingers, that he need only release, have nature do its metaphorical business, dispense with all preliminaries and, in a word, *go*, but when, whether unexpectedly or in fulfilment of some conscious apprehension in himself, another man pushes through the door and assumes the apparently obligatory position alongside him, never far enough away, perhaps grunting something, perhaps grunting nothing, perhaps unable to conceal a fluster as intense as the first man's, perhaps triumphantly affecting a virile indifference to all around him, as he unzips or unbuttons his own ineluctably interfering member, all purpose dwindles for the first man, all concentration and all hope.

One of two courses of action, or rather inaction, then tends to ensue: either the newcomer blithely gushes forth, pissing up the urinal to his tool's content, and leaves the first man as if transformed to stone, standing in pained self-consciousness with his untrusty, non-performing plonker still in hand, knowing no water will come to pass till the newcomer has finished and completely vacated the scene, or the newcomer, having manoeuvred the troublesome item from his trousers, comes to realise, to his own no tiny mortification, that he has been peremptorily dammed up in turn. Perhaps it is not surprising that little is said or written about the absurdity of two grown men, standing next to one another, with their penises dangling uselessly in hand. The silence that emerges, as both consider their aims undone, continuing awhile to stand alongside one another, not peeing into thin air, scarcely even able to think, soon grows intolerable. (*What is this like? Waiting to catch a bus? Expecting the arrival of a loved one? Seeing it as someone else's problem and hoping the technology will sort itself out? Why does this happen to me? Or, conversely, why should a man ever be expected to be at ease standing next to a stranger in this forced intimacy? And how can I bring it to an end?*)

Such was the scene in which Nicholas Royle and Nicholas Royle found themselves that evening, in the basement of the International Anthony Burgess Foundation, in the immediate aftermath of their joint reading. One had arrived before the other, it hardly mattered who. The embarrassment of one failed public performance now gave way to another.

— Next time you get that out you'll lose it altogether.

The older Royle could not hear as well as he used to. But then again, he had always enjoyed the possibilities of creative mishearing.

— I beg your pardon?

— I said next time we get called out we'll do this all better.

They attempted for a time to stand beside one another pretending not to be constrained in the slightest.

— You mean responding to Osmer?

Yes. (*Not that he'll be turning up to any future gig we might be doing.*)

(*Has he started peeing yet or is he in the same state of paralysis as I am?*)

(*How long are we going to carry on with this?*)

(*Looks like we'll be doing this till death us do part.*)

(*Does he think Osmer was referring to both of us, when he produced that offensive show-stopping remark?*)

— Do you know him at all?

(*I wish I'd noticed him going down the stairs. He can only have been a few seconds in front of me. I could just have stopped for a quiet minute or two in the basement, taken in the oddity of the Burgess typewriters under glass, read that notice on the door about access to the archives. Anything to avoid this ludicrous scenario.*)

— Me neither.

And then they did the gentlemanly thing that two mutually afflicted gentlemen in the gentlemen's do, in this pathetic situation: feign having successfully unburdened themselves, then tuck away their futile protuberances and retreat to wash their hands. Each had somewhere else to be: the local author was spending the evening with a couple of writer friends; the professor and his wife were having dinner with Matthew Frost.

But once out of the gents and back in the basement they paused, in friendly unison, realising they would likely have no further chance to talk that day. The younger man gestured towards a poster of Stanley Kubrick's *A Clockwork Orange* just behind them.

— Ironic all these fetishistic typewriters when it's the movie that made Burgess his fame and money. Same as J.G. Ballard, I suppose. Or Ishiguro, come to that.

— You don't believe in the art of the novel?

— It's not that. I care about it more than ever.

— So how would you define 'powerful writing'?

The younger man smiled over his goatee and considered for a few moments before responding:

— It's writing you believe in. With characters – or a character – you're interested in simply because you believe in them. It might be deeply rooted in a particular place, so deeply it's as if it's grown out of the earth there, like ivy or convolvulus bindweed.

The younger man seemed to read the other's quick scan of the basement, all spick-and-span glass cases, cabinets and polished floor, no sign of parasitical growths about to erupt beneath their feet.

— Or not set anywhere at all, but involving some drama taking place in someone's head and that head feels similarly like a real place. It's about truth, lies about truth.

— Sounds like Jean-Paul Sartre.

— I mean a story that reveals some truth about the real world. It needn't be set in the real world, but it will relate to the real world. It might be strange, but it doesn't have to be. It will probably affect you emotionally; it might make you laugh, it might make you cry. It will probably remind you that life is precious. And short.

Although he didn't say so, the other Royle, the one who, when Osmer's 'Double Whammy' was published less than three weeks afterwards, would be dubbed 'the woodlouse', was impressed. He was struck by his namesake's sense of commitment – perhaps that was Sartrean as well. And he felt mildly envious at the younger man's ability to encapsulate things with such clarity and brisk efficiency.

— And what do *you* think, Nick?

— I think it's a can of worms. What's 'powerful writing' for whom, when, where? Would you say that *Mein Kampf* was powerful writing?

— No, Hitler's prose is crap.

— But plenty of people find the Bible or the Koran, or Shakespeare, Dante or Rustaveli unreadable.

— Rasta who?

— You know, the twelfth-century epic poet from Georgia, Shota Rustaveli.

— Never heard of him.

— That's what I'm saying. Powerful writing is—

— Sure, OK. But *what is it for you*, I'm asking.

— Well, I don't know – it's all the things you just said it was. Only—

— Yeah?

— I'd like to write a novel that would try to do justice to the reality of birds.

— What do you mean?

— I don't know. I think it would be the death of me.

— You mean, like, Icarus without the wings?

The woodlouse laughed, then tried to explain:

— I dream of a writing that would not really be human. It would try to foreground the importance of non-human animals, especially what we call, in a nauseating appropriation, our feathered friends. If there's post-truth, there's post-fiction. I would like to write a post-fiction novel about love and death, spectrality and the poetics of extinction. I fantasise about a book that would be a new form of music, a transformed birdsong, a work of many voices – mixed sexes and identities in flight – a completely new species of literary psittacism.

— *Sick* what?

— Psittacism. You know, to do with parrots. Only it couldn't be a novel. I don't know what it would be. I dream about the idea of a hide.

— Jekyll and Hyde?

— No. Well, yes and no. You have to reckon with what Stephen King calls 'basement guy' – (and at this point the woodlouse flashed a smile at where they stood) – but the idea of a *text* that would hide, that would *be* a hide, a place from which to look out and look in, a secret place from which it would be possible not only to observe the activity and behaviour of birds and humans, say, but also to observe the novel itself, a kind of screened-off or embedded space within a novel in which it would be possible to explore the relations between birds and words, birdwatching and wordwatching.

The younger man seemed genuinely intrigued.

— What form would this hide take? Would it be located in the lower part of the page, like a running commentary or sub-text below the main body of the novel itself?

— Ideally, yeah, it'd be at the bottom of the page. The hide wouldn't be a sub-text, though. It's not a matter of providing the real or underlying meaning, some fixed or final message that lies beneath the surface. And it wouldn't be commentary either. I think of the hide rather as a kind of drone. Not the unmanned aircraft kind of drone with which drugged-up US military personnel kill and maim people of different ethnicity and religious belief via a computer thousands of miles away. I'm imagining a kind of weird textual drone, the hide as a new way of thinking about surveillance, including self-surveillance – but something that would be neither destructive nor indiscriminate.

— And what about the novel? You said the hide would be screened-off or embedded… What would the rest of the novel, or the novel itself, be about?

Taken aback, the older man looked suddenly perplexed, as if this question had simply never occurred to him.

— The novel itself? I haven't the foggiest idea.

Meanwhile, upstairs, Stephen Osmer had made his getaway before anyone could harass him with any tedious follow-up. In his haste he quite forgot about Lily. He was some distance down Cambridge Street, looking for a taxi to take him back to the friend's place where they were staying that night, when he remembered. Returning to the performance venue did not seem an option, he told her afterwards. He texted but got no response. Of course she had switched off her phone for the event. It had been quite chaotic in the aftermath. As Lily tried to spot Stephen (already gone) in the swirling eddies of people and coats, she found herself accosted, in perfectly courteous fashion, by the man with the twirling moustache. Would she care for a malt whisky, he asked, with a twinkle in his eye that seemed to countenance no denial. Would she be interested in a copy of *The Uncanny* for a tenner, with a generous dram of Bruichladdich thrown in? She had no intention of taking up this quirky offer, but before she knew it she was being introduced to Professor Royle's wife, a woman whose name she failed to catch.

And then Frost began to regale them with further jokes:

— Old man on a long journey with a horse and cart, gently swishing his whip, absolutely huge amount of manure in the cart, enters a village and is slowly driving past the pub and a fellow standing at the door says, What have you got there?

The old man says, I've got a ton of manure. And the other says, What are you going to do with that? The man says: I'm going to spread it on my rhubarb. The fellow outside the pub considers for a moment then replies: Round here we pour custard on it.

— A man takes his Rottweiler to the vet. My dog's cross-eyed, he says to the vet, is there anything you can do for him? Well, says the vet, let's have a look at him. So he picks the dog up and examines his eyes, then checks his teeth. Finally, he says, I'm going to have to put him down. What, says the man, because he's cross-eyed? No, says the vet, because he's really heavy.

— What do you call a deer with no eyes? *No idea.*

— What do you call a deer with no eyes and no legs? *Still no idea.*

— How many surrealists does it take to change a light bulb? *Fish.*

— What do you call a fish with no eyes? *Fsh.*

— Terrible news about all these schoolchildren in Bradford and Leeds, injecting Ecstasy directly into their mouths in order to avoid detection. It's called 'E by gum!'

Sensing his listeners beginning to weary, Frost shifted tack again:

— How many PhD students does it take to change a light bulb?

He contorted his face and mock-wept, exclaiming:

— *You just don't understand!*

There was something charming about the sight of the two most beautiful women in the room laughing together at the same time. Lily's laughter fused a semi-wincing knowledge of Stephen's futile travails in the domain of doctorate-production with the feeling of personal relief at a difficult road untaken. Portia (to put a name to the professor's wife) could be readily amused by the reference to PhD students because she had been one herself. But she had also known the teller for some years and heard the joke at least twice before. What on this occasion especially delighted was the screwed-up moustache face and the bizarre resemblance Frost's gesture managed to bear to a frenzied image of screwing in a light bulb under immense psychological pressure.

The group's Person from Porlock was a mousy, furtive-looking young man evidently hoping to take advantage of the book-and-whisky offer. Reluctantly, Frost broke off to make a sale. And Lily excused herself, but only after talking a little longer with the delightful-seeming Portia. The two women had been thrown together by laughter and something, at least for a few minutes, stuck.

The problem was that Lily had actually enjoyed the evening. That had not been her word. Shortly after arriving at the friend's flat, she said, not *really enjoyed*, she knew that would not be the most diplomatic formulation, but she had found it a *really interesting* evening. Stephen practically blew a gasket. It was the tiny but explosive detail of a moment. She was riled at having been deserted by him in a large and unknown city at night. She might also, with hindsight, have sought to check his mood before giving voice to her own. It was not *what* she said, she was convinced of that, but *how* she said it.

— I didn't say *enjoyed*, I said I found it *interesting*.

While she might not have used the word, Stevie was right to infer it. She had known from early on in their relationship that he had a temper. In general she had immunity: it was something he directed at others. Along with extraordinary powers of articulation, he could also be a man of few words.

Indeed he had only succeeded in getting to where he now was, swanning around the cultural heart of London, through an impressive capacity for discretion. But in private, when she and Stevie were alone together and he gave vent to his feelings, she found him on occasion alarming. There was never any suggestion of physical violence, but still she felt affronted. She was glad at this moment that there was no one else present – the friend was still out somewhere for dinner – but to be shouted at like that, in a stranger's flat, to be told it was intolerable, to be shoved by the fierceness of Stephen's feelings in this manner, when she was already upset... They were clearly both tired and edgy, not knowing when the friend might turn his key in the lock.

She retreated, like a snail with antennae cruelly flicked. She was going to bed. And then he, abruptly remorseful, apologised. An uneasy reconciliation followed. She was, in any case, asleep by the time his friend rolled in: the two men, old school-friends, duly bantered over a whisky or two before bed. It was an early train back to London in the morning. Between Lily and Stephen there was a cooling of affect that lasted several days, and it was during this period that he had dinner with Brian and then spent the rest of the night spinning out his 'double whammy'.

Osmoses

Osmer soon enough re-immersed himself in the everyday demands of magazine production, organising copy, dealing with subscriptions and advertising, reading and editing material, corresponding with contributors, making sure they got paid. But that evening at the Burgess Foundation changed him. He had been involved in numerous memorable events over the preceding couple of years: Ian McEwan, Salman Rushdie, A.S. Byatt, Jonathan Franzen, Julian Barnes, Hilary Mantel, Alan Hollinghurst – so many of the names of the day. These evenings with authors, sometimes staged at the *Gazette* offices but more often at bigger venues like the British Library or the Barbican, had been the highlight of his job. Stephen relished meeting the authors, listening to them read, and being able to discuss their work with them in a public forum. And often there would be dinner or drinks afterwards and the additional pleasure of more informal and sometimes indiscreet conversation. S.B. Osmer could, in short, a tale or two unfold.

But something had now altered in his conception of these events. Gone, after Manchester, was any sense that they ever were or ever could be productive occasions for the staging of arguments and ideas. They were merely narcotic. They were about the systematisation of literature as celebrity cultural production. They were about transforming the potency of fiction into what Stephen called 'program personality'. By this he meant the kind of personality a literary author was obliged to have, in order to be successful on the circuit. It was personality as program and program as personality. He ought to write about that.

It was crucial to make clear the reality of 'author readings'. Such occasions were about people and personalities, not about arguments and ideas. They served the interests of the marketplace, bolstering the cult of the author as celebrity in an entirely empty fashion. Of course, as co-ordinator of 'evenings with writers' and 'art events' in London with the *Literary Gazette* over the past several years, he had not failed, from time to time, to entertain such thoughts. But that Royle gala performance had truly scraped the scales off his eyes. The Royles were not of course celebrities of any kind, but still they were a part of the infernal program. What was needed was a focus on political reality, social responsibility and economic justice, not a literary fashion-show. Novelists and critics had a duty in this context, and the stand-up double-act in Manchester was a rampant dereliction of that duty.

So, more or less, had run the additional paragraph that the managing editor cut from the final copy for his essay on the topic.

Osmer wanted to bring all this to bear on the events he chaired with acclaimed authors, but how was he to do it? Towards the end of April there was an evening with Don DeLillo. The American read a couple of passages from *Point Omega*. Stephen wanted to get him to talk about the relationship between his novel and the 'war on terror', but was not sure how to angle it. He quoted for DeLillo's benefit a couple of lines of his own dialogue: 'The sixties are gone and there are no more barricades,' says one character. And the other replies: 'Film is the barricade... the one we erect, you and I. The one where somebody stands and tells the truth.'

What is *Point Omega* saying about the relation between film and the novel as an art form? What is Hitchcock's *Psycho* doing in your book? Does film 'tell the truth'? And what about real barricades, Mr DeLillo, for example in gated communities, or around finance centres in London, New York and elsewhere, or around the Palestinians in Gaza? What about the barricades that can still be manned? And what about all the metaphorical but no less powerful barricades between the ruling classes, on the one hand, and the working class and underclass, on the other?

He couldn't do it. This new experience of pornographic abjectness – the sense that he was actively contributing to this 'celebrity nihilism', as he sat in the polished leather armchair facing the great American novelist – was unreal. It brought him out in a sweat. He felt as if the very air was readying itself, oiling up invisible utensils preparatory to skinning him alive. Was he unable to deal with certain feelings of anti-Americanism, despite his best intentions? Was it a peculiar fury he felt in response to this novelist in particular, a writer perhaps more capable than any other in English of honing his prose to the most pencil-fine elegance? Was it a new sharpness of disappointment about DeLillo's writing in a political context? Was it that unctuousness, that very facility of refinement and meticulous aestheticising in his writing, its calculated straddling of high art and high theory? Osmer supposed he must, for the first time in his life, be having a panic attack. He could not look out into the audience. His heart felt like a boxing glove trying to punch its way out of his chest. Everything was dazzling, dizzying

– the lights overhead, the metallic hum and throb of the microphones on the table in front of them, the stirrings of the audience as of a soundtrack that has been suddenly turned up – and waves of a kind of paralysis ebbed over his face and hands as the sweat trickled down his face and streamed inside his shirt.

A fortnight later was no better. It ought to have been the easiest thing in the world: a bookshop event with Andrew Motion, talking about Edward Thomas. Stephen told himself the DeLillo was an aberration, a nightmare evening to move on from, and he felt perfectly at ease as he cycled over to the Piccadilly Waterstones with plenty of time to spare. How can anything go wrong with this, he asked himself, a chat with Andrew Motion?

They were talking about Thomas's relation to Robert Frost and everything was going along fine. Sir Andrew recited 'Adlestrop' to the assembled multitude. (About a hundred people had shown up.) It was almost the end of the evening. They were talking about the poem in a perfectly relaxed fashion, and then, as if a fuse had blown, Stephen lost all sense of reality. It might as well have been a poem by J.H. Prynne or, come to that, a sonnet by Saatchi & Saatchi. Was it something about repetition? Motion had already duly impressed the audience by delivering the lines by heart. But now in the course of talking about the poem, he cited again the lines about the steam train pulling up and then leaving the deserted platform:

Yes, I remember Adlestrop –
The name, because one afternoon
Of heat the express-train drew up there
Unwontedly. It was late June.

The steam hissed. Someone cleared his throat.
No one left and no one came
On the bare platform. What I saw
Was Adlestrop – only the name.

And the celebrity author, respected biographer and former poet laureate was making elegant remarks about the enjambment, the poignant torsions of the prosaic, the quietly magisterial character of the 'Unwontedly', the passing away of this shattering industrial intrusion, and all Osmer could think of was the name, the absurdity of 'Adlestrop', the dismal self-advertisement of a poem about that name that calls itself by that name, 'Adlestrop', a brain-addling lad's trope, ladling on the post, a strop on a pedestal, this crazy obsession with a lost Englishness, a lost history that the poet appeared to be affirming and now Motion appeared to be affirming in turn. Stephen was completely scattered, thrown into a kind of dissolution by this word 'Adlestrop'.

He felt as if he were committing incest in public. He was certain the audience could see how pale he was and shaking, and he thought he was going to black out. Motion came to a halt. Stephen felt as if the bookshop was about to be blown to smithereens. Every bookshelf, every face on which his eyes settled teetered and started to dissolve. But after a pause which might have lasted five seconds or five minutes – he had no consciousness – the poet smiled and blinked benignly in Stephen's face and suggested they might leave it there. Everyone clapped. As if no one had looked up and noticed, the whole disaster passed over like an isolated toxic chemical cloud.

In general, Stephen had a deep-rooted dislike of wordplay. He associated it with all things frivolous and inane. In a literary and cultural context it was inseparable, for him, from the sordid resourcefulness of bourgeois self-indulgence. Still a certain double-think prevailed, as so often where something is fiercely rejected. In these respects, there was a homology between the mind of S.B. Osmer and the tabloid newspaper. You could hardly expect the *Sun* or *Daily Mail* to devote extensive and regular column space to exploring the idea of paronomasia and the intricacies of language in shaping people's experience and their understanding of the world. Nowhere is a narcotising contempt for the richness and power of words more evident than in the pages of such publications. And at the same time virtually every news item is headlined with some abject pun, alliteration or other ludic effect.

For the linguistic thuggery of the tabloids Osmer felt only distaste. He was driven, as few committed socialists are, by a passionate conviction of the capacity of language to change people's lives. But this carried with it a marked scepticism whenever someone started playing with words, accelerating into vituperative rage the moment he deemed such activity to be in the service of the machinery of capitalism and ideological control. This, for Stephen, was liable to prove the case anywhere and everywhere, from crass versifiers in mainstream poetry magazines to ingenious copywriters in the advertising industry, from up-themselves academics to content-free red-top journalists.

The maniacal disintegration of the word 'Adlestrop' was thus quite foreign to him. He was perfectly capable of wordplay in the private gymnasium of his head, but what often first came into his mind was quite different from what he wrote. In his mind he was given to wordplay of a rather simple and banal kind, but he regarded this as less tabloid, more Dickens. In keeping with the great novelist's proclivity for artifice in the realm of character-naming (M'Choakumchild, Pecksniff, Cruncher, Podsnap, the Barnacles, the Dedlocks, the Veneerings and so many others), Stephen had developed an array of common names adapted to his own particular uses. Thus in his head he would refer, for example, to a *banker* (something or someone, like Lily, you could bank on), a *booker* (a topic inciting such a degree of anger that, if needed, you could write a book about it) and a *thinker* (a period of withdrawal and considered judgment, at a distance from other people). A more intricately probing mind than Stephen's might have observed the consistency with which these acts of naming entailed distorted meanings of common nouns ending *-er* and gone on to speculate how far they might thus figure as echoing or rhyming with his own surname. Stephen did not dwell on such fripperies. His *os* might signify 'mouth' and his *mer* the 'sea', or any number of other nice contentions and conjectures, but this went quite beyond his range of interests. His very electing to use initials, to be S.B. Osmer, was impelled by a desire for a name as flat and workmanlike as possible.

Glider

Stephen Osmer needed to go on a thinker, and how better to do so than ride in the calm of the early dawn? Its calm gripped him, literally, between the legs as he cycled, laden with panniers, building up calf-muscle hour after hour trekking out one Thursday in late May, leaving London, leaving Lily, leaving everything and everyone, for a weekend alone in Norfolk. The boss had without hesitation given him permission to take two days off: he wondered if she could tell somehow that he needed the break, for she didn't press him for reasons. He headed out to join the Lea Valley towpath from Limehouse, cycling up as far as Dobbs Weir (and early lunch at the Fish and Eels), before winding his way through a string of villages with quaint names (from Much Hadham to Little Hadham to Clapgate to Starlings Green), and stopping over that first night at the Crown Inn just outside Saffron Walden. This was what he needed, a day of splendid isolation, sweeping through the sunny lushness along English country roads in green and flowering May, concluding with a leisurely bar-supper and couple of pints in a comfortable old pub, before turning in at around nine o'clock with aching limbs, exhausted but content. Next morning he pedalled on to Cambridge, where he put himself and his Allez on the train in order to reach Great Yarmouth by the late afternoon.

Glider

He had booked for two nights at the Royal Hotel. He was well aware of its historic connections. Dickens had stayed two nights in 1849: out of that brief sojourn came significant elements of *David Copperfield*. Stephen was planning no major work of autobiographical fiction, but felt that there was indeed something vital, some further labour of composition stirring within him. He was not in Norfolk to write, however, but to think. On the way to Great Yarmouth his aim had been clear: to become physically exhausted, balancing himself along the towpath of the Lea Valley, unwinding down those winding country roads towards Saffron Walden. And, now that he had arrived at his coastal destination, his task was to embark on the thinker proper. He had duly resolved to spend the rest of Friday in or around the hotel, then set out early next day and cycle up the coast, returning via a loop that would take him through a section of the Broads. He ordered a pint of Aspalls and sat with it in an armchair alongside a large tropical fish aquarium in the corner of the hotel bar. Immersed in the rhythms of coming and going, rising and falling in the cool shadow-life of the tank, Stephen tried to come out in his mind. He felt very much like the catfish lurking under the ornamental bridge in the sludgy green bottom of the tank – and then again as fearful as a guppy in the midstream, as it darted out of the way of who knew what. He sipped from his glass of ice-cold, fine dry cider and reflected.

He appeared to be in uncharted waters. Was he heading for a shipwreck? He had never had a panic attack before, if that was what it had been. He dreaded the thought of a recurrence. It had to do, he realised, with the physical confrontation with celebrities and an unprecedented feeling of paralysis. Like most Englishmen, Osmer felt personally sick at the thought of psychotherapy. He had a pretty fixed idea of it: self-indulgent, expensive, and not for him. How could he face up to even broaching such a thing with Lily? Or to telling Brian and others at the office? *Stevie isn't in this morning till eleven, remember, he's seeing his shrink.* Or: *Always thought of him as such a strong, independent young man who could deal with anything thrown at him.* Besides, he knew that he was smart in ways that would make counselling or therapy ridiculous. He'd ride loops and circles around anyone who thought they could tell him what was wrong. Only over the phone with his mother could he air something of the anguish he was experiencing. They spoke at least once a week, sometimes more frequently. He had called her the night before he came away, gathering courage from her voice and no-nonsense easiness. He knew that there was a point at which her church-strong upbringing constrained her, just as he knew what he didn't have to tell her for her to know all he needed her to.

Eyes sunk in the cool shadow-life of the tank, Stephen saw that getting away to Norfolk was no getting away from himself. Ripples of sadness passed through him. He had never felt so solitary. Dickens, at least, had not been alone here. He thought of the song by Mark Lemon, his companion on that trip in 1849: *Oh, would I were a boy again...* But nothing, in fact, was more alien to Osmer than such Victorian sentimentalism. Even his beloved Dickens failed him in that department. Nostalgia just didn't agree with him. Still, was something telling him his days with the *Gazette* were drawing to an end, and that it was time to look to some new position and a different kind of challenge? And could he discuss these things with Lily or should he, as he so far successfully had done, keep them to himself until he was clear what he wanted to do?

He consumed a fish supper in the bar, mildly irritated that the vegetables were from frozen, not fresh. He drank a second pint of Aspall's, then retired to his room. This opened on to a small balcony over the seafront. He poured himself some whisky from the hip flask he had brought with him and sat out in the late spring evening air. This was a town that had, he knew, voted overwhelmingly to leave the European Union. Few current inhabitants, he surmised, would concur with Dickens' description of Great Yarmouth as the most wondrous sight his eyes had ever beheld. The balcony was noisy with Friday night traffic and groups of drinkers in the street below, and Stephen soon withdrew. His plan was to read in bed for a while, but just before undressing he found himself flicking through the hotel information pamphlet on the bedside table. Some whiff of the estranged recent past was to be caught here: *All of our staff speak English.* He was wryly amused to discover that the hotel had originally been called the Victoria but had changed its name on account of the fact that the Prince Regent (later King Edward VII) had visited with his mistress Lillie Langtry. He hadn't intended to text or call Lily, but the appearance of the lovely forename in the otherwise banal paragraph summoned up her absent beauty in intoxicating fashion. As for Edward and his lover, the only thing Stephen could recall was the alleged exchange in which he had told her, in exasperated tone, that he had spent enough on her to build a battleship. To which Lillie Langtry replied: *And you have spent enough in me to float one.* The recollection of this crudity made his own Lily still more desirable in his mind.

He'd told her he needed to take a long bike ride and wouldn't be about that weekend. He hadn't explained himself any further. She was going to be staying in town. She had something at the South Bank on the Thursday evening but no other weekend plans, she said, a quiet Friday night in, watching *Fitzcarraldo*, she thought, at home in Clerkenwell. (She was doing some research on Werner Herzog, in preparation for an upcoming series of events.) But when he texted, then phoned, he got no reply. He would try again later, he decided. He got into bed, enjoying the coolness of the sheets and thinking about how unlike a mistress Lily Lynch seemed to him. He was suddenly flooded with love for her. And he realised, as never before, how much she meant to him. They truly belonged together. Their relationship had all the solidity and firmness of a marital bond.

Propped up in bed he poured himself another whisky, then summoned his book on his Kindle and was quickly captivated. He was reading Matt Taibbi's *The Divide: American Injustice in the Age of the Wealth Gap*, having recently devoured the same author's *Griftopia: A Story of Bankers, Politicians, and the Most Audacious Power Grab in American History*. Replenishing his glass of scotch on the bedside table, he felt himself gliding through the text. That was the thing these days: with a tablet you didn't need to scrutinise the pages, you could just glide. Instead of a book, Stephen thought, you could call it a *glider*. It was dark beyond the windows now, but he kept going and, every twenty minutes or so, poured himself a little more whisky. Soon enough he was rather drunk. This bender was to be a mender: he was on a thinker. He felt his mind swirling. His banker was Lily. His booker would be about the financial catastrophe of 2008 and its continuing aftermath.

Taibbi's work was instructive. He highlighted the enormity of what was happening in the United States. But like so many Americans who write about global issues, acknowledging that the financial meltdown could not be confined to a single country or region of the world, his writing retained a maddening inward focus. For better and worse it was addressed to a ghostly American middle-class intellectual who might be awed and shamed into some directly productive and meritorious response. Taibbi was saying what everyone should know. It was a shocking account of how much, how far and how brutally the so-called financial players, in the US in particular, had gambled with everyone's money but their own, messing about with huge non-existent funds, destroying people's jobs and vocations, taking away their futures. Taibbi foregrounded the absolute, intolerable injustice of the whole thing and how much it depended, like a novel, on fictional figures, structures and effects.

The global collapse had been wrought by *financial players lying to investors*. And this proliferation of fiction, fabrication and story-telling was made to depend on the idea of knowing what someone else was thinking, on *proof of the mental state* of the player. Call in the lawyers, the bankers' best friends forever. The collusions of the legal profession and financial speculation had a long and sordid history: *Bleak House* and *Our Mutual Friend* rolled into one. But Matt Taibbi turned not to Dickens but to Graham Greene for a key term in his argument. *The Divide* was not about the working class, but about the *torturable* class. For Taibbi there were now just two classes: the Wall Street class and the financially torturable class. What about the torturable class of Great Yarmouth? Taibbi was no stop-at-home Americanist. He had spent time in St Petersburg for example, back in the days when it was still Leningrad. But he couldn't describe the catastrophe of what had happened in 2008 in ways that stretched beyond a US readership. Taibbi was right about plenty of things, but he didn't go nearly far enough. It was up to S. B. Osmer to make these truths count. Stephen would write the book or essay – at any event the piece of writing – to change it all.

His ride the following day went well enough. It was dry at first, a mix of sun and fair-weather clouds, with light winds. He took the loop route he'd planned, along the coastal road past the huge wind turbines out to sea at Scroby Sands, up past Horsey Windpump as far north as Sea Palling, then down along the west side of Hickling Broad National Nature Reserve back into Great Yarmouth, via a brief stop-off to see the remains of the Roman fort at Caister-on-Sea. It was a grand day. No punctures, no snags. He kept himself steady. He cycled fast enough to set the May breeze and sun streaming in synch, cooling and warming by turn. Feeling at liberty, feeling strong, he cycled at one with the magnificent flatness of the land and vastness of the sky. He encountered a small warm rain for a few miles between Ingham and Sutton Mill, but then the sunshine returned and breeze enfolded him.

The train back to London next day was sweaty and long, with a change at Cambridge as well as Norwich, but he felt OK. He buried himself in another book about what people call, without apparent irony or misgiving, the finance industry, Michael Lewis's graphic exposure of high-frequency traders, *Flash Boys*. It was good to have cycled so much. He'd felt he was in his element. It was a brilliant weekend, he told Lily later that evening over the phone, forgetting even to ask where she'd been. He had got stuff sorted.

Crypt

After about six weeks or so came a reversal of which the Woodlocks themselves were scarcely conscious. Silas became fed up with wintry shopping expeditions and wandering streets strewn with people less mobile than himself: his sociality was less developed than his wife's. He hadn't retired to an out-of-the-way anonymous little town on the south coast in order to foster valuable new friendships with other members of the human race. He wanted out of the Great Rats' Nest of London, he wanted done with the mind-numbing, body-aching decades of heading up Woodlock & Sons, he wanted nothing more than some proper, long-term peace and quiet. It was a large enough house that he was able, for the first time since he was a boy, to have a room of his own, a den in which he could play his *Night at the Village Vanguard* or *Station to Station* or *Exile on Main Street* without troubling or being troubled by anyone. The couple now in effect switched places, so that Ethel was the one off fetching the shopping and generally mooching about town; and, unlike her husband, she was soon enough exchanging smiles with neighbours, talking with shopkeepers and striking up acquaintanceships.

She worried that Silas was becoming withdrawn. She knew well enough that retirement could make you ripe for depression. Wasn't she wrestling in her way with the same thing? You enter upon your twilight years and suddenly can't see why or what you're supposed to be doing or for how long. There was still plenty to be done to the house but once winter was over, she knew there would also be the garden. She wanted it all to look nice, especially for when Ashley came down as he promised, bringing Rhoda with him, for a long weekend.

On Sunday afternoons it became a regular thing for them to pop into the Wellington for a drink. Weather permitting, they'd start with a walk along the seafront, though it was the busiest time of the week, with couples and families, locals and day-trippers, dog-walkers and wheelchair-users, cyclists and young children on scooters. Even then Ethel was keenly aware of what all the bustling covered up: *nothing but the waves and the cries of seagulls*. It was bracing to get some of that sea air, and the comfort and indulgence of sitting by the fire in the pub was heightened as a result. Ensconced in the warm chimney-corner one Sunday towards the end of March, Silas with his pint and Ethel with her chardonnay, she put it to him:

— You see at the Crypt they're doing watercolour workshops and writing classes for people?

The Crypt was a rather remarkable thing she had stumbled upon more or less by chance. You'd never know it was there, a nondescript modern building tucked in behind the tourist office and police station. Only later did she realise there was a front entrance, situated on Church Street. But she first came across the place as she was walking home from the supermarket, having decided to see if there was a shortcut. Buried in a corner of a car park, it transpired, was the back entrance to the Crypt. There was a small porch affair and an open door. Without further invitation she went in. There was a small exhibition area featuring work by local photographers, along with a couple of further rooms at the front. But at the heart of the building was the Crypt itself. Beyond a large, battered, ancient oak door off the exhibition area, a series of uneven steps, not wheelchair-friendly in the slightest, led down into a shadowy chamber, a thirteenth-century vaulted room with seating for about thirty people. Its existence, especially encased in such incongruous surroundings, seemed implausible. It took Ethel at least two visits to come round to the idea that it wasn't a replica. Her husband had countered:

— Why would the town council construct a *fake* medieval chapel in the middle of a bog-standard 1980s office building, love?

Little, in fact, was known. They were less than two hundred yards from St Leonard's church, which went back to the thirteenth century and beyond, but there was no established connection. Local historians suppose that the Crypt had served as a private family chapel, part of a much larger domicile of which no other traces remain. Ethel liked it. It took her down into herself. Its initial impact on Silas was of another kind. Having stooped, as he had to, to get into it, he stood in the cool, dimly lit stone enclosure beside his wife and realised that he, they, neither of them so far as he was concerned, had given consideration to the question, *where to be buried?* So when Ethel said *crypt*, before pausing to take a sip of her chardonnay, that was where he was led. She went on:

— The workshop is just fifteen quid, plus a donation for materials. I imagine the writing classes must be about the same.

Silas did not revisit the question of their final resting place until some days later. His immediate impulse was rather to query why there would be a donation for materials for a writing class. He was being obtuse, she was talking about the donation for materials for the painting sessions, she didn't know offhand, she hadn't noticed what the price was for the writing classes but think, Silas, you've often in the past said you'd like to paint or write something – why not now?

Not in a month of blue Sundays would Silas Woodlock have signed up for an art class in Croydon. But while his initial reaction to his wife's suggestion was one of faintly scornful dismissal, by the time he'd drained his glass he was coming round. It called, if only unconsciously, for a second pint.

The creative writing classes were run by a young man from Hastings called Jason, who made clear his industry and credentials by informing the group that he was author of several novels as well as a collection of short stories and also ran classes in Eastbourne and Brighton. In that same opening session Jason went round the group (they were actually seated in a pleasant but anonymous, brightly lit room at the front of the building) asking what people did with their time, were they working, did they have previous experience of writing, and the rest. Of the ten or so present, all but a couple were in their late sixties or seventies and no longer working. For some reason the tutor, when he got round the table to Woodlock, seemed to think him still in gainful employ, asking with vague insouciance:

— And what do you do for a living?

— For a *living*? demanded Silas with a vehemence that visibly took others aback.

There was something about the man's bulky frame, his height and stooped shoulders, and about the unexpected abruptness of his echoing Jason's question, that precipitated a psychic drop in the temperature of the room. The tutor was not going to press the matter, but Woodlock paved over the sudden quietness by observing, in distinctly more friendly fashion, that he had recently retired and never written a word of fiction in all of his natural. He was not inclined to declare himself to the world at large as a former undertaker. It was quite irrelevant to the occasion and, he well knew, only likely to produce a negative effect on the proceedings. He wasn't there, in any case, to make friends. Indeed he was already weighing up whether this first creative writing class (all Ethel's idea) was also to be his last. But as the session went on, and no one made any further attempts on his private life or history, Silas somewhat softened and, at the end, paid for the full half-dozen workshops, running fortnightly till the end of June.

Silas remained generally aloof from others in the group. After class it became customary to repair to the Old Plough for a drink, and he was one of only two or three who consistently gave their apologies. He felt conscious of having left Ethel on her lonesome for the evening, but he also found the class itself unexpectedly demanding. To be put on the spot and challenged, there and then, in the company of a dozen strangers, to dream up ideas, words and paragraphs about sometimes quite alien topics, took it out of him. He struggled with the sense that he was back at school and, fifty and more years later, no different in any respect from the way he was then.

Jason Winslow's writing exercises seemed by turns insipid or impossible. The first one that really brought something out of Silas was when they were given a line from some dead poet called Basil Bunting who apparently once remarked that *it is easier to die than to remember*. That struck a chord. They were asked to keep a journal over the following week, listing things that were difficult to recall because it was easier not to. So Silas started putting pen to paper, at various moments of the day, jotting down memories of things he had resolutely put to the back of his mind or had not, in some instances for decades, even realised were available for recollection. This exercise didn't appear to lead anywhere in particular, but Woodlock found it interesting. And then they were each asked to take a specific story and read it over the course of the fortnight ahead and, at the following session, report back on their experience. Silas was asked to read something called 'The Drowned Giant'. He had heard of the writer's name, J. G. Ballard. Ethel had gone to see *Empire of the Sun*. She'd often taken herself off to the pictures, at Grant's or down the Purley Way. The name of Ballard had come up then, but he had never read any of his books. It turned out that Winslow was a big fan.

Silas had never encountered anything like 'The Drowned Giant', and he enjoyed reporting on it to the group. It was an account of a drowned giant (what else would you expect?) washed up on the beach. It was about how all the people travel to the coast to see it, and are filled with curiosity and a sense of marvel, and then about how gradually they start desecrating the body, and different body-parts end up serving different purposes, like showpieces in hotels and golf clubs, circuses and museums. Silas found it sad but was also able to admire the care that the author had put in, the writer's precision concerning the human anatomy and the descriptions of the cadaver. He wasn't surprised when the tutor said that Ballard had done medical training as a young man.

Where to be buried? Silas kept this question to himself for a few days. But it seemed incredible that he, they, neither of them had given it their attention before. Of course the topic had come up in passing from time to time, but they'd never sat down and made any decisions. For all the encouragement they'd given others, down the years, to make prudent provision and pre-paid plans – but that was often the way, not putting into practice your own good advice to others. They'd seen to their own parents at the allotted time but would Ashley see to them? Would Ethel even want that? He could recall that they had, on one or two occasions in the past, mulled over the question of burial or cremation, and had agreed that they'd want to be buried together, but where?

One morning shortly after their first visit to the Crypt, he had set out on a walk without telling his wife where he was going. It took him longer than he had anticipated, but he was a fit and vigorous man for his years and enjoyed the amble. He walked west along the seafront and then made his way inland to the village of Bishopstone. It was a sunny, blustery day and the daffodils were out in St Andrew's churchyard, all jostling in the breeze. He'd read up a bit beforehand about this squat Saxon edifice nestled in the foot of the Downs. Over the porch stood an ancient sundial, inscribed with the name of Eadric, king of Kent in 685. He stood for a good couple of minutes wondering at that, before stepping inside to take shelter from a sharp shower.

Reading a few weeks later about the beached cadaver brought home the desirability of a decent burial, Christian or otherwise. You wouldn't want to be strewn all over the place, like Ballard's giant. Silas had liked the feel of St Andrew's churchyard. Despite the rain, he had been struck by its tucked-away location, the quiet and dignity of the place. He could see him and Ethel ending up there. He had meant to tell her that same week, but never got round to it.

Crypt

As April turned into May there were the gulls to contend with. One spring afternoon they'd taken a walk along the seafront to the Salts, a park with a café, a kiddies' playground, an outdoor gym, tennis courts and playing fields, and Silas had got himself a can of cloudy lemonade and his wife an ice cream. They were standing outside the café when a gull swooped on Ethel from behind and took her 99 cone clean off her. And then just a few days later he had been standing on a ladder in the garden, stupid in retrospect, with a cheese sandwich in his hand. Ethel was in a world of her own, a few feet away, potting up geraniums. He was just ascending a couple of rungs in order to check on a bit of paintwork he'd done earlier that day, when a gull (probably the same one, laughed Ethel afterwards) nabbed it or tried to. The sandwich landed in the begonias. Silas was incensed.

But that was just the beginning. The gulls were now mating and nesting on the rooftops all around them. The Woodlocks couldn't believe the racket they kicked up. All hours of the day, starting before it even got light, they cawed and squawked and screeched. The old couple had never known such a cacophony. The house was tall and stood in a rather narrow street, and the back garden was surrounded on three sides by further high walls. This seemed to create a kind of echo-chamber that preserved and accentuated all the noise. By the time summer arrived, Ethel was practically going round the twist.

There was a stretch from late May through June when the weather seemed to have simply broken down. It had an eerie quality that brought back memories of the desiccation of the summer of 1976, when they had the extended hosepipe ban, rivers dried up, and lawns and churchyards turned brown and arid. You could scarcely dig. But this was different from the earlier drought, because you knew it wasn't natural. You could feel it in the air. You could sense it in your bones. Probably the gulls sensed it too. What was it, Ethel asked more than once, what were the government calling it now? Was this the tipping effect everyone had been tipped off about?

For their final assignment on the creative writing workshop everyone in the group was supposed to write some poetry or a piece of fiction. What Silas really wanted to do was try his hand at a detective story, but the gulls got in the way. He decided to write about them instead, envisaging it in the style of a kind of report, like Ballard. He followed Winslow's recommendations and bought a notepad to keep a record of his impressions. He kept it on the bedside table and when he got rudely awoken, as happened, day after day, or shortly before, in the twilight before dawn, by the dystopian scratched record of the gulls, he would remain still, like one of the stone effigies of blokes lying down in Southwark Cathedral, and rack his brains to think what on earth these discordant sounds were like, what words to use to describe this incessant din. By now it wasn't only the cawing and shrieking of the adults, it was also the plaintive mewing of the newcomers, hatchlings that seemed to double in size overnight, then double again the next.

After about a month and a good deal of effort, writing and collating and rewriting, checking and researching reference works in the local library, he managed to put something together, something he felt he might be able to show the tutor. For Winslow had said, at their final session, that if anyone wished to send him a printout of their work, up to six pages but no more, with a stamped addressed envelope for return postage, and receive a professional opinion on it, they would be more than welcome to do so. Silas had written his piece by hand, so it would need to be typed up anyhow. Ethel would be happy to do that. But first he wanted to read it to her, to see what she thought. So, armed with the first fruit of his creative labours, he took Ethel down to the Wellington. It was the middle of the afternoon and the pub was quiet. Other customers had chosen to sit out in the sunshine, but they sat inside at their usual table, in the cool of the chimney-corner, where now of course no fire was lit. It was a strangely exhilarating occasion, as much for Ethel as for Silas. It called for more than one drink. It was his first proper piece of creative writing, and Ethel had no idea, as he cleared his throat, what he was going to say.

Icebergs

Lily Lynch loved Stevie Osmer. She loved his mind, his ability to put things into words, his political passion, his spiritual and physical generosity, the sort of gentleness he had while hardly knowing it. And she was drawn, too, she could not deny it, by the allure of someone whose reputation was gathering such steam, someone who spoke for his generation and whose words might come, in due course, to have some effect on the world. She loved him, but she was young. *Love before marriage is like an excessively brief preface at the start of an endless book.* She couldn't recall where she'd come across that witticism – an old French poet, was it, her mother had once quoted? That was what Lily was like: someone who wanted to fully experience the brevity of the preface. Her mind could skip, talk in different tongues, lift thoughts from different spaces and registers. She maintained numerous strong friendships while also keeping to herself. She could listen to the radio, read a book, knit a multicoloured hat and hold a conversation with Stephen, all at the same time. He found it, on occasion, maddening. She was part-Arab, her mother francophone, which must account for something.

What should a woman like Lily do? The Arts Council was in an interesting place. Why should anyone fund the arts these days? And what arts should the Arts Council fund?

Wasn't 'the book' over and done with? Shouldn't money be going into film, digital media, the virtual reality construction industry (as she thought of it), public forms of pleasure of the kind with which everyone walking into the Turbine Hall of Tate Modern could get their hands dirty? These were issues she thought about, and had to talk about with others, more or less every day, and she relished everything it entailed.

Stephen had not actually raised the subject of marriage. He had not said, in so many words: *Lily, how do you feel about tying the knot some time in the next year or so?* But she inferred its presence in his mind. He seemed older. Or, at least, he seemed to have grown older than her in the couple of years since they had been together. It is difficult when one is very beautiful. Lily mostly denied that she was, even to herself. But if beauty is in the eye of the beholder, it also has something of the non-negotiable. Many a flower might still blush unseen, but not so easily in Cambridge or central London. If you're a supermodel smoking forty a day to suppress appetite and boredom and the money is piling in for your face or legs, that's one thing. But if you consider yourself shy, as Lily did, public places could be onerous. She mostly disliked the sensation that she was being lusted after. It could be such a hassle fending off attention. She had to be careful, whoever she was talking to. The boss of this gallery or that museum might appear not to be interested in her body, but still she had to be on guard. From a thousand signs, even if she did not understand why, she knew the rest of the world found her intensely desirable.

She mostly preferred to think of herself as a bit dim. This consideration was crucial to the balance of her relationship with Osmer: she allowed him superiority on more or less every topic or question they ever discussed. Conversely, she knew that, while he might be fêted as the cleverest young man in London, he was hardly the most handsome. Life, for her, was easier that way. In fact, of course, she was very smart. She hadn't achieved a first at Cambridge, but that was because she hadn't tried: she had been too deeply involved in other things. Quite apart from what being an acknowledged belle invariably required in an ancient university town, there was editing, drama and even, for a couple of terms, the debating society. She studied human, social and political science, specialising in sociology. Unlike many of her peers, she also enjoyed reading for pleasure. As finals approached, she was more likely, indeed, to be found in her rooms (for she stayed in college throughout her three years) reading J. M. Coetzee or Ali Smith than studying Emile Durkheim or Robert K. Merton. Her foray into biological anthropology in particular had been a mistake. She had somehow conceived of herself as a scientist at root, but by the end of her undergraduate studies she was less sure.

Still, there were things she understood as few women and fewer men do. She was possessed of a peculiar unconsciousness that flipped into luminosity. So she knew that her dimness was indoctrination. With two older brothers it was easy enough to see, growing up, how much self-confidence, assertiveness and ambition were male attributes of an especially insidious and fake kind. In her time at Cambridge she came to a more profound apprehension of how far the world was organised around the delusions of patriarchal posturing and destructive virility. Her final dissertation at college was on the subject of hoaxes in media and culture. It was marked down because it took the subject too broadly. Not willing to stick to specific examples, such as Sokal or celebrity death hoaxes, or even to range more generally across urban legends, email scams or stories going viral on the internet, Lily Lynch wanted to argue that the hoax was everywhere, starting with the superiority of the *homo* and going on to the *sapiens*.

All of this happened in her body. She lived it without fully appreciating how much it illuminated her. Without thinking, therefore, she was a vegetarian, and it was then simply a question of time before she came, as she did at university, to pull together the reasons why she should not feel able to eat meat. A softly spoken young man at a dinner party one night on Mill Road (where, for everyone else, the main course was chicken) happened to use the word *carnovirility*. She had never encountered it before. The others laughed like hyenas. But she could have slept with the shy boy who said it. Perhaps not the world's most elegant word, it nonetheless brought together two major fundamentalisms. And she understood, with disarming simplicity, that consuming the flesh of other animals and having puffed-up penis-structures symbolically strutting about giving orders was not the future. She didn't need to wait for the authors of *Farmageddon* to tell her what was already crystal-clear: if humanity was to survive even the next century or two, it would require a radically different conception and use of land and resources, a fundamentally altered estimation of the human male, a new politics. Without perhaps yet having the words in which to say it, then, her sense of *Que faire?* was no less revolutionary than the passions driving Stevie.

But she herself was still changing, still coming to terms on *her* terms with the sort of fix in which everyone, and especially women, found themselves. So she was working for the Arts Council, but she might soon enough be led elsewhere. For the moment, she was involved in a project about the idea of intention in film. That was where the Herzog came in. With a friend from the British Film Institute she had dreamt up this series of events on *Cinematic Intentions*. Stephen had asked, with a furtive smile, what she intended by it.

— Intention, she replied energetically (while checking for messages on her phone), is something that is being transformed. And film is one of the places where you can see this, but people don't seem to have noticed.

Stephen thought the whole thing frankly crazy. It took her a while to convince him that the guy from the BFI wasn't just going along with it because he, like Stephen, found her the hottest woman he had ever laid eyes on. But when the three of them met, one Friday evening in early June, for dinner in the restaurant at the top of Tate Modern overlooking the river and St Paul's, Adrian Franton was as gay as the day was long and wore a wedding ring for all to see and talked with great animation about his other half while showing no sexual interest in Lily Lynch whatsoever, besides the charming affinities a loquacious gay man can have with a beautiful straight woman, and Stephen's mind was put at rest. The conversation moved on to the project that had brought Lily and Adrian together.

— It was Stevie's inspiration anyway, she pointed out, as they sat at their table, not yet having picked up their menus.

And in that split-second she coloured, only now seeing that 'cinematic intentions' had, perhaps, a marital resonance that she hadn't considered. Was she prompting Stevie to make the proposal she had already inferred was present in his mind and which she was already determined to reject? It was a strangely dislocated moment as the two men looked at her and she in response picked up and stared furiously at her menu. Each man felt differently perplexed. Then they followed their noses and joined her in that curious anthropological space of prospective diners looking together at their menus. Within half a minute it transpired that no one was having a starter; Adrian was electing to have the *confit* of free-range rabbit, *Sarladaise* potatoes, *ragu* of artichokes, broad beans and cherry tomatoes; Stephen the corn-fed chicken breast, young peas, Emmett's smoked bacon, vegetable and herb stock; and Lily the pearl barley risotto, smoked garlic and slow-roast tomatoes – the solitary option for the vegan she now was.

But so much of the meaning and future of the world is contained in a restaurant menu, or at any event in deciding what to eat, and on what basis or conditions. This half-minute could readily be expanded or slowed down to half an hour, as if miming the title of Herzog's short about the dangers of texting while driving, *From One Second to Another*. For entire lives are played out in this eerie interval, in which no one perhaps says a word but the most primitive, dishonest, vicious, tender, deadly feelings are at work. No film-maker is capable of gathering this archive, no matter how complex her intentions. To resort to the voiceover would be moribund travesty. In this less-than-thirty seconds a world explodes. Who would be its curator?

The frantic scrivener, the perspiring dark figure bent double, records that *Sarladaise potatoes* are potatoes cooked in fat; that *Sarladaise* is a word derived from a town in the Dordogne; that *Emmett's* is a shop which, while currently very much in vogue, actually dates back to the 1820s, selling smoked ham and bacon, in Saxmundham, Suffolk. To this a note is added to the effect that Adrian could tell Lily and her boyfriend, in case they didn't know and knowing might tickle them pink, that the Queen Mother had given the shop a Royal Warrant for their sweet pickled chutneys back in 1970.

— Absolutely random, by the way, Adrian concluded in self-deprecation; I haven't the *slightest notion* why I should be a party to *that* little gem.

Ignoring that intervention (for such palpable devices deserve only the widest berth, the whole point being that what happens in these thirty seconds is not just uncapturable on film but also entirely alien to the voice, to the voice or identity of any one person, man or woman, dead or alive), the scrivener gives due consideration to a comparison and contrast of scrivening and texting, to the madness of a royal warrant, to a complete itemising of other dishes on the menu, to how all the diners are struck that each main dish is accompanied by the recommendation of a specific fine wine or beer but are held back, as by some invisible skein, from articulating this. And concerning this skein a brief disquisition is appended on the nature of embarrassment and, in especial, on that form stereotyped as *peculiarly English*. But first and foremost the dark scrivener, perspiring out of the limelight, seen only in thought, details the process by which the diners in this silence eliminate from their gustatory enquiries each of the menu items in turn.

Mentally rubbing his hands together, having all too soon set his mind on the rabbit (and made a mental note that, if there *were* to be dessert, he would be opting for the pistachio and roast apricot tartlet with apricot sorbet), Adrian proceeded to a brisk assessment of the bright young man some ten years his junior, seated opposite. Slightly taller than himself, granted. But no looker, definitely not. Still, trim and quite muscular. Swims a lot, perhaps, or cycles. Adrian wondered how much Lily had already told him about their ideas for the project. And now for the first time he reflected on her surname, suddenly baffled as to why it hadn't occurred to him before: could she be related in some way to *the*? No, surely not: someone would have said. His thoughts trailed off into his rather limited knowledge of the biography of the creator of *Eraserhead*.

Stephen momentarily pondered what Lily's problem might be. But his prime focus, now that they were sitting down, was how beautiful she looked, and the thought of how, later that evening, in her flat in Clerkenwell, he might slowly divest her. He was radiantly conscious of how alluring she was not only to himself but to any and everyone else in the vicinity. A longish, captivated gaze at her from an older man dining alone at a nearby table pleased him almost as much as looking again at her himself, and feeling his ownership of her sensual warmth literally inches from his side. Admittedly it had occurred to him, for a fraction of a second, that here he was, yet again, about to order meat. Even if it was only chicken, still he knew she found it impossible.

And your smoky bacon, Stephen, don't forget to save that: too tangy, too tasty ever to renounce. Buried not so deep, the going against your father's religion, about which your mother seemed actually guiltier than her husband: boyhood memories of her driving and stopping with you at a diner somewhere on the road to Chislehurst, where she presented you with *a secret to keep from your dad*, a heavy white plate of glistening greasy bacon and eggs, with scalding-hot tomatoes and fried bread. How many times did that happen, you wonder, the outing to that roadside greasy spoon? Its latest revamp: the sizzling, salty speciality bacon sandwich from the café near the *Gazette* offices, an occasional treat you simply couldn't give up.

Lily had challenged Stephen about meat-eating and animal welfare, on and off, for at least the first six months of their relationship. It was a conversation topic that had, however, come to a dead end. Literally, in this instance, for the chicken with its unheard squawk, and the pig, sweating and grunting then squealing and groaning till the shadows are all descended. As often happens in intimate relationships that last, there are unshared passions about which, from early on, little more is said. She dreamt of a world in which it would not happen. The option would not even be on the table. She gave her order to the waiter and listened as Adrian and Stephen placed theirs. She reflected on the brutality: *confit of free-range rabbit* and *corn-fed chicken breast*. The *confit* intimated that the rabbit was cooked in its own fat: what a soft and gentle word for an operation so vile! With vague echoes of comfort-eating and confectionery, *confit* and *free range* together had a real concentration-camp compactness. Who would have thought a rabbit could be anything *but* free range? But once the phrase has been tacked on to the creature from the old-gold common it surely becomes difficult not to entertain the thought that rabbits previously eaten were not free-range, but were like the chickens in that vast factory in Alberta, Canada, supplying McDonald's restaurants in the US with their eggs, video footage of which she had recently watched, or tried to watch, on YouTube, countless thousands upon thousands of creatures confined within or indifferently beyond an inch of their lives, in the living death that is so blithely labelled *factory farming*. In the absence of any specification as to provenance or welfare, on the other hand, *corn-fed chicken breast* seemed to suggest that this was not free-range, but a chicken choking on its incarceration of lost-all-pecking-order in the endless chopping aisles of Alberta or some other paltry-poultry-killing-complex probably not a hundred miles from where they were sitting. And *corn-fed chicken breast* evoked in her mind one further grimness, surrealistically projecting the image of a breast bred and fed in a separate space, like a pig's heart pulsating on the surgeon's table before being eased into position in the body of a man.

We are icebergs. We never get the measure of others or ourselves. The sounds we make as we collide we hardly start to hear. The speed at which we are melting we quite fail to see.

And then, before the unfolding of a single napkin, the conversation about cinematic intentions resumed. Lily recalled, if only for Adrian's benefit, how Stevie had shown her a famous essay about what was called the *intentional fallacy*. She remembered Stephen's very words, and now recited them: *To read a book in terms of its author's intentions is to embark on a wild goose chase*. That was what had got her started. Wasn't it quite naïve for film theorists to have adopted the term *auteur*, without taking on board any idea of a fallacy?

She and Adrian were already past the planning stage, but they talked over dinner as if they'd only just skewered the thing on their forks. This phrase *cinematic intentions*, for him, accommodated *all manner of playful possibilities*. And Franton proceeded to enumerate them at such length and with such panache that Stephen finally wanted to throw himself from the window (not a customer service that the reinforced plate glass and general watchfulness of restaurant staff on Level 6 of Tate Modern readily facilitated). There'd be a whole *package* of different *kinds* of events, not just in London but around the country. There'd be screenings and *symposia*, real-time online events, *chats* and tweets, catering to a range of audiences, from the everyday movie-goer to the academic film theory buff. What's cinema *for*, after all, Adrian enthused, what *designs* does it have on us? How is it different from books or TV or a conversation among friends? How do directors talk about their intentions? What do realised intentions *look* like, for heaven's sake?

The hope was to have Laura Mulvey and Peter Bradshaw in discussion, and they were also making progress towards getting Herzog to agree to do something as part of a one-week cluster of screenings, installations and other events on the South Bank...

Stephen's attention was drifting – off somewhere between lust for Lily and the return of the rage he had felt in the event he had recently hosted with Don DeLillo. How was any of this talk about intention and intentionality in movies in any remotely interesting way connected to the completely terrible situation that the world was in and the pulsating urgency for political action? In his vague reverie, Osmer no longer noticed which of them was saying what.

— It's quite *comical* in some respects, if you think about it: in a way that is *just* not possible in a novel, the screen displays the *face* of intention – the would-be killer gazing malevolently at the *murder* weapon, the vampire *salivating* to sink his teeth into the gorgeous heroine's exposed white neck, the *hysterical Hitchcock girl's* desire to flee, to get out of the room at all costs. But is this even *comparable* to what a *director* intends, both at the *macro*-level of the movie as a whole or in the context of a single scene or still? ... Do we believe what a director says when he tells us what he intended to do with a particular image, character or scene? ... And then, what about *unconscious* intentions?

— Unconscious *bollocks*! Stephen finally spluttered out, tuning back into what was being said and unable to contain himself any longer.

The evening thereafter drew rather quickly to an end.

— Intriguing choice of phrase, Adrian had replied, more than a little stung.

It was, in truth, another of the sticking-points between Lily and Stephen – that she, in his view, went along with a cartload of crap about psychoanalysis, stuff she seemed to have picked up from the sick and twisted world of sociology. Lily loved him, even as this peremptory rudeness went against her own sense of civil manners. But she was changing. Things had already changed for her in ways she had not been able to bring herself to explain to him. It was difficult enough understanding it in herself. And an involuntary flush came to her lovely face as she recalled once more the irony of the phrase that had presided over their conversation that evening: *cinematic intentions*.

Restoring the vestiges of an amicable dinner, they split the bill three ways and stood up to leave, Adrian to his husband in Kennington, Lily and Stephen to unexpectedly passionate love-making in Clerkenwell. Happening to catch, without immediately recognising, her emerald and gold-stitched silk shawl reflected in the windows, Lily imagined for a moment she saw on the twilit Thames a shifting procession of huge green icebergs. What was she doing to Stephen? Shouldn't she tell him? But how?

Unmarked

A busload of people had come in out of the sun, raucous, unseeing, disturbing the peace. They occupied tables in every direction. They seemed to have no thought for the quietness that had prevailed before their arrival. Ethel and Silas had already downed a couple of drinks. They probably should have called it a day. But in vague defiance they plumped to stay on for one more. It had, after all, been a singular occasion. He'd read her the story. She was really impressed. And they'd laughed over some of it, especially the ending where the man puts a sheet over the woman's head.

— Reflects all that reading you've done down the years, she told him through tipsy, shining eyes. And all that note-taking you did up the library, burying your nose in them reference books and that – what was the name of it – an ichthesaurus?

— It's a thesaurus, my dear. An ichthyosaurus is a sort of fossil fish, many examples of which I believe we saw in the Natural History Museum one time, donkeys years ago.

— Well, whatever it was, I'm proud of you. I honestly am. Though I confess I don't understand half the flaming words. You must send it to that Winslow fellow and see what he thinks.

Whether it was the third pint and third glass of chardonnay (or could it have been the fourth?) or the flustering influx of people all of a sudden changing the whole atmosphere of the place, it wasn't until later, when the couple were preparing to turn in for the night, that Silas appeared, wondering where she'd put his 'Gulls', and Ethel categorically knew nothing of its whereabouts. And then with a sudden qualm Silas realised he must have left it in the pub, on the red-velvet-padded chair beside his own. There was still a good hour until closing time. He'd pop down the road and pick it up from that nice young barmaid whose name he could never remember, with the blonde hair and the pretty smile. As he entered the lounge bar he looked first at the table and chairs where they had sat, now unoccupied: no sign of his manuscript. He glanced also at the fireplace: the grate was empty, no fire made there in months. Ambling towards the bar, he saw that the staff had changed. The barman knew nothing about it. Enquiry was made.

— No, nothing handed in... She'll be back in tomorrow at twelve (the girl who was working earlier), if you wanted to call in or give us a ring.

Woodlock duly wandered in the next day, though already with a defeated feeling.

If you were the girl your name would be Sylvie and you'd recognise him as the tall, saggy-shouldered old guy, who has asked your name on a couple of occasions but never seems to remember, with the big sunken blue eyes you can't decide are creepy or friendly. In the company of his wife he is a familiar enough sight in the pub, especially as he is invariably dressed the same, black trousers and baggy old shirt, but never this early in the day. And as he approaches you wonder what on earth he is about, as he doesn't look like he's come in for a pint and his head is hung down, but when he looks you in the face and smiles and says good morning, sorry, good afternoon, there is a sadness in his expression that makes your heart go out.

And when you disappoint him, as you are obliged to do, because you haven't seen, and nor has anyone else, a slender sheaf of scribble held together with a paper clip, just half a dozen pages, written in blue ink, with the word 'Gulls' at the top, you watch as his face goes through a peculiar set of turns, like someone who is trying to chew something but gives up, and witness the forlorn figure he cuts as he makes his exit, even though you do your utmost to express your sympathy and sense of helplessness, even though you offer to take his phone number and give him a call if it turns up, on account of someone coming in having found it somewhere on the street, say, or of someone in the pub yesterday having put it in their bag by accident, though how likely would that be really, you ask yourself, you can't remember who sat at that table after he and his wife departed, no one as far as you can recall, until your shift ended.

It was a significant blow. He retained a photographic impression of the empty red-velvet seat and the adjacent spick-and-span fireplace. For the first couple of days in particular this image stayed in his head. He couldn't believe the misfortune. It had been so much effort. And who in their right mind, anyway, would see such a thing and think of nabbing it? Why would anyone do such a thing? But then again, why would it not be behind the bar? The inevitable question was gently put to him: could he not just write it out again? But this triggered such an incandescent response that Ethel in defence, if now a little guiltily, could only recall her own sense of outrage the night Ash was born, at the Mayday, when Silas draped one arm around her shoulders as she, on hands and knees, was enduring the overwhelming waves of pain of heavy contractions, and he remarked, as if from an entirely different world:

— This is alright, isn't it, love? We should do this again!

No, he couldn't just write it out again. His memory wasn't up to that. He didn't even want to talk about it. He had a crystal-clear picture of the fireside seat where he must have left it, but, for the writing itself, he struggled even to remember the precise course or point of its opening sentence. He had his notes scribbled down somewhere by the bedside table, but they were no basis for a proper reconstruction. He'd pretty much changed everything as he was going along. He would simply have to let the thing go. He might have chosen to write something else, completely different, but he felt strangely disabled by the loss. Something inside him had gone away.

For two or three weeks it was a notable non-subject in the house. Ethel knew well enough to let the topic be. She followed his anger at a distance, pained for him but loath to intervene. In those days, and especially in the evenings, he played 'Paint It Black' a lot in his den. And then one morning he'd been out and about town and he strode in and said, with a semblance of the rosy smile of his old self, that he had enrolled for the watercolour workshops. Ethel brightly offered to donate a tenner to the cost of materials.

The mad weather, the remorseless day after day of sweltering sunshine, so unlike England, accompanied by the relentless squawking gull-life, came more or less to an abrupt end at some point in August. The fledglings evidently required six weeks to ready themselves for flight. Then, one day, the Woodlocks awoke to find them all gone. And as if by a vicious, faceless removals company, the sun was swept out and winds dumped in, a chill in the morning, summer seen off overnight. That was how this tipping effect, or whatever it was they said we should think of it as, made its impression, not just with stretches of manifestly artificial weather like a computer virus filling the sky and air with regimental scorching heat, as if the globe had been tilted round to give England Spain's weather non-stop for weeks on end, he remembered what it was like, didn't he, that time they were on the Costa whatever they said, the Costa Living as she joked, too hot to bear, supposed to be there a fortnight, first and only foreign holiday after Ash was born, and had to come home after four days, terrible, the heat, just awful, and now it's plonked down on the south coast of England, *fiasco total* – no, not just that, but the lack of transition, that was what made it stick out: no period of grace, no lull for a shift from summer to autumn, same with spring to summer, never the same again, just jolts and disintegrations.

But they forged a *modus vivendi*. Ethel's health seemed better, probably the sea air, she said, even if it does come with the toxic fumes from the insanerator, as she called it, the huge old-technology newly built incinerator churning its unknown waste into and down from the skies just a couple of miles away at Newhaven. The only major new construction project in the area, she more than once pointed out, apart from all these enormous assisted dying homes they keep putting up.

— It's living, love, he said. Assisted living.

Silas went along to his painting classes, but his interest flagged after a few weeks. He learnt a little, however, and found he was able to dash off a few not completely hopeless seascapes and landscapes. They had bequeathed their old Rover to Ashley when they moved, so Silas was reliant on walking or public transport to get him to interesting locations. The woman running the workshops was called Marion. Silas considered her snooty, imperious and annoying.

Through her, nonetheless, he was introduced to the work of a local artist called Ravilious, who had apparently produced celebrated paintings of the Downs close to Seaford back in the 1930s. Silas's most successful picture was based on a journey he took to a place not so much off as very close to the beaten track, yet still largely invisible. It was some miles inland. In Eric Ravilious's day it was known as the Asham cement works. Now it was the Beddingham landfill (or, more precisely, landfilled) site. The cement works went on to become an absolutely vast rubbish heap and then the absolutely vast rubbish heap was covered over again with chalk, buried in what Silas thought of as an unmarked grave. Unmarked, in that it was very difficult to know you were there when you were. No helpful sign to inform you:

You are now standing on top of millions of tons of domestic and commercial detritus, mounds upon mounds of stuff from the cosmetics and pharmaceutical industries, millions of disposable nappies long since disposed of, numberless BSE cow carcasses, countless car tyres, and indeterminable quantities of asbestos and radioactive waste.

It was also difficult to access. The quickest way, it transpired, was to take the train to a little village called Southease, then continue on foot, part of the route requiring him to walk along the verge of the busy A26 and get hooted at as if he were an inconvenient stray dog. Still, a fitting place to paint as a surprise and give to Ethel at Christmas. He had it framed in oak and attached a note on the back: *Unmarked (Asham Cement Works, Beddingham Landfill), with love, Silas.*

Screen Potatoes

At Cambridge Lily had had several lovers. These affairs were flings, experiments, erratic ecstasies. In the now more than two years she had been with Stephen she had indeed, until recently, only been with him. He himself was completely set on her. It was, she knew, different for him. It was not always her way to be forthright, though she certainly liked to appear so. Had she been five years older she might have been candid sooner, or gentler, more sensitive in her dealings with him. Time and the heart never truly rendezvous.

As for Stephen, he had journeyed through a groggy night of body and soul and now, he believed, come through. He had thought he was going to die in a chair sitting opposite Don DeLillo, and then, of all the softies in the British Isles, Andrew Motion. People joked about going to East Anglia to die, but he had found solace there or, at any rate, in the cycling to and about. He was better now. It had probably helped that there were no other celebrity author events lined up in the coming weeks. His only public appearance was a 'discussion evening' on J.D. Salinger's *The Catcher in the Rye* at the British Library. This would involve only himself: he anticipated a straightforward, rather low-key event. He had already scribbled a few questions and topics for debate: What makes *Catcher* a classic? Why is it still seen as subversive, even banned in certain places in the US? Is it a communist novel? Or is it a deeply reactionary and conservative work? How relevant is it for understanding youth today? He would have little to do besides chair the discussion and adjudicate between members of the public giving their views. He was also scheduled for a couple of events at the Edinburgh Festival later in the summer, but these, of course, were not to be.

It was early June, a week or so after the dinner with Franton. It wasn't usual for her to stay at his place. The Bloomsbury bedsit was tiny compared with the loft in Clerkenwell. They ate pizza and watched one of Herzog's early films, *Even Dwarves Started Small*. Afterwards they argued about it. He couldn't see the point at all. It was distinctive and zany, sure, but what was its political import? Life's an insane asylum? She on the other hand was affected, as she hadn't been when first watching the film as a student at the Arts Picturehouse, by the manifest ill-treatment of animals, especially the mock-crucified monkey carted off in wheels of fire. She wanted to talk about what she'd been reading that week, a disturbing book about the extent to which the entire film industry was based on dead animals, starting with the gelatin from which film itself was manufactured. And he wanted to tell her, not what he thought or what someone else might think about some irrelevant post-surrealist experiment from the '70s, but about the essay he was beginning to plan in his mind on the subject of the banking crisis and financial meltdown. He told her the title he was envisaging for it.

She was no more conscious that he, in his heart, called her his banker, than he was aware of the holocaust she had already lit in it. The celluloid was already frying. Their argument was as much about what was not being said as about what was. Eventually she remarked:

— I've – we've – been invited to a party.

It was by the sea, a spectacular setting, she'd been led to believe, an old farmhouse up on the cliffs near Beachy Head. There was so much she couldn't say, but she had to say something. It would be on Midsummer's Eve. And then the day after that was – if he remembered – when she was going to Australia with her parents for a month. Of course he remembered. They'd discussed it at length. He'd made clear how torn he was, how much he'd appreciated her father's inviting him to accompany them – tacitly granting that her father was hardly strapped for cash, not with their grand house in Beaconsfield and the flat where Lily lived at a piffling rent, and the pension of a retired ambassador. It was a generous gesture but he couldn't. He was committed to devoting the remains of his allotted annual leave to getting this essay written.

— Who knows, he added, it might even turn into a book.

If cinematic intention is contentious, what of the telepathic? There is no archive – besides perhaps the dark scrivener's – in which to investigate the strange effects that fall without name, the silent thoughts and feelings that two people might share in response to something on a screen. Lily and Stephen scarcely ever watched TV together, but next morning as he came out of the shower, careful not to trip straight into the bed, he saw she had switched it on, so he positioned himself as lithely as he could beside her, and they viewed together, he with his towel around him, she still nakedly entwined in the bed-sheets, the news apparently, or some eerily damaged metamorphosis of the news, impossible to be sure if it was current or historic, in which a man-and-woman team were telling you that in a minute they were going to interview a woman who three years previously had suffered terrible facial injuries (this, Lily noted, hot on the tail of a piece about stalkers and new changes proposed in the law with a view to tougher sentencing, recognising stalking as a phenomenon affecting all of society, not just celebrities, everyone in favour of change, what ho, even the snortling minister into whose department it fell) and was so badly defaced it was clear as a bell to doctors that she would never through her left eye in her lifetime see again; but the woman, now it seemed the minute was coming to an end, for she had been shunted into position on the pertinent couch, adjacent to the newsreaders, no longer of course the great beauty she once was but garishly bold in pinks and purples, restored to the public eye, was going to recount, she wasn't doing it yet, they were just showing her sitting there beside them, just a couch away, with her fixedly coy eyes lowered or to the side, smiling suggestive of simpering, a simpering constructed for TV by TV, the camera didn't have a mind of its own but there was no stopping it mentally getting carried away, so it tried to keep a cool hand even as the smut, to give it in Edwardian English, traces its filament over the screen a little in the manner of those toy faces you can ornament and remake by jiggling iron filings, *the model* after all was the name that had been assigned to her, ravishing model, you were unsure for a split-second whether they actually used the word *ravishing* or if it was merely subliminal code, the pornographic switch-word encrypted in the scene, ravish me, ravish this woman, this ravishing model, gorgeous-looking bird, and at the same time a digital boxing out, where the screen breaks up into a fragmenting nude descending a staircase like a huge decurved beak protruding out of the picture, they were going to do it after all, it was supposed to be brunch in Covent Garden but now there was to be sex, erotic passion, touches of anger, redden all up the dark too, all the way, love, to be made, she was wet already, and she hadn't said anything, and another week was going to pass without her doing so, hard enough to say the party, we've been invited to a party, heartbreaking love of it, let him once more, crucify her, just hold it there, love the stillness in him, not her, hold the image of the model who was going to recount, in just a minute, the story of how she was watching something on TV, thereby opening up a new line of unconscionably tedious Russian dolls, the snooze-mode hypnopompic suggestion of the power of TV by TV, the edifying or restorative magic of the box, as their grandparents used to call it, as their parents recalled their parents used to call it, don't underestimate the potential of TV to change your life, you simply cannot afford not to keep watching, a box-set you come to be part of. She was watching a programme about stem-cell research and a doctor who was pioneering the treatment of various forms of blindness, for the viewers' model on the couch, now theirs thanks to the insidiously but gloriously erection-pulsing patronising way in which the camera and newsreader discourse had captured her, the capturing of the dream of men, eureka moment, the moment of revelation when she apparently saw that this could be her, she could be the one, the model of a model to be peered and pioneered upon, and so sought out the doctor in question, practising somewhere in the States, and you were given sight now of footage of the doctor, at first unclear whether this is the documentary that the model saw or a documentary made about the model when she saw the doctor, all part of the great hypno-lottery of life for the TV viewer, a calculation for TV by TV aimed at telecommanding attention, remote control head on a plate, now clarifying itself unexpectedly into a combination of the two, a commingling which began with one kind of footage and ended with the other, enough to lose your footage, a bit of the other, the model with the doctor four weeks, it turned out, before the surgery she was to receive and now, shifting back to the studio and across from the newsreaders to the victim on the mirror potato couch, it was three months after the operation and how do you feel, they asked, how successful was it? So that finally, after what had seemed like a couple of full feature-length purgatories of repeating the storyline, the time-frame, the raw-as-an-open-wound facts, and crawling like a rodent, tricked, poisoned and exhausted, back and forth between what the newsreaders were telling and what they were promising to tell, between their heavily made-up but thank God, they think to themselves, unreconstructed faces and the clips of the documentary, between the documentary this beautifully stalked victim saw and that of her being seen, you were going to have the privilege, for by this point it seemed you were expected to regard it as that, of gazing at what was left of the face of the woman herself and hearing from her own lips, insofar as they were hers, how she felt and how successful the treatment was. And even as you knew it would not happen, you wanted to hear her say, without hesitation, thrusting her face forward for all to see the excruciating poignancy of this still manifestly deformed face, this face with such care and dignity restored thanks to the skill of the plastic surgeons and the costs covered in part through money raised by public donation: *Fucking awful, look at me, I feel like fucking death, how would you feel?*

Out of Season

Perhaps the sea air helped to scumble his own impressions of small-town life. Unless he was steadily, without realising, turning into one of the old codgers for whom he had been so ready to feel disdain on first moving into the new place. Silas Woodlock couldn't think of himself as in the same boat as the shaky guy with the stick or the dilapidated fellow on his mobility scooter delivered into a second childhood threading his way between other elderly citizens down the pavement of the main shopping street, but he was at least partly conscious of accommodating himself to a different sort of populace. And he didn't miss the relentless hubbub of central Croydon. A predominantly ageing or aged population had other advantages as well. Along with an unusual concentration of pubs within comfortable walking distance there were also many cafés and other eateries. He and Ethel soon came to realise that, while no one from out of town really came in to shop, plenty came for the cafés, the breakfast places and little restaurants. Everyone could afford a cup of tea and no one was in any great hurry. Silas and Ethel became quite particular about where they liked to have their coffee and Earl Grey, about which establishment sold the best cakes, best breakfast, best lunch and the rest. Life was mostly quiet and simple. They established certain rituals. Along with the Sunday afternoon drink at the Wellie, they had breakfast together at Pomegranate on a Tuesday, and once or twice a week shared a pot of tea and a slice of cake at the Front Room. But Silas was perfectly capable of taking off by himself and spending a couple of hours sitting in a quiet corner of the town library, or in a café by himself with an old detective novel he'd just picked up for a song from a nearby charity shop. He was happy to be the loner.

Ethel on the other hand liked to meet up occasionally with one or other of her new acquaintances, have a nice cup of tea and sandwich somewhere. And she was unwavering in her custom of taking a walk along the seafront every afternoon or dusk, unless the weather was just too bad. Sometimes Silas would accompany her, but more often she went alone. She came to appreciate the particular loveliness of *out of season*, the cold, windswept, dark days when she could take herself off down to the sea and gaze off left and right and see not a single other person in either direction. She came to love the midwinter days when she could retrace her steps towards the town, with the lighthouse at Newhaven twinkling away at the end of the pier a couple of miles distant, and witness the disappearing orange of the sun slinking magically back into the sea.

— According to Rhoda it's good for the pineal gland, she more than once remarked to Silas. But Silas appeared, while mumbling assent, not to be remotely interested.

Their new house, actually early Victorian, had a wood-burning stove in the main sitting-room. They had had nothing like that in the old flat in Croydon. It was a delight to them both, on cold evenings, to get it lit and settle beside it in their armchairs, him with his book and her with her thoughts. It's true she would read something occasionally, some history or biography, or do a bit of sudoku, but mostly she was content to sit by the fire, with a blanket over her knees, peaceably gazing into the flames. Other times the old man would take off to his den and she might spend an hour or two watching TV, catching up on the news or mockudentaries or whatever they called them. Now that he had his own place to listen to his vinyl records in peace and the rest, she was more prone to watching TV. Soaps were anathema, but in the course of that autumn tipping into winter she developed an unexpected soft spot for property programmes. Perhaps it was due to having recently gone through the whole house-moving palaver themselves, she could better enjoy watching the stress and trouble of other couples, young and old, trying to make momentous decisions about where to live, what to do. Dot came down a couple of times, and at Christmas Ashley drove down with Rhoda and stayed a couple of nights.

Through January and into February, however, the weather violently lurched off again. The skies opened and stayed open all day. The Woodlocks began to see the point of the Latin motto on the Seaford coat of arms – *E ventis vires*: From the wind, strength. The seafront was the worst. If you weren't going to let yourself be blown all the way down the beach to Newhaven, you needed strength. But elsewhere in the town, too, there were pockets or passages where the wind suddenly came at you, threw you, took your hat smack off your head. And the rain wouldn't stop. It wasn't normal downpour, Ethel could see that. Anyone with their head half-screwed-on could see that. It was weird. The streets were awash, streaming from arrows of rain like the Battle of Battle or Hastings or whatever it was called and overflowing gutters from one hour to the next. It was the tipping effect tipping it down, day after day, night after night.

112

With the spring tide the town was in danger of flooding. There were flood alerts all over the country, rivers bursting their banks, coastal defences breached, whole swathes of England underwater. For a couple of days the little town seemed to tremble. People stayed in their homes, hunkered down. Precautionary sandbags appeared in the entrance-ways to properties on and leading up to the seafront. And at the same time it was mild. You wouldn't bother to light a fire, it wasn't cold enough. This lent the Woodlock household a troubling atmosphere, at once agitated and hushed. Silas became embroiled in some new Scandinavian noir detective novel, a bit of a departure for him; in the usual run of things he tended to stick with more classic stuff such as Christie, Sayers or P.D. James. Ethel was having none of it.

— You were the one spouting the Latin town motto, *E ventis vires*. It's not strength *to* the wind, it's our strength *against* it. I'm off.

And, dressed in as much rainproof garb as she could muster, she practically stormed out of the house. She could be like that, he knew. She was likely responding to the quip he'd made the previous evening as they sat eating their macaroni cheese and mixed salad together to the sound of improbably large raindrops lashing the windows, about how she had always wanted to live by the sea. The remark was a standing joke between them by now. She'd struggle her way down to the seafront and be fine. When he'd finished the chapter he was on, he'd prepare some soup and warm some bread, ready for her return.

There was something eccentric about it, but she was in her element now. There was no point seeking protection in any of the seafront shelters. The tide was so full and the winds so high. And she was alone. No one else had been foolhardy enough to venture out on to the beach in these conditions. She was barely able to stand, but, cowering into herself, she remained more or less on her feet. The onslaught was a kind of ecstasy. She could scarcely see out from under her wind-battered eyelids, air and salt water together swashing over her cheeks, into her mouth and nostrils. With eyes squeezed almost shut she could just about make out the colossal waves rising up and shattering over the lighthouse and all along the smudged black line of Newhaven pier. The sea was a kind of lunacy, advancing between her eyelids, a whirl of giant snails foaming at the mouth, spuming death.

— Leek and potato, my favourite. You *are* good to me, she was saying half an hour later, after coming home and taking a hot shower.

For several weeks it seemed as if the end of the world was indeed upon them. It wasn't just a spell of bad weather, it was manufactured, she told Silas more than once. It was time the government stopped pulling the wool over our eyes.

He couldn't say it would blow over, because he shared her feelings about it. These were record-breaking rainy days and nights, storm-force winds and flash-floods, mounted up in some kind of holding pattern that wasn't right. He was glad they were retired. They worried about how their son was faring and spoke to him over the phone on a number of occasions. No fun, a funeral, at the best of times, but the laying in and the digging and the ritual standing about and the ruined floral tributes and the rest in these torrential times scarcely bore thinking about. Pity people couldn't get a bad weather exemption certificate, allowing them to peg off later.

With the turmoil of the weather the old couple quite failed to register the absence of the gulls. But any respite was in fact short-lived. The weather quietened down with

improbable abruptness towards the end of February, and
March had scarcely begun when the breeding and nesting
season once more got under way.

— Don't waste time, do they? muttered Silas, as he and
Ethel stood together in the kitchen being eyed by a full-
grown herring gull just a couple of feet above them, sitting
in a sort of aggressive complacency on the neighbour's
extension roof.

It was the start of what they variously referred to, in their
lighter moments, as the Second War, the Dawn of the Dead,
the Mother of all Mating Seasons. The preceding spring and
summer had driven the couple to their limits. Hadn't he
been obliged, in the end, to take that bizarre course of action
that he had candidly described in that piece of work for his
writing class? Hadn't the noise and the permanent proximity
of these inhuman neighbours completely got the better of

them both, prompting an agreement that if it really were to be like this again the following year (which, however, they simply couldn't believe), they would devise strategies for dealing with the situation? They would contact the council. They would get spikes and netting put up on their roof. They would acquire a bird-scare humming line or other inexpensive newfangled technology to install in the garden. He indeed went further, proposing to buy an air-rifle. But he knew, even before speaking, that such a course of action would never be countenanced by his better half.

As it turned out, this year was, if anything, worse. They were taken by surprise. It was distressing, like being out on a walk and caught short. They were vexed with themselves and one another for not seeing it coming, for not taking preventative measures when they'd had the chance. They put it down to the terrible storms and how their sense of the calendar had been totally blown off balance. They had hardly blinked, it seemed, before gulls were nesting all around them, like military emplacements, every one of them sitting smug and ugly, a categorical fixture, like the cannon on the Martello tower down at the seafront, and nothing you could do about it. They phoned the council and looked into possible courses of action but they were advised against doing anything at all, as *the herring gull is a protected species* and it is *a criminal offence to disturb them* once they have begun nesting. Although Ethel and Silas were prepared to give credence to the claim that herring gull numbers across the UK were dwindling, their impression was that the missing complement had merely moved to Seaford. More couples than ever had chosen to take up residence within screeching and defecating distance of their abode. And every week felt like the further ratcheting-up of a foreign occupation.

Doubtless this was in no small measure due to the accumulative effects of sleep-deprivation, for the ageing couple were both seriously afflicted by it. Especially as the mornings got earlier, or lighter, or whatever it was called, the squawking bloodcurdling ear-sickening orchestra started up before you'd ever got sufficient shut-eye and seemed to dictate the mood of the day from dawn to dusk.

On top of this, one of their neighbours took to feeding them. Whoever it was, apparently from a second-floor window, started throwing stale bread, cold fish and chips and other waste food on to the extension roof adjoining the Woodlocks' house. It sent the gulls berserk, and the Woodlocks in turn. They would watch and wait, then a window would open and the air explode in a havoc of white and terrible clamouring, flapping and skittering, but the couple in their twilight years couldn't be sure exactly which window it was and so never succeeded in establishing the identity of the perpetrator. For the personal safety of the individual involved, this was perhaps just as well, given the stoked-up state into which Silas was sliding.

Towards the end of May they looked into their finances with a view to taking a holiday, a break in the strongest sense, somewhere cheap but different and far away, like Thailand. But this looking provided only a further twist of the knife: they discovered that they had significantly less money to play with than they had supposed. A long-established savings account in which they had set aside money for a rainy day transpired to have been decimated, a blind casualty of the financial triple-dip run-off-over-the-hills recession, or whatever it was the government weren't calling it. And even their monthly outgoings, it seemed, were working out greater than was realistically sustainable. *Living beyond our means*, they thought, in unspoken dismay. Financial worries on top of physical exhaustion generated real wobble. They even considered going back to the flat in Croydon and staying with Ash for a week or so, just to get some relief, catch up on all the broken mornings, but that seemed, at the end of the day, ignominious and absurd.

They invested instead in a couple of pairs of headphones, which gave going to bed a sort of whimsical astronautical quality. It also had some mitigating effect, though not as much as they'd hoped. In their sleep the headphones tended to work themselves off. Silas in particular found himself waking up early in order to adjust his headphones and, in the fiddle-faddle of doing so, woke himself up further, thus intensifying the sleep-deprivation he was struggling to beat away. They had different tactics during the day. From late May onwards, Ethel took to swimming in the sea early in the morning. The water was still very cold, but she claimed it helped to take her mind off things. Silas made it his business to spend at least one hour every day sitting with a book in a quiet café away from all the blare and clamour of home. And occasionally, on drier, warmer days, he took himself off on treks inland, sometimes as far afield as Alfriston and Firle.

It was just a day before midsummer when the Bomb dropped. That was how she thought of it, though in truth it was silent and she wasn't there to witness it. The weather had turned hot. They had talked the night before of moving to a room lower down the house where they wouldn't be so much affected by the heat and noise. They wondered why they hadn't thought of this sooner. In truth, each had thought the other would think that to forgo the room with a view, the so-called master bedroom with its splendid sea vistas, was a sacrifice too far. But just as they hadn't readied themselves for the return of the gulls, so now a sort of veil of impenetrable lethargy had begun to envelop them once more. They couldn't move the bed, after all, without getting help. Perhaps next time Ash was down. They didn't, after all, want to vacate their own bed in order to install themselves in the guest bed which, they agreed, was uncomfortably smaller. And then its mattress, also, they were both aware, was pretty much gone for a burton.

As had become his enforced custom, Silas staggered downstairs in an under-slept torpor to make himself coffee. Only now did he become aware that his good lady had already taken off for a morning dip. He must, as he sat in his armchair by the unlit wood-burning stove, have nodded off for a time: his coffee was only partially drunk but stone cold. It was another scorching day, the sun heavy and garish, all ready to kindle a dry and thirsty land. He thought of following Ethel down to the beach. She'd no doubt be taking a sunbathe and, knowing her, a catch-up snooze on the hot stones. But he decided, after all, to head into town. On his way to the café where he'd planned to get another cup of coffee, he stopped outside a second-hand bookshop he hadn't visited in a couple of months.

There was a little table of books set up on the pavement. Nothing of any interest there. Still, he wandered inside. He was absentmindedly casting his eye about the fiction shelves when his attention alighted on a cheap paperback of 'uncanny stories about birds'. Riffling through its pages he came upon what made his blood boil.

Fore

It was almost twenty-four hours before Silas was able to act. Ethel tried desperately to talk him out of it. He had discovered the address, putting two and two together from a conversation the previous evening with a fellow up at the Cinque Ports and what's her name, Sylvie, in the Wellington. I hear what you're saying, love, but it's my personal integrity. It's not for you to be involved. You have to let me do this. I won't. You can't just take the law into your own flaming hands. You sit down and listen to Ethel. Take stock for a day or two. Let's make enquiries and see if we can't. I've made enough enquiries already. Stop standing there like a demented scarecrow, your coffee's gone cold. Sit down and let's consider the whole matter in the calm light of day. We've already talked it to death, love.

Infuriating that they no longer had the Rover. Whatever had possessed them to move to the seaside without a car? In the midst of all this sleep-deprivation, each new day now bringing spasmodic sensations that bits were literally falling off his body, he could not for the life of him locate their copy of the Ordnance Survey Explorer Map 123. Earlier that morning he had searched high and low with a mounting sense of out-of-focus fury. It was as if his eyesight had deteriorated overnight and, trying to look then look again through the pile of maps on the little table in his den, his fingers had shed all nimbleness. In the end he gave up and took himself off to the local branch of Sussex Stationers, plucked 123 from the shelf, spread it out over the aisle and pored at such length and so awkwardly over how best to reach the place on foot that the assistant had to come and politely ask was he intending to purchase the map or, if not, would he kindly return it to its rightful place on the shelf before it got creased and damaged? No easy thing for such a sprat of a girl, confronting a big craggy old guy like that. Woodlock scarcely heard what she said. Information mentally stored, he muttered a heartfelt but virtually inaudible thanks as he swept out of the shop.

Ethel had done everything she could think of, short of taking the keys and preventing him from leaving the house. She appreciated how incensed he was, she shared his feelings of outrage, but it was a matter for the police, a matter for the courts. We'll get justice, dear, I know we will. But he wouldn't listen. His eyes had that coldness in them that she'd seen only once or twice in all their years together, moments of grief as much as anger, like when the little black kid ran out in front of the Daimler or when his sister nearly died from her drunk husband's pushing her off that balcony. It wasn't a matter for the police, it was a matter for his own sanity, he said, with a clenched expression of his jaw and a stark staring eyeballing of his wife that made her want to shrink into the woodwork like a spider tapped on the spinnerets and stopped in its tracks.

A few years ago she'd have insisted on coming with him, but her knees couldn't have withstood it now, not going up those cliffs. Took enough out of her these days just having a dip in the sea.

Once again it was a far warmer day than made sense. He'd meant to be out of the house first thing after breakfast.

But then Sussex Stationers didn't open till ten, and there was Ethel to deal with. He finally set off from the house shortly before noon. The sun was belting down. It wasn't a direction he was prone to go in. It wasn't the precipitous nature of the cliffs and headlands up there; he was hale and hearty enough for all that. Before they'd moved he imagined he would be walking up there on Seaford Head at least a couple of times a week. But in fact he had not been up that way in ages. It had to do with the golf.

He was, as his dear wife had put it just before he'd blundered out of the house, in a right old state. Like a man possessed, he strode along the esplanade with the dazzling sunshine bouncing up at him off the white concrete, down to where the precarious white cliffs began and the kittiwakes were crying their high, nasal-sounding *kitti-wee-ik! kitti-wee-ik!* from their colony on the high, inaccessible cliff faces of chalk.

At the end of the esplanade he swerved off to the left, propelling himself up the cliff-edge steps past the ruins of the red-brick Victorian hotel and on to the – you couldn't call it *sward*, so dry it was like an affliction of the sun. He was dressed in old black trousers, a baggy white shirt and a cloth cap he thought might be sensible: keep the sun off his head. *Oh, my old man's a dustman...* (with an unconscious tip of the old cloth cap). Many are the afflictions. Where was that from? And of course he had his canvas bag. *Many are the afflictions of the righteous*, quite right, must be one of the Psalms. But by the time he was crossing the great swathe of parched grass prior to the clamber up Hawk's Brow the cap was already too much, come sunburnt pate or not. He took it off and carried it folded in his left hand. He wondered at what point he would stop perspiring. Perhaps, as he began scaling the heights, the breeze would cool him down. Then, at the top, he could re-don his cap.

Scarcely aware of doing so, he planted himself down, for there was after all a wooden seat *in situ* for precisely such occasions: retired gentleman out for the day, on a hike, like today, more challenging on the old cardiovascular than anticipated, take a short breather here on this bench dedicated to the memory of Marjorie *who loved to sit here*. He wondered would Ethel do the same? Would she take it into her head to establish some memorial for him, an inscription on a personalised bench? But where? Here by the sea or back in Croydon? Lay my ghost to rest with a bench in beloved memory of Si— Lordy lordy, what's going on, heart racing around like a lump of mercury in a matchbox. Hadn't he kept himself in pretty good trim down the years? Plenty of opportunities to witness the work of the ageless bogeyman Obesity. Seen too many out of their street-wear up to double or treble natural life-size. Lay my ghost to rest with a bench and the rest, lay my ghost to...

He must have fallen asleep. He peeled back the sweat-soaked cuff of his left sleeve to see that it was nearly two-thirty. Where did *that* time go? Good job he'd put the cap back on his bonce, or sunstroke the order of the day. Can't remember doing that. It's the sleep-deprivation is what it is, not a shadow of a doubt. Them – he could hardly bring himself to say the word, even in the silence of his head – them *gulls*. And a day like today, of all days, what a time to doze off, all the days of my appointed time, to nod off with this prospect ahead. No one else about, at least there's that.

Besides the golfers over the brow.

This was in truth the most irksome detail of his journey. Ethel was right: he hadn't really thought things through.

He hadn't wondered, for example, what would happen if he found the place and there was no one home. That possibility simply hadn't occurred to him. Too late to turn back now. It was these golfing types that were the trouble. Get past them and the rest would follow. Not an issue. It was a superstitious terror, irrational he knew, a fear seeded in him while on holiday as a boy walking with his mother along the promenade of a northern seaside town and him thinking like your average ten-year-old of nothing other than the double vanilla cone with a fat chocolate flake in it she'd promised they'd get at the ice-cream van just a hundred yards further on, when a shout was heard, as if time shattering in reverse, as if sound travelled like an airborne tumour, quick through the blue air, picked up too late, for a voice crying *Fore!* that seemed to come after the shattering, the disastrous world-splitting realisation that a golf ball had struck his mother full pelt on the side of her head and she stumbled as he had never seen a grown-up do, except in Westerns when a cowboy received an arrow in the chest or back, his mother crumpled, and in the midst of all the fluster of people confounding for who witnessed if anyone had seen it if anyone happen or been aware of something like an asteroid crashing into where the picnic was, people came up and flurried all round, and eventually the golfer himself, an Englishman, unless one of those Scots speaking in a snooty sort of voice more English than the English, stiffly wishing to defend himself, he'd shouted *Fore!* after all, dreadful error, most awfully sorry, but by that time his mother was on her feet again, she hadn't died, she hadn't come back from the dead, the golf ball had hit the frame of her glasses just at the top of the wing, the right-hand lens smashed to pieces and she naturally a bit shocked, but completely unscathed.

Fore

Whereas Silas from that day forth took into his head a horror of golfers, so that venturing up the Head was a kind of torture, a disincentive-laden exercise to mount the higher echelons, is that what they were called, escarpments, no, *lynchets*, clamber the upper lynchets till Seaford and everything to the west, as far as Brighton and beyond, was out of sight, and there on the top of the cliffs stretching east was the expansive turf of Seaford Golf Club with at least a couple of the holes absurdly close to the grass track along which members of the public were supposed to be able to stroll with all the nonchalance in the world. From his very first sortie up here he'd thought what a travesty it was to have a golf course so close to a public footpath meandering along the edge of the cliff. Granted, after a while the golf course, like Seaford and Brighton and the rest, slipped in turn completely from view. But for about half a mile Silas Woodlock had to pick his way, mindful not only of that day with his mother but also two prior experiences up on the Head. On the first, in the company of Ethel, as they were returning home, coming back within sight of Seaford Bay once more, a man ahead of them, who transpired to be a German tourist, was hit on the leg by a ball bouncing beyond the green and cried out in pain and surprise and in brief conversation afterwards concurred with Silas's own sentiment exactly: how crazy to have a golf-course up here right next to a cliff-edge where people walk.

— Crazy golf, said Ethel, with a bright-eyed laugh that the foreigner failed to appreciate.

On the second occasion, one fine morning literally up with the larks, early enough, he'd hoped, not to encounter any golfers at all, a deadly white object not much bigger than an eyeball, belatedly accompanied by that spine-tingling

Fore! as if shouted directly out of his boyhood, bounced with incongruous friendliness up to within a couple of feet of his boots. That was when he knew, as he explained to Ethel later that day, that it was just his having been thinking so fixedly about it that made it happen. So now, as he stole along this treacherous half-mile, he knew he couldn't give the slightest whisper of a thought to the bunch of old farts, in truth his contemporaries, in their check trousers and plain chinos with Teflon finish, in their striped polo shirts and sleeveless sweaters with cube designs, in their perforated golf caps, knitted beanies and waterproof bucket hats, carting their loads at the edge of his vision like overgrown children carrying folded-up push-chairs down the fairway, because if he gave them the merest chink of attention, if he so much as glanced or dispatched a split-second's thought in their direction, it was certain, as one of their horrible number retracted arms for a full firm sweep with a seven-iron, the unleashed ball would fly crashing straight between Silas Woodlock's eyes.

Moving on along the cliffs without incident, he recalled planting a distinguished old golfer, a former headmaster of some well-known public school, out in the bone orchard down Caterham way, the grimacing quip made at the service by the man's best friend about the eighteenth hole and the clubhouse, and the peculiar satisfaction, at the end of the day, of burying the clubs with the body in the box, no common-or-garden nose-squeezer for him.

Party Going

— Odd wine, ventured Nigel Newton.

It was midsummer's day and the party was in full swing, if by that phrase is understood nothing entirely straightforward, with credence given to a thought of gibbons never so cute as they might appear aloft, briefly embracing, before falling fifteen feet to reassemble in a posture and location as if always anticipated, preening a moment before launching again into another tree, and given also to the way words' swingings wing into one another so that, in the pleasant crush, fine things are heard that were never said and things said unheard, not just from the sheer volume of voices, music, glasses, plates and cutlery, but out of the subterranean chasms of what someone would like to have said, almost mouths, begins to intimate but the swing shifts, the heart folds up or unfolds a fresh linen tea-towel and an alluring woman turns away without a word or a man you've never met before obtrudes a mildly inebriated but beatific smiling face, watery blue eyes studded with indefinite loss, and the blooming but precarious stem of talk that had been swaying before you snaps. It's swings and roundabouts, a party in full swing with how many friendships or love affairs never begun thanks to the missed golden segue, one entire mountain range after another sinking without trace.

Academic parties used to be common events. They don't really happen any more. This particular gathering on the longest day of the year had its fair share of lecturers, professors and students, as well as locals and family friends. It was styled less as party, in fact, more simply as afternoon drinks – a rather orderly and old-fashioned get-together. It began around two o'clock and everyone was expected to depart by six. The supposition was that people might initially convene inside, before easing through to the garden. It took place at Cuckmere Haven farmhouse, where the literary theorist Nicholas Royle and family were fortunate enough to live, up in the seclusion of the South Downs. The house was situated down a long single-track lane off the sea-road between Seaford and Eastbourne. A rather fine and rambling eighteenth-century property, it was set back a few hundred yards from the white Sussex cliffs, with a view of the oxbow river flowing gently out across the Cuckmere valley to meet the sea concealed by a sloping field of Bluefaced Leicester sheep.

Newton had passed his verdict initially unaware of any *faux pas*. He was standing by the drinks table, addressing a beautiful woman who, so far as he knew, was another visitor like himself, and their talk had picked up quickly, less from anything said than from the unspoken recognition that both spoke with an American accent. Not a straight American accent, however, but a special model, in her case, evidently shaped by years spent in the south of England. He pictured it, fleetingly, as fluted by sea-winds like trees on the Downs, a couple of which were indeed visible through the window behind her, tenacious occupants of ancient boundaries. Newton was there more or less by chance. Royle knew him not so much as the chief executive of Bloomsbury Publishing, but rather (and then only slightly) as a fellow colleague, an honorary professor at Sussex. He'd heard that Newton occasionally visited the area. They had happened to bump into each another, out walking the previous afternoon: *We're having some friends over for drinks tomorrow afternoon. Why not come along?*

Newton had not realised that his interlocutor was the hostess, even now *en route* to tend to a batch of brownies and chocolate chip cookies in the kitchen from a snatched conversation with her husband about the recessive pleasures of Faulkner. Only an American well-immersed in some of England's quirkier literary productions would have called to mind at this moment Richard Curtis's *Skinhead Hamlet*, where thousands of lines of Shakespeare are collapsed into a couple of pages, including most entertainingly, she thought, the Ghost addressing his grief-stricken son with the brief epithet *Oi! Mush!* and then Queen Gertrude, in the final scene, sipping from the poisoned glass and remarking, *Fucking odd wine.*

Portia Piper recounted this without hesitating over the expletive, and he, being unfamiliar with the Curtis, found it funny and delightful, especially in her singular mid-Atlantic. Of course he knew his wines, and indeed still maintained a business interest in vineyards at St Helena, California. The wine in truth was foul and no wonder: the 2004 Darriaud Rasteau was a *vin de table* that should have been consumed years ago. Portia might have tried to explain – one of Nick's graduate students must have opened it, imagining it appropriate for the occasion, but it wasn't supposed to be for drinking, it was the last remaining bottle from the reception after Nick's father's funeral in 2005 – but she was fearful the brownies were getting burnt and excused herself before the visitor could say any more. Newton discreetly poured himself a glass of a perfectly decent-looking St-Emilion and drifted into a conversation involving Petrina, the Namibian wife of a Newhaven fisherman, who was talking with Ben, a local builder, about two *huge* shoals of mackerel out in the bay, and *that* was the reason why the shoreline was awash with dead whitebait: nothing *weird*, she explained, just the mackerel chasing the whitebait into the beach and the fishermen chasing the mackerel.

Just a few feet away, though it might have been the Bermuda Triangle (for such are the deceptive spaces of a convivial occasion with a roomful of some seventy-five or eighty people, in which someone has been telling you about the benefits and drawbacks of their new smartphone and if that handsome young graduate student proffering a tray of miniature scones with strawberry jam and clotted cream hadn't distracted you at the moment you'd planned to effect a sidewise shift to the intriguing knot of three people immediately to your left, you would never have got exposed to the argument that the universe, essentially, at the end of the day, is *very, very, very flat*, as a Danish astrophysicist – whose presence at the party seemed something of a mystery to everyone – was now vigorously summing up), the incorrigible twirling-handlebar-moustached Matthew Frost was remarking to Nikki Tate, an attractive woman in her mid-forties, with long blonde hair, an expert in Bowen Technique:

— … and he said to me, *Don't go any deeper please, you're bruising my man-cervix*.

And then, too, there is the person who is indeed not listening to *you* but to the conversation *over your shoulder* and who, when speaking, supplies less than fifty per cent of their attention, leading you in response to make each and

130

every word you say a little less sincere, until the travesty of the exchange ends with a parting of the party-waves, sometimes retaining the vestiges of civility, other times more curt, leaving you stranded, just your luck, until the next game fool, kind soul or kindred spirit is washed towards you on the afternoon tide. Matthew Frost had a foot in this treacherous category but with such small toes that many felt, looking at them curling as he spoke, they couldn't really deny him a second (looking over your shoulder) or even (doing it again) a third chance, for the reward would come not so much *at* as *after* the end. Such was his gift of timing, the infectious curling, the twirling and the twinkling eye. So it came when, on the verge of entirely nonplussing Nikki Tate, he added:

— We laughed for a not inconsiderable period of time.

Her husband, the travel writer Rufus Pinner, was a poor eavesdropper. With his slightly impaired hearing he occasionally spoke more loudly than he might have wished. But his enthusiasm for the intricacies of speech and the lives of others also made him quite exceptional, the sort of listener from whom the Ancient Mariner might have received genuinely helpful feedback. An arm's stretch away from her, Pinner was deeply engrossed in a conversation with the poet Keston Sutherland and an artist from Siberia called Olga Sorokina who had just said:

— Bring it on!

This was her peremptory response to Sutherland who, with great verve, had just recited a passage from one of his odes to the code of a defunct model of tumble dryer, TL61P:

— ...involuntary flinching from algorithmic traders, iffy qualms with quant developers, instant revulsion at options data analysts, hard-won hang-ups about life and health actuaries, automatic melancholy when confronted with corporate actions specialists, nuclear abhorrence of continuity managers, petty incredulity at transitions co-ordinators, complex disaffection for performance improvement operations professionals, real hatred of transformation managers, waning displeasure at heads of decision support, discreet pique at heads of client integration, evangelical vexation at asset servicing specialists, irresponsible annoyance about transfer agency operations managers, fruitless fretfulness over distressed debt fund analysts, mealymouthed misdoubt of credit sanctioners, overdue animus for debt markets writers, harrowed disbelief at credit partners, plangent repudiation of restructuring reporters, gruelling denial of structured credit surveillance analysts, necrotic mockery of assurance managers and irremediable illness of disposition toward regulatory affairs consultants getting social housing down to the last unfuckable man means that you don't really want the communism you say you want.

Pinner was compelled to ask:

— What do you mean *Bring it on*?

He appeared to have no doubt at all as to what Sutherland had been detailing. The poet for his part, however, quite failed to realise that Pinner was not addressing him. Rufus wanted Olga, who had already told him a little about growing up in the small Arctic town of Snezhnogorsk in the 1980s, to confirm what she was saying about communism. And so, a little more loudly:

— You're referring to communism, yes, and you're not saying *Bring it back*, you're saying *Bring it on*? Fascinating. That's *really* interesting. And *party going*, you said, *all parties going*.

Then, turning to Sutherland:

— Marvellous poetry, by the way. *Not in utopia*, eh, quoth Wordsworth, no *subterranean fields*, but *in this very world*. Absolutely! Marvellous stuff. Bring it on!

Phillip Quick loitered a little dizzily in the wings, still recovering from an experience of roundabouts he hadn't for a moment seen coming. Olga's husband was a mild but meticulous man, tall and thin as a beanpole, determined to consume as many of the brownies now doing the rounds of the room as he reasonably might, without appearing victim of an eating disorder. His metabolism demanded that he consume Portia's baked goods, or others discreetly extracted from one of his deeper blazer pockets, at a rate of at least three an hour. The hostess had made an entire extra batch with this insatiability in mind.

Quick's height and solicitous manner led him to stoop slightly in conversation, adopting a pose that seemed initially indistinguishable from a GP's unctuous dealing with a private healthcare patient, but shifting gradually into a more sturdy friendliness of demeanour, teetering at moments on the impossibly complicitous, when he would clatter into joyful laughter at something his interlocutor hadn't even noticed had been said, and a clarification would be called for. The genial and good-hearted man was still reeling, however, from having overstepped the mark in a manner thoroughly mortifying to him. While known by friends to advocate the most stringent agnosticism, Quick especially liked to converse with strangers of a religious disposition. He was reeling in this instance not so much from something said or mis-said, as from a tiny gesture horribly misunderstood. For in a languorous – and doubtless, for the monk himself, overlong – discussion of the psychological and physiological benefits of monastic retreats, the pleasures of evensong, the values of quietness and meditation, and the practicalities of building one's own dwelling according to now easily available online Anglo-Saxon architectural drawings, Quick had touched very lightly, graciously, a little way down the side of the man's head just below and back from his left ear. He did so purely affectionately, with the happy aim of highlighting a contrast with his own shaven-headedness. At which the monk, till then all pleasantness and decency, flashed out, to a face-reddening that passed so fast it seemed to ignite not only the violator but several other visages within a couple of yards' radius:

— Fuck off my tonsure.

The commotion soon enough subsided, as Quick repeatedly murmured words of apology, *sorry, I'm so sorry, really, no offence intended in the world,* before moving away to the kitchen in search of the solace of another brownie and a word with host or hostess concerning his acute embarrassment.

With his departure a gap needed filling. Bystander and sympathetic blusher Tony Fletcher was a big-boned, bear-like, smiling man in his mid-fifties, local purveyor of alternative and renewable energies. Derailed from his conversation with Portia's Aunt Mae and family friends Andrew Bennett and Ulrika Maude, the smiling man leaned over in the direction of the disconsolate monk and exclaimed loudly but with unexpected sweetness:

— All is good!

The group then sought to resume conversation. Maude returned to showing Fletcher pictures from a recent trip to the Far East:

— It's the Ryoanji rock garden, my favourite place in Japan.

Aunt Mae, a child psychoanalyst and expert on the work of Sándor Ferenzci, who was in England for a week or so to attend a conference, swung off in a new direction, asking Bennett what sort of work he did. Enunciating in a brisk deadpan apparently aimed at foreclosing any further discussion of the topic, he replied:

— I'm writing about suicide. In the novel, I mean.

Phillip Quick had picked out a brownie, pocketing a couple of back-ups in the absence of the hostess who, by this time, had not only linked up fleetingly with the host, but vacated the downstairs altogether. To her husband she had just divulged the conviction that she should, years earlier as a student at Berkeley, have pursued a reading of Faulkner's novels in terms of transgenerational haunting. It might have formed the basis for an illustrious academic career. And Royle, without a moment's reflection:

— Have you considered haunting that runs forwards?

— But that's what I meant by recessive pleasures.

Playing host is invariably a bathetic business. So much energy is expended on ensuring that everyone knows where to stow their belongings, has a drink and something to eat, can find their way to the toilet, gets to meet so-and-so, stranger or old friend. So many questions impose: Is the music OK? Are people having a good time? Is the food or drink about to run out? And why is everyone still congregating in the house, like a backed-up drain, and not moving out into the garden? Are the children (in this case at least a dozen, mostly out in the sunshine) behaving themselves? Who has not yet arrived and why? What to do with the bottles and flowers and other unexpected gifts? And so the spectacle will have passed, with the hosts little more than dazed onlookers. It was with a sense of this dislocation, and with a further, deeper feeling of unease, that the host had been eyeing across the crowded main room, more than once, the figure of Stephen Osmer.

And here lay a quite different question. There had been a cursory hello exchanged on Osmer's arrival, but would they actually converse? Stephen had come along very much, as he saw it, to please Lily. It was their final day together before she was to go away for a month. He'd assumed they would spend that night together in Clerkenwell, though she had procrastinated when the topic had been raised. She seemed very preoccupied – busy in part, no doubt, getting ready for the trip. He wasn't especially enthusiastic about the party in Sussex. He had mixed feelings about it all. He had thrown a verbal brick in the host's face in Manchester, but he had no intention of apologising or retracting that remark. And indeed, in his essay in the *Gazette*, he had been pretty brutal too. He presumed the old woodlouse must have read it. He wondered whether his intervention had had any beneficial effects. If Royle had indeed read 'Double Whammy', how could he fail to see the challenges it posed? *No sense of history*, Osmer had proclaimed, *no engagement with social or political actuality*. Might he have inspired this old theory-boffin to rethink? His joining Lily that afternoon was thus motivated in part by what he considered an ethical and philanthropic impulse. You can't have a true revolution without changing people's world-view, and he dared to hope that his essay, in hitting a number of sensitive spots, might have helped the old theorist see the light.

For Royle, on the other hand, what was there really to say?

At the same time, Osmer appeared to be rather engrossed in a discussion with Robert Rowland Smith. Smith had been introduced as 'the philosopher and management consultant'. Other implausible combinations had flashed upon Stephen's consciousness, as they shook hands: '*Daily Mail* journalist and brain surgeon', 'primary school teacher and arms-dealer'. Smith amused him well enough, however, and they had plenty to talk about. Strange not to have crossed paths before. They even shared the ambivalent distinction of having grown up in the same patch of south-east London. But then Osmer noticed Royle lumbering towards them.

— There was no end to Doreen.

— No end to? asked Osmer. He couldn't have been giving it his full attention.

— There was no end to Doreen, reiterated Smith, and beamed with that intense, almost gleeful mischief in his eyes that had drawn in so many admirers down the years.

What did it mean, *no end to Doreen*? But now the host was with them.

Royle knew Osmer's general political views well enough from reading the *London Literary Gazette* and remarks attributed to him on social media, the duller as well as more celebrated soundbites, the gossip-column anecdotes and so on. Here in the openness of his own living room at a friendly gathering in the midsummer afternoon sunshine, where nothing more than easy and relaxed conversation among friends old or new need be anticipated, however, he felt first and foremost a sharp division in his consciousness – between a sense, on the one hand, of where, elsewhere, his presence was now required, and, on the other, of a subtler but more profound unease at his being there at all. The moment seemed to expand, but in a peculiarly encrypted manner, like the glimpsing of a passage down into the underworld. Royle knew that it was a question of tone, and the first breaking of silence between them would be decisive in ways exceeding anything either could predict or control.

And meanwhile, to be picked up alongside them, Phillip Quick had become embroiled with the Bowen Technique woman, the conversation having sped from her misconstruing the beanpole man's raised eyebrows at the phrase *Bowen Technique* (he'd thought she was talking about the Anglo-Irish novelist) and defensively saying, *I have found that working with the body in this way can, surprisingly, go far deeper than the conventional talking therapies*, to her interlocutor's unmanageable enthusiasm in relating how one of his friends had got into such a frustrated state while awaiting surgery that *she was looking forward to having her leg off*.

In preparing to negotiate his contempt for the intellectual self-indulgence, the wordplay and jargon-infested stupidity spouted by the academic woodlouse, Osmer was at the same time struggling to keep apart the perhaps merely random relation between having a limb amputated and there being no end to Doreen. Royle had, in fact, not been entirely unhappy with 'woodlouse' when encountering it in the pages of the *Gazette*. 'Louse' had always struck him as an oddly debasing name for a creature so roundly prehistoric, so dignified in its incorrigible trundling, its humility, its proto-hedgehog capacity to roll up in self-defence. The American equivalent, 'potato bug', was perhaps a different matter.

Suddenly overcome by the feeling that he had left things long enough, even too long, the host donned an expression of hurry and concern to check on the party of children now occupying the rear lawn, and veered by. In doing so he just missed Sarah Wood's first and only contribution to the conversation with Osmer and Smith. Eerily chiming with Osmer's wondering to himself if Smith qualified as a *bona fide* example of a financial sector worker, Wood gnomically intoned:

— The truth will out – blood will have blood.

Now in Midsummer

Glancing out at the garden where all seemed fine, he took the stairs by the back door and stealthily ascended. He retracted a key from his left pocket and turned it in the lock of the bedroom door. It opened softly, without a creak, and he was not sure at first whether those inside had even noticed his entrance. Ordinarily the pretty leaded windows looking out towards the sea would offer a good view of the garden where, just at present, children could be heard playing tag, but the curtains had been drawn far enough across to provide invisibility from the outside world and comforting dimness within. The first thing he noticed as his eyes acclimatised were a couple of screwed-up balls of paper on the rug. He hesitated before picking either of them up. He wanted to be sure he had been seen.

But there was a warmth in his face and running over his chest. Already he was aware of a delectable strengthening below. Despite himself, despite his best efforts to remain detached until the last possible moment, the women had already upended him. She was, he now saw in the dimness, kissing her. Portia was kissing Lily on the bed, and he couldn't tell if she was choosing to ignore the fact that he had entered the room as a ploy to build him up or if she was so taken up in the sweetness of kissing the younger woman that she was simply oblivious of his entry.

He felt, in the flushing of his limbs, paralysed in the moment. Most arresting of all was the detail of Lily's look, over his wife's shoulder, her eyes catching his and appearing to him to be fainting with pleasure. She was gazing at him with a longing he felt completely unprepared for. But then, how could anyone ever be adequately prepared for the gaze of Lily Lynch?

No sooner had this thought crossed him than she was blind again, as if she had never registered his presence. Lily's was the pert and superb body of a beautiful twenty-three-year-old woman. She was lying back on the biggest bed in the house, her short dark hair in the pillows, as his wife kissed her mouth, softly, repeatedly, letting her tongue drift into Lily's, finding the roof of Lily's mouth and making it difficult for the young girl to articulate anything, even had she wanted to, beyond faint gasps of pleasure. He was not, he soon realised, too late. His wife was still wearing her white button-up shirt and jeans, though he could see that her belt was loosened, as she straddled the younger woman. Lily's clothes appeared still untouched. She was wearing the light summery red linen skirt and matching top that had already downstairs been well noted, designed as it was to show off her dark waist, bare shoulders and lovely neck.

The girls, as he thought of them, must have waited as long as they could. If his encounter with Osmer had seemed to be in slow motion, it was above all because he had been thinking about this scene, fearing that they couldn't desist from acting alone or, more narcissistically, that the very prolongation of his absence had sharpened their desire and precipitated the scene he now believed had not yet occurred. It was a relationship, this intoxicating arrangement with his wife and Lily, stretching back several months. It had its seed, as passionate affairs often do, in a delicious haze, a reaching back into memory that they enjoyed talking about, even if it tended, more often than not, to trouble as much as reassure him. That night in Manchester, when Stephen had brought the evening to its abrupt but reverberating close, the women had been introduced to one another and spent twenty minutes or more in conversation. It happens. They were both beautiful, eminently clever, lovers of art and literature, and passionate about the inequities and injustices of the unbrave new world in which they found themselves. But in truth neither had ever before fallen in love with another woman, at least not to the extent of its bamboozling them into what is described, with juridical dullness, as a physical relationship.

They liked to recall, nonetheless, that they experienced, that first evening in Manchester, a peculiar rapport, as undeniable as it was surprising, and this perhaps had something to do with how Lily had first caught Portia's eye without exactly meaning to, as if Portia conversely had caught hers without actually being aware of it. And if Lily tried to attribute the remarkable sense of something happening at that first meeting to an inadvertent glance, trapped like a leaf by the playful paw of a kitten, the other woman would gently remind her of the unprecedented touch. For at the end of that twenty-minute conversation when they had, perhaps without giving it much consideration, exchanged contact details, had Lily not finally, as they were parting, touched Portia in a manner that made them both even later that same night flush to remember?

Had Lily not, like a girl in a cloud of mosquitoes, perplexed by her own bodily presence in the moment, put up her hand and waved it gently but incomprehensibly across the older woman's left cheek? Had she lost balance, in the rush of the moment, realising that Stephen had evidently already left the building and conscious of the need to go after him, trying to gather up her bag and coat, determined not to forget anything, while also wanting, in a way mysterious to herself, to imprint some sense of the encounter having happened, of something having existed between them that she had not previously felt at any point in her life? Was it some unconscious gesture evoking compassion, miming a retraction or requesting forgiveness for her partner's remark about the brick in the face? Had she even subconsciously not meant for her hand to end as it did in this strange caress of the other's cheek? Might she not rather have intended to trace something in the air between them, not sure herself what to make of it?

Certainly in the first place it did not seem possible for either to mention the matter to their respective partners. And indeed, on at least the first subsequent meeting, there was no physical connection made of any kind, beyond the conventionality of a brisk social hug. A few days after returning from Manchester Portia was going up to London. It was something she had been planning for some time, needing to get a visa stamp in her passport in preparation for a trip that summer. She and Lily agreed to meet for coffee at the end of the afternoon, at the Serpentine Gallery, where an exhibition of photographs of gardens was running. And they had met again just a week later when Lily had texted to say she had to be in Brighton for a meeting with someone from the South East Arts Council. Initially there was obvious excitement in a shared secretiveness, a giddiness neither was quite yet willing to name without either of their partners knowing about it. They sat with skinny lattes in a small café in the North Laines talking for an hour and more about coffee, food and travel, books they were reading or wanted to read, the attractions of living in London versus by the sea, without even a mention of their partners or love-lives.

Their conversation was as simple and enjoyable as either had ever known. Why was it so easy for women to talk to women?

And then Lily shot to her feet: she hadn't realised the time, she had to get the train because Stephen was chairing an evening with Alan Hollinghurst and she'd promised to be there, and perhaps it was the young lesbian couple, one with bright pink hair, both with enough piercings to bring down a Zeppelin, but the older woman stood up, as if to music, delayed in time, saying, yes, of course, don't miss it, and kissed Lily on the lips.

And here Portia was, several months later, still kissing her, eased down now on top of her, Lily's arms around her, shoes long since slipped off. Except that now her husband was also there, as he had been on such occasions for some time. Soon enough, in the early flowering of illicit passion, the guilty lover confronts the fork after which all other paths in the garden diverge less darkly. That confrontation might last a mere split-second, a week or years, but the route, once taken, determines all. For Lily the thought of telling Stephen about the affair was simply not to be borne. She knew that if he knew they would be finished. There was no question. The strong and in so many ways fulfilling relationship with him, confirmed and reaffirmed over many months, would shatter like cheap glass, were she so much as to try even to broach the subject.

For how would it work? *Stevie, there's something I have to...* Ridiculous. Or: *You know, Stephen, sometimes I find that when I am with another woman, especially an older woman...* Impossible.

Of course, just as unreasonable was the prospect of explaining to him that the object of her pash, the person for whom she had developed an infatuation beyond anything she ever imagined she was capable of feeling for anyone of the so-called same sex, was the wife of a man he execrated. And doubtless there was something additionally thrilling about the whole arrangement, not only about Stephen's not knowing, but also about the egregious nature of her object-choice.

Had she unconsciously sought to make up for the brutality of Osmer's dismissal of the literary theorist, his authoring of a defacement arguably stretching to the wife in turn? Lily saw the neatness of such a rationale, even if it could scarcely pose as master-key. She was perfectly open to Freudian or post-Freudian speculations on this and anything else. After such knowledge, no return: no mothballed Eden, no regression or pretence, no mindless denial or side-stepping for her. In this she had always been at odds with the young man from the *LLG*: one of the things that had helped make Stephen Osmer a cultural and media celebrity was his consistent, often acerbic and funny dismissal of psychoanalysis.

She had also read some of the woodlouse's work and formed an opinion rather more favourable than Stevie had. From the beginning indeed, listening to him read and talk about his relationship with his namesake that evening in Manchester, she had had no gut feeling of revulsion: he had a rather nice reading voice, she thought, and she liked the way he laughed. She had tried diplomatically to make a case for him again, when seeking to persuade Stevie to come to this party at Cuckmere Haven:

— He's simply not the abject reactionary you make him out to be. And anyway I'd like you to meet his wife. We've become good friends.

That last detail, to be sure, was surprising news to Osmer. Lily wasn't about to reveal the depth of this friendship, let alone of the other man's role in it. But the pressure of keeping the friendship altogether under wraps had gone, she realised, far enough.

Was this to be the quickest striptease yet? 'Striptease', however, carried a sense of frivolity and exploitation entirely foreign to this impassioned love triangle. Moreover, it suggested nothing truly risky, whereas what was happening here in this upstairs room, to the sounds of children laughing and playing in the garden below the windows and the reverberations through the old wooden floor of a buzzing party below, felt wonderfully dangerous. For how long, in fact, could both host and hostess be away from the so-called main action and it go unnoticed, without query or investigation?

He was blushing he knew but, in this fleeting space of time in which he verified the women's awareness of his presence, he bent down, plucked up one of the balls of paper and uncrumpled it, hands slightly trembling. This was how it had been now on a number of occasions. It was part of a choreography by which they all became differently intoxicated, an inebriating elongation of longing. *So long?* asked Portia, when this joint provocation was first mooted. For the pattern proposed entailed an experience of perseveration, a waiting game almost, at times, strangulating in its sweet long-drawn-out-ness. Its drafting had originated in the early encounters between Lily and Portia and developed through the strategies adopted to deal with the various idiosyncrasies of the different parties.

The women had quickly committed, just a week after the kiss in the Brighton café, to meeting again. When Portia visited Lily at her flat in Clerkenwell, neither had quite supposed how rapidly and explicitly things would escalate, before the visitor indeed had taken much more than a sip from one of the glasses of freshly squeezed orange juice her new friend had set rattling with ice on the low table before them. If the precipitate behaviour had at first been the older woman's, it was now something akin to Lily's return match – precisely as if her own lips suddenly kissed in that shocking fashion just a week earlier were from day to day meanwhile readying themselves for this sweet and unequivocal revenge.

Portia, on the other hand, had felt waves of embarrassment tumbling over her more or less every day since she'd done what she'd done in the café – mixed, it is true, with strange flows of excitement, even a curious pride in her audacity. It had not occurred to her that Lily Lynch would respond with such heart-in-mouth directness. It was an escalation as sumptuous as it was unforeseen. And so she let Lily. She met Lily's lips with her own. She let this completely new and shocking experience of kissing another woman, a beautiful woman perhaps ten years younger than herself, take its course, or more precisely she rose to the invisible heights of the occasion, standing clinching hotly kissing as if this were an oasis in another world and she didn't care for any soft voice suggesting it was a mirage for, if so, so what? Wasn't this the shimmering reality of all passion?

For Lily this was also an experience of the utmost unexpectedness, a soaring departure from anything that had ever happened to her, an outstripping of any crush she had felt for any of the girls she had known at school, a shock of excitement like surfing a green collapsing wall of icy water or plummeting in a bungee jump for which she had not exactly volunteered, and yet also unprecedentedly warm, this immersion in the arms of a woman whose beautiful face and limbs bespoke a maturity and sensitivity come from her extra years. A pain aflutter in Portia's heart was not, however, to be just brushed away. Lily, in a passion that was really more girl-like than the older woman knew what to do with, was still kissing her mouth but, as she did so, was letting her hands run down Portia's back and caress the seat of her jeans as they stood otherwise still in this seemingly unending embrace, caressing and pressing herself speechlessly into the visitor's body as if she lacked the vocabulary to know how to arouse the desired response or even to be sure what response she might be seeking. But, as the dark-complexioned young beauty was fingering Portia's thin black cashmere sweater that discreetly, almost inadvertently showed off the still shapely loveliness of her breasts, full but small, much in fact like a younger woman's such as Lily's own, flustering at the front of her sweater with a blind desire to demonstrate, to dishevel, to slide up and off, to reveal Portia's sweet breasts and fall on them, softly, in pleasure, kissing and sucking softly, one nipple hardening after the other, the fluttering in the older woman's heart made her put out her hands in sudden unconscious exhaustion and hold Lily abruptly in check.

— We can't, she said gently but plainly. We can't do this without Nick knowing.

Such is the predisposition to read ourselves in others, smuggled by lightning in the mirror of the moment, that Lily, for all her sensitivity to ambiguity in books and movies, did not for a fraction of a second waver over what Portia was telling her. Bolstered, no doubt, by her own conviction not to reveal anything of this affair to her own partner, but indeed to delve and take pleasure in a clandestinity that a week ago she wouldn't have imagined possible, it took her a little while to assimilate that Portia was not voicing her anxiety that her husband could not but find out, that he would, inevitably, come to be aware of this liaison, and that therefore the liaison, such as it was or was threatening to become, should be abandoned. But then the thing did become clear, after Portia put herself momentarily back in the hot stuffy interminable afternoon Latin classes at high school and parsed the sentence – *it's called parsing*, she told Lily, laughing, *listen to how Portia parses*:

— I'm not saying I don't want to do this, and I'm not saying we cannot do this without my husband discovering and all hell breaking loose. I am saying I would like to do this but I can't, without his being in on it.

What *in on it* signified was perhaps more or other than Portia had, at this juncture, either intended or even begun to contemplate. And indeed this was another facet of the mirror-show: in the very act of explication, you say something new and strange even to yourself, seeking merely to reflect or reiterate but actually articulating something that sounds and speeds off in an entirely different register. By *in on it*, echoed Lily Lynch, did she mean what Lily thought she meant? Turning to their glasses of orange juice, the women sat down in a flush, the air, their arms, filling with flowers of possibility. Portia had ventured something she had certainly not planned or quite possibly meant. At any rate, this *in on it* resounded with an erotic ambiguity neither of them felt, at least for a time, equipped to pursue further.

At first, back in March, it had been a piece of mild provocation, a decision that Lily should come to the farmhouse one Friday after work, when she knew that Stephen was away for a weekend literature festival up north. It would be an opportunity for her to meet Nick and drink some wine and she could stay over in the spare bedroom and head back to town some time, perhaps after lunch, the following day. The early stages of falling in love may be tricky enough in the case of two lovers, but the addition of a third generates a veritable vertigo. The women might work together, at least up to a point, in stealth. So vodka tonics had been consumed, dinner was close, wine had been poured, and the man having left the dining room for a couple of minutes, returned to witness his wife brazenly kissing Osmer's girlfriend on the sofa by a well-stoked log-fire. Ruffled but rising to the occasion, Royle had remarked that, if this was what they wanted to do, they should write first asking his permission. Dinner was not spoiled but certainly delayed. The seed had been planted, in any case, and provided the template for their subsequent dalliances. Each of the girls would write on a single slip of paper. As brief as a recipe, though perhaps of a singularly *haute* cuisine, each sketched the fantasy of what they wanted – to do, say, play, and the others too. And the two papers would be folded or screwed up and left for the man to choose.

So now with hands all tremulous – from the excitement of seeing them already on the bed together in each other's arms kissing, from a sense of the pleasure he knew this business of writing gave all of them, from the sense of danger in having fixed on this tryst in these circumstances at all (since he imagined they might have minutes at most before someone, a fellow party-goer or one of the children, would come upstairs looking for one or other of them) – he uncrumpled what, in a thrilling flash, he recognised as Lily's handwriting. In truth Royle had never succeeded in entirely vanquishing feelings of a deep but peculiar unease that had been haunting him now for some months. There was, in the first instance, the continuing sense of wonder, the feeling that Sir Thomas Wyatt describes in the memorable words, *It was no dream: I lay broad waking.* This was what Royle himself had written about years ago, in one of his books of literary theory, as the strangeness of what is 'too good to be true' – the assumption of being past it, too many years on his back to appear sexually attractive to one so youthful, the overwhelming excitement of this erotic triangle, of making love to not one but two beautiful young women, one much younger than himself, the power of arousal in seeing them making love, finding sexual fulfilment without him, and then of having one or the other or both at the same time, in whatever choreographed scenario prescribed. And then there was also, unavoidably, a distinct kick to be got from the fact that he was fucking Osmer's girl, like a titillating reversal of Chaucer's tales of worn-out old men, vigorous Nicholas making a cuckold of the guileless young celebrity.

But this sense of wonder was accompanied by a more troubling feeling, a less definable unease. It was the mystifying but apparently undeniable experience of a peculiar estrangement. Was it derealisation or depersonalisation? Could there indeed be a psychological state that somehow combined or oscillated between the two, never quite one or the other? He could think, at times, of no better way of describing it than that he was 'living in the pages of a novel'. Others around him seemed real enough, he considered, but in recent months – ever since starting work on the project of writing the hides – he had become haunted by a sense of his own irreality. He couldn't share this with his wife, or indeed with the new girl. It was too strange. It was as if he lacked an interiority that others had.

Lily had got to work with Portia's silk scarves before he finished reading. After securing his wrists behind him at the foot of the bed, the young women now positioning themselves on the rug, out of reach but in full view of him, returned to their former pleasures with new excitement. Portia soon came. After sliding up the younger girl's skirt and slipping a hand into her white cotton panties, stroking her in a tantalising manner for little more than a couple of minutes, she fell back and pleasured herself, unable to hold any longer, as Lily leant above her, kissing her mouth and rigid nipples with soft, wet, hungry lips. Portia then, in her intoxication, gently lay her lover back on the rug, shaking off her little red top and finally pulling off the white underwear, kissing the beautiful darkness of Lily from tip to toe but lingering soon enough at her pulsing core, sliding her tongue to where and how she knew Lily most loved it.

After she too came, and eyes lit in that gaze of desiring fullness he relished perhaps as much as anything else in all this lovemaking, the girls proceeded to take turns counting to seven. As Lily's note had stipulated, it was now time for 'the burning roof and tower'. Both kneeling close to him with breasts exposed, they tinkered, playing intolerably with time, over lapping tongues of flame, counting seven for the other, at one time too quickly, at another achingly rich to the verge of exploding slowness.

At which point there was a sound behind the door. Did he lock it? He could not remember. There was a firm and sickening knock.

— Who is it? called the host.

— It's me, Rufus! a voice declaimed, loud and agitated. You've got to come!

Gulls

Untied and dressing himself, already in forgetfulness of lost time, as the women pulled on clothes and composed themselves into a conversation on the bed, he opened the door. He attempted a hurried explanation about Lily being upset and she and Portia in the midst of girl-talk that he, the host, had not meant to interrupt as he'd popped upstairs to fetch... But none of this seemed of any interest to Rufus Pinner.

— The thing is, Rufus said, it's *a bit* weird but, there's this fellow who turned up at the door (as they make their way along the landing towards the main stairs, leading down directly into the main reception area), apparently he just showed up at the door and he is *demanding* to see you. Says he's not *for* the party, he just needs to speak to *you*. He seems pretty het-up and, I don't know, *odd*, if you ask me. Says his name is Silas Woodcock.

The name meant nothing to the host, but as he reached the bottom of the stairs he saw that the stranger's presence had come to all but dominate the room. All sounds of conviviality had fallen away. Everyone was looking in Royle's direction and then back towards the figure in the open doorway, the rolling green of the South Downs visible behind his bulking silhouette. Tall but a little stooped, this craggy-looking man in his mid-sixties seemed frozen on the threshold.

— Hello? called over the literary theorist at last, in a questioning but friendly enough tone. Can I help?

— *Help?* echoed the big fellow in a voice that seemed at once trembling and incandescent. You are…

— I am Nichol—

— I know who you are!

— And you, sir? A Mr Woodcock? enquired the host, determined to maintain a level of courtesy, but a little unnerved by the size of this shadowy stranger and his manifestly troubled state.

Someone took the executive decision to extinguish the sounds of Itzhak Perlman performing Bach's Second Partita for violin that had been, till then, still audible. The party had fallen silent.

— It's Wood*lock*, you bloody bastard. You should know who I am. Silas Woodlock. Ring no bells?

— I'm really sorry but I just don't—

— You're a nasty piece of work, Royle.

— What are you talking about?

— I'm talking about fakery and I'm talking about thievery.

At this juncture the figure in the doorway shifted his feet and the host became aware for the first time of the vaguely ominous canvas bag hanging from Woodlock's long, limp but powerful-looking right arm. Royle certainly couldn't recall having ever seen this man before. There was something forbidding about him, with his pale perspiring cheeks and wild, sunken blue eyes. His expression was oddly distorted. It was as if some tic or machine were generating small but constant convulsions in his face.

— You took my work, Mr High-on-Your-Pedestal Professor, you took my own writing and you published it under your own name. Yes, ladies and gentlemen! This mighty Mr Royle here is a fake and a thief. A plagiarist, as I believe it is known in technical terms, and a full-scale breacher of personal legal copyright!

By all of this the accused was visibly shaken, simply muttering:

— I don't know what you're talking about, I'm sorry, perhaps there's some mistake.

The man who worked in renewable and alternative energies came forward, perhaps the largest person in the room besides Woodlock himself, evidently seeking to demonstrate support for his host, and to see the situation sorted out without any trouble. Tony Fletcher was a man who needed to be able to say, as often as possible: *All is good.* And so now, with his radiant smile and winning melancholy, he extended his bear-like right hand, exclaiming with a charming hint of a Scottish accent:

— Well, Mr Woodcock! Come in, won't you, and join us for a glass of wine!

Largely unnoticed in the background, Lily and Portia had by this point discreetly descended the back stairs and reappeared to witness the proceedings.

The stranger's right hand remained limp and motionless at his side, still holding the old canvas bag. No shake forthcoming, Fletcher let his own hand drop as the man replied, with a molten stare at this new buffoon:

— It's *Woodlock*. Are you all deaf? Silas *Woodlock*, retired funeral director.

— Wow, perked up Fletcher, his interminable innocence settling on a new object: you're an undertaker!

— He *was*, Tony, he *was*. He's just said he's retired.

This was thrown out as an aside by his friend Rufus, who had not spoken since coming back downstairs.

Gulls

But now Pinner went on:

— When you say breach of copyright, Mr Woodlock, can you explain a bit more?

There's only so much interest that a party of people, many of them already two or three glasses of wine down and enjoying a midsummer afternoon up on the Downs by the sea, can take, in a joined-up attentive fashion, especially when it comes with the phrase 'breach of copyright'. As with the tiresome admonitions about video piracy before the start of a movie, people mentally switch off. The newcomer was not a figure of indifference but in a crowded room of around eighty people, unless you are close to the action and able to follow who says what to whom, and when the conversation you were in the midst of was, after all, perfectly engaging, you can without too much of a struggle return to it, as numerous guests now did.

One woman, noticing Lily, impulsively smiled at her and commented on the loveliness of her attire. Another, a bespectacled Zimbabwean, plunged back into the conversation she was having with Phillip Quick, rushing out the words:

— There's something in the air right now – could it be the revolution?

Entertaining a small knot of postgraduates in the doorway to the kitchen, the literary critic Peter Boxall smiled broadly as he declared:

— It seems strange at first, and then you get used to it.

The students nodded, furtively glancing at one another. It was evident that none of them could recall what he had been talking about. And, a few feet away, Bethan Stevens, another Sussex colleague, returned to a discussion she'd just begun with two women whose names she had yet to learn:

— I just can't wear brooches. But I love them. The really spectacular ones, you know.

But others, especially those in reasonable proximity, were very drawn to what was going on between the host and this rather unnerving figure in the doorway. Robert Smith turned his mischievous grin on Osmer.

— I say, Stephen, in what social class would you place an undertaker?

But S.B. Osmer evidently wasn't interested in this question. In fact a bit rudely, Smith thought, he pushed off at this point, like a punt, gliding between bodies right and left till he was standing directly behind Pinner and Fletcher, in full sight of the party-pooper.

Evidently still in high dudgeon, but somewhat mollified by the request to supply details of a more formal nature, Silas Woodlock advanced a couple of steps into the room, and proceeded to relate the circumstances of his grievance. In sum: the antithalian accusant had given up his lifelong occupation in south London and moved with his wife Ethel to the town of Seaford. Things had been going along well enough until the breeding season began among the seagulls. Woodlock's life would never be the same again. They survived that first summer by the skin of their teeth, but this year had been even worse. More gulls breeding, more born, more nests on their roof, more noise, more disturbance, more tempers fraying, less sleep than ever. But that was another story. A year ago he had written about them. He would never have done so, were it not for his dearly beloved wife. It might help take a weight off your mind, she said. So he wrote something. It was only a few pages, but it was a lengthy, significant and complicated labour. And then Ethel asked him to read the piece out loud. One quiet Sunday afternoon down the road at the Wellington he duly did just that. That was when the thing went astray. He must have left it in the pub. When he went back the barman hadn't seen it. No one else knew anything about it. He'd made no copy, just those five and a half pages. He asked after it again at the pub and at the police station, but it never showed up. And then yesterday, browsing in a second-hand bookshop just off Broad Street, he came across this book of stories about birds. Lo and behold, there it was, in print, in black and white for all to see, his very own piece of writing. And at the top of it was the name of a complete stranger: Nicholas Royle.

At this point Woodlock stooped down and extracted a copy of the book from his canvas bag. *Murmurations*, ran the title, while murmurs ran through the crowd: *An Anthology of Uncanny Stories About Birds*.

What was to be done?

Now by a nice coincidence it happened that one Laura Ellen Joyce, another contributor to *Murmurations*, was also in the room. Indeed, in accordance with the natural egotism of authors, she had already noticed a copy of the book in question on one of the shelves just a few feet away from her. Accordingly she slid it out and, smiling as she did so, came forward and handed it to Royle, who looked entirely nonplussed. Accepting the volume from her, he appeared strangely bereft. Of course there would be those in the room who would be surprised to hear that their host, the respected literary theorist, was the author of any fiction at all, let alone in an anthology of short stories about birds. He was certainly not known to have avian interests.

In any case, the pause at the end of Woodlock's speech had by now lasted long enough and it was Stephen Osmer who, seeing each of the men with a copy of the book in his hands, made a suggestion:

— Since our host appears to be at, er, a loss for words (laughter, some uncomfortable, at this) and Mr Woodlock appears to be so sure of his case, and since we have the text, as it were, to hand, how about if, beginning with Mr Woodlock, we were to be treated to a reading aloud of the work in question?

— Hear, hear! chipped in Smith at this point, evidently sensing fun. What a grand idea!

Tony Fletcher, coming round to what was happening, added with sudden energy:

— And if he truly is the author, it should be audible from the manner in which he reads, from the nature of his rendition of the piece, no?

Osmer's proposal, then, was met with numerous exclamations of approval. Woodlock seemed gratified: he nodded his agreement. Royle himself, however, remained stony-featured and speechless. But the general desire to hear a story carried the day.

And so again the room fell quiet. There were even a few voices calling for quiet, *a speech*, *a speech*! As someone finally closed the front door, Mr Woodlock lowered his bag to the floor with the faintest, scarcely audible clang, found the page and, still standing just a few feet inside the entrance-way, proceeded to read, starting with the title and emphatically altering the name of the alleged author:

Gulls, by Silas Woodlock.

I never dreamt, when we retired to this old house by the sea, what trouble there'd be with the gulls. I'm talking about the big ones, the new urban thuggish variety that have been buying into the heart of seaside towns and establishing themselves willy-nilly, come hell or high water, in recent years, that mug you for your sandwich or ice-cream, peck and tear apart rubbish bags, wheel over you too close, screeching incessantly. These are the type that have learnt to stand their ground, with violent yellow eyes that don't blink or bear looking into. Like a new breed of rat, only gulls, super-gulls. In the space of a mere couple of decades they seem to have been morphing into some new species altogether. That's what my wife thinks. As if a genetic trigger were being released, part of a plan, like a government experiment. Or, she thinks, if it's not the government, it's climate change, unprecedented evolutionary acceleration thanks to a tipping effect. All this feeding on human garbage, heavy metals and other nutritional goodies, it's thrown the bird-world off kilter, resulting in a new phenomenon along the south coast, a geneticist horror story unveiling its frightening face before our very eyes but with most of us too dim or drugged-up on everyday crisis management even to notice.

In any case, it's not the seafront muggings or ripping into litterbins or daily screeching. It's to do with the night turning into dawn. Someone told me it started with the old school they knocked down, the gulls no longer able to build their nests on its extensive rooves. Rooves, roofs. Which is it? Neither sounds right to me. But who cares any longer about proper language or pronunciation?

At first we were hardly aware. But then the breeding season came. The house is narrow but tall. What possessed us to buy a place with so many flights of stairs I'm not sure. Space for the grandchildren, my wife said. We don't have grandchildren, I said. And then she says, If you're going to be by the sea you want somewhere characterful and solid. My wife always wanted to live by the sea and now she has her wishes. We sleep at the top, in an attic room that looks out over all the other roofs for miles around. Or rooves. Roofing. The roofscape. There's the occasional triangle of sea in between, but the principal outlook is rooftops, flat and sloping, in every direction, and, for weeks now they've been covered, I kid you not, with nesting gulls. It's been crazy, an open-air mental-hospital-cum-hotel-cum-departure-lounge for squawking, mewing, frantic birdlife. Even before the day begins we get to hear them scuffling and sliding on the roof above us, landing and taking off, pattering and skittering about dislodging tiles, besmirching the windows with their filth, making their cacophonous din.

It's never one sound, but a swirling ubiquity. It keeps shifting, whining, whinnying like ponies, cheeping like chickens, cicadas, a cockerel or two, a goose, a swamp of frogs, mallards, mewing, trilling, screeching a siren, human infants crying. There's something diabolical about it, an auditory *ignis fatuus*, a sound-shifter. It's a barrage of sound, an erupting of bar-rage, vicious sheep *baa*-rage, at once distant and near. It's a gluing, a galling, a sawing of plastic with a quiver of backsound, a *koo-ip* that flips into scoffing. It's an aggressive self-cajoling, a plaintive parody, ridiculing the plaintiff. It's a cawing triumph of maniacal croaking, a black magic wedding, an apocalyptic glutting. I connect it with the image of a descent quickening, as of something dropped or thrown down the stairs: unspeakable gullet.

It's been weird weather too, hardly a splash of rain. And every beginning of the day it's identical, the cacophony of the gulls and this feeling of the end of the world. I can't say it any clearer than that.

Woken up, a tympanic attack, an assault of sound: what is it? where am I? who's making this racket? I'm taken in every

Gulls

time. Have I been drugged, transported through the night and woken in the depths of Amazonian jungle? Or in a fairytale with peacocks? Or surrounded by penguins and **sea** lions in an Antarctic nightmare in which everything is melting from my face? Or is that a human baby in agony, horribly close by? The sounds are appalling, incomprehensible, pipers gulping oxygen twisting asphyxiating struggling curdling cries at every window because in the heat you have to leave them all open, and I've been gulled again.

Waking up used to be a kind of freedom. Even setting an alarm on your bedside clock you're waking up on your own terms. But this is waking up on theirs. Every daybreak, or still earlier. More regular than clockwork, quicker than time. No alarm can beat their larum. *Larus* larum *laridae*. I'm caught out, duped every time.

It's not even morning, it's this dark milky nothing and: what is it? where am I? who's making this racket? Ethel and I have stopped talking about it. We know what the other one's thinking. We're on the same page.

Happy as Larry they make a mockery of Latin and every other language I ever came in contact with. Larum *larus, larus* larum, *laridae* never die, Larry larynx never say die. *Larus argentatus*: silver gull quicker than quicksilver. It doesn't matter how little or well I sleep, how hard I try to anticipate them, they are out there in advance, tripping the light, screeching ahead. The other day I was reading: 'Herring gulls are very noisy and famed for their raucous laughing sound…' Laughing? Who's laughing? And famed? Is there some TV series I've been missing? What is it, *Celebrity Rooftops*? Ballard writes somewhere of the 'sea-wearying gulls': a charming turn of phrase. Don't worry, be weary. But be wary of this weariness, it will have you for breakfast.

163

It's truly an omnivorous word. Gull (verb): cram, gorge: hence (possibly), delude; (noun) cheat, impostor, but also the one cheated or duped. Gull: throat, gullet. Gull (verb): to swallow, guzzle, devour voraciously. To wear down or wear away.

I wake up in an underworld of shrieking monkeys, a ferocity of broken piped music, elderly folk groaning on their deathbeds in some twisted NHS Hieronymus Bosch dystopia.

I'm worn down completely. In the past few days I've scarcely slept. If I shut my eyes, it's to the horror-tilting yellow of the eyes of gulls.

Gull sounds have clocked, clucked, clotted everything. I hear voices below me in the street, but they disintegrate into gulls echoing in the gully: donkeys braying, flooded engines turning over, coyotes and hyenas. There's the incessant *kyow-kyow-kyow*, as ornithologists call it, trying to sound scientific. But goodbye to all that, I say: it's looping loony tutti-frutti tutting, tooting, tooting bec beckoning, screeching as if the rooftops suddenly were awash with fish, herring, herring aid, hearing gulls, and next thing pterodactyls, crooning, craking, creaking, squawking, strafing, the demented snatch of a band of native Americans crying off across a vanished prairie two hundred years ago, it's warpathological screaming scrying genetic transformation, swallowing hole, a phantom downloading generated in the gullet. It's drunken arid chanting charging changing, oneiric pestering bickering busking bantering, murderously battering wearying sound into a new source, new sauces, pickled hearing aids, a human cry, collapsing walls of sound.

It's dry as dust, too hot to go outside. I've confined myself to the house, in mew as people used to say, wandering from one floor to another trying to settle in a chair somewhere for a few minutes, unable to read or think. Then I look out of the window

Gulls

again at neighbouring rooftops. Young ones, silent or mewling, all brown and downy, I see: armadillos on stilts, gigantic artificial insects, moths obviously manufactured in China.

The fledglings stand about, bored out of their miniature brains, waiting forever to fly. They stoop their shoulders when they mew, in a mimicry of the old and vulnerable.

A few weeks ago Ethel called them 'the new lot' and wondered what'll they be like a year from now, with a further genetic shift, I mean: what are the next new lot going to be like?

Too much life, she went on to remark, gazing out.

But we've stopped speaking to one another now.

I just passed her downstairs. She was sitting still at the table with the sunlight streaming in. You need help, I thought to myself. I looked around for something. As if she were a hawk, I've put a sheet over her head. I'm letting her sit like that for a while.

Woodlock stopped, then added in an aggressive tone:

— That's it. All my own work. Every word of it.

The applause was hearty and the accolade consistent. In one voice after another the audience averred that it was an extraordinary rendition.

— Extraordinary rendition! exclaimed Rufus Pinner.

— Wow, said Tony Fletcher, yes: that was an extraordinary rendition, thanks a lot.

— Hear, hear! Freedom! Democracy, totally! (This came from Portia's Aunt Mae, somewhere near the back of the room.)

— What a rendition, said Nikki to Sarah. Altogether extraordinary. No other words for it. Extraordinary. Rendition.

And now Aunt Mae called out with vigour, 'More champagne!' Which was funny, since there hadn't been any in the first place.

Royle and Osmer had clapped enthusiastically at Woodlock's reading, though neither had yet spoken. With obvious relish for this unfolding spectacle (he was already picturing a paragraph he might write up on it for the *Gazette*), Osmer now more explicitly assumed the role of impresario.

— So, Professor Royle, what do you say? Do you wish to comment regarding Mr Woodlock's claim? And would you care to offer us your own reading?

A rather painful hiatus then ensued, as the theorist seemed to be examining the carpet. It wasn't clear that he had even heard the challenge. Finally he spoke.

— This gentleman's claim is entirely groundless. I agree that his reading was remarkable and I very much enjoyed it. I am the author of this text, however, and never saw or heard of Mr Woodlock in my life before this afternoon. I have on occasion had a pint at the Wellington, but I have never seen him there and certainly never picked up his manuscript.

While the host was formulating these remarks, Woodlock himself remained stock-still, staring stonily at the accused with his unnerving, sunken blue eyes, his face still perspiring from the physical efforts of his reading.

Sleep, as the poet says, is a blessed thing, but who knows why consciousness sometimes just cops out completely? Even among those who are fortunate enough not to suffer from epilepsy or other recognised forms of seizure, many people demonstrate a cataplectic capacity, suddenly keeling over, whether or not biting their tongue in the process, whether losing consciousness for only a couple of seconds or blacking out for far longer. Such incidents are more common than is perhaps supposed, especially in crowded spaces. Portia, at any rate, passed out. For some, like Stephen Osmer, such an incident could have no deeper, so-called unconscious significance. For others, including Aunt Mae, it seemed charged with meaningful possibilities. Was it really by chance that the moment her niece chose to pass out, if choosing may here be allowed, was just when her husband uttered the words 'his manuscript'? For was that allusion to a manuscript, and the attribution of ownership implied in the same breath, not a revealing slip of the tongue?

It took a little while before the collective assembly became properly aware of what had happened to their hostess, and it took their hostess even longer. The beautiful Portia was out cold. She didn't come round. If it belonged to the family of the swoon it appeared to be of the mammoth species. Her husband was very soon kneeling at her side, quickly joined by Lily and others. Variously loud and tremulous voices were raised: was there a doctor present? It seemed that, while there might have been at least three dozen doctors of philosophy, there was no medical doctor in the house.

Osmer could hardly conceal his frustration. It was obvious that the contest, if that was the word for it, had come to an end. Pinner and Fletcher took command of the situation with almost casual ease. The former began:

— Look, I'm sorry, Mr Woodlock, really you're going to have to leave. Your reading was terrific, absolutely brilliant, but you can see this is no place now…

— That's right, said Tony Fletcher, joining in. I'd say, to be perfectly honest, if you want to take this business further, you'd be best advised to pursue it through a solicitor.

Osmer made one of those faces you'd associate with a TV comedian's shrug. Drained of all expression, Silas Woodlock picked up his canvas bag, stowing away his copy of *Murmurations*. As the uninvited guest was making his wordless way out of the door, back into the sombre green majesty of the Downs, Tony Fletcher raised his bear-sized arm and rested it on the unflinching undertaker's shoulder with the friendly valediction:

— All is good, Mr Woodcock, all is good.

Whatever had afflicted Portia did not, in fact, last so long. If mammoth, it was, in retrospect, baby mammoth, like the one she had seen and been so moved by, as if fainted away on its side, discovered miraculously preserved in the permafrost of Siberia and now lying in the museum at St Petersburg. She came to after three or four minutes, out of a long sweet dream, and behaved quite as if nothing had happened. The incident had a sobering effect, however, and it was a little while before the conviviality of the room regenerated. The host, greatly relieved by his wife's recovery, exchanged with her looks at once tender and perplexed. And at the same time he was not overwhelmingly keen to become embroiled in a long cross-examination, either with her or anyone else, on the subject of 'Gulls'.

— I'm so glad you're all right, he told her quietly. I think I'll just check out the garden and see that the children are all OK.

Smothering Whites

At his escape into the lovely sun and shade of the garden, the literary theorist felt a kind of wonder. How amazing, to step into a world of children. And looking about at the dozen or so youngsters, aged from three or four up to young teenagers, variously spread out, playing, talking, singing, laughing in the garden, it seemed to him in some strangely euphoric way, just for a moment, that there was no pattern, and that this absence of a pattern offered a fresh way of thinking about how and why the world of children was so important. Then he noticed that the back gate was open and his heart flopped in his chest.

He'd told them all, the older children especially, and he now felt like a machine repeating it, he and Portia had both made it absolutely clear that no one, for any reason whatsoever, was to open the gate or go out on to the Downs. If a ball happened to bounce over the hedge, they were to come inside and let one of the adults know and someone would come and retrieve it for them. He rapidly surveyed the garden, trying to establish whether there was any child obviously missing. He asked one of the oldest girls, Alice Corbin's daughter, had anyone gone out through the back gate? The girl shrugged and said no, she didn't think so.

Royle was feeling, in truth, seriously disorientated. He walked over to the gate, for no useful reason thinking of the sound of *ajar* in Wallace Stevens (*I placed a jar in Tennessee...*). As he ventured out to look he instinctively sought to step back, but it was already too late. So close that the sweat on his face stood glistering in rivulets, wheels of flame in his eyes, Woodlock had moved with almost preternatural speed to block the younger man's return through the gate. Soundlessly, he lowered the latch, then thrust Royle backwards into the hedge. It took him a couple of moments to recover his balance.

— Checking up on all your pretty ones? Sooner rather than later, I reckoned, you'd be looking for a breath of fresh air.

The literary theorist now saw that Woodlock was holding something, a dull silver object evidently extracted from the canvas bag that lay on the path beside him. The craggy stranger went on:

— Know what this is?

Royle was rather slow of speech at the best of times and Woodlock was obviously not in any mood for whittling away the afternoon. He answered his own question with savage precision:

— It's a three-inch stainless steel skull-breaker. And if I tire of using that, I have a nine-inch bone mallet and some bone-cutters I think you'll like the sound of.

Royle ran. He was as slow on his legs as he was in his speech, in the ordinary course of events, but this moment, had he paused to reflect on it, would not have qualified as ordinary. He ran as he had never run in his life. He might have screamed. It might have proved particularly efficacious to have done so at that juncture, within earshot of the garden and, who knows, possibly even someone inside the house (though by now the festive mood was re-establishing itself and Portia, partly in a bid to make herself feel better, had put on Bob Dylan's *Modern Times* and just turned up the volume for 'Rollin' and Tumblin''). He *would* scream, but that was later. For now, he ran; his heart and soul were set on running. He was on home turf up here on the Downs and he felt, in accompaniment to the thudding terror imposed by the figure now pursuing him, an underlying conviction, a lifesaving confidence in his ability to give this man a run for his money, or for his mallets, and circle back round to the front of the house, barricade him out and call the police. If he tried to smash his way in, Tony and Rufus and other friends would help deal with him.

There was nothing of a potato bug's trundling in him now. The gray-haired professor veritably shot down the path, along the edge of the garden, towards the outbuildings. There was a barn, for it was still a working farm, even though the farmhouse itself had long been in unattached residential use. He would take cover there. He would head for the far corner, where he knew there was a small side door.

In any other circumstances the swooping of the swallows and the odours in the barn might have been bliss, for the mixing of hay and dung in this barn was always capable of transporting him to his boyhood, to a family holiday at a farm bed-and-breakfast in Dorset, to some vague but erotic morass of memories: summer heat, a girl staying there with her parents, the girl on horseback, the girl at afternoon tea, scones with strawberry jam and clotted cream, across the dark-panelled dining room, but she had to leave after just a couple of days, the high-pitched twittering of the swallows, twilight and earliest day, seeing badgers for the first time, milking a cow by hand, drinking the warm frothy liquid straight from the udder. He would get out through the side door and thence switch back to the house. His assailant would very likely not even spot where he'd gone, in the cavernous depths of the barn.

A straggly black cat, asleep in the sunny entrance, shot off in fright. Royle had gained a few yards on the older man, clunking along with his canvas bag, and now, diving into the barn, he tried to make up further ground. Dodging round a tractor and some old milking equipment, he reached the side door in the gloom. It was locked. How could it be locked? It was never locked. He couldn't open it. It couldn't be locked. But still he couldn't open it. Was it jammed? *Crunch*. Woodlock struck the literary theorist. In the darkness it was difficult to see. He had hoped to hit him on the head but in fact smashed the man's left arm, wrecking the radial bone. Royle lurched clear. The blow elicited a scream, heard only by themselves. The pain leapt through him, then leapt again. He looked about for some object with which to defend himself but could see nothing. Then the tall, older fellow pushed him over. All power in his left arm gone, Royle went down like a bowling pin.

For a long time it has been understood, at least in principle, that a man can be adjudged sane and yet commit the most terrible of crimes. A man can murder dozens of people on account of racial hatred, be tried and found guilty, and duly sentenced on the basis that he is in fact sane as he goes about bombing and gunning down men, women and children, sane as he expresses the racial hatred that has supposedly driven him to this mass-killing, and sane when he finally declares in court, on receiving the jury's verdict, that he is sorry he didn't massacre more people. For his crimes he receives a prison sentence of twenty-one years. Woodlock's mind was now moving in mysterious ways, but there was no doubting a certain undertow of lucidity. Seventy-seven murders, divided by twenty-one, what is that? Roughly three and a half murders per year. If I do away with this man, this liar lying on the ground before me, will the custodial sentence be three or four months? Probably not. If I'm lucky I might get five years. (At which, in his head, David Bowie's *Ziggy Stardust* starts up.) No, even at the early stages of his outing, when he was toiling up Seaford Head and wondering about the memorial bench, he had had second thoughts about the nature of the tools he was carrying with him. He had contemplated the gravity of the deed at some length. The desire to murder Nicholas Royle had kept him awake all night, along with the racket of the screeching gulls and mewling new ones nesting on the roof right at his head. He didn't pack his bag with necropsy equipment for an afternoon picnic (*pick Nick: that was funny*). He never expected there'd be a party in full swing (*Careful with that mallet, Eugene!*). He had actually imagined the thieving prof would still be at his place of work and he'd just hang about discreetly till he turned up. Hang about discreetly, he thought: *story of my life*.

In fairness, Woodlock was no straightforward cold-blooded killer. Certainly he was enraged by the theft of his manuscript, and sleep-deprived by the gulls to the point of a kind of craziness. But now a chance discovery acted upon his mind like petrol thrown on flames. In a trice, the idea took possession of him. Just inside the barn-entrance was a big, new-looking, shiny green and yellow machine, a John Deere ProGator 2030A: he'd noticed the key sitting in the ignition. He could eliminate all trace of his assault. He could make it all look like an accident. (In fact the vehicle belonged to the local golf club. The farmer, Jack Ticehurst, let them keep it there at a peppercorn rent, plus a free dinner once a year at the clubhouse with his missus. The groundsman would use it for hauling, and for spraying and top dressing. Had Woodlock known, he would doubtless have been chuffed: a chance to exploit the golf club for nothing.) And now he stooped at the younger man's ear and observed quietly:

— Make another sound and I'll bash your skull till your eyes slop out of your mouth.

This seemed to the literary theorist to be, on balance, a persuasive speech act. He knew, in any case, that no one would hear any cry for help from where they were. He wanted to address his assailant but suspected that this would not be the cleverest moment to do so. Woodlock began dragging Royle by his feet towards the bright green and yellow vehicle. Its newness and compactness made it look like an oversized toy. Woodlock stooped once more, picked up the injured man and set him down in the cargo box. Then he clambered on, started the engine and took off.

It was a glorious afternoon. The sun was a little less fierce now, and a welcome breeze was blowing in from the sea. As they drifted across the sky, a few cotton-wool white clouds supplied their scudding shadows to the sumptuous rolling hills. And skylarks sang, far overhead, pouring their invisible liquid notes into the air. Not that any of these things made any special impression on the two men. It took Royle a minute or so, batted about as he was in the back of the little truck, to become aware of what was going on. Woodlock was bumping at full throttle along the bridle-path, directly towards the sea. There was nothing to be seen on either side except a wall of blackberry and gorse bushes. Royle thought, however incongruously, of Sylvia Plath's poem, with its alley of blackberries *going down in hooks* to the sea. What else could he remember? Something unpleasant about *intractable metal*. The pain in his left arm was intolerable. It was difficult to maintain any sort of composure unless he lay on his back, submitting to the bumps generated by the vehicle speeding over the uneven ground.

Speed flutters in the pulse of the perceiver. For Royle's chauffeur, the journey was almost cerebral. If anything, Silas felt he was going along at a rather leisurely pace. He derived curious pleasure, too, from the macabre progression of this unusual form of conveyance. Hearse-like, it made him nostalgic. He glanced back from time to time to check that his customer was still with him.

Very soon, Royle thought, they would reach the end of this tunnel of hedgerow and come out on to open ground, perched above a steep bank of rough grass, stones and heather, leading down to the grassy purlieu of the main footpath. That would be the place to jump out. That would be the place to shout. There might very possibly be tourists, joggers, people walking their dogs – someone, at any rate, to help him escape from this madman sitting upfront, staring back from time to time and meeting his eye with a ghastly, glassy pleasure. Coming to the top of the bank Woodlock abruptly stopped, and admired the heavy-duty hydraulic disk brakes enabling him to do so. For a moment he felt like a cowboy in an old Western, surveying the lie of the land, scoping out the horizon. He checked the switches and levers on the machine. The path dipped down to the smooth grassy expanse of the main coastal footpath before sweeping up again through heather and long grass, pockmarked with rabbit-holes, to the chalk cliff-edge.

— Not a soul in sight you'll be pleased to hear, he shouted back to his passenger. Let's do this thing!

As Woodlock made off down the stone-strewn slope, the injured man supposed he might be thrown out of the cargo box by the sheer emetic bounciness of the ride. He tried now to get to his feet to facilitate such a contingency, but the truck jolted at just that moment and threw him back to the floor, with an agonising thump. He cried out in pain, but Woodlock only glanced back to confirm his cargo was still intact, then pressed down on the accelerator, speeding over the open ground. On his feet again, now in desperation, Royle threw himself sideways out of the cargo box and landed awkwardly on the grass. Woodlock immediately caught this manoeuvre, however, and braked heavily. Then he calmly changed gears and reversed, hitting his erstwhile fare just as he was getting to his feet. The rear bumper smacked into his legs and the high and mighty Prof was floored once again. Woodlock might have carried on reversing over the victim's body, but that would have spoilt his plan. Instead he stopped the vehicle, strode around and reloaded his victim, now visibly and audibly the worse for wear.

Clicking the rearguard of the cargo box into position, Woodlock remarked:

— That was what Americans, I believe, call a fender-bender. You'll find it easier not to move. Lie back and think of England.

As Royle lay groaning, Woodlock continued up the final jutting incline, drawing the vehicle to a halt just a couple of yards from the cliff-edge. Two or three crows flapped languorously away. Woodlock swung the ProGator round to his right, then backed up to the precipice. The vehicle had a powerlift that was operated, as he had already been pleased to note, by a switch mounted on the dash. Not so very different from whooshing-off a coffin at the crem.

177

It was time to part. It was time for his fare to face the music, the quick, sad music of humanity.

— You need to listen to me, Mr Woodlock! cried the man slumped in the cargo box.

And now Royle propped himself up a little in an attempt to gather his wits about him and ensure he could be properly heard. The pain in his elbow and legs was so intense he was surprised he was still conscious. Adrenalin was presumably pumping through his body, his sympathetic nervous system responding to fear. But in other respects what was happening, this entire chain of events, threw to a new height his strange feeling of unreality. In a court of law he could have declared without hesitation that he was the author of the text published in *Murmurations*, and yet – and yet and yet, as the Wallace Stevens poem goes…

Already, as the craggy old man was giving his public reading of the story, the professor had experienced a new effacement of his own identity: he had been affected by the simple but disturbing sense that, if he himself were asked to read the piece aloud, he could not imagine but doing so in *exactly* the same way, emphasising *exactly* the same words or syllables, pausing at *exactly* the same moments. But what troubled him even more was the audience response – the ubiquitous iteration of the same single phrase, *extraordinary rendition*.

It made him think of his namesake, of something they'd published a few years previously in a magazine called *Patricide*. Each had furnished the other with details of a personal experience he'd had, and then the other had been charged with writing this up in the first person singular, precisely as if it had happened to *him*. Each Nicholas Royle, that was to say, became the author of memories that were not his own. He wondered if that experiment somehow presaged what was now happening. His namesake, after all, had also edited *Murmurations*, the anthology in which 'Gulls' had appeared. He had not been directly in touch with Nick since Manchester, beyond the exchange of a couple of emails of a professional nature. He felt a sudden desire to talk to him, to tell him about how strangely his life had gone since he had begun working on the hides.

Secretly extraditing prisoners from the United States to foreign soil (Jordan, Egypt, Morocco, Syria) in order to have them abused and tortured without the American government being held to account: such is the standard meaning of 'extraordinary rendition'. For the literary theorist, it had historic resonance: it spelt the end of the US as the more or less legitimate keeper of world order. This sense of the phrase seemed grossly incongruous in the context of some retired old codger reading a story about seagulls at a summer drinks party. Royle supposed that someone must initially just have meant that Woodlock's rendering of the text was impressive and then, as responses proliferated, people were simply not thinking, picking up the phrase from one another in a sort of mental contagion. But now as he thought back, he wondered if he hadn't been hallucinating: whether he alone had experienced its reverberating echo around the room, whereas perhaps only one person (Tony, had it been?) had actually said it. And now in his physically shattered state, as he gazed up at the crazy figure on the mower, sitting above him at the cliff-edge, Royle felt something quite new: he felt for the first time a creeping uncertainty about the idea that he had indeed written the story.

— There has obviously been some funnel-mental confusion, Mr Woodlock...

Royle had at last begun to speak, but the words seemed to dribble from a corner of his mouth. Perhaps he had received some facial injury without realising.

— Can't hear a word you're saying, Prof!

Royle mustered up all his strength to declare:

— I think I'm starting to see, Mr Woodlock. The trouble is – and I promise you I've said nothing to anyone about this, not even my wife – the trouble is I…

He wanted to say that for months it was as if he'd been drugged and was only at last coming around, it had been all in his mind, his mind trying to tell him, it was he, not Woodlock, who was the subject of extraordinary rendition, for while in other circumstances a literary theorist like himself might work up a little article for a peer-reviewed journal along the lines that *extraordinary rendition* is a way of describing the violence and illegitimacy of what a writer does, in order to render a place and time, in order to render a character, to give himself or herself over to someone else, allowing the character to take possession, actually in this case, the opposite was true, for it was he, Nicholas Royle, who had been flown in without knowing, head hooded, held in this alien environment, without explanation or justification. Finally everything seemed clear. But at the same time Royle realised that no talk of this sort would make the slightest bit of sense or difference to Woodlock. It was all quite delirious. In the end he simply said:

— The trouble is… really, Mr Woodlock, I shouldn't be here.

For someone who had made a career out of studying and teaching the rhetorical structures of texts, Royle certainly did not choose the best phrase with which to conclude. Silas

Woodlock not at once responding, the broken man at last exclaimed in more pleading and pathetic tones:

— Please, Mr Woodlock, please, really, *please* don't!

The driver gazed back at him over his shoulder, his eyes glowing with inscrutable passion, before simply replying:

— Ah Prof, I tell you: your flesh profits nothing. It's too late now.

— What do you mean, 'now'? retorted Royle, desperately trying a new tack.

— Stop quibbling, literary theorist. Your days are done.

And the man in the driving seat would have activated the powerlift at that very second, were it not for an unexpected development. Cliff erosion along this stretch of the South Downs was a serious problem. The gardens of the coastguard cottages, a little further along the cliff, were disappearing into the sea at a rate of a foot or more every year. For the same reason the Belle Tout Lighthouse, on the other side of the estuary, had recently been dismantled and rebuilt a few hundred yards back from the cliff-edge. Every year there were landslips and, indeed, anyone walking on Seaford Head can readily observe the deep telltale fissures in the chalk or soil at the cliff-edge. Doubtless from the weight of the vehicle perched where it was on the jutting heights, where the land was carved into its perilous overhang, doubtless on account of the lack of rain in recent weeks and the friability of the soil, the entire edge, extending several feet, began to give way.

Woodlock had his wits about him, revving up in order to move away from the precipice. He had forgotten, however, that he was still in reverse gear. The sheared chalk and cracked topsoil crumbled away in great clumps; the vehicle shot backwards. As it did so, Woodlock bellowed his last words:

— Let it come down!

Whether by fluke or design, the ProGator 2030A made a remarkably orderly descent. Neither driver nor passenger was forced out of his seat in unduly premature fashion. The vehicle remained on a curiously dignified even keel. Having slid into the offside back corner of the cargo box, Royle clutched with his right arm on to the side-panel – not for dear life, he couldn't really go so far as to suppose that, but clutched on just the same. Despite the well-nigh uselessness of his left arm and both legs, he was thus able to sit up, his right arm over the outside of the side panel supporting him, as the vehicle plummeted.

Eerie in many respects, thought the misplaced figure, hurtling downward. Strangely clear and easy, like sitting in one's favourite armchair at home. Or in the bath as little boys. Yes, no doubt, whole life flashing. But images or words? Is there flash without verbal recall? He glanced at Woodlock, still bolt upright facing away, like that cloaked figure in Coleridge, lulled by the, wakened by… *Sits mute and pale his mouldering helm beside*. Perhaps not so odd, die looking at someone's back, probably common phenomenon. Face death, face to face with death: desperate stuff really. As if death had a face, look you in the eye. Smothering whites. Wuthering heights. Language try anything. Fall over backwards to reassure you of some ultimate—

Woodlock's exclamation, as he found himself careering over the edge with his hated passenger, related to the sort of plague-on-both-their-houses logic whereby, looking back over the course of the past twenty-four hours as he now very rapidly did, this particular untimely and unintended destiny acquired a kind of revolting sheen of predictability. Fine mess for a post this'll be. Floater or otherwise. Was it prudent to bring along those bits and bobs, that bag of tricks dating from his time with Paul as mortuary technician apprentices? Back in the day. Anatomical pathology technologists now. *Let it come down!* He shot a glance from the dizzy machine to confirm what he had already intuited: hundreds of feet below, the tide was out. Rocky landing ahead. Ultimate rock and roll. Imagine Ethel making that quip. He sought solace in a snatch of music, strain of something, anything, his dead starman rushing again into his head, then the Stones' 'Gimme Shelter', Sonny's saxophone on 'St Thomas', Miles Davis's 'Agitation', but no needle would repose in the groove, what groove, what will Ethel do? *His manuscript*: the scoundrel's very phrase, someone must have noticed, follow it up and I'll be vindicated. Turn to cast one last curse of a look? Couldn't be arsed. Whosoever liveth and believeth in me shall never. Where's all the gulls anyway? Sheer white cliff and not a nest to be seen, not a screech to be heard. Some swansong. Mine eyes shall behold. Your face, to—

Before the vehicle crashed into the rocky shore and exploded in flames.

Obits

Ben and Jane offered to pay for their son's flight out to Sydney and a week's accommodation in a decent hotel. Over the phone Stephen had told his mother enough for her to feel real anxiety on his behalf and talk the thing over with her husband. They knew he was stuck on Lily as he never had been on any previous girlfriend. They even imagined there might be some announcement before too long. Stephen knew that mere talk of a church wedding would be thrilling, not just for his mother, but for Grandad and Grandma, doddery as they now were. He knew too, however, that his father was different, not simply on account of being Jewish (and already parentless), but also as a man determined, if in spite of himself, to keep up with the times. Ben Osmer was acutely sceptical about much in life, having years ago lost his belief in communism and party politics, not to mention the mainstream media. Stephen's parents still loved one another. Yet they were well-matched, in part, because they were so unlike.

If they had their lives to live again, would they have married? Wasn't marriage one of the great Christian strangleholds from which the world needed to loosen itself if it were ever to become a place of true equality? This was one of the themes that his father had pursued with Lily herself on the single occasion they met, when the Osmers came up to London for Stevie's birthday the previous spring and took the young couple out to lunch at Carluccio's, in the Brunswick Centre. From that conversation Ben gathered she wasn't thinking of settling down any time soon. But perspectives change, convictions shift, Jane told him on the train shuffling out of Paddington back to Moreton-in-Marsh in the late afternoon. And wasn't Stevie divided as well? Had he not around that same period declared he could never marry and then at home, apropos of nothing, in the quiet of Boxing Day evening as she sat with him in the softness of the white lights from the Christmas tree, staying up with him a while longer with a small glass of port because he was heading back to London early the following morning and every minute with her son was precious, didn't he then out of the blue with admiration remark on the fact that Marx himself was a married man, having tied the knot with his beloved Jenny at St Paul's Church in Bad Kreuznach, before going on to have seven children together?

— Of whom three scarcely lasted a year and two of the others committed suicide.

Stephen had been surprised at his mother's knowledge. But it came easily enough to a woman who was a nurse by training, with a love of reading, married to his father. Was her remark a kind of sarcasm? Did she mean to imply some criticism of Marx's parenting skills? Or sympathy for the grim poverty and conditions in which the revolutionary thinker and his family were obliged to live? As the years went by, Stephen had come to see how fuzzy at the edges was his understanding of this unreservedly loving, complexly self-effacing woman.

— We were literally on our way out of the door, his father began.

— Hello, is that you, darling? We're just off to Cirencester to meet Sarah.

There were two phones and they had picked up at the same time. It was maddening to Stephen when this happened. His father never stayed on for very long, but still it was infuriating having both parents on the line simultaneously. All sense of turn-taking was destroyed. You never knew who was supposed to speak next, or why the silence, or which thread of conversation to follow. Everything got mangled. It made you want to scream.

On this occasion he considered querying his father's *literally*. Literally on the way out of the door? Since when was the phone in the front-porch? But in truth he was too fragile. He merely enunciated the briefest *Hi, Dad, hi, both*. And so these were the last words exchanged between father and son. Later, in the flinty retrospections of grief, Ben would wonder why he had to be in such a hurry, why such vexation at the incursion of a phone call that delayed them for a few short minutes from setting off for a leisurely lunch with their daughter, why walk away from what would become the last time he ever heard his beloved son's voice?

At any rate, Stephen's father went out and sat grumpily waiting in the car while Jane tried to grasp what Stevie was talking about. It was unusual to hear from him in the middle of the day. He was on his way to have lunch with someone, she didn't catch the name. It wasn't a particularly good line and some of the details remained unclear, but she could tell he was troubled. Lily had sent an email from Australia announcing that their relationship was over. Jane knew the couple had had their ups and downs, but these were never any more than what she mentally termed their tiffs and spats.

Of course he was not telling his mother everything, but there was sufficient raw pain in his voice for her to persuade Ben, on the drive into Cirencester, that they should offer to help him make the trip down under. She accordingly called him back that afternoon, but he couldn't accept their kindness, it was over, he'd have to come to terms with it. Less than a fortnight later he was dead.

As for the Sussex academic, an obituary was provided by the novelist who shared his name. It appeared in *The Guardian*, as one of their 'Other Lives', and comprised three short paragraphs:

He disliked the term, but the writer, novelist and academic Nicholas Royle was known, by some at least, as a literary theorist. In his books Telepathy and Literature *and* Veering: A Theory of Literature, *he helped us appreciate narrative in new ways. Perhaps his major work,* The Uncanny, *tackled a complex subject with charm, invention and infectious wit. He was an authority on Jacques Derrida and also wrote on Elizabeth Bowen, E. M. Forster and Shakespeare.*

Apart from gamely accepting a couple of commissions to write short stories for anthologies, he remained almost exclusively a non-fiction writer until 2010 when he published his first novel, Quilt. *In it he wrote about bereavement and the peculiar, uncanny qualities of rays, in particular the manta ray. For Royle's readers it was fascinating to witness him putting some of his narrative theories into practice.*

As a writer and an academic, Royle was sometimes confused with his namesake, who also wrote and published and worked in academia. With his passing

I feel a profound sense of loss. Above all I have an acute awareness of how he might have felt had I been the one to go first.

—Nicholas Royle

The old man himself, Silas Woodlock, received no obituary at all, besides what was reported about the 'tragic cliff death' in a couple of the local papers. As he had foreseen, the whole business of post-mortems was messy. And to a patient legal eye its conclusions were likewise untidy. No statement forthcoming from his widow, no provable case of murder, no particular point in trying to establish the purpose or deployment of weapons of minor destruction, the macabre tools of trade of the anatomical pathology technologist discovered in the burnt-out remains of a canvas bag some yards along the shore. Everything else was smashed, fragmented and charred beyond recognition. It was, all in all, a rather sordid and distasteful affair, and death by misadventure was recorded for both parties.

By a nice stroke of chance Woodlock, or what was left of him, did in fact end up in the churchyard at Bishopstone. Ethel discussed the matter with Ashley. She didn't want to take him back to Croydon. Nor did she see it as necessary for her son to be involved in a practical way. Given the complications of the post and the rest, it seemed easiest to organise funeral arrangements locally. Silas, she thought, would want to be close to me here by the sea. She ordered a taxi – it was one of the things she managed on autopilot in the days following his death – and asked to be conducted around the various local options. Seaford Cemetery, heading out of town on the way to Alfriston, seemed all a bit anonymous and exposed, though she appreciated the fact

188

that it had public toilet facilities. They might come in useful, she considered, for herself obviously. Then there was the churchyard at East Blatchington, but that was overgrown and, besides, looked full. St Leonard's, in the town centre, was full too. There was Lewes, but that was too far afield. There was the cemetery at Newhaven, but that was more or less bang opposite the hideous great rubbish incinerator. Silas surely wouldn't have wanted that. But then finally, on the road back from Newhaven to Seaford, the fellow turned off left and wiggled up farm lanes to St Andrew's church at Bishopstone. Ethel tumbled out of the taxi into the sunshine and felt right away that this must be the place. What capped it was the fact that, quite contrary to expectations, from the churchyard you could see the sea, green and shimmering on the horizon, nestled between trees.

How you deal with trauma is as singular as a signature. You might be blessed with a remarkable capacity to continue, in large measure, as if nothing has happened. There is a peculiar parallel here with the workings of the media. A café full of people is blown up, a lone gunman goes berserk shooting schoolchildren, a landslide wipes out an entire village, and the media coverage invariably includes some note of surprise at the extraordinary way in which *life, for those who have survived, carries on pretty much as normal.* Isn't this media impulse to affirm the ordinary and unchanged something of a projection? Whatever happens, the media itself remains invulnerable. There is, apparently, never any question of the trauma as a trauma *for* the media. The business of reporting and representing, imaging and storytelling, carries on as if unaffected. But this is precisely where trauma trips up. Being *in shock*: this is a thought that the media likes to keep at a distance.

If you are Lily Lynch, you strive body and soul not to be likened to those Americans (military or tourist) who nonchalantly declare, apropos tomorrow's return to what was once called the Land of the Free, *I'm outta here!* You have no wittol for a boyfriend. You are in love with Portia and were at least half in love with a man who's just been packed off over a cliff-edge. Enduring grief, you are also, thousands of miles away, committed to the thought of returning to London to work on the cinema project with Franton. But that is only a beginning. And in the meantime your life, your sense of the earth, is being transformed by these weeks in Australia. You feel as never before that the future of the planet depends on what you are able to do, in league with others, in breaking up all the machinery of vile and virile. You are newly born. For you there is no resting-place. You are an arrow in the night.

You send Stevie a long, sad email, at one in the morning on the night of arrival. Traumatic for sender and receiver. You'll be in Sydney for ten days, then heading off to different places, including three days in Tasmania. It is best if there is no further communication. You would appreciate it if he did not write or call. There is nothing more to discuss. Your mind is made up and the reasons need no spelling out. But you spell them out anyway. A fortnight later, on hearing of his death via a text message picked up in Exmouth where you have just been swimming with whale sharks at Ningaloo, you feel a terrible conflict of impulses, but you know you cannot attend the funeral. Your candid email severed you from any future with his family or friends.

It might be ventured, without undue exaggeration, that the obituary of S.B. Osmer took the form of his own essay, the follow-up to his 'Double Whammy'. He had given it the somewhat provocative title 'The Holocaust of the Bankers', and his boss at the *Gazette* thought hard about its viability. She took legal advice as well as consulting with other colleagues. But she also knew that this was a scoop and there might be nothing else like it in her lifetime. It would outdo any headline in competing publications – the *TLS* or the *LRB* – or even in the national dailies. Who could say where it might not lead? He had talked to her about it the day before he died. He told her it was coming. He specified the title. Even over the phone she felt herself quake: *holocaust*?

The final decision was hers: publish and – what would come would. She ran the piece in the very next issue, unabridged, just as it appeared in the file on Osmer's computer. She had no idea it would have the remarkable effects it indeed went on to generate. The rest, as the idiom goes, is history.

The Holocaust of the Bankers

We are living at a curiously awful time. It appears to be, among other things, a dangerous new era of demagogues. There used to be people, however, known as public intellectuals. They were invariably well educated (Oxbridge or Ivy League), yet taken to be representative. They would write in newspapers and magazines, and even appear on TV, and give their considered views on a range of literary, cultural and political topics. The names of Frank Kermode, Raymond Williams and Edward Said come to mind. An epoch has come to an end. It is not that we, the public, have necessarily lost our faith. Nor have we lost our appetite for knowledge and insight. Yet something has fundamentally changed.

This can, I think, be attributed to three specific shifts in public and cultural life. First of all, multiculturalism: we are suspicious of the idea of anyone in particular being representative and authoritative, of embodying and speaking on behalf of the interests and concerns of culture and society as a whole. Second, there is gender: it is doubtless not by chance that the names evoked a moment ago are all those of men. For a while it may have seemed that a woman (Germaine Greer, say, or Jacqueline Rose) could fulfil the desired role, but this was in truth a naïve supposition. Thatcher may have brought us the nanny state, but the intellectual world – above all in its direct plug-ins to political life (advisers, spin doctors and so on) – remains at root very much a male preserve. Third and finally, there is the impact of technology – all the new gadgetry and new media by which information and ideas can be conveyed. No one can keep up with who's who. Andy Warhol's fantasy of everyone being famous for fifteen minutes has come to look almost quaint.

If globalisation means anything, it is atomisation. The internet, celebrity culture, blogging, tweeting, Facebook and all other forms of social networking: each involves a new and different kind of emptiness. But we do not relinquish hope. Is it true, in fact, that the public intellectual has disappeared? Can this figure really be dead – any more than the author, despite the brittle soundbite of a certain flamboyant Frenchman? There is a public hunger to believe somebody or something, to be stimulated, guided and even inspired by a particular individual, a unique voice. This idea thrusts us right away in the direction of religion. But the public intellectual is neither saviour or messiah, nor mere iconoclast. The figure of the public intellectual is important precisely on account of his or her distance and impartiality as regards any organised religion. And at the same time the need for enlightenment and stimulation cannot ultimately be separated from social and political questions.

This was why, at least for a while, the name Slavoj Žižek seemed so alluring for many people. Here, it seemed, was a philosophically trained, effervescent public speaker, who could talk and write about cultural and political issues in provocative, dynamic and brilliant ways. It took people longer than it should have done to twig that he was really just a sort of Hegelian conman or Lacanman, jumbling jokes, psychoanalysis and politics in a cocktail of turgid self-cancelling prose. In his own words, if phrased with uncharacteristic modesty, Žižek should really just have remained 'a mediocre philosophy professor in Ljubljana' (*The Guardian*, 15 July 2011). Žižek seemed to have a quotable opinion about everything. And many people looked to him as a teacher. For that is what a public intellectual ought, after all, to be: a figure of inspiration and education. In another interview, in August 2008, he was asked what was the worst job he ever had. It was 'teaching', Žižek said: 'I hate students, they are (as all people) mostly stupid and boring.' And as for the most important lesson that life had taught him? 'That life is a stupid, meaningless thing that has *nothing* to teach you.'

Still, the example of the man from Ljubljana is illuminating. Žižek's tortuous, grim but complacent prose draws its life-blood from a cultural emptiness and negativity that it half-perceives and half-creates. As a teacher and philosopher, Žižek is admirably representative of the mess in which we find ourselves today and to which we seem to go on adding. Times are bad. The world itself seems to be teetering. Our curiously awful time could be said to take five basic forms:

(1) It has to do with the collapse of the banks – both of the banking system itself and of our faith in it. We now understand, as never before, that the financial world, as much as the world of religion, is essentially a question of faith – of 'fiduciary issues' – 'credit', 'confidence' and 'credibility'.

(2) It has to do with the 'return of religion', a phrase I take to refer to a newly inflated sense of the importance of this or that religion and of its incompatibility with other religions. People of different faiths find it increasingly difficult to live side by side, to accept that others have other faiths.

(3) It has to do with climate change, and with diminishing natural resources, especially oil, drinking water and clean air.

(4) It has to do with the ongoing population explosion, the bare statistics of which we acknowledge but then stare at as if it were something happening on another planet. And finally,

(5) It has to do with the concomitant egregiousness of poverty, deprivation and hunger affecting a massive proportion of the people on earth.

The writings of Slavoj Žižek recognise these things. Such recognition is a necessary starting-point. But there is another essential requirement for any public intellectual truly deserving of that title, namely clear and accessible language. The public intellectual has to talk and write in a lucid and considered manner. His or her discourse should be elegant and memorable, as well as intellectually probing, sceptical and critical. It will not do to conceal one's mediocrity behind the big names or philosophical systems of the past.

Nor will it do to sidestep truly radical arguments when they are needed. Permit me to limit myself to a single illustration. At a revealing moment in his book *Living in the End Times* (2010), after foisting upon the reader a tangled string of rhetorical questions (one of his more tiresome strategies for not saying anything), Žižek writes:

Maybe José Saramago was right when, in a recent newspaper column, he proposed treating the big bank managers and others responsible for the global financial meltdown as perpetrators of crimes against humanity whose right place is before The Hague Tribunal. Perhaps one should not treat this proposal merely as a poetic exaggeration in the style of Jonathan Swift, but rather take it absolutely seriously.

This is as clear an example of sidestepping as one might imagine: it's all about the feebleness of that 'maybe' and 'perhaps'. It also offers a characteristically patronising and facile engagement with the literary or poetic. Žižek dismisses Swift's 'A Modest Proposal' – and would presumably dismiss Dickens and all other cases of literary satire – as 'merely' a 'poetic exaggeration'. Slavoj Žižek couldn't tell the difference between poetry and a brain tumour.

My concern in this essay is of a quite limited kind. I wish simply to reopen a debate about the role of the intellectual in Britain today and to provide one or two practical suggestions about dealing with our curiously awful time. I begin by offering some reflections on the state of the English language, as I believe that a commitment to linguistic clarity and precision is vital. And this is also where we can remind ourselves of the value of literature and see how the novel, for example, can still or perhaps better than ever provide a basis for conceiving social and political change, indeed for justice and equality in a worldwide context. The awfulness of our time is reflected in the awfulness of the writing it talks about it in. If the preceding sentence suggests the image of something ugly goading itself in a mirror, my purpose here is perhaps beginning to unfog. If we were reliant on the prose of Žižek for an understanding of culture and intellectual life, we would never get beyond a recklessly smashed-up elementary mirror-phase.

It was under Margaret Thatcher that schools stopped teaching grammar. By now many millions of people have gone through education without knowing how to identify the subject or object of a sentence. Most people in Britain could not look at a sentence and say which word is the main verb, which a preposition, adjective or adverb, and so on. We are living in a bizarre update of hard times, to echo the title of Dickens' great novel of 1854. Dickens ridiculed an education system in which children were instructed in the most mechanical and deadening manner. The grim teacher at the heart of that novel is Mr Gradgrind. Nowadays the Gradgrinds are not the teachers. Everything is more insidious. Gradgrinding is what happens behind the scenes: it is what the government makes management makes teachers and academics do to themselves. I have not met a schoolteacher or college lecturer in Britain who, however much he or she may still enjoy teaching, does not consider the excess and obfuscation of administrative duties anything less than *death by form-filling*.

And meanwhile it is the pupils who are neglected. When I hear teenagers talking today, on the street or in some other public place, the most vital word in the English language is apparently 'like': 'I was walking, like, down the road, like, when this guy, like, came up to me, like...' If Jonathan Swift were writing today, imagine his laughter and contempt! He might spin an incisive tale of extraterrestrial visitors who observe everyday English and speculate that 'Like' is the name of a deity, to be sounded as often as possible in every sentence. In truth it seems a poignantly empty code for transmitting several things at the same time: I cannot construct a proper sentence without breaking it up and looking around like a moron, like; I want you to listen to me and like me, so I say like a lot, like, like you, moron; I have never heard of simile and I have no practical knowledge of any other rhetorical figure of speech because if I did, like, I would realise how immeasurably more interesting and powerful I could be in what I say to you, like; and so, like, in short, what I'm saying is, I'm not worth the air into which my words are delivered and nor are you, why don't you kill me, like, now, like? Beyond any efficacy it may ostensibly possess as what linguists term a *focusing device* or *quotative particle*, 'like' becomes, then, a merely vapid figure of self-destruction. It mimics the inflictions, like, of self-harming language. Language should not be a source of oppression or incapacitation. It is a force for discovery and transformation. And it is in this spirit that the public intellectual speaks and writes.

How much the Gradgrinding of technology has to answer for! Already impoverished in their knowledge of vocabulary and grammar, people are losing the art of conversation. Indeed there will be readers who may feel inclined to raise an eyebrow at the very word 'art' in such a context. Samuel R. Delany's science fiction once explored the possibilities of conversation in outer space, but it seems as if outer space in recent years has come to earth. People talk to each other on their mobile phones as if their co-ordinates were the principal subject. 'I'm on the train... We're about to go through a tunnel.' 'I'm walking towards the building now. I can see you.' And when there *is* something resembling conversation on the phone, it is either a rant or a forlorn series of monosyllables. The mobile phone seems to divide people into two types: those who listen, merely testifying to their ability to do so ('yeah', 'OK', 'right') and those who go on and on and on, as if they were giving the first speech in history.

On mobile phones, as anyone can confirm, people's bodies change. If they are on the street or in some other public space, they become weirdly oblivious not only to their own surroundings and to other people who happen to feature there, but also to their own gestures and body movements. It is difficult not to smile, if a little grimly, at the American English term: the *cell*. People turn about, pull up short, walk back and forth, and stagger away, as if the inanity of the so-called conversation were being registered in the excesses of this involuntary expressiveness. There is a general surrender to the machine.

The Holocaust of the Bankers

Each to their cell – where everyone keeps as a solitary prisoner, in Walter Pater's phrase, their own dream of a world. Without people having much awareness of the fact, the mobile phone, along with email, texting and so on, has eerily altered who they are. It is the twenty-first-century opium of the people. How often do you hear someone use a mobile phone in a way that inspires anything other than boredom, exasperation or indeed perhaps a violent impulse to snatch it out of their hands, throw it to the ground and mash it to pieces under one's feet? George Meredith speaks in one of his essays of 'the lively conversational play of a beautiful mouth': how often these days, out and about, do you witness such a thing?

Occasionally one hears something memorable. I recall the words of a man sitting across from me on a train a couple of months ago: 'I'm not having a go at you, but are you telling me you are just now, at the very arse-end of May, getting to the April invoices?' A roundabout sort of question, complete with a snide instance of paralipsis ('I'm not having a go at you, but…') – unpleasant, in short, but also, one suspects, effective. The man spoke in a soft and gentle voice, too, as if he might have been talking of some leisure activity such as gardening – forgetting to plant the sweet-peas last month. Quite differently, on the bus just a week ago I heard a man exclaim: 'Oh, bloody hell! Stop fighting yourself… When will it pass?' But then I realised that there was no phone about his person. I suppose he was experiencing auditory hallucinations. Still it was a more memorable line of conversation than 99.9 per cent of what one has to put up with. Email, texting and so-called social networking seem merely to be hastening the extinction of the art of conversation.

Moreover, it is not simply conversation, it is critical discourse itself. I recently picked up a magazine and read an essay by Frank

Hunter, allegedly one of Britain's most 'sensitive', 'humane' and 'intelligent', etcetera critics. (As it happens, Hunter is not based in Britain at all these days: he teaches at Stanford.) It was, I freely submit, the usual piece of patronising intellectual mediocrity. But it also struck me as very much of its time, in other words of our curiously awful time, in which the critical essay itself is morphing. Conventions of critical decorum and evaluation seem to be giving way to a sort of US melting pot model of personal-memoirs-cum-rant. In this particular instance it was Hunter ranting, in his inimitably self-regarding way, against religious ranting. Frank Hunter is a notable specialist, indeed, in the oxymoronic art of what might be called the bland rant. If the art of conversation is dying, so too is the art of the essay.

The reader may in turn rightly wonder where the present essay is heading. I have sought to reaffirm the value of the public intellectual. This, as I have suggested, requires a mode of public discourse that is clear and probing – sharply, even memorably phrased. I have also suggested that this discourse (whether written or spoken) should constantly be attuned to the most pressing concerns of the day. Above all, it must confront and seek to transform the reality of an unjust world, especially in so far as this reality is based on massive inequalities in social and economic life. More than ever, the public intellectual must be, in Antonio Gramsci's resonant phrase, a *permanent persuader*.

I wish to conclude with a straightforward practical proposition, though some readers initially might consider it outlandish. In these pages and in the companion essay 'Double Whammy: On the State of English Literary Culture Today' (published in *LLG* earlier this year), I have underscored what I consider to be the most fundamental and ingrained problems with contemporary society – to do with the repressive character of the so-called education system, the effective containment of public revolt at the level of speech, the all-pervasive effects of teletechnology as a means of controlling behaviour, upholding age-old social class hierarchies and inequalities, and maintaining effective levels of public ignorance and apathy. It is clear, I hope, that this critique bears no particular allegiance to any of the major existing political parties. The reader will perhaps nonetheless have detected a certain affinity with the intellectual spirit of Karl Marx, but this is a Marx, I submit, whose views should be shared by all, in the same way that a love of Dickens might be shared by all.

It will be evident too, I hope, that my final remarks go some way further than any kind of liberal bleating or radical-chic prevarication à la Žižek. Let us cut to the chase – to the Chase Manhattan, J.P. Morgan, Bank One or any other merging of pseudo-identities of any and every bank under the sun. There can be no solution to the present global crisis unless it addresses in a radical fashion the entire question of capital and finance, and of the banking system whose collapse precipitated the intolerable place in which we now find ourselves. I suggest a complete clear-out. I propose to designate this as the *holocaust of the bankers*.

Now I am aware that, as soon as someone says the word 'holocaust', a cluster of quite specific images and assumptions comes to mind. It remains the case, in Europe and North America, at any rate, that this word principally connotes the Jewish holocaust, the genocidal atrocities practised by the Nazis and their allies in the years leading up to and during the Second World War. A significantly smaller proportion of people may think also, in this context, of the Armenian holocaust that took place in the years leading up to and during the First World War, involving the systematic extermination of a million and more Armenians. Often, in fact, the term 'holocaust' is avoided or denied in this case, and reference is made instead to the Armenian genocide or, especially in the US, 'the Great Crime'. But the word 'holocaust', we should remember, literally means 'burn all': originally it meant a sacrifice consumed by fire. The Tyndale Bible of 1526, for example, speaks of 'a greater thing than all holocausts and sacrifices' (Mark 12: 33). In the King James Version of 1611, these holocausts became simply 'burnt offerings'. In the novels of P. G. Wodehouse, on the other hand, a cottage or similar abode going up in flames is regularly described as a holocaust. In *Thank You, Jeeves* (1934), for example, a cottage burns down but its garage is said to have avoided 'the holocaust'. And in *Joy in the Morning* (1947), regarding a thatched residence called the Wee Nooke catching fire, Bertie Wooster comments: 'Well, everybody enjoys a good fire, of course, and for a while it was in a purely detached and appreciative spirit that I stood eyeing the holocaust.'

There are dangers, that is to say, in deploying this word solely with reference to the Nazi extermination of Jews in the 1940s or in speaking of *the* holocaust, as if there were only or could only ever be one. Even if we restrict the conception of holocaust to the systematic extermination of a people, it would be necessary to acknowledge that there are various holocausts in operation at the present time, in particular in relation to the numerous tribes being decimated in Amazonian jungles. But who thinks of them, any more than of the monkeys and other apes being wiped out at the same time? In a more newsworthy analogy perhaps, no one who has tried to visit what is not yet the state of Palestine can fail to notice the profoundly disturbing similarity between the way in which the Palestinians are confined and oppressed by the Israelis today and the way in which the Jews were confined and oppressed in the 1930s. It is difficult not to feel that the goals of Israeli policy in this context are anything much short of the systematic extermination of the Palestinian people, and that what is being enacted today in the Gaza strip and in what are laughably called the 'occupied territories' is a re-enactment of the early history of what was perpetrated upon the Jews a few decades earlier. I write these words as the loyal and loving son of a Jew.

I propose, in short, a holocaust. The greatest revolution might prove the most peaceful. I am no advocate of violence, despite the blaze of rage at social inequality and injustice that surges through my veins at every moment at the so-called 'current administration' and 'political life' of Britain today. The workings of this 'administration' and this 'life' are in many ways subtle and even invisible – especially, as I have tried to suggest, with regard to linguistic corralling (the oppression of the lower classes through insidious but rigorously orchestrated impoverishment of discourse), teletechnological entrapment (the capturing and silent ransoming of subjectivity through the delusions of freedom provided via mobile phones, social networking, internet shopping, etc.) and, last but hardly least, an education system that would be the envy of any dictatorship on earth in terms of an absolute rigidity in maintaining a centuries-old system of privilege and deprivation, promoting massive inequity combined with almost total social acquiescence.

Education, we know, is an excruciatingly gradual thing: we are all slow learners, and every mewling and puking infant seems like a reinvention of the wheel. No immediate or short-term action in this context is going to affect anything one jot. But there are reasons for supposing that concerted action on a more specific and readily remediable front might have more pervasively beneficial effects on society more widely, and it is in this context that I want to address some concluding remarks to the topic of the banking crisis and collapse of financial markets such as we have been witnessing in recent years. Let us not 'lose the name of action', as Hamlet might say, in thinking too precisely on the event. At the very heart of this curiously awful time, I would contend, is the fact that a comparatively tiny number of extremely wealthy, inordinately greedy individuals called bankers – merchant bankers, hedge fund managers, stockbrokers (I leave the reader to extend the inventory of virtual synonyms or grotesque variants here) – have messed around with the livelihoods, the personal savings and investments of the large majority of ordinary citizens.

Of course, you may say, this is nothing new. Dickens' fine line from *Nicholas Nickleby* comes to mind: 'four stock-brokers took villa residences at Florence, four hundred nobodies were ruined'. That was written in 1838. But the scale of what has happened in the past ten years or so is without precedent in world history. These professional criminals have suborned unthinkably large sums of money. In the US, in Britain, across Europe and beyond, ordinary people have paid and are continuing to pay for this crime, literally and figuratively, with their own personal savings, through their taxes, in higher pension investments, and in higher prices for everyday goods. Ordinary people have paid and are continuing to pay for these outrageous embezzlements, compensating the banks for the very acts of theft for which they should be held morally and financially responsible. The irony of such a scenario is staggering. It is nefandous.

And yet here is something even more dazzling and incredible: there has been no palpable reaction. There has been really no organised expression of outrage, injustice or call for revenge. This is baffling in the context of a country such as England (though it is hardly in splendid isolation on this matter), whose culture is still so wedded to talionic law, in other words to the principles and logic of an eye for an eye, a tooth for a tooth, and so on. Or at any rate it would be baffling, were it not for the devious and profound machinations mentioned earlier. If I am thinking here chiefly of England or the UK, a corresponding case can readily be made for the US. The machinations of *its* mind-and-body control through education are also no doubt very different. We should never lose sight of the idea that the United States is, in many respects, the most insular country on earth. Nonetheless, as Matt Taibbi has made clear in *The Divide: American Injustice in the Age of the Wealth Gap*, the US is identical to the UK in this tiny but extraordinary detail: of all the thousands of criminals-cum-bankers who have creamed their millions and billions off the rest of us, not a single one has gone to prison. As Taibbi puts it: 'Since 2008, no high-ranking executive from any financial institution has gone to jail, not one, for any of the systemic crimes that wiped out 40 per cent of the world's wealth.' (And at the same time, as Taibbi also points out, there are now some six million people in the US in prison or on parole – 'more than there ever were in Stalin's gulags'.)

I should stress that I have no sympathy whatsoever with those who systematically uphold talionic values and act on talionic impulses. On the contrary, I would argue that the force of such law – the logic of retaliation and revenge – has been the single most destructive manifestation of human violence and self-violence in history, not least since 9/11 and the absurdly named 'war on terror'. The obscenities of talionic conduct – if one can indeed dignify it with such a phrase – are as much in evidence in the British tabloid newspaper front pages screaming for vengeance in a particular case of murder or child abuse as in the endless chain of US military reactions to 9/11.

Still, talionic desire is deep-rooted in every one of us. If we could daily exercise a free hand of vengeance on those by whom we felt abused, we would all be mass-murderers by lunchtime. And then, in albeit displaced guise, talionic desire fuels the grisly machine of inequity, social network engineering and tele-entrapment. Such is the seemingly benign and natural face of 'like for like': I want the new iPhone, the new BMW, the new flatscreen TV, I want this so that I can be just like my friend or colleague, rival or role-model, and so on. An educational provision explicitly critical of talionic desire might be one way of improving our currently awful situation. I leave it to the appropriate experts to pursue such a scheme. A short course called Talionic Studies might prove notably more useful than piling up yet more modules in 'Citizenship' or 'Life Skills'.

It is not my concern to lay out the finer details of how far the holocaust proposed might exemplify the talionic. Philosophers tell us that a sacrifice is always the sacrifice of something we love. Must we not, in fact, always have loved the bankers? Is not a banker the object of our love? Let us bring to the surface, let us mobilise the unspoken reverence for Mammon. Let us philosophise with fire. To repeat: I propose a holocaust. There is a difference between 'propose', on the one hand, and 'urge' (let alone 'wish to incite') on the other. I do not want to see anyone suffer, even in the case (let me make it quite clear) of the bankers themselves, the despicable cheats and fraudsters, so readily classifiable as the loathsome tricksters who have made off with so many people's savings, their incomes, their livelihoods and their pensions, their futures and their children's futures. But let us work with the tools at our disposal. Let us acknowledge that retaliation and revenge is the only message some people will listen to. Let us start from this point. Even among the many others who rightly consider themselves more civilised, the talionic impulse is present and indeed in crucial respects, I would argue, irreducible.

The Holocaust of the Bankers

So let us put all this unspoken love, this intense hatred and gut desire for revenge to worthy ends. Psychologically, spiritually and ethically, we have to be able to recover from the criminal enormity visited upon us by the bankers. Tinkering with current legislation offers no social justice here, any more than voting to leave the EU (committing referendum UK *hara-kiri*, as I have described it elsewhere) helps the poor or impacts on the bankers themselves one iota. Let us organise a public movement to bring about the restitution of lost monies. Let us launch this movement in the UK, the first modern home of capital and empire, with the hope that similarly motivated people, in other countries across the world, will organise accordingly.

It hardly need be observed that one of the more outrageous aspects of the financial crisis in the UK has been the revelation of the widespread phenomenon of the 'non-dom', in other words the fact that many of the bankers and other individuals who have sucked and stowed away the most money from the people of Britain do not even pay their own taxes in the UK. Related to this, of course, is the sickening extent to which UK public services, utilities and assets are actually owned or significantly controlled by foreign banks and other sovereign states (especially China, France, India and the US). The national farce called UKIP, spearheaded by former commodities trader Nigel Farage and focused on discontent with perceived levels of 'immigrants' (once a commodities trader, always a commodities trader, you might say), is a feeble postscript to the chilling pantomime ('It's *behind you!*') wherein the UK is already, to all intents and purposes, in foreign hands, and in foreign bankers' hands in particular. You don't have to live in London to realise this: check out James Meek's recent study, *Private Island.*

It is all coming to an end.

If governments cannot collaborate and take joint action, we require people-power. Across the UK, North America, Europe and beyond, we must adopt a more radically unilateral approach. But, all being well, this will not prove necessary.

Here in the UK, I propose the following. Let every banker or anyone else working in financial services who has, in any year since the first day of January 2000, managed to siphon off more than £50,000 in excess of her agreed actual annual wage return the money to the British taxpayer within a specified period of thirty days. (You may be tempted to say that the year 2000 is already going back a fair way. If so, you are thinking in the dim-witted way that the bankers want you to think. Bankers themselves pretend, in this respect, to have the memory capacities of young children. We may here recall the chief executive of HSBC talking in 2015 of 'historical events' and meaning by this all the fraud, tax dodges, advice on tax-dodging and wealth-concealment that went on, year after year, until 2007. Let those who have felt and continue to suffer the effects of the financial meltdown be the judges of what is 'historical' and what is still palpable.)

If the cash cannot be raised within thirty days, transfer of property and other goods will suffice. If the banker in question has already passed away, let us go to their estate and their inheritors. A complete transformation of the banking system must ensue. Let there be no more banks for profit. Let bankers work for people, for the common global good, not for themselves. Let money be for equal distribution and social wellbeing, not for salting away in Swiss villas or Mayfair apartments or second or third homes in the otherwise economically deprived English countryside. Let the bankers return our money to us forthwith. In order to force the British government into action on this no doubt challenging venture, what is needed in the first instance is evidence of popular support. I therefore propose a public petition, to be set up online but also available to anyone without an internet connection. I propose that this campaign be called 'The Holocaust of the Bankers', a phrase intended to command attention and force a response from those in government.

My hope is that this simple ultimatum would be enough. I am confident that the proposed petition would gather millions of signatures. Let me reiterate: I imagine and fervently hope for a solution without the need for any purpose-built incinerators. Few creatures are more cowardly than bankers. When trouble comes, they run, slime, slink, squeeze and sneak themselves out of harm's way, dissolving the pseudo-identity of one financial company and taking up shelter in another. Once cornered, however, they are anybody's. I believe in threat, in the power of threatening language for the higher purposes of freedom. Just as the bankers have injured and disfigured our lives, and the lives of the coming generations, so counter-threat can rebalance the books. I believe there are still things we can learn from the Cold War and especially from its 'rhetoric of deterrence'. Liberationist transformation can be effected through counter-threat. My proposal and my unequivocal wish, in short, is for a velvet holocaust.

But if the petition should fail to galvanise our democratically elected representatives into producing a satisfactory outcome, let us, in the name of a greater justice, take the measures we all know to be genuinely robust. The threat (like that of the US and Soviet military establishments in the Cold War) must be seriously made. Let us hunt the bankers out, track them down, one by one, every single last banker, and let us kill them all. Just a few thousand heroic individuals might make up the clandestine organisation required, operating like resistance fighters or Nazi-hunters – if needs dictate, beyond the law. Ironically, in this context, there would be a need for insider dealing. For there will surely be a banker with a conscience. That is my dream. I dream of a banker with a conscience. My banker would tell me the truth. We would establish the whereabouts of all those refusing or ducking repayment, one by one. If they flee abroad, let us run them to ground. Let us find them out in the cities and villages, in the deserts and forests, on yachts or private jets, in bijou apartments or mountain caves. To play your part you would have only to deal with a single banker. Find your banker and, in the name of justice, put that banker to death: lethally inject, shoot, knife, poison, run over, smother, or flay like Marsyas in the painting by Titian with airy and fantastic music. And finally set alight. For *everybody enjoys a good fire.* And as they burn I would have them endure the flaming retribution with the words of *Nicholas Nickleby* ringing in their ears, ringing them all to death: *for gold conjures up a mist about a man, more destructive of all his old senses and lulling to his feelings than the fumes of charcoal.*

Ethel's Wharf

Walking east along the esplanade, past the Martello tower and sixty beach-huts painted in improbably bright yellow, green, blue and orange, you come to the foot of the cliff, where all attempts to fend off the ravaging power of the sea terminate. To the left a path leads, gently at first, up the side of the cliff, around the red-brick ruins of an old hotel, towards Seaford Head. This is the route that Silas Woodlock took, on his last afternoon. The esplanade itself ends in the shadow of chalk cliffs, at what is rather prosaically called Splash Point. Here an old groyne, much of it washed away, stretches out a short distance, like an amputated arm, into the sea. Beyond the railings at Splash Point a wild terrain of unmanageable chalk cliffs and inaccessible coves runs off east to where the ProGator 2030A crashed and, beyond that, towards Beachy Head. All along this coast the relentless, moon-minded waters press. Once sand and salt-marsh, Seaford Beach today is mostly pebbled. But the sea is constantly working over this shoreline, churning it up and dragging it away. Every winter and early spring dump-trucks and diggers manoeuvre clumsily, like huge, dying yellow ants, up and down the beach between Seaford and Newhaven, carrying back stones that have been washed westward by the tides.

Just thirty yards from the groyne at Splash Point is another, also of timber and stone. Visitors and locals alike tend to disregard this projection, preferring to walk to the end of the esplanade, the final outpost of the town. It is hard to say which groyne is in a worse state. Differently precarious, both are falling to pieces. Most of the time they are half-submerged beneath the waves. Much of the more westerly of these structures is barred off by railings. About halfway along hang a host of signs. One sign is visibly older than the rest, a white board with red trim that states simply but firmly: *Warning Slippery Surface Beyond This Point.* The others are more recent and hysterical incumbents, fastened to the railings like a row of cards. White, with a black and red image of a robotic policeman's head and big black outstretched hand held up, the first declares: NO ACCESS BEYOND THIS POINT. Next to this are three signs in garish yellow, each with a black stick-person in trouble, falling, drowning and so on, to accompany its shouty, capital-lettered warnings. DANGER DROP, says one, DANGER DEEP WATER, says another, and DANGER HIGH WAVES FAST TIDES, says the third. Beyond these railings and warning signs, the more westerly groyne assumes the character of a slipway. Then after ten yards or so there is a slight drop and a further, narrower stretch where not even the most intrepid fisherman would think to go. This last section, only exposed at low tide, wrapped in a vivid treachery of slimy green, ruddy-brown and black seaweed, comes to a halt with what appears once to have been a beacon, now blackened and emaciated, rising some twenty feet or so in the air.

While the more easterly structure can readily be identified with Splash Point itself, the other has no name besides the official designation *Seaford Terminal Groyne, Grid Ref. TV 48800 98205.* Ethel is frankly flummoxed as to why the government should give it such a name. As if you'd say to your partner or loved one, should you be so fortunate as to have one: *Just popping out for a stroll down to Terminal Groyne.* Or: *Fancy taking a breath of sea air down at TV 48800 98205?* And what does any of it have to do with the television?

As far as she is concerned, in any case, it is Ethel's Wharf.

Why she thinks of it as wharf, rather than groyne or jetty, is unclear. She likes the sound of the word.

It is late January, seven months since her husband's death. Ethel Woodlock comes down to the seafront, walks past all the stray members of the public and straggling dogs and heads for her wharf. What does an Ethel say? *Wharf, wharf.*

Ethel has turned her back, for now, on the flaming world.

Every late afternoon, come rain or shine, she makes her way down the promenade and on to the wharf, then stands, with her back to England, till the light fades and day is eliminated. Unable to trek up the cliffs themselves, she is confined to staying around sea-level. Jutting out further into the sea than the groyne at Splash Point, Ethel's Wharf is the closest she can be to where her husband went. Of course there is also the plot in the churchyard at Bishopstone, where she plans to join him in due course, but she can't get over there so easily – she'd had a taxi drop her off, just twice, and walked back on her tod – but in any case it was too much, too painful to see him dead in the ground. She prefers to think of him still alive.

Yesterday the light was green. As if bathing her tired eyes in the serene chalk reflections of the cliffs, she stopped before the host of signs and leaned against the railings of her wharf, looking east. She noted, as she had every day now for several months, the absence of the kittiwakes, due to return from America next month, to nest on their narrow ledges high in the chalk. The cliffs now were as uneventful as the grave, just a crow or two flopping about the edge. And then atop the solitary great clump of chalk in the sea, that outcrop or whatever they call it, stack, atop that blank reflected double in the emerald, five cormorants stood and preened.

She stooped and ducked, as was her wont, through the railings, past the stupid cluster of warning signs, and ambled on. Then, having come like clockwork to the end of the shiny black slipway, she paused, resting an arm on one of the large, split and weathered oak posts buttressing the wharf. She gazed with affection at the lower, final section of jetty with its half-disintegrated beacon, four rusted black metal struts rising to an apex like a burnt-out tepee. The tide was coming in. Around the base of the beacon the waters lapped and slapped. This swirl was the most striking sign of movement in the scene. Behind her, waves were quietly breaking on the shore. Before her, over the sea, big clouds were piling up at the horizon, neither mountains nor forests, yet not like clouds either. This was her Channel, in truth facing out here as much towards America as France. The green reflecting chalk light of the cliffs to her left extended its ghostly sheen far out across the unwrinkled surface of the water. To her right the orange sun was setting, streaks of coppery yellow and rose casting their reflections, glistening and glimmering almost into the green mirror of white cliffs. And then directly ahead, around the beacon, blue and black shadows of clouds amassed, the water a vast, coldly stirring cauldron, reaching almost to Ethel's feet.

Just a month after Silas went, it must have been, a young one got stranded in the garden. Changed Ethel's feelings about *them gulls*, it did. Fallen from the roof or flip-flapped in staggered fashion, roof to wall, to branch, to ground – for it landed unharmed. Already sizeable but fluffy, soft, flecked gray, speckled white, it was lost, cut off from its parents on the roof above. For three days the fledgling waited, mewling or silent. The mother knew her inadvertent delinquent was below. She scrawed and screaked: *you offspring, my one of two, come, bird, come back!* For on the roof there was still another chick, apparently oblivious to the perilous situation of its sibling. But the mother and father knew, they peered and knew and screeched. Breast-bursting, exploding skyward from their gullets they cried: *come back!*

And the cries would bounce back up from the garden like echoes without starting point: *you yes, I hear, come back, come back!* They arose and fell again from the mother on the rooftop, and sometimes from another rooftop the father. Unless it was another mother. That wouldn't have surprised Ethel. Who knew what these creatures got up to in their surrogated communities? The sounds spiralled, blind from the rooftops: *where are you, why are you there, come back!* But to all these cries the fledgling in the garden could in fact no more than *mewp*.

With nothing of the strength of sea-going gulls at ten, twenty or even thirty years calling over the waters, the reedy thinness of the fledgling's cry seemed to Ethel as much human infant as anything else. Trying crying, plainting, peeping, mewping for help, the premature skedaddler for much of the day stood stock-still as a garden gnome. But then suddenly it would step, at once dainty and firm, startled by a breeze or sparrow in the bushes, or reanimated by cries from the roof above. Flat-footed vulnerability: so much for a powerful web presence. Soon enough it returned to its crazy sentry, default gnome.

...And those we miss, you'll surely pardon – for what was this misplaced creature to do, with its skittering, half-formed clattering of oversized feet and diminutive downy wings, aspiring to avian jumbo jet in a space offering no runway and no refreshment facilities? It was perhaps just a week from flying, or already capable if properly cajoled, waved on, jump-started if needs be, terrified into flight. But how do you jump-start a jumbo jet?

Silas would have known; probably something with bits of wood, turn the garden into an amateur circus arena. She made an attempt, setting a plank to slope upwards from the ground to a table she'd dragged into the middle of the garden, but it was useless. Jumbo jets don't walk up hills.

Every morning, first thing, Ethel passed quiet as a mouse through the back door into the garden, hoping the young gull had taken flight in the night. Several times each day, in trepidation, she unlatched the door, stepped out into the eerie, claustrophobic space, and listened. Sometimes she was guided by the mewling. Relief that the creature was still alive combined with incredulity that it was still incarcerated. And other times, especially on the third day, it was not a matter of being led by sound but of venturing as unobtrusively as possible from one part of the garden to another, peering into the rose-bed or wisteria, or around the corner by the fir tree, before spotting the solitary, silent, flightless being, now sprung into sudden clumsy movement, as if cornered, awkwardly snagging on a branch perhaps, or faltering and sliding unmanageably from a vague perch it had assigned itself, an upturned flowerpot or small pile of stones in the shade by the fir.

No relation to Ethel, none at all. But equally it seemed unrelated to the screecher creatures overhead. In its downy, blackberry-eyed softness, it seemed to belong to a species all of its own. What could a woman well past her prime do but whisper words as soft as possible, come on you lovely foolish thing you can't stay here and nor can I. If your parents see me with you they'll likely desert you, if they haven't already.

Such was the dilemma: if she put out food, the mother would abandon its offspring altogether. At the end of the first day she called an RSPB helpline and heard just what she expected: *do not touch or feed the bird; the mother will keep an eye out and make sure it gets food.* This advice sank like lead into her already black-hole-heavy heart. She wished she could believe. All day the mother had done nothing but screech to the fallen one from the roof above, as if scolding, as if in desecration, launching repeatedly a cry from the gullet, a mad monotony of *come back!* But there had been no indication that this mother had brought food down.

Next morning, for a period of several hours, parental absence reigned. Ethel alone was watcher. But then out of the summer sky, cloudy, but with enough blue to make a sailor a pair of trousers, cries came again, tormented or tormenting, not only mother or father but other gulls too, perching on ledges and chimney tops, whether in scorn or sympathy or blank seagull rage. This uproar strangely revived her.

But without food how long can a baby gull survive? Two days at most, she thought. And after nightfall? The idea that the mother might under cover of darkness fly in some rescue package seemed unlikely. In an act of daylight robbery in reverse, while the mother was not overhead, Ethel crept out and left bread. This was a gulling worth its weight in gold. The bread gone before you could say Jack Robinson. *A herring gull can fly at forty-two days, if not sooner,* said the voice from the RSPB, and Ethel now resolved to keep up this deception, putting out food every day until the fledgling took to the air of its own accord. It could only really be a matter of days.

And so twice on the third day she put out more bread, which was scoffed in a twinkling, and that night she put a piece of frozen cod in the fridge to thaw out by next morning.

Hardly slept, heart in mouth, Ethel stepped out once again into the dewy, snail-tracked newness of another scorching summer's day. Amid the chatter, as she paused to listen, of blackbirds, thrushes, starlings and sparrows, as well as gulls calling from the air and rooftops, she looked about to check that the orphan was still there and had not magically flown away, before placing the food on the ground, and there underneath the wisteria she saw it, isolated on the ground a single wing, as if a fabrication, a collage of balsa wood with feather and down, stuck on a harp, a hope-warped heart taken off in the night. For a moment Ethel had the crazy thought that the young bird could have taken off in the night and might be alright, without a wing. A wing and a, what was that phrase? A wing and a…

About the dewy garden she wandered, slow as any Eve, less walking than afloat, eyes in dread until alighting on a flowerbed some yards distant, in the shade under the rosebushes: the rest of the body. In state, she thought. In a *rigor mortis* of utterly confuddling dignity, the legs straight up like a bird out of the oven, the remainder laid out on the flowerbed without the slightest sign of gore. And when she picked it up she could not believe she had. *Light*, she said dully aloud to herself, *as a feather*.

Pollicide? No: *prolicide*. That was the word. It must have come up at the time of the Dawson killings, almost thirty years ago, else how would she know? A mess, Silas said,

like he'd never seen: the phone threats, the baby bier, armed
police at the funeral, not to mention all the blood everywhere
in the first place. The impulse to blame the mother was
overwhelming. Where was she?

Only in the afternoon, when Ethel was up at the top
of the house trying to get some shut-eye, did she attune
to the mother screeching and screeching from the rooftop.
Only then did Ethel think through the imprint of the night:
this parent witnessing death in the dark, from its bird's-
eye-useless height, must have temporarily abandoned the
appalling scene and come back now because, what else?
Where else was there to go? Ethel wished her husband could
have been with her to experience the loss, to share this new
appreciation of the gulls, their rooftop and roofdrop life. She
told him as much.

Today is different. The distance from one day to the next
might be a year. It can't only be his death, it must be the
tip effect, the climate topping or whatever they call it. All
tranquillity of green light and soft orange sunset one day,
then raging storm, high winds and dangerous seas the next.
No sign of that coming. Ethel doesn't listen to weather
forecasts any more. But it wouldn't have deterred her in any
case. She sets off in the late afternoon and struggles through
the wind-tunnel at the end of the Causeway, eyes streaming
from the rain and wind driving the sea into the air. She hears
the tumultuous crashing waves well in advance, but still the
sight of the sea is a shock. The esplanade is deserted. There
is a savagery in the air.

And as she squints to make out through the soaking
sloosh the goal of her journey, she catches from this distance

something about the wharf she'd not seen previously. She can't see at all clearly, but this phantom assault, as wind and rain and sea-spray beat her face, now reveals the profile of the farthest section of the wharf, lower than the rest, as a black casket half-submerged and sloping down into the sea, while the struts of the beacon suddenly resemble, seen slit-eyed in the blast, the skeletal, charcoal line-drawing of a bird's beak. Why has she not noticed this before? In the past it has just looked like a burned-down wigwam or the face-cage the man wore in that film she saw with Dot, what was it called, *The Silence of the Moths*. How can people look so much, so often, and see so little? Funny dunny Dunnock, she tells herself – *me little sparrer*, you used to call me in our courting days – what people don't think, however many times they see something.

More than ever she feels contempt for the warning signs pinned to the railings: DANGER DROP, DANGER DEEP WATER, DANGER HIGH WAVES FAST TIDES. Really, she thinks, on a day like today? Well, well. Whoever would have imagined?

The waves cascade over the wharf in great surging, lunging movements that seem to have no rhythm or reason at all. She clings to the boards between the oak buttresses as she inches her way along.

It is not advisable, as the government would say, to venture on to the slipway at any time, let alone in this storm. Still, she does. She stoops and ducks between the railings, gripping tenaciously as she goes. With her back to it and all its recent unprecedented events that no one should have foreseen, she has not forgotten the world. Nor has she forgotten Ash or Rhoda or the baby Clifford who just three months ago squeezed into it. But she is not ready for any of that, not yet, not now.

She can hardly see anything. Seen better days, that much for sure. She is soaked to the skin and every minute another huge wave smashes over the side, unsteadying as it crashes over her from head to foot. The tide, the, what do they call it, neap, whatever that is, no tide at all, no tidings to all, completely helpless, as far as she can make out, shooting up the wharf, swirling and withdrawing. It's her Channel to channel. Station to station – she thinks of that song, and the one time Silas took her to a Bowie concert, at Wembley it was, as she stands clinging at the end of the wharf, *dredging* your what was it? Your *dead star-man* you called him, all teary you were, when you heard he'd copped it: *lost*, where was that, in your *circus* was it?

Ethel is in regular communication with Silas. She speaks to him and channels his responses. She doesn't bear a grudge against the Nicholas Royle brigade, not the one who published the book with her husband's story in it without naming him as the author, nor the one who filched the story in the first place: it's too late. That's all water under the wharf. You don't like to talk about the day you went and I respect that. We prefer to remember all the days long before, all the golden years, don't we, Si? Once there was, what's the line, something about sun birds, was it? We're still on the same page, aren't we?

In yesterday's twilight, away to the right she could observe the twinkling eye of the Newhaven lighthouse and the fainter lights of Brighton far beyond. Not now.

Standing on the slipway, treacherous at the best of times, her boots submerged by the oncoming waters, holding on like a barnacle to a shoulder-high post, Ethel looks into the Channel filling the air. Seeing at sea, she registers: boiling cashmere, shattered webs of giant spiders, momentary blancmanges of foam, shooting and spouting, swell and tumult, icing over hell, skeins sucked like hideous dishwater draining away at lightning speed, the murderous lashing agitation of the water, brown and yellow closer to the shore, green-gray and bruise-blue and blackening out beyond.

Back home she takes a hot shower, lights the wood-burner and makes supper, heating up some of the leek and potato soup she took out of the freezer to thaw first thing this morning. Afterwards she takes her seat by the fire. From the little table she reaches for the sheet, folded up beside her sudoku and reading-glasses. She unfolds and arranges it, neatly, over her head. She listens to the faint hiss and crackle of logs in the stove, flames now barely shadows. She thinks of the weightless fledgling in the garden. She thinks of the gulls mating, all the kerfuffle of snow-white feathers and scrawking, till the sudden calm of the one on top of the other, the female implausibly still, looking off to the side in fathomless irony. She thinks of Silas making love to her, the full weight of him on top of her, beneath, behind, beside, upside down her, the complete gamut, on the same page, pressed into her. She lets herself sit like that for a while.

PART TWO

The Hides

Hide 1

Things move as soon as one speaks. It is better not to speak, in the hide. The moment a voice says *hide*, everything has already gone off like an atom bomb. Listener A thinks *hide* refers to the act of concealing. Listener B thinks it is skin. Listener C, with a historian's ear, hears in it the measure of land in ye Olde English tymes considered large enough to sustain a free family with its dependants. Listener D has no doubt but that it is the name of a hut or other screened-off location for the observation of birds.

In the unfurling of the split-second before *hide* is heard, split beyond all sense or recall, A hears what B is thinking and has to pause, B hears what A is thinking and has to pause, C hears what A and B are thinking but couldn't really care less, and D hears what C is thinking and considers it the mark of someone curiously hidebound. When listener A hears that B thinks that *hide* refers to skin, the pause given gives paws: A is sidetracked by images of the skins of animals, including the human variety, Nazi lampshades, the flaying of bodies, raw or dressed, and the pity of a paw, the peculiar punctuation of proceedings that a raised paw provokes, the question of the relation between paws and skin, the pores. When listener B hears that A thinks that *hide* refers to the act of concealing, it is hardly a matter for surprise. B wonders, however, if A is not concealing something in the very act of thinking, with or without knowing it, such as whether listener A considers the *the* as equivalent to an *an*, as in *an act*, any old act of concealing, for example a bar of chocolate or a corpse. And listener B is sceptical, also, because *hide* need not in truth be tainted with intention: there is, to be sure, keeping a fact or object from the observation or knowledge of others (listeners B, C and D, for instance), but there is also keeping something from view, obstructing vision without any implication of intention, as in the case of *a stretch of coast hidden by trees*.

Listener C hears what D is thinking and likes the sound of it. At any rate the image of a hide as simply a noun referring to a hut in which to observe birds has, C must concede, a certain charm. This conception of *hide* is sympathetic to C, on account of those forms of dry intellectual passion, arcane simplicity and quiet hermeticism too hastily considered a historian's innermost perversities. When listener D hears what A and B are thinking, a vague warm feeling ensues. This is the radiation effect of what enabled listener D to have had, in the first place, *no doubt* but that *hide* is the name of a hut or other screened-off etc. From this it may be suspected that listener D had effectively subsumed what A and B thought and shifted the conversation, as it were, on to another level. Other significations had been pondered and judgment reached. That such a trial occurred might also be inferred from the fact that listener D specifically reckons with *hide* as a *name*. It is perhaps by virtue of this occupation of another level that D is led, in turn, to consider C hidebound. But all such suspicions and inferences fall apart. This is not just a game, some abc of magical chairs. Whether this other level be higher or lower is, then, a moot point.

For listener A the idea of *hide* as a place for the observation of birds is completely maverick, as though D were dallying in a foreign tongue. This is because A is thinking in American English. For her the correct word in this context is a *blind*. Listener D is muddling his hides with his blinds. In any case she would like to ask D how a *screened-off location* could find its way into the picture without the merest suggestion of *hide* in the sense of concealing. Listener C would like to ask B if the epithet *hidebound* might not more accurately attach to the original ruminator on the subject of skin, that is to say to B *in propria persona*. Listener B would like to ask D on what basis the hide should be construed merely for the observation of birds and not, for example, gorillas. Or, come to that, teenagers hanging out on street corners or novelists tapping at their keyboards. Listener D feigns blind regarding the idea of the blind and seeks to perform some mode of reverse psychology on A, speculating that her mental ramblings on the image of the paw amount to a displacement activity: the fertile acoustics of the word have been drowned at birth, pushing so many kitten or puppy paws down in the bucket and keeping them there, together with little mouths and noses, so long that Emily Brontë's Hareton himself would be proud. In short, listener D would like to ask A: What about the poor?

Listener B would like to ask C: Who are you calling *ruminator*? Listener A would like to give D a good hiding. Listener C would like to know who made the remark about whether the level is higher or lower being a moot point. Listener D would like to avoid any kind of physical confrontation and, with all due respect, acknowledge that he may have misunderstood what A was thinking. Listener B would like to know when D is going to answer the gorilla question. Listener C would prefer to ignore the threatening tone of B's accusation regarding the ruminator. And listener

A would like to know who made the remark about whether the level is higher or lower being a moot point.

Still puzzled by the proposed invocation of the largest and, while arboreal, most ferocious of the anthropoid apes, listener D attends instead to the question of how many listeners there in fact are. Listener C wishes to postulate surprise that no one seems to have picked up on the disclosure that D is male and A female, and furthermore to advocate that it would be only fair that they all now tick that box. Listener D is silent, evidently riled. Listener B is silent, still ruminating on the ruminator. Listener A would like to make it clear that remaining silent is neither helpful nor in fact new, since no one has yet said anything. Listener D wants C to know that *postulate* smacks of the lingo of someone who read history at Oxford and never really found their *métier*. Listener C wants it to be understood that he won't be drawn by such petty skirmishing but is minded to advocate establishing listener details appertaining to age, ethnicity and social background, as well as gender. Listener B prefers *sex* to *gender* and is faintly appalled that someone with a university education should not know the difference, but just to clear up any possible misunderstandings is happy to volunteer she is a woman. Listener A wants to know who *wouldn't* prefer sex? Listener D would like to know who made the remark about whether the level is higher or lower being a moot point.

With the caveat that statistics are not everything, especially not for the rigorous challenges of historiography, listener C is perfectly prepared to disclose that he himself is of Indian background and a graduate of the University of Melbourne. At which point listener A is curious to know if she is the only one who had failed to identify C with an

Australian accent. Listener C wishes to make it abundantly clear that no one has actually heard him speak. Listener B would like to know who made the remark about whether the level is higher or lower being a moot point, while listener D considers it high time to bring the conversation back to the question of the hide.

Listener A is struck that no one has yet made any connection with the *Hyde* of Dr Jekyll fame. Listener B is suddenly worried by the thought that *hide*, at the very start, might actually have been an order, a cry or shout, accompanied, if written, by an exclamation mark – *Hide!* – thereby carrying a firm indication not so much of dappled sunlight in the morning orchard and laughter with other children in sturdy shorts or cotton frocks racing gleefully away in uncatchable directions in an idyllic game of unending summer as of an imperious cold command, issued from unseen loudspeaker, to take cover immediately, scramble, scrabble, anywhere you can find, before being scooped up by the midriff, prior to being teethed in a singularly unenjoyable crunch.

Listener C, still indignant, wishes it to be understood that he has not come along to be interrogated about his sense of national belonging and is minded to express this in the somewhat oblique form: You think this is why an Aussie, of whatever ethnic extraction, or an Indian, of whatever deracination, is interested in Old English conceptions of servitude and land-division? In the thought of this retort he is half-aware, however, of an unintended alignment with the apparently un-British mental linguistics of A. At the same time, in more philanthropic mode, he is keen to obviate widespread panic and reassure everyone that the speculation about *hide* constituting some sort of terrifying practical imperative should be treated as just that, speculation, and moreover, if that had been the tone of the original pronounce-ment, at least one of them might reasonably be expected to have noticed.

Listener D is inclined to add that, if this had indeed been the tone of the original pronouncement, they might all reasonably expect to be dead some time ago, an inclination immediately seized upon by listener E who wishes to criticise as simply ungrammatical the hypothesis that someone could *expect to be dead some time ago*. In other circumstances the abrupt intervention of a new listener might have generated ubiquitous gulps, mental if not actual. Instead, however, listener D resolves to try to sway attention back to his own pet subject, making it clear as he does so that *pet* is ironic, since the last thing he is interested in is configuring the observation of birds as a variation on keeping pets. In which case, listener A has to wonder, why introduce the idea of pet subjects in the first place and, while on the subject of subjects, why has D still not responded to B's puzzlement that he should assume *hide* to refer to a construction designed for the observation only of avian life and not, to give a further example, otters? Listener C surprises even himself by determining to stick up for D at this point, given that their initial rapport, if not entire relationship, revolved around the esoteric allure of feathered creatures. Besides, how much know-how does A have on the practicalities of observing otters, particularly of the marine type, as they forage as deep as twenty-seven metres for sea urchin and abalone? Is it now incumbent upon them all to envisage an *underwater hide*? Where would be the sense in that? But then again, why not?

Listener A is suddenly tantalised by the possibility that listener E might have some shadowy link to the afore-mentioned Mr Hyde. Listener C, sharing her thought, wonders if that wouldn't make listener D Dr Jekyll? At which D's immediate impulse is to tell C that they are frankly a million miles away from the melodramatic murderous double-talk of late nineteenth-century Scottish horror fiction. How could C, a trained historian and responsible scholar, even entertain an idea of such naïvety? All of which leads listener B to wonder whether the listeners are not beginning to divide up along what they would doubtless term *gender lines*. Listener A wishes to stress that there are no lines anywhere, gender or otherwise, and that she would love to give *everyone*, E included, a good hiding.

With respect to B's earlier passing allusion, listener D is now minded to interpose that *hide and seek* is odd, for the one who hides is not the one who seeks: there is something awry in the name of the game. But listener B is oblivious. She is indeed so preoccupied now by the possibility that they all mistook *hide* as a soft, equanimous promise of welcome, as distinct from a terror-inducing throat-strangling cry to make themselves scarce, that she thinks she hears, all of a sudden, a bird fly up out of the turret. Listener A feels she must do her best to calm B down by declaring, albeit falsely, that she herself noticed nothing, whereas C wants to know more about the provenance of the turret, and D can be of little or no assistance at this juncture, since he has mistaken provenance as *province* and therefore assumes listener C to be, like B, losing the plot.

Listener B, no fool, wishes to call A's bluff by stating in no uncertain terms that she, listener A, is no fool and must have heard the bird. Listener C would like to know if the turret might be another name for the hut or screened-off location to which D wished to allude at the outset. Listener D wonders at his own fierceness but, in the most friendly possible way, can listener C just *shut it* about the turret? And listener A finally snaps and wants to know why D should feel so aggrieved that someone else is taking an interest in the nature of *his* hide, especially in the wake of witnessing a bird? *Hah*, listener B is impelled to retort: so you *did* hear it fly up! Listener C feels bound to propose (*postulate!* listener A would like to say, delighting in the mock-correction; *postulate!* listener D is sorely tempted to chip in) that if, as seems increasingly clear, they are not going to discuss the mootness of the remark about levels (had they perhaps already quite forgotten about it?), they should at least give serious consideration to the fact that no one has yet emitted a syllable: in sum, with all due respect for the energies put into what has been perhaps the longest recorded non-existent conversation in history, there is little or nothing to show for it. Bullshit, nonsense, poppycock, listeners A, B and D are immediately disposed to exclaim, oblivious to the elegance with which C has returned the discussion to a semblance of calm.

Listener A feels the force of C's proposition, but is inclined for the moment to conceal her true emotions, including the strangely powerful physical attraction she feels towards him. Listener B, anxious as ever to save her own skin, nonetheless finds sufficient inner steadiness to wonder if there are by this point any remaining grounds for doubting that they all heard the bird: in which case, was this not *de facto* confirmation that listener D was right all along? Even so, listener C is curious to know if he will ever be invited to talk in any real detail about the hide as, in the first place, a place or division of place, for example as a quantification of how much land could be tilled with one plough in a year, not yet understanding that, as and when listener A's feelings towards him are reciprocated, she will be happy to listen to him discoursing about hides in Bede's Ecclesiastical History, the Domesday Book, or Anglo-Saxon and any number of other old chronicles till the cows come home. Listener D feels a pleasant flush at the apparently emerging consensus that, first and foremost, *hide* would be a hut or other screened-off location in which to observe birds. After all, had not a case in point flying up from a turret told them so?

Never one to rush things, especially in the arena of love, listener A would like to revert to her earlier query by asking if it isn't time to attend to what listener E, evidently keen to keep his cards well concealed, might have to contribute. Listener E wants to laugh, happily prepared to wonder whatever makes A suppose that E is a he or even human? And given that the assembled listeners couldn't arrive at a simple decision to discuss the question of who made the remark about whether the level is higher or lower being a moot point, that they hadn't thought to enquire who had actually begun the conversation in which they found themselves, and that, in any case, even by their own admission they ought to have been dead some time ago, wasn't it high time to turn to other listeners and start again?

Such is life, before a word is spoken. All is relish, all is passion. That's how things are in the hide.

Hide 2

The hide is dark but not uncomfortable. There are numerous places to sit, including benches with cushions where people can put their feet up (after removing their shoes), should the desire arise. There is even a sort of visitors' book, in which people can leave a note of their name and the date of their visit. Comments are also welcome, but the tendency is to forgo this option. Visitors find it difficult enough to write their names, let alone scrawl some remark that they will never see and is anyhow likely to be illegible. As may be testified by anyone waking from a dream, determined to write it down in the dark, even with paper and pen conveniently to hand, such a task is never easy. The peculiar anxious pleasure of taking up a pen to become a dream-scribe, feverishly in the moment while not yet fully conscious, tussles with the growing consternation that one word or one line is being super-inscribed upon another, thereby rendering it unreadable, or that the word or line, initially believed finished, has stopped short, or else grown overlong and veered off the paper altogether.

The visitors' book – though it has never been called that – is a rather remarkable object, when all is said and done. It rests on an elevated table in a corner of the hide. The table is unusually sturdy, as it must support the book, which is immensely heavy, with a spine and covers of solid oak encasing many thousands of pages. The table has robust ridges at each edge, in the manner of a lidless box, in order to prevent the book from sliding off, and there is a modest but perfectly effective felt-tip pen attached by a length of string to the book itself. The good working order of the felt-tip is verified every day. If it should happen that the pen runs out of ink, it is true, the writer would have no means of knowing. In the ordinary course of events, however, there is little to prevent a visitor from logging an inscription in the book, besides the difficulties occasioned by the darkness. After all, the visitor may reflect, what is the point of recording my name and comments in this book? No one will read it. Even if they did, what is there to say?

Nice hide. A bit dark.

Or: *We loved it here. So quiet and peaceful.*

Or: *Difficult at first, especially with young children, but after a while...?*

It should also be pointed out that the table is unusually high. In order to access it, a visitor is required to ascend a ladder and balance on the top rung, while manipulating the covers of the book and trying to locate the pen. It helps, of course, to take your own writing implement up there with you. But, in any case, in the dark it is impossible to know at which page to make a fresh entry. The book feels as old as the hills. Only a complete nincompoop would suppose that there is space for a new entry anywhere in the opening pages. If someone standing at the top of the ladder makes vigorous efforts and, holding on to the table with one arm, manages with an athletic flourish of the other to sweep open the book about three or four hundred pages in, the paper feels beautifully crisp and smooth to the touch, but there is no certainty that this is not what a thousand other visitors have done before and the page in question mere inky chaos. All in all, it is no visitors' book for the fainthearted.

Visitors' book is misleading, however, since it may suggest a castle or fine country house or simply a bed-and-breakfast, in other words a place you pass through, having spent just a short time before going on your way. In some respects it might be more appropriate to refer to it by the French term, *Livre d'or* (literally, 'book of gold') – not so much on account of any suggestion of grandeur, but rather for its closing sound: a book *door*: a *door-book*. In other respects it may seem apt to think of a *record of sojourn* or *tome of visitation*. But all these names are lame ducks. None of them begins to do justice to the extraordinary distortions, explosions and foreshortenings, loopings and collapsings, shrinkings and elongations of time to which people are prone, in the hide.

Occasionally someone comes in with the express purpose of writing. This gives rise to a variety of scenarios, funny or dire, depending on case and point of view. The visitor in question makes straight for the corner, in order to secure the ladder up to the book for which no descriptive phrase seems fitting. They do so without having allowed their eyes to adjust to the darkness and tend therefore to stumble into someone else on the way, or, in more slapstick fashion, to trip over a rucksack or bench and fall flat on their face. In any event, the ladder is almost always in a different corner from the one towards which the visitor blindly gravitates. This is because the hide has seven corners, making good fortune less likely than in Russian roulette. But these are trivial deterrents for a serious writer. The woman or man who has entered the hide specifically to write cannot easily be stopped. Soon enough the ladder has been located and the visitor is clambering up with all the enthusiasm of a young sailor wanting to get their first experience of a crow's nest.

Their enthusiasm has been known to get the upper hand. More precisely, they can be seized by a literal delirium. By the time they reach the highest rung and stretch out hands to open it, the book has indeed turned into a crow's nest and in the succeeding barrage of squawking and screeching and battering of enraged wings the visitor loses grip and falls. Serious injuries have ensued and, on occasion, death is the sorry learning outcome. It should be added that, in circumstances of this nature, no one in their right mind wants to stick around. It is not pretty. It is not just that the injured or dead person needs attention that you are very likely ill-equipped to provide. It is not just that the screaming of the crows and cries of the fallen make for an intolerable cacophony. It is not just that getting a medical team out to the hide presents almost insuperable logistical difficulties. It is also that the crows just don't know when to stop. Whether it is merely a couple of broken legs, a spinal fracture or, alas, the final countdown (over before you can say *Stone the crows!*), the creatures won't let you rest in peace.

That is how it is with crows and ravens. People dying on battlefields have known this for millennia. Not for millennia as regards their own demise, but *it has been known for millennia* that people who die bloody deaths are not neglected by the local carrion population, whether on a battlefield or in some other field of endeavour, such as finding oneself victim of a hit-and-run car accident, or doing a spot of rambling, alone on the hills in a remote area, and stumbling or otherwise succumbing to mortal misfortune. Notions of human dignity and decorum, or even the corvid equivalent of a minute's silence, have no purchase here.

Carrion carry on regardless. The celebrated British comedy team missed a trick there: *Carry On Carrion*. You may at this point feel a strong temptation to carry on without a thought of carrion. Who could blame you? Carrion can, after all, be death personified. Call him carrion or Charon. Or don't call him: let him call you. As an otherwise unmemorable sixteenth-century poet once put it: *Seeing no man then can Death escape [...]* / *We ought not feare his carrion shape*. In any case, carrying on or carried off, you don't need to die a glorious military death, trip over a ravine, or slam unavoidably head-on into an oncoming SUV driven by a drunk (with or without valid motor insurance) on a lonely country road miles from anywhere, undiscovered for

twenty-four hours or more. Variations on the theme of Corvus and death abound. There is, for example, the newspaper account of the Bridgwater blacksmith who went out shooting in his home county of Somerset, on Christmas Day 1767: *On Pallet Hill he espied a large flight of old ravens, fired and killed two, which so exasperated the rest, that they immediately descended upon him, and plied their bills and claws so dextrously about his head and face that notwithstanding all possible care was taken of him, he died.*

It should be emphasised, however, that mortalities sustained in the hide in this context are not real. We are dealing here with writers and, more narrowly, with the very small proportion of that dreamy tribe who allow their enthusiasm to get the better of them and become prey to delusions of literality. In reality there are no crows' or ravens' nests, although it is not unknown, in fact, for a bird to enter the hide.

The point, in any case, is that there are those who enter the hide driven by a desire to write and, in the main, they succeed in their ambition. The visiting writer eventually locates the ladder and reaches the top, while minding their head on the ceiling. (Tall writers need to be wary of this and stoop accordingly, unless they positively enjoy the non-*feng shui* sensation of the ceiling grazing the top of the skull.) He or she then valiantly opens up the book, feels about for a page, with varying degrees of grace or clumsiness, touches base with the appointed felt-tip, and gets to work. Such a visitor might spend many hours in this manner, deeply absorbed and hardly caring if the page on which she is writing is blank or already crammed with words, if the words he is inscribing are set out in a legible linear fashion, or if the ink is actually flowing at all.

241

In these circumstances, nonetheless, problems may arise. It is not impossible that, without ever being exposed to the kind of lethal enthusiasm already described, the writer has a moment of over-excitement or frustration or sheer tiredness and loses his or her footing and clatters from the ladder. The consequences of such a misfortune – this time happily minus the carrion team – require no reiteration. To be grounded without harm is not the norm. Alternatively it may be that writers get so mentally transported by what they are writing that they start to sing, moan or groan, in the manner of Glenn Gould at the piano, and this will infuriate others in the hide who are, naturally, keeping their own counsel. It is perfectly acceptable to whisper a few words from time to time but, as a rule, people are expected to maintain a respectful hush in the hide. It is not the Sistine Chapel, with guards exclaiming *Silencio! Silencio!* as tourists' collective whispering rises in a crescendo as serpentine and hissful as Milton's Hell. Nevertheless the unspoken supposition is that it should be possible to stand or sit in the hide and hear a pin drop. No living creature outside the hide should be able to hear any sound within it. Writers who sing, whine and so on, get short shrift. Ejection is speedy and automatic.

Another problem, admittedly unusual, is when two writers enter the hide, or at any rate lay hands on the ladder, at the same time. What happens in such instances can be entertaining to those already in the hide, whose eyes have adjusted to the darkness. The writers, being new to the dark, fail to spot one another and collide and fumble, often in a quite risible fashion. As they cannot see the other's face or the sweet irony of their coincidence, there is no need even to turn a blind eye. They begin to climb the ladder as if the other did not exist, or at any rate should vanish forthwith like a phantom. This is not helpful. However prone to dream and fantasy, writers have bodies. There is not sufficient space on the ladder for two at the same time. One writer must cede to the other. (As a matter of academic interest, it is very often the less intransigent writer who produces the more nuanced and valid commentary when eventually set free upon the page.)

Finally, it can happen that a writer goes gaily up the ladder only to discover another writer already in residence. The encounter with the other is thus an encounter with muddy footwear and trouser-legs or skirt. The writer in residence has no way of knowing whether this groping in the nether regions (for that is how it feels) emanates from another aspiring writer, or from a visitor intent simply on leaving a note of their name, or from some other creature, such as a badger. Whence this image of the badger, who can tell? – for badgers live in setts not hides, and in truth there are, for better or worse, currently no badgers in this particular neck of the woods. And, in any case, badgers do not scale ladders. This is not a children's fable. Moreover a badger might nuzzle or even root, but could hardly be said to grope. Badgers have sharp teeth, however, and can inflict severe injury if so disposed. (They also have a singular predilection for nightjars' eggs, but that is not germane here.) It is perhaps for this reason that a badger came to mind. In the dark, and especially when you are high up in the rafters in the full flow of scribbling, oblivious of all around you, the sudden apprehension of bold and lively movement around your lower legs can trigger all sorts of speculation, of which the most troubling, to be sure, is that you are about to be eaten alive. Happy to say, in more or less every case, pragmatism wins out. The penny drops, the Johnny-come-lately backs off, and the writer at the table can continue in peace a little while longer.

The desire to write is perverse at the best of times, but this is especially manifest in the hide. The sad fact is, no matter how good the writing may be, and no matter how much should eventually transpire in legible form, a writer will have missed the most important thing. In short, they fail to experience the hide. Of course writing can, in a different way, itself be an experience: why otherwise would these passionate types be so incorrigibly clambering up the ladder? But that is a secondary consideration, akin to the badger's fondness for the eggs of the nightjar. The truth is, if you are writing, the hide will elude you. The hide will always hide. Nature, as Heraclitus said, loves to. It makes sense not to write, in the hide. It is best simply to observe.

Hide 3

No one hide is the same as the next. That much will be evident to anyone who has sat in tears surprised by joy in the hide at Loch Garten in Scotland or, in the United States, has acquired from L.L. Rue Enterprises their own *ultimate photo blind, in woodland green camo or all-terrain digital gray camo*, complete with *two photographic snouts* and *six screened viewing windows*. This portable American blind, it should be noted, is large enough for two people, so, if you don't already have one and are interested in making a purchase, you should not hesitate to talk about it with a friend and consider going Dutch. Save discussion of multiple occupancy for later.

Hide 4

Alternatively, take a ride in time in a submersible hide. Check out the alterities of the twilight zone, before descending into midnight. Life begins not at forty, or fifty, but around the alkaline hydrothermal vents near the Mid-Atlantic Ridge, down on the remotest ocean floor. Out of those depths emerge the lungfish and subsequently reptiles that veer off into birds and humans.

Hide 5

You enter the hide. It is peaceful and immediately tranquillising. The door closes softly behind you, in the dark. You quickly lose a sense of time and space. You have no idea how many you are. Nor do you have any clear notion of the scale of the place. You might be all alone, or there might be twenty or thirty others with you. You might be able to touch the ceiling with hands upstretched. Or the hide might be of tremendous proportions, akin to the home for the world's largest colony of bats, Bracken Cave near San Antonio in Texas. (Bats are not birds, in case of any possible confusion here: the point is about the size, space, volume of a *hide*, not about the kinship or non-kinship between feathered vertebrates and those lucifugal mouse-like quadrupeds famed for the thin membranes which extend out of the fingers to form wing-like structures, enabling them to fly in their own weird, zigzag, jumpy way.)

You need to be quiet and take care where you step. You don't want to make an idiot of yourself, like some of the writers you've read about. You suppose there are benches, bodies, rucksacks, walking-sticks and other obstacles. As you grow more accustomed to the darkness you think you can make out hunched silhouettes – people sitting at the front, figures standing. The hide feels big. You hear murmurs here or there. You build up an impression of the number of people gathered. It is never fixed, however, for there is always someone, a shadow away to one side or another, entering or exiting.

Eventually you seat yourself on a bench at the front. You listen and watch. It is like nothing else. Momently you recall wandering into a church as dusk falls on a winter's afternoon when there is no one else about, say, or a childhood hideaway with an old mattress and bits of plywood, plastic milk-crates, carpet remnants and discarded bed-linen, down at the bottom of the field, beneath the trees, a tank concealed amidst a jungle floor of stinging nettles affording protection from imaginary intruders and seclusion from real grown-ups. Or you think of other joys of early childhood, in still fainter flashes: a princess in a silk tent, a pirate up a tree. But no image or memory measures up to the singularity of the hide.

As your senses absorb this new environment, you cannot be sure if what you see is a thing going on, in fact, in front of you. You cannot tell how long you have been sitting. You feel oddly warm and comfortable, as if you had already drifted off and are not to be disturbed. The hide has begun to subsume who you are. You detect neither screen nor stage, neither page nor glass. But you feel as if you are seeing and reading at the same time.

You observe: *On December the third the wind changed overnight and it was winter. Until then the autumn had been mellow, soft. The leaves had lingered on the trees, golden red, and the hedgerows were still green. The earth was rich where the plough had turned it.* Whose voice is this? There is a softness to these words despite the drastic change they announce. Winter arrives overnight. It is in the wind. Yet the emphasis remains with what was before. With what is mellow, rich and golden red, and with hedgerows still green, you pick up echoes of the *soft-dying day* of Keats's autumn, and, in the alliteration of leaves lingering, the unlikeliness of such phrases in everyday speech. The tenses tangle. Winter comes abruptly on the morning of December the third, and still something hangs, sliding and repositioning itself in the shift from *had been* to *were* and *was*, so that you cannot say if the earth that the plough has turned is or is not still rich.

Alfred Hitchcock read these words only once. You see them through his eyes, from his point-of-view. He was already responding to them as film, the apocalyptic scenario lapped up in the link of an eye. Every movie is a blast chance saloon. You slur read with him. You see the words and pictures sliding and shifting one on top of the other, like birds coupling. You see the words he read but did not use, you see the words she used and no one watching reads. You see the scene he made that speaks only in squawks or silence of the eeriness she dreamed. You see the text and read the film, sensing listenings and layerings of other texts and other films, all at the same time, sitting in the dark, mind adrift, attention and intention spectralised, lost in the hide. In the drunken Irishman's singsong, with its mixture of comic and terrible: *It's the end of the world.*

The director was well hitched. As was du Maurier. For he worked closely with Daphne's father in the '30s and she had already provided him with stories for two movies. The title is overhead from the start. He cannot improve on hers, if it was his and not Evan Hunter's, if it was hers and not Frank Baker's: *The Birds.* You see and read *The Birds.* Returning to the air, the words belong to no one.

You think of *stories to be read with the door locked* and picture a seeping dread, overwhelmed by claustrophobia.

You think of *stories to be read with the door locked* and fill with pleasure, womb-like, cut off. There is a sense of foreboding, for sure, already brooding, but it is as if you were afloat, feelings lulled, at a distance. It is 1952, a couple of decades before anyone is talking about nuclear winter, but du Maurier makes time a wintry catastrophe from the start, easing into view Nat Hocken with his wartime disability, working three days a week on a farm, eating his lunch sitting on the cliff's edge where he can watch them. The birds. The *watch* in birdwatching never tells the hour but gives much more: study and immersion, uncertainty and alertness, keeping guard or vigil, tending and looking after the dead.

The war is over. You can see that. And then, after the war, after the war to end all wars, the birds.

At the end of the world the seasons migrate. In spring the birds move inland. It is migration with a mission: *they knew where they were bound, the rhythm and ritual of their life brooked no delay.* You falter at this *brooked*: it is not watery. Once it was, the repose of a word that meant enjoying, now merely bearing or enduring. This vernal brooking no delay loops oddly back, identifying the birds with the sudden intervention of winter. It's climate chaos. Your man Nat prefers the autumn: *In autumn those that had not migrated overseas but remained to pass the winter were caught up in the same driving urge, but because migration was denied them followed a pattern of their own.* Du Maurier's phrasing, easy and deceptive, casts shadows over belief. You try not to get into a flap. How to conceive these creatures called *birds*? How to speak and not project, not feather them in the trappings of human psychology? What is the *pattern of their own*?

No mention has been made of birds migrating overseas, only of flying inland. It is something elemental as the wind, some great *driving urge,* but perhaps not natural. The birds have been *denied.* And then: *Great flocks of them came to the peninsula, restless, uneasy, spending themselves in motion; now wheeling, circling in the sky, now settling to feed on the rich new-turned soil, but even when they fed it was as though they did so without hunger, without desire.* The birds appear to be *without hunger, without desire.* And with desire *denied* to them, all is up in the air again. Everything is *restless, uneasy.*

You feel a sexual frisson in the *spending themselves in motion.* The mistress of suspense suspends this spending, this spilling of strange seed: *The restless urge of autumn, unsatisfying, sad, had put a spell upon them and they must flock, and wheel, and cry; they must spill themselves of motion before winter came.* The unnatural and supernatural mix. Autumn's is a magical urge: you see, everywhere, birds under a spell.

Nat Hocken dissolves. You know he has no place in Hitchcock's film. You are trying to watch the movie and at the same time decipher the palimpsest of Evan Hunter's script, but in walks Mrs Trigg. The name suggests neatness and no-nonsense. But a *trigg* is also a wedge or stop. There is something blocked, like a trigger arrested in mid-flight. She thinks Nat's account of the bird attack the preceding night is merely a flight of fancy. *Sure they were real birds,* she asks with a smile, *with proper feathers and all? Not the funny-shaped kind, that the men see after closing hours on a Saturday night?* She suggests he write to *The Guardian* about it. Then Nat's wife hears about it on the radio and tells him, *It's not only here, it's everywhere. In London, all over the country. Something has happened to the birds.* Cornwall, England transforms, before your eyes, into Bodega Bay, California.

You watch du Maurier's words infecting Hitchcock in every direction, at every level, and you register too the cross-contamination, knowing you cannot read the text of 1952 without interference from the film of 1963. It is in this very simultaneity that you are experiencing the end of the world. *Something has happened to the birds.* With this comes the blockage, the dread, the futile preparations for the worst, the phobia and horror, the birds gathering, sharing strange knowledge, breaking in, the blood and dead bodies, inside your room, having to touch them, being touched by them, birds killing themselves in a frenzied attempt to kill you, starting with a tap at the window, then the splintering of glass, the outside becoming the inside, the screeching, flapping, squawking, pecking out your vile sweet jelly babies.

The silence of the hide is virtually pounding in your ears. *They kept coming at him from the air, silent save for the beating wings.* Silence broods behind everything, behind every sprig of conversation, accentuated by the very artifice of noise. Nat helps his wife make supper, *whistling, singing, making as much clatter as he could,* in an attempt to cover up all *the shuffling and the tapping* of the birds, on the roof, outside the windows, at the door.

And what a dire success, what a disaster movie Hitchcock makes of it all. From the start, of course, perversity marks it out as no one else's. It bears a pattern of its own – from the scratchy melodramatic credits, bird silhouettes frantic, the excess of their screeching and scrawping, to the maverick juxtaposition of Rod Taylor and Tippi Hedren in Davidson's

Pet Shop in San Francisco, implausibly flirting over the possible purchase of love birds. Any fidelity to du Maurier is shattered in this showily Californian, whimsically unreal romantic encounter. Still, like the comic image of the director himself plonked down in the opening sequence, walking surrealistically out of the store with two lapdogs on a lead, something keeps sticking, an imprint of the strangeness of du Maurier's work rattling Hitchcock's cage.

No politics for his birds, apparently. You see that plain as day. Mrs Trigg connects them with Russia, something to do with the Arctic Circle. *Like the air-raids in the war*, thinks Nat.

In August 1961 an area around Santa Cruz in California was invaded by sooty shearwaters. Thousands of them transpired one morning dead or dying, along the sea's edge, in the streets, in people's gardens, disgorging the contents of their stomachs, anchovies eaten or partially digested, everywhere stinking with dead fish from dead birds. As Wally Trabing reported next day in the *Santa Cruz Sentinel*: *Dead and stunned seabirds littered the streets and roads in the foggy, early dawn. Startled by the invasion, residents rushed out on their lawns with flashlights, then rushed back inside, as the birds flew toward their light.* Over the streets and lawns and housetops, dead birds and vomited fish. An explanation was proffered by Ward Russell, museum zoologist at the University of California: the birds must have been confused by a blinding fog that engulfed the bay that night and they became disturbed while feeding and all rose up flying as a flock towards the light given off by the streetlights, houses and businesses onshore. This theory never seemed particularly plausible. Hitchcock heard about the incident and asked for a copy of the *Sentinel* to be sent to him. It was *research*, he said, for his *new thriller*. The current consensus on the why of the massacre, you recall, is Amnesic Shellfish Poisoning.

Then comes the travesty of the ending. His is a whole Hitchcock-up, as if the sun could set and let you watch, as if the sun could be shown setting on what he had shown, on what was happening to the birds. And at the same time you observe du Maurier, keeping things small and personal, focused on Nat, his wife and children. Time has split in pieces. It is not clear who, besides Nat himself, is watching. *Still, as long as the wife slept, and the kids, that was the main thing.* Asleep, you think. But the wife is apparently awake again as the story ends. Nat is going to smoke that last cigarette, he tells her: *He reached for it, switched on the silent wireless. He threw the empty packet on the fire, and watched it burn.*

The point, you sense, has to do with the silence. Both author and *auteur* do something sickening with sounds: the tapping of the birds, their scuffling inside, flapping, flopping, the uncomfortable strangeness of a bird trapped in a room. It might be enough to make you stop watching or reading, and wake up. There is only so much you can take of being trapped in a room with birds. They belong to the open air. That is their abode.

Unable to know how to finish, but knowing that the demonstration of this inability is crucial, du Maurier stages conflagration in little: Nat *watched it burn*. And, with an imaginative sensitivity to the birds that seems to you largely absent from Hitchcock, she lets the immediately preceding paragraph continue to vibrate and splinter, playing over these flames. The birds are coming in: *Nat listened to the tearing sound of splintering wood, and wondered how many* million years of memory were stored in those little brains, behind the stabbing beaks, the piercing eyes, now giving them this instinct to destroy mankind with all the deft precision of machines.

You picture, coinciding with the publication of Rachel Carson's *Silent Spring*, Hitchcock aloft on the success of *Psycho*. You picture him with the money and impulse to go it alone, ignoring the advice of friends and financial backers, setting aside his *commercial instincts* (as the absurd phrase has it), and making a film about human-inflicted avian genocide. That is what you see in the hide. In this projected remake, Carson's spring is a silence sprung in Hitchcock. Deep in the hush of your mind's ear you pursue this silence, like a vanishing nodal point, in the figure of Mrs Bundy. Described by Hunter as *sixtyish, wearing walking shoes and a tweed suit, a very masculine-looking woman with short cropped white hair*, she is the benign metamorphosis of Norman Bates and his mother. She is the woman-man who knows too much. She has very few lines but in her you pick up the acknowledgement of deep time: birds *have been on this planet* for *a hundred and twenty million years*. Through her you listen, as in a maze of the cinematic brain, following her awareness of the size and potential of *brain pans*, into the silence, sensing the segue of dinosaurs into birds, and humans a mere aberration, a tiny blip in the descent of species.

The body of Mrs Trigg's husband, Jim, is found beside the telephone: *He must have been trying to get through to the exchange when the birds came for him*. Nothing works. No more telephones, no more wireless. Nat *switched on the silent wireless*. In the darkness you feel yourself scratching your head, or feel something scratching: *millions of years of memory*. Something has happened to the birds and it has to do with what is stored in the memory. Tracked in the silence: *What he had thought at first to be the white caps of the waves were gulls. Hundreds, thousands, tens of thousands... They rose and fell in the trough of the seas, heads to the wind, like a mighty fleet at anchor, waiting on the tide.*

You wonder what is going on. Did someone turn the lights off? But then you remember that you are in the hide. You suppose it must be time to leave. You fumble across towards where you came in, taking care not to bump into other people or their paraphernalia, into benches or the foot of the ladder. You are amazed at how dark it seems to have become. You reach the place of entry but it is no longer there. You feel your way around the seven sides of the hide but cannot locate an exit. You think of shouting or calling out loud, or at least of trying to communicate with someone else in the hide. But they are mere silhouettes at most, you can scarcely make them out. It is still dark, and everything has gone back. *The Birds* is starting up again.

Hide 6

Let's suppose I've invested in a photo blind in all-terrain digital gray camo. I invite you along. Like the advert says, it's large enough for two. Except that you wouldn't say advert, because *advert* is British English, and here in the US it's an *ad* or *advertisement*. Also, in England such a piece of merchandise would accommodate two people only if I were slender as a lady river-nymph or my fellow-occupant some fellow skinny as a greyhound. At best it would be a tight squeeze. But in the US *large enough for two people* means decently capacious. Space in the US is different. I don't just mean *personal space*, though that remarkable American idiom must be part of the story. Not only are things bigger (cars, shops, streets, houses, drink cartons, plates of food, photo blinds), but there is also more space *around* stuff.

This blind, in any case, is *roomy*. Only in America. No wonder the advert boasted of *six screened viewing windows* in addition to the *two photographic snouts*. But, before we set out and actually test this new product in the field, we need to complete one other item of housekeeping. You say *blind*, I say *hide*. Nothing I ever say will change things in this respect: American English and English English, foreign tongues in one mouth. Two tongues making love and war in the same blind. I mean hide. The blind is blind to hide, the hide hides blind, the blind is blind to blind, the hide hides hide. I have no desire to call the whole thing off: I would merely request that you let down your barriers over this single word and allow it passage, as an illegal immigrant, a foreign worker, a verbal chancer, a tiny vocable meaning no harm, into your enormous beautiful language, just for today. Hide!

While seeking out a good hide, I came across this: *Some wildlife refuges, or state parks, have pre-built blinds that you can use, but these are fairly rare. If you want to take advantage of a blind, chances are you will need to make one yourself or buy one.* This confirms what I was just saying: there are no hides in America (or, at any rate, not until now, not until this one here), but even if we were talking about *blinds* (and I have to remind you, *we are not*), pre-built versions are *fairly rare*. Only in America. Only in America would someone say something that sounds so bizarre but is meant as matter-of-fact: *pre-built blinds* are *fairly rare*. Let's consider another website example: *Pop-up hunting blinds make for cheap photo blinds*. This sentence takes the biscuit, as we say in England. Rather than hack about trying to find yourself a hide by searching *photo blind* websites, make things easier on yourself: you just need to get a *pop-up hunting blind*. It's cheaper. It's the economy, stupid. Get yourself a well-priced hide that you can use for *birding* (as you call it) but also for *shooting and killing*. A classic case – to use a phrase familiar in British, American, Canadian, Australian and so many other varieties of English (and we must return to it) – of *killing two birds with one stone*. Pop-up hunting blinds make for cheap photo blinds! Only in America.

And this would also be an obvious place to say something about gun law. Gun law and gun lore: the two inseparable, a mirage made in heaven. Such is the *naturalisation* of the gun as an object welcome, in effect, in every household. Hunting talk is blind to the blindness of gun lore. Slip a word like *hunting* into your blind talk and no one so much as blinks.

Suffice to say the only hunting I am advocating today is *word-hunting*, where a word-hunt, like a ghost-hunt, is a game of two halves or at least of reversibility: words hunt you, as much as you hunt them. The words you hunt down will have hunted you down. Keep your eyes skinned.

I've invested in a photo blind in all-terrain digital gray camo. Why not woodland green? you may ask. Because *all-terrain digital gray camo* sounded so American: the expansionist, spatially boastful *all-terrain*, the happy artificiality of *digital gray* and the military kudos of the *camo*.

How can anyone live with the term 'photo blind' and not go completely *c-c-c-r-r-a-a-a-a-z-y*?

Hi! Do you hear?

Hey, bud! come see! It's a white ibis and you are totally photo blind.

I tell you, American English *is* photo blind.

It's so completely photo blind it has no place to hide...

Until now! For this is a hide, and we are in it together – just you and me. (We can invite others later, if you want. We can work out multiple occupancy. Everything's possible.)

Hide-de-ho!

It may not look very different from what you're used to, except that it enables you to see things you wouldn't otherwise. It's a personalised hide from which you can look out and see America differently, one snout for you, one snout for me, starting with the realisation (which comes with a five-year warranty!) that space isn't what it used to be. There's a gun lobby and there's an oil lobby, but there's also a language lobby. Seeing this is one of the things that the hide enables.

We can go anywhere across these thousands of miles of your enormous beautiful country, from north to south, east to west, crosshatching in any and every direction. We could sit in our hide beside a lake in Seattle and watch poetry and philosophy together. We could zoom into the study of the prehistoric birdman, birds, gods and people in ancient Native American crosshatching art and inscriptions on the Cumberland Plateau in Tennessee and a dozen other cave locations. We could sit in the White House, the digital gray camo blending in perfectly, move up to the president's desk monitoring every word, every shade of body language. Or we could get out into the fields, into the mountains, on to the plains, down to the shore, into the creeks, deep in the woods, far into the forest. We can observe the blue-gray gnatcatcher, the ovenbird, Bullock's oriole, the common redpoll, the blue jay, the purple martin, the orange-crowned warbler, the black-billed magpie, the sooty grouse, the mountain bluebird, the northern mockingbird, the green-winged teal, the Acadian flycatcher, the black-necked stilt, the greater roadrunner, the American oystercatcher, the Harris's hawk, the Clark's nutcracker, the cedar waxwing, the northern flicker, the prairie warbler, the common poorwill, the ruby-crowned kinglet, the great blue heron, the bushtit, the herring gull, the American white pelican, the least sandpiper, the green jay, the summer tanager, the tufted puffin, the red-breasted sapsucker, the chestnut-backed chickadee, the black-chinned hummingbird, the downy woodpecker, the great gray owl, the turkey vulture, the glossy ibis, the mourning dove, the pygmy nuthatch, the tufted titmouse, the phainopepla and the American woodcock. Take it all in through one or more of *six screened viewing windows. Too-too-too-too* much!

But the hide lets us think differently, first of all, about space. It's about alterations of scale. Across this enormous beautiful country mass-extinction is under way. In England it is easier to spot these things: everything is so cute, it's *so small!* Here in America the poetics of extinction has been in slow motion, not because that is the actual speed, but because of the perception of space. A solitary hummingbird appears in the sun-dappled leaves of the maple tree in the park – hide-de-ho! Anna's hummingbird, what a stunning creature! – but then is gone. Gone into the thousands of miles, into all the air miles and country miles you think you can't need to think about. The American't American. For birdwatching in America everything is significantly less certain than in England. The hide lets us realise that populations of all of these birds are declining at a much faster rate than the language lobby can tolerate. The poetics of extinction heads toward fast-forward.

I spoke earlier of *pre-built*. I should have been clearer. It is not so much a pre-built hide as a hide we make as we go along. And now I am going to leave you: it will be up to you to carry on with the hide. Carry on. Don't count on me. Whatever you're doing, wherever you are: take a distance from the language lobby. Think: *hide*. Pop it up.

Hide 7

Counting is ghostly: the cuckoo knows this.

Hide 8

Personalised hides have a well-established history. Our understanding of the life of cuckoos is crucially dependent on the portable twig-construction used by Edgar Chance and his team of merry men at Pound Green Common in Worcestershire, in the early 1920s. With cinematographer Edward Hawkins (in the hide itself), together with celebrated photographer Oliver Pike and additional assistance from hide-bearers Simmonds, father and son, Chance shows how timing is everything. In the film he directs, *The Cuckoo's Secret* (1922), we see a meadow pipit's nest on the ground, then a female cuckoo flying into it: she lays an egg and is gone. It's all over within eight seconds. Timing shows how chance is everything.

Hide 9

Language is variously anthropomorphic and ornithomorphic. Anthropomorphism may seem to spread its tentacles everywhere, but what about ornithomorphism? Think of Mozart. He kept a starling and he knew backwards what he was talking about, dreaming of singing and composing twinkle twinkle requiem. Think of Dickens. He kept a raven and he knew backwards what he was walking about, dreaming of scriving and croaking the voices of the streets and the oppressed, police rookeries, sniff-pecking and missed flights. But hold a space, too, for the other way round, the starling that kept Mozart and the raven that kept Dickens. People speak of a man whose wife has proved unfaithful as a *cuckold*, for example, with little or no awareness that this is an ornithomorphism, deriving from the Old French (*cucu*) for cuckoo. But then in a silly or slightly mad anthropomorphism people also appropriate the bird in order to designate someone as silly or slightly mad. For Wordsworth, on the other hand, the cuckoo embodies poetry itself: it is *a wandering voice*, an *invisible thing*, a *mystery*. Cuckoo! Cuckoo! A word can be a hide.

Hide 10

Consider this a hide for wordbotching. Of all the idioms whereby English speakers abuse the avian world, none is perhaps more nauseating and abject than *killing two birds with one stone*. In general this figure of speech is taken to refer to the advantages of getting two things done at once, by means of the same action. A trip to the shopping mall, for example, would allow the consumer to purchase a new pair of jeans at the same time as calling in at a barber's for a much needed haircut. Making this trip, rather than seeking the haircut more locally, enables the consumer to *kill two birds with one stone*. Or making this trip, rather than seeking denim legwear closer to hand, enables the consumer to *kill two birds with one stone*.

Already certain complications show up. Such is the nature of an example. How far off is the mall? Does the consumer actually need new jeans? Or the haircut? To what extent is going to the barber at the mall a short-cut, so to speak, a cheapskate option dictated by practical consideration of location? How many people have had a haircut they were really pleased with, from a barber in a mall? Isn't the consumer's hankering for an expensive new pair of jeans driving the need for the haircut, as much like being dragged through a hedge backwards the latter might transpire to look?

These, in any case, are questions in which the consumer is unlikely to be much interested, for the decision to describe the proposed trip as *killing two birds with one stone* indicates that, at its heart, lie feelings of ambivalence. On some level, however fleeting, the literal meaning of the idiom is mobilised: the outing will be an act of savagery, not only with respect to the destructive manner in which malls have usurped local independent shops or designer jeans manufacturers make vicious use of cheap foreign labour, but in the otherwise apparently free-floating mental life of the shopper and to the detriment of birds. On some level, however unconscious, the shopper indeed contemplates the reality of throwing a stone, whether by their own hand or by resorting to some contraption such as a catapult, and hitting two birds, whether in a tree, for example, or in mid-air, thereby violently terminating the lives of the creatures

in question. Why would anyone wish to kill a bird, let alone two at the same time?

Of course the platitudinous answer is: for food. If invited to pursue the analysis, the perpetrator might reflect that the birds involved would be on the diminutive side. It is unlikely that the consumer could kill two ostriches with one stone, even in a prospective shopping rage as towering as Tokyo Midtown. It is unlikely that he or she could kill even two chickens with a single, well-aimed, flinty shard. Without naming names, we are talking about sparrows, finches, larks, nightingales, the sorts of vulnerable little beings that people have been proudly killing for even longer than they have been proudly talking about killing two birds with one stone. Who knows, perhaps this is the origin of the idiom *Pride comes before the fall of a sparrow*? (Or at least it would be, if that saying were ever to acquire currency.) In any case, why? Why would anyone want to eat little birds like that? Why would they want to eat bigger ones, like chickens? The short answer – because the consumer is a consumer and there is nothing else to eat – has some traction as and where such vicissitudes obtain. But in the general course of daily life, for the majority of humans who go shopping, this is not an issue.

Such indeed is the cruelty towards chickens in this context that many people harbour the conviction, or at least entertain a belief, that they are not actually birds at all. It is these people whose chickens, not surprisingly, never come home to roost. They are barbarously many. (The people, naturally, not the chickens.) Perhaps the consumer is one of this breed, perhaps not. Perhaps we should speak not of breed but of massive, macabre flock. It is, after all, well known what birds of a feather do. That idiom, while perhaps less immediately troubling than the *two birds with one stone*, has its own sickening dimensions, but it is difficult enough just staying focused on the bird-killing. It is difficult, it should be stressed, not so much from the perspective of the observer, but rather from the projected vantage point of the flock.

The point here being that a very large number of people, indeed the majority of the world's human population, pass their entire lives in a state of criminal disavowal and dishonesty on this front. As to where this criminality begins, where do crimes against non-humanity ever begin? It would be tempting to say simply: open your eyes, listen up, look, listen down, get those eyes tested, you have a problem, Houston, likewise the ears, take a whiff of this, touch it, this is your doing, this is what you have brought upon yourself, yes *you*, and upon those around you, your friends and family, and your enemies too, even if that doesn't matter to you, as it should, since thinking about your enemies is the quickest route to realising how much you share with them, how much your own squirming barbarity, your own criminal, abject and sickening *modus vivendi* (to dress up your predicament in a fragrant Latin garnish) is theirs too, you are in it together, all of you in one complete chicken-in-a-basket-case, enemies reunited.

At any rate, if you are one of the aforementioned flock (a parson's nose is in there somewhere, sniffing out your life), you will acknowledge that a chicken *is* a non-human animal, even if you cannot bring yourself to recognise that it is a bird. Crimes against non-human animals begin with the presumption that *Thou shalt not kill* means: *Thou shalt not kill other human beings*. Rest easy, brothers and sisters: you can kill as many *other* sorts of animal as you like, any time of the day or night, 24/7 shopping sprees, no need to be an early bird, you can kill 'em to your heart's content all the livelong day.

Here it is necessary to observe, at least parenthetically, the fleeting appearance of another idiotism: *the early bird catches the worm*. EBCW, as we may designate it, if only in a gesture towards a more general endeavour to foreground and ridicule the deathly inanity of contemporary bureaucracy (one small hop for mankind), is the sort of nasty jingle that might start up in your mental headphones when you come across *blinking light and drizzle, the song of thrushes and blackbirds, the plundering of worms and the green, faintly twinkling, still-dewy expanse of the cemetery*, evoked in the context of a certain cremation in Cheltenham. A pernickety idiom-cruncher might wish to stamp his feet (rather like the herring gull in earthworm-summoning mode) and insist that it is the worm that has to be earlier, for the bird to be there to catch it. Let us here set aside such paradoxes of chicken and egg. Earliness is not the point. We would merely like to observe that the *catches* in EBCW is a ludicrous anthropomorphism: the early bird is not a fisherman. The bird detects the worm first of all by *listening*. The thrush does not tilt its head and glance rapidly about simply because it has picked up signals of your infinitely questionable presence on the scene, but because it is listening to *sounds in the ground*. National Security Agency eat your wormy heart out. The *early* is a further laughable projection, as if birds could show up late for breakfast or even on occasion prematurely, while it's still dark. EBCW might also readily be construed as an oblique insult, a thoughtless diss to all birds that don't eat worms. Just because you do not tune in to hermaphroditic representatives of the *Phylum Annelida* first thing in the morning doesn't mean you cannot be early.

Closely linked to that world of crime, we were saying, which is among other things the criminality of most religions, is the outrage of naming. People say *chicken* in the singular when they are actually talking about *chickens* in the plural. Mixing their metaphors in a vague toilet panic, they try to flush out – meaning flush away – their knowledge of what they are doing by resorting to an abstract plural, a strictly fictional turn of phrase, as part of an elaborate strategy to gloss over the reality of what they are doing. In this seemingly small but telling detail they behave precisely in the manner of *headless chickens*.

Who knows what the headless chicken sees? In any case it is obvious enough that you are not and very likely never were reading this, you of the huge macabre flock, you for whom criminal disavowal and dishonesty are as thoroughly embedded as the proclivities of a deranged paedophile, you who deem yourselves so ethically, mentally, physically *free range*, at liberty simply to declare *I like chicken [sic] because it tastes good*, as though the same rationale might perfectly well apply in the saturnine contention: *I like child because it tastes good*. Why, then, you may not ask, are you still being addressed here? For even if you transpired to be one of the odd bods, one of those who happens to stray, however inadvertently, and chew, seriously, one of the chosen chewing, even for twenty seconds, on the possibility that you have been, for too long to bear contemplating, a collaborator and participant in atrocious cruelty and suffering, constantly, day and night, week after week, year upon year, decade beyond decade, you'll chicken out at the last moment. Sick birdbrain that you are.

If we then submit for critical reflection a brief statement from bird scientist Tim Birkhead, it is not in the supposition that *you* will be reading, but rather with an eye and ear towards a future reader who might be more of a human being in being less, and less in being more. Yes, we confess: the dream of a new and other humanity is what eggs us on. Merely human readers are of course welcome, but are not expected to make much progress. It is Not Within Our Remit to persuade or dissuade. We are simply concerned with observation. People may think they know why the caged bird sings, but when a cage goes in search of a bird things are more enigmatic.

Birkhead assesses the question of whether birds can feel pain:

> *Studies of chicken, however, provide rather convincing evidence that birds can experience the feeling of pain. Chickens kept commercially at high densities often resort to pecking each other's feathers, and sometimes to cannibalism. In an effort to prevent this, the poultry industry amputates the tips of the birds' beaks... Beak trimming is a rapid procedure performed with a heated blade that simultaneously cuts and cauterises the beak. It appears that trimming results in a period of initial pain lasting two to forty-eight seconds, followed by a pain-free period of several hours, which is then followed by a second, more prolonged, period of pain.*

Next time you get a haircut, think of it as getting your beak trimmed. That is the sort of tone in which the distinguished ornithologist presents it. Beak-trimming is a *rapid procedure*, quicker than a haircut at the mall. And the *heated blade... simultaneously cuts and cauterises*: you half-expect him to make a passing quip about killing two birds

271

An English Guide to Birdwatching

with one stone. But of course the great thing here is that beak trimming doesn't *kill* any birds, it merely inflicts excruciating pain, on and off, over a very prolonged period. Indeed, you could and probably would say that it is a positive boon for the fluffy little creatures, since it virtually eliminates worries about cannibalism.

A certain bluffness is *de rigueur* for scientific discourse, a cool insanity in the face of the dispossessing powers of language and quiet acquiescence in the conniving cruelties for which it can be deployed. We will not dwell on Birkhead's use of *however* or the even more innocent-looking *rather* (*Studies of chicken, however, provide rather convincing evidence…*): suffice to observe that he is intent on appearing to be scientific, not willing to be completely swayed one way or another. Just a couple of pages earlier he offered apparently contrary evidence – that a puffin can be mauled and killed by a peregrine without any show of suffering. Others might speculate on cataplectic paralysis, but he is content to leave the thing like that, all rounded up in a smooth, putatively knowledgeable discourse that seems to weigh up the different sides and betray no awareness of dead weight and the death-dealing obscenity of language.

Chickens kept commercially at high densities: how much is packed in here, what a history of evil! In its succinctness and seeming felicity of alliteration (*kept commercially*), the scientist negotiates a way of retaining the traditional and familiar idiom of *keeping birds* while doubtless knowing very well that the kinds of industrial conditions in which these birds are confined or coffined is a nightmare world away from the modest farmer keeping a few chickens ranging freely in the yard. What is painfully elided here, as in other such purported science writing, is the enormity of agency, in other words of a mechanised process of torturing and gradually putting to death countless thousands of birds, a process that must appear not to be governed by any individual human agency. Comparisons here with throwing people into ovens or gas chambers are perfectly legitimate. Thus Birkhead writes: *the poultry industry amputates the tips of the birds' beaks.* At least he calls a spade a spade and says *amputates.* If he had resorted here, once again, to the egregious euphemism of trimming (*The poultry industry trims...*), the vile whiff of the burnt body, flung scorned and cauterised, the bill of no rights and squawking hell salon might have been too difficult to miss. But who does the wicked work of amputating the millions of beaks? Human individuals are not involved, it is the *industry*.

All of this is but a scratching about, to spare a passerine thought for science and the military. The military? Has even a mention been made of the military, honourable or otherwise? It could scarcely make happy reading. Things are painful as it is, excruciatingly so, on and off, over a very prolonged period, in truth all the time, not simply on and off, as if once you have had your beak amputated you could have it put back on again, but off, the phantom limbs of phantom beaks, permanently off, if not for this commercially kept creature then for the next, all the time, daylightless day after day, week after week, year upon year, decade beyond decade.

What goes for the scientist goes for the military: a fine case of *killing two birds with one stone*, you may say. But, to be fair, an old bird like you would be unlikely to feel like saying anything much at all, in the immediate aftermath of having had half your mouth amputated. And yet, if this is not the place to elaborate on the relationship between ornithology and the military, on scientific and military discourse, on the military or quasi-military killing of birds down the centuries, where would be? And where better, too, to sample the toxic cocktail, the mutually backslapping special relationship of American and British English in its most lethal forms?

Bracketing off for a rainy day extended rumination on the immense, farcical dependency of the military on ornithomorphic language, thanks to all those small unkind acts of naming everything from muskets to snipers to cockpits, hawks to doves, aircraft wings to tails, jet fighters to missiles (the Harrier jet, the Hawk TMk1, the Sea Sparrow RIM-7 missile), anything that flies and kills, the slow and torturous putting to death of names in the service of the military, let us for the moment simply ask: why would you choose to put a military airbase next to a bird sanctuary, any more than you would choose to put a nuclear power station on a major earthquake fault-line?

In this context, an appreciation of the *seaside surrealism* of 'The Kestrel and the Hawk' by Nicholas Royle (b. 1963) might be notably enhanced by consulting the official Royal Air Force website description of the story's location, RAF Valley. Consider, for example, this account of the Bird Control Unit (BCU):

> *The BCU uses a variety of methods and equipment to scare birds away from the airfield and in particular those critical areas where birds may endanger a departing or arriving aircraft. This variety is essential to ensure that the flocking birds do not become complacent and accustomed to the scaring methods. Methods include the Digi-Scare, which simulates the distress call of a bird caught by a predator, thus scaring other birds away. This is generally the most*

efficient method. The Vari Pistol, which uses shell crackers to disperse a large flock of birds, is also an effective method. General habitat management is also important in deterring flocks of birds from settling at the airfield. This includes the maintenance of the grass by ensuring that it is kept to an appropriate height as well as using weed killer to kill the plants on which birds may feed. However, the height of the grass may easily be affected by long periods of sunshine or rain and so constant monitoring is needed. Inspection of the surrounding area ensures that the habitat is made unfavourable for birds, thus preventing roosting. All bird activity for the day is recorded in a log, which is then compiled into statistics on a monthly basis which are audited annually by the CAA, Safety Regulation Group.

Discover for yourself, discover yourself. Enlist! Join up! You too could have fun with the BCU, not just with endangered birds but with endangering them! Never let these birds become complacent, soldier! Simulate the distress calls for yourself with our state-of-the-art Digi-Scare. Or just shoot 'em up with shell crackers! Wipe 'em out with weedkiller. And don't forget: *grass grows*. Classic effect of sun and rain. Look it up, soldier, constant surveillance, never let a detail go, check it out, all part of BCU responsibilities, note it in the log, preventing roosting, statistics and auditing, monthly basis, habitat management, make it totally unfavourable. Bio-acoustic bird dispersal systems R Us!

'The Kestrel and the Hawk' has been the subject of unwarranted criticism: the young man from the *Gazette* speaks of *prose of jaw-sagging ineptitude*, for instance, declaring it *ill-formed, flatulent and haphazard.* For us, on the contrary, it is one of several thoughtful and intriguing short texts with an ornithological bent that Royle has penned, including 'Gannets', 'The Goldfinch' and 'The Bee-Eater'. We would suggest that the journalist in question might better have set his sights on the sort of RAF prose just quoted. Give the author of 'The Kestrel and the Hawk' a break. Not only does he suffer from confusion with someone who shares the same first and last name, the author of 'The Kestrel and the Hawk' is not even the only Nicholas John Royle. For there is at least one other bearing those nominal appendages who also has a thing about birds. Nicholas John Royle (b. 1971): researcher in behavioural ecology, PhD on gulls ('Reproductive Decisions in the Lesser Black-backed Gull *Larus fuscus* and Their Effects on Reproductive Success', University of Durham, 1998), author (as Nick J. Royle) of 'Hatching Asynchrony and Sibling Size Hierarchies in Gulls: Effects on Parental Investment Decisions, Brood Reduction and Reproductive Success' (*Journal of Avian Biology*, 1998), and other works. *Seaside surrealism*, as we were saying. Runs in the name if not the family.

Was it not Patti Smith who once remarked, *I'm a hundred per cent fucked-up, and a hundred per cent military*? Smith meant this as a point of information based on contraries. This was, we now recall, at a poetry reading in Greenwich Village in late June 1977. Someone in the audience had accused her of being fucked-up. She was not close to her microphone at the time, but returned to it in order to make the observation. Despite being fucked-up she was also, in spite of that, at the same time, completely military.

It is possible that what is military is, however, fucked-up, in a different way, militarily speaking. It is possible.

It is not very fashionable or even prudent to speak of the military as fucked-up. It can get you into trouble. But it is still possible. It can land you in a dark place, a space of solitary confinement closely akin to what in medieval times, that is to say in an era when the occasional French idiom was acceptable to English-speaking people, was called an *oubliette*, somewhere worse than a tight corner, something at first glance like a blind (as they say in the US), though on a considerably more constricted, less comfortable scale, and not conceived in such a way as to enable you to look out at the world and observe, but rather confront, in the dark, the consequences of having looked and having been judged to have observed too much or to have allowed others to observe too much, to have said too much about what you observed or to have allowed others to say too much, leaving you in a situation very much like someone kept commercially, as in a sweatshop, at a high density population of one person per oubliette, a hole in the ground, no bigger than a broom cupboard or allotted space on the factory floor, as if you were not, from the very first day, kept commercially, completely in the public eye but in the public eye to be forgotten. It is possible.

There are oubliettes and there are oubliettes. This one, for instance.

It is possible to be a yellow bird and speak of being a yellow bird and be fucked-up as well as military. It is possible to speak of military fuck-up and also of the military as fucked-up. But to be fucked-up in that way you have to be military. You have to be really fucked-up. It is possible.

But how fucked-up, in fact, is that? Why not give US citizenship to starlings? Why not grant them the same rights as other, earlier settlers, of the human variety? This is the focus of an article by Rachel Carson published in *Nature Magazine* in the summer of 1939. She makes the point that, since its introduction into the United States in the early 1890s, *Sturnus vulgaris* has established itself as the most effective avian destroyer of insects considered an enemy to American farmers. She highlights the fact that the US Department of Agriculture itself has heaped praise on this cheerful, industrious little creature. So, as the title of her essay puts it: 'How About Citizenship Papers For The Starling?'

It is not only the sad timing of her question, thanks to the military, thanks, as always, not to *the war*, but to what D. H. Lawrence (making this same distinction) calls *the imbecile wantonness of the war-masters*. Inevitably US newspapers and magazines appearing in the autumn of 1939 and several years thereafter were not likely to be all a-chatter with the matter of recognising this good work on behalf of the American people, and weighing up the pros and cons of granting citizenship, or at least refugee status, to a bunch of birds. The question of military interference on that front was obvious. But it is also clear that the strategy Carson adopted was awry: an attempt at a certain kind of military intervention of her own, admirable up to a point, was also manifestly naïve, if poignantly childlike. No amount of literal or straightforward anthropomorphism can pass muster in the military fuck-up of language with which we are here preoccupied.

It hardly needs to be pointed out how what is fucked-up is the military fuck-up militating towards a bigger military fucked-upness. This is not a matter of some miserable one-off clusterfuck. It is simply a basic element in the monitoring. Keep quiet, look out and soon enough the images parade into view. Yes, here they come now. In the first instance it's mostly men, in poverty traps (like rings around birds' feet, not totally debilitating, capable of writing their name, *joining the military* as the seemingly seamless saying has it), kept commercially, designed to kill other people, these days mostly women and children, but also other men, and fuck them of course, or think they do, and fuck them over and fuck them up so badly that if they're not actually dead they may as well be, they and them amounting to the same, there no longer being in this scenario anyone non-military, no human on earth exempt from exhibiting a military meaning, civilians as much as non-civilians fucked, every single one of them, man, woman and child, starting with the fact of being *kept commercially*. Fuck that, you may be thinking. If we can't sort out dignity of life for chickens, what hope the humans? But don't fret: you're not actually reading this, even if for a moment you imagined you were.

Military bird-killing is hardly a recent phenomenon. Put to one side the issue of grouse or pheasant seasons, the quasi-military organisation of the so-called countryside and birds bred up to be shot down in warm blood in their tens of thousands (on such swathes of England and Scotland as are kept commercially to be fit for purpose). Take the case of the sparrow. As a Victorian gentleman had admirably set out before him, while he partook of a post-prandial port and cigar at his London club, reclinin' in his armchair in February 1865, castin' an eye over a paragraph in the latest copy of the St James Magazine: *Sparrowcide is not a modern crime, but was extensively practised by our forefathers.* And in the subsequent century this crime was to be repeatedly practised, all over the world, from the Sparrow War in Boston, Massachusetts (1889–99) to the mass exterminations demanded by Chairman Mao in China in the 1950s (with millions killed in the countryside, plus a modest 800,000 or so in Beijing itself). War, after all, is never merely about humans. In terms of the sympathy stakes, compared with human genocide, the massacring of birds is always going to come second. But sparrowcide is a thing of the past. Like art, it has been so successful its point of reference is all but gone. Perhaps, as a recent study by Kim Todd puts it, *the house sparrows and the insects that feed them are failing under some unknown aspect of the urban environment that will soon affect people, too. Perhaps the vanishing sparrows are telling us something about the state of the cities that we can't yet perceive with our own senses.*

Science and the military go hand in hand, botching English, speaking the same drivel. Try to get the miliscient or scientilitary to sit down and read a couple of phrases of Shakespeare, for instance, and observe the happy catastrophe that ensues: *We defy augury. There's a special providence in the fall of a sparrow.* Your average military man, even if he were English-speaking, these days probably wouldn't even recognise the words in question. But let's speculate for a moment on someone who's up for it, a sort of fantasy militia type, needn't be too advanced in years, but no mere stripling either, handsome fellow, prime of life, seen a fair bit of action in Iraq and Afghanistan, no life-threatening injuries sustained but witness to plenty and more, a man who reckons he studied *Hamlet* at school or at any rate saw a performance and has an at least vague suspicion that Shakespeare might possibly have something to say about war and national sovereignty and the machinations of power, about the different *-cides*, from suicide to genocide, all of them coming together in a grand finale to be de-*cided* in true military fashion, blood everywhere, bodies piled high, good clean conventional massacre, thoroughly beguiling *cide*-show for all the family, run through with poison or blade, mothers and uncles and unborn children and everyone lying on top of one another ready for collection at the end of the day, at the end of the road, Basra road-side bombing cider with rosy remembrance it till the day I die.

Uphill battle to bring our fantasy militia man back, even in shuttle diplomacy, if we were to slip the name of Horatio into the discussion, such a damned fine military name, smacks of top brass, think of Nelson, think of Hornblower, damned clever chap Shakespeare, managed singlehandedly to turn Horatio into the name of a hero, militarised indefinitely, like contamination from depleted uranium in UN weapons in Iraq and Libya and Afghanistan drifting into future generations. So let us simply suppose that Hamlet is addressing his words not to his beloved friend but to someone, anyone who happens to be listening, or if they're not listening that's perfectly fine too. *We defy augury*, he recalls, and this military gentleman is no one's fool or rather yes, of course he's a fool, utterly stupid, but not merely on his own account, he's a kept fool, a fool kept commercially by no one in particular ('the industry', as we may call it) and therefore, in that respect, no one's fool, as we were saying this military fellow has the sort of brain that is currently being commercially developed in the miliscient or scientilitary field of prosthetics research specifically in order to enable it to configure objects and movements, for example in a desert, sweeping by in one's tank, as one does, or in a prospective sniping scenario on a street in Baghdad or Beirut, to allow the military man's perception to be enhanced so that he can take in more of what his brain, being a bit ahead of him so to speak, has taken in without having time to tell.

He has registered, in other words, that *we defy augury* is not something that the protagonist fellow, the tragic dude Hamlet, says near the beginning, it's a sure-fire case of last ditch, yes, lights out, all coming back to him now, the end is approaching and it's the moment the hero is finally manning up, manning up, did I hear someone say, get back in your oubliette, you heard what I said, are you disobeying me, captain?

We defy augury, thinks our military fantasy man as he starts to loosen his belt, having already deposited his handgun in its appropriate place of regulation safety, and set himself up for a regimental smoke and tipple before turning in: does that mean Hamlet means there is a tendency to defy predictions, *we* being people besides himself, he himself being a bit aloof from the battlefield? Or is he saying *we*, meaning all of us, we all have a tendency to do this? I mean to say, *Is it? Do we?* Or is he saying: *Right now, for the first time in my life really, in a gesture so remarkable that it behoves me to deploy a sort of royal plural, though what I am about to say amounts to throwing to the winds any chance I might ever actually have of becoming king, I hereby defy augury*? And come to think of it, a bit cuckoo as it may sound, can you defy augury, as a matter of fact, without *not* defying it? I mean, as is clear from instances of military prowess down the ages, an act of defiance is an act based on knowledge of what a fellow is defying. How could a fellow defy augury without being wrecked by a recce, I mean to say, without an acknowledgement of the reality of what he is defying?

What I mean is *how* can what-the-devil's-his-name, Hamlet, or Shakespeare, make three simple words so damned un-straightforward, sounds for all the world like a simple statement of defiance, meet with it all the time these days unfortunately, not surprising of course with all the men kept commercially in such intensive conditions, cooped up for the rest of their decades what with post-traumatic stress disorders of ever-proliferating subtlety and variety as more and more of the ignorant beggars come to their senses if they've still got any to come to, eh what, but it's defiant beyond the call of duty, can't for the life of me make out who's speaking and about whom or what, dammit, birdlime wordlime, makes a booby-trap of my brains as to what is going on in the *augury*, bird-word if ever one flew up from a thicket, bound to be a sniper, shoot it down, soldier, snipe it, shooter, I mean to say does one or other of them, author or character, or both at the same time, dammit, double vision now, stymie blimey, scarcely see the glass in front of my face, I'd like to know, does one or both of the blighters already have the sparrow in mind before there's the scarcest mention of augury, that antique business of divining via the flight of birds still perched or aflutter inside each one of us with every flash of the future echoing or imagined, every inaugural gesture, every word we breathe, if we are on song?

Where were we? Ah yes: *It was mid-July and the dawn chorus of sparrows had been going on for some minutes.* Come upon a matter-of-fact statement of that nature, think nothing of it. Just another daybreak, nothing new under the sun, motley crew of sparrows starting up the diurnal chirrup once more. But any moment perhaps the last. Your sparrow knows it as your *homo sapiens* never does, till the end perhaps, days all a haze, incapable of a true thought of the sparrowhawk or other heartstopper, must be what old age is like, finally start to realise what it's like to be a sparrow. Never actually arrive of course. Blind date, eh what?

Completely squiffy and hawkeyed at the same time. Real bruiser of a headache coming on. Pop something quick. Best you could hope for is, Bede was it? Quip about a fellow's life the duration of a sparrow's flight through the officers' mess? Would the bard have needed Bede for the Prince to be a sparrow? Absolutely, quite. You see, I mean, ambush! Ambush!

I mean to say *in the fall of a sparrow*, not just your standard military prudence and foresight but something out of the ordinary, *special providence*, special forces eh what, and not just the fellow on stage saying it or the bard or Bede, but the Lord himself, or whoever the wise old owl is, concealed behind St Matthew's gospel when the good book says, *Are not two sparrows sold for a farthing? and one of them shall not fall on the ground without your Father.* Which I frankly take to mean not that God falls, gung-ho wrestling match on the deck with a couple of feathered friends rather the worse for wear, won't catch me making that sort of rummy blunder, but sparrows in Damascus or Galilee or Jerusalem or wherever it is we're talking about here are cheap as chips, at least back in the day when chips were cheap, and you could buy yourself a sparrow-supper, decent portion, brace of birds, eh what, for the then local currency equivalent of an Elizabethan fraction of a penny, especially if you're paying in US dollars, we'd be talking about a dime, less than that, less than a cent, a giveaway is what I'd understand the Christian message to be, and even at that rate the Lord himself, overseer of all napalm and surgical bombing, fair game for mutual assured destruction, master of the universe and all its parallels, watches over, all his ducks in a row, and thus knows and can teach the world to sing that there's a special providence in the fall of a sparrow and it's entirely irrelevant, seems to me, whether the bally bird in question consists of one or two sparrows, and whether it's Matthew or Bede or Shakespeare, Hamlet or the Lord himself, or some delirious chorus of sparrows taking out two humans with one rhetorical flourish, one in the hand, two in the ambush, entirely irrelevant whether or not the sparrow or sparrows fall to the ground before you buy them, unless they're off, something rotten in the state of sparrow-meat, little Cockney devils, don't want your dinner spoiled that way, awake half the night puking your guts up, pull yourself together, manning up, I said get back in that oubliette this minute, soldier, back off. Just as it's frankly unclear, in my current state, whether what happens is in point of fact a deadly fall, terminal tailspin, or a swoop, calculated mock-flutter to the ground in which the plucky fellow, takes after me after all, survives the fall, having really just feigned death, staged a dissimulation like the proverbial actor strutting and fretting, as if for the sparrowhawk who keeps a vigilant bird's eye view over all the proceedings, including God and Matthew or whatever the voice of authority is, can't question it, soldier, orders are orders, if a fall is a swoop or a swoop a fall that swops with a swoop, air tattoo, too-too! too-too!

Always be Farnborough, even after I'm gone, practically see it from the garden, not that I'll see it after that, not that I can picture being gone, into a passing out tale-end, immortal immaterial, right in front of my eyes, stymie blimey, not the slightest operational planning decisive action idea what Shakespeare is on or on about. I mean is it a godly or ungodly remark, a respectful confirmation or quiet devastation of the words of the good book? Does the defiance of augury inaugurate the bally observation about the sparrow? Or was the bally sparrow in someone or other's mind or minds already in position before the defiance, if it is defiance? And why on earth would anyone think of telling the future via the avian? Have a flutter for whom the bird tolled, don't tweet us we'll tweet you, war bling and warbling, fly in the face of meaning, terrible mistweetment, mushroom cloud oubliette and freedom fries, so stoned I can't think, brains shuffled off their mortal perch, must be all this military chat, stonechat and yellow-breasted, only way to kill it I say.

Watch out for the time-zones, soldier. New world yellow-breasted chat (*Icteria virens*) singing by moonlight in its white spectacles from bright yellow throat eerie insomniac *Witchety, witchety, witchety! cherrk eeeep! Woo-woo-woo! Chek! Wok! Ank-ank-ank!* The other, old world stonechat (*Saxicola torquatus*), first thing in the morning, call of the male resembling the sound of two pebbles being struck together hence its name, two stones with one bird. Simultaneous mutually assured bidirectional intercontinental missile only way to get 'em, soldier! Prepare to fire.

Hide 11

It is a raw winter's morning on an exposed stretch of Norfolk coast. There is brilliant sunshine but a bitter wind. She is wrapped in her warmest winter coat and boots, prepared as best she can for a freezing walk and standing about with her mother's old field-glasses, picking out an avocet here, a sandpiper there, in the shallow water of the intertidal pools and on the adjacent sandflats. She takes a seat in the hide as if finding her way at a theatre after the lights have gone down. She is vaguely aware of other bodies, huddling up this side and that, enabling her to plant herself somewhere near the front and gaze out at the waders and other birds. She stuffs the field-glasses back into a deep pocket in her coat.

She hadn't expected to find herself here. She feels trepidation. She is no birder. Serious birdwatching is to her as foreign as trainspotting. She knows next to nothing about the interior life of twitchers, with their feverish binoculars and telephoto lenses, mist nets and ringings, sightings and list-compilations. If she were in a novel she would have some distinctive, rather enigmatic name such as 'Penelope Menace' – 'Penny' or 'Pen', for short. But she is not in a novel. She is in a hide.

There is a quietness that recalls the undirected anguish pervading an empty corridor in a hospital, or the laceration of leaving the September sunshine and going through the big red door on her first day at primary school. She thinks of London taxi drivers who have the Knowledge, and of birders who have theirs. There is knowledge she will never have and, in the half-light of the hide, it is pressing in on her from all sides. Her mother liked birds but was no Phoebe Snetsinger: she had a good pair of binoculars and carried them when out on long walks in the country, or visiting bird sanctuaries. But it was an interest the daughter had observed and humoured rather than shared. Real birders were obviously men. They must start picking it up from early boyhood. Boys and their fathers. There are, she notices, a couple of mothers and girls here in the hide, but they figure differently. She doubts that they *have the knowledge* in the same way. Ornithology is a man's world, or it is, at least, by and large, written by men.

She is not crazy like Virginia Woolf when the birds start singing to her in ancient Greek. Still something is happening.

You might die tomorrow or before the hour is out. She has thought that very often for many years. But now death appears differently. It has moved distinctly closer, even at moments, it seems, within smelling or tasting distance. It resembles a troubling version of that children's party game where you are at the front with your back to everyone and try to catch one or more of them moving when you turn round. You look at – a woodland scene, a crowded railway station, your room with its simple furnishings. Only death brings death near. That thing, called by whatever fugitive name, has edged up, in camouflaged closeness, but you cannot see where or how.

A girl behind her, who can't be more than thirteen, whispers something to her mother and giggles. Somewhere to her right, one birder mumbles something to another. The woman looks ahead, trying to set aside the mild intrusiveness of other people, the collective smell of rain-jackets, rubber boots and tweeds. In her peripheral vision she picks up the profiles of people with raised binoculars, close to the window. At the same time the hide remains shadowy, and for a moment it is as though some gyrating snowy mass of shadows were passing over her eyelids.

She is not crazy like Woolf when the birds start singing in ancient Greek. Still, as a character called Penelope Menace, she would pass the entire duration of a novel walking about in the Sussex Downs around Rodmell. Every detail of flora and fauna, weather and feeling, history and culture, space and time-consciousness should feature, along with dozens of digressions. On her rambles she would see the stranger painting on the hill. She would follow him through her field-glasses. They would meet. In the end, however, she would be alone. She would wander out into the brooklands to stand at Asham Wharf. She would stand and wait and wait. She would wait at Asham Wharf for Woolf to come washing into view, bubble up from the stony depths and sing to her. But she is not in a novel. She is in a hide.

There is a pressure, a closeness in her chest, as if she were at high altitude, not sea-level. She would like to go to sleep. That would be ridiculous, as she has only just arrived, and in any case there is nowhere to lie down. As she looks out, the pools and sand-flats seem too bright. She takes a deep but quiet breath and apologises to the man sitting on her right, upon whose bulk she fears she may, momentarily, have dropped off.

She recalls, because she was perhaps just dreaming, the extraordinary black and white reeling of *The Private Life of the Gannets*, the sweep of aerial and slow-motion photography of Grassholm, the remote island off the coast of Pembrokeshire, in 1934, the plummy lost world voice of Julian Huxley describing gannets, the time-lapse imaging of the chick breaking out of its egg, its neck for weeks too weak to raise itself. She extracts the blue notebook from her coat pocket, to check the phrase he uses, locating her scribbled reference in the half-light of the hide with pleasing speed: *the most uncanny sense of direction of any living creature.*

She gazes out again into the brilliant cold Norfolk day. Gannets can live to the age of fifty, but in the case of Alexander Korda's film, each one of them is, like all the adult humans in a '30s movie, dead as a dodo.

Why dodo? Why not dead as a *Didus ineptus*, as Linnaeus brutally named it, as if its extinction were mocked in its name, noted in advance? And what of *Homo ineptus*? It's do or die, deed or died, Didus without issue, the oddity of a four-letter word that marries with the four-letter *dead*, double-declutch of impossible egg never hatched to avoid the full-on collision with the four-letter word that repeats itself like a marriage vow deprived of all subject: I do, I do, dodo.

She thinks of the famous comedian, the one who made her father roar with laughter, the absurdity of the dissatisfied customer as the pet-shop owner tries to fob him off with the stuffed bird, the non-existent Norwegian blue parrot *pining for the fjords*, and she thinks of its scarcely audible undersong, an elegy for the eligibility of words. Why *dead*? Why not *bereft of life* as a dodo, *deceased* as a dodo, *expired*, perished, passed away, exanimate or done-for as a dodo, checked out as a dodo from the impossible Hotel Dodo, mortified as any dodo might be bearing, as it has had to, the colossal ineptitude of this deed of naming on its pitiful frame for nearly four hundred years, stuffed stupid name for stupid, dodo as a dodo, doomed, defunct, liquidated?

But if other than *dead* is *no can do*, why pile everything on the dodo's solitary sunk head? Why not *dead as a dusky seaside sparrow*, like the tiny slumped creature in a glass bottle she'd wept at in the Florida Museum of Natural History, its legs stretched out improbably further than it could reach, extinct since 1987? Why not dead as a society parakeet, dead as a paradise parrot, dead as a Mascarene gray parakeet, dead as a Cuban macaw, dead as a laughing owl, dead as a Puerto Rican barn owl, dead as a Mauritius owl, dead as a bushwren, dead as a Guam flycatcher, dead as a nightingale reed warbler, dead as a crested white-eye, dead as a mysterious starling, dead as a slender-billed grackle, dead as a black mamo, dead as an elephant bird, dead as an upland moa, dead as a King Island emu, dead as a crested shellduck, dead as an Amsterdam duck, dead as a pink-headed duck, dead as a New Zealand quail, dead as a Tahiti sandpiper, dead as a great auk, dead as an Eskimo curlew, dead as a Hawkins's rail, dead as a red rail, dead as a Tristan moorhen, dead as a Mascarene coot, dead as a Colombian grebe, dead as a Bermuda night heron, dead as an Olson's petrel, dead as a Guadalupe storm petrel, dead as a passenger pigeon, dead as a Sulu bleeding-heart, dead as a red-moustached fruit dove – all of them eliminated since the dodo walked out of the world, initially without even being noticed, in 1662?

She will never write a book like Helen Macdonald or Mark Cocker or Tim Dee or Esther Woolfson. She doesn't have their experience of birds or ornithological knowledge or indeed any desire to publish her name, let alone her ideas. She is content to observe. Still she cherishes the notebook in which she has been gathering jottings, mainly from essays or books by others, along with a few reflections of her own.

She lowers her long, slender neck (always, she's thought, one of her more attractive features) and returns to the much-fingered blue notebook. Now she sees that the man who was sitting to her right has moved away. The hide feels quieter, colder too.

She has had since girlhood a love of words and poetry. She imagines literature reconceived through flights, songs and visions of birds. With the passing of her mother she has gone back to things, she has followed her to places she scarcely noticed or entirely suppressed at the time. She feels that she is living, as Phoebe Snetsinger felt, on borrowed time. Birdwatching on borrowed time.

In a novel she would wreak havoc. It would not be able to accommodate her. She would weave, singlehandedly, a Penopticon™, transforming the way people see. She would fall in love with a small dark scrivener and have many beautiful children, even if he'd prefer not to. All of them would be a complete menace – not just *in* the novel, but *to* it. *To-to-to-to! Too-too-to-two!* She would give her name to a new kind of writing, a penny menace, in the spirit of the Victorian penny dreadful. It would make all the borders of the text dissolve. Everything would become transparent. A penny for your thoughts – and all for the birds. But she is not in a novel. She is in a hide.

She has a notebook entry on *stream of consciousness*, recording its original appearance in the writings of William James:

> *When we take a general view of the wonderful stream of our consciousness, what strikes us first is the different pace of its parts. Like a bird's life, it seems to be an alternation of flights and perchings.*

For the woman in the hide, on borrowed time, the weight of this *like* has given way, a tiny desiccated twig, *like a bird's life.* Instead there is, in the philosopher's wording, a new reality, already in flight, the bird no more or less metaphorical than the *stream*, in thought's *alternation of flights and perchings.* She imagines this other world, at once new and ancient, in which the privilege blindly handed to the human dries up, the fences, walls and turrets of reason dividing the literal from the metaphorical crumble into ruins. In her chest there is a feeling of something at once irreparable and uplifting.

As James goes on, he seems to recoil from the force of his own poetic insight:

> *The rhythm of language expresses this, where every thought is expressed in a sentence, and every sentence closed by a period. The resting-places are usually occupied by sensorial imaginations of some sort, whose peculiarity is that they can be held before the mind for an indefinite time, and contemplated without changing; the places of flight are filled with thoughts of relations, static or dynamic, that for the most part obtain between the matters contemplated in the periods of comparative rest.*

Her mind meets with another world, not of a Jamesian orderliness where thought is confined to the sentence and every one closed by a full stop, but in a wilder, stranger, less closed movement in which to meet is also, as it was for Chaucer in his *Parlement of Foules*, to dream. Poetry meets with science.

It may be decades before this vision becomes intelligible to others, she supposes, but the study of birds, with all its dream-poetry of resting places, lines of flight, thoughts of relation, is establishing a new conception of the human, of scale and intelligence, space and time. Another knowledge is hatching. The entire regime of the literal is disintegrating. The *like* of *like a bird* is no longer a convincing way of partitioning human from non-human. It is no longer possible to believe in some true and proper language in which to net and capture the life of birds. Never has *like* seemed more like nothing.

In the half-light she winces at the exclamation mark she has inserted alongside the title of John M. Marzluff and Tony Angell's book, *Gifts of the Crow: How Perception, Emotion, and Thought Allow Smart Birds to Behave Like Humans.* From this, as well as from their book *In the Company of Crows and Ravens*, she has learnt all sorts of things. But the chain-dragging heaviness of *how perception, emotion, and thought allow smart birds to behave like humans* reminds her of why she could never write a book herself. Perhaps it is not the authors themselves but the publisher, the insistence on a subtitle that depends on this moribund *like* (to *behave like humans*) and the crass violence of an evocation of avian wonder through an implicit comparison between smart birds and smart phones. As if *perception* or *emotion* or *thought* were secure from the deranging effects of *the gifts* of which these authors write! (Wince!)

Marzluff and Angell are, however, hardly isolated cases. Tim Birkhead's *Bird Sense* makes a corresponding gesture with its apparently blithe but absurd subtitle: *What It's Like to Be a Bird.* It now occurs to her that this tic-like *like*, perhaps more than any other word, signals the massive metamorphosis underway.

The fleetest observation of the red-throated diver, the wagtail, the little grebe beyond the window of the hide confirms that they inhabit the world with an ease and grace unavailable to humans. Ah, dodo, ah, *homo ineptus*! Regardless of how long we remain challenged by the existential anguish of humans not being at home in the world, we must now reckon with the alien actuality of the birds alongside the avian energies of the human mind. *Their fate is our fate*, as Peter Doherty says. But it is not only about *how*, as that impassioned immunologist explains, *birds foretell threats to our health and our world*. It goes all the way down and all the way up. Ethological revolution is in the air. The very language and understanding of *consciousness*, *sense, emotion, thought* and *perception* are on the wing. All of her reading in these few months has pushed her, with a sense of exhilaration as well as almost unbearable sadness, in this direction.

She thinks of Humboldt's parrot, the first and last of its tribe, worthy of a true diatribe. Travelling in South America in around 1800 Alexander von Humboldt encountered a parrot that spoke the language of an extinct tribe, that of the Atures: a true Ature, the only one. That is the beauty of the parrot of the ghosts of words. She recalls Rimbaud's phrase, the sounds of its letters rippling and rearranging themselves in her mind: *Je est un autre, je est un Ature*. Suddenly she pictures a tidal wave, a sort of psychotic oceanic lyricism in which humans might finally live, talk and love, mourn and die in flashes of birdsong. She is not crazy like Virginia Woolf. She is not crazy *like* anyone.

Do, do the dodo. Do the *pollies* in different voices.

She had hoped for a chance to peruse others – spot the twitcher, eavesdrop on bits of conversation, smell out something of the curious reality of the birder and his friends or family relations. But she is so lost in her own thoughts and in the pages of the blue notebook that she scarcely even notices that the hide is emptying out.

She flickers through other scribblings:

Nutcrackers and jays can remember for months the tens of thousands of locations where they cache pine seeds each year. (Marzluff and Angell)

Pigeons are at least as good as humans at memorising and categorising visual images. (Birkhead)

Flamingos can sense rain falling hundreds of kilometres away... So far, no one knows what sense flamingos and other birds use to detect distant rain. (Birkhead)

As we coevolve with other species, not only do we become better at reading their actions, they become better at reading us. (Marzluff and Angell)

Is the feeling of the encroachment of her own death – the sense of its shifting up closer, when she isn't thinking – a peculiar effect of having been increasingly drawn into an awareness of the domain of birds? Or has her research into the world of ornithology and birdwatching, sometimes harried, sometimes patient, been driven by this encroachment?

Consciousness is not the special preserve of the human. It is clear, for example, that crows and ravens think. Her eyes alight on another observation from *Gifts of the Crow*:

The interesting premise that a crow might know what another being is (or is not) thinking is a mental attribute known only in people and our closest primate relatives. This complex cognitive property is

*called possessing a 'theory of mind', and it requires
being able to imagine and consider what others know.*

The eerily mindful corvid, especially the raven, has
always been with us, even if we hadn't noticed. Aristotle
speaks of its *emotive eyes*. The association of ravens with
second sight and unearthly knowledge goes back at least to
the ancient Norse god Odin with his two raven attendants,
Hugin (Thought) and Munin (Memory) – spies who fly away
and gather secrets and come back to perch and whisper into
the god's ears. But now the science is catching up. Another
passage copied out from Marzluff and Angell:

> *The ability to think about the past and plan accordingly
> for the future, projecting oneself forward in time, is
> considered by many to be a unique feature of humans.
> The impressive, integrative prefrontal cortex of our
> brains may enable this handy trick. But given our new
> understanding of birds' brains and the apparent way in
> which their executive centre works like our prefrontal
> cortex, it seems at least possible that birds like corvids
> may employ true time travel.*

Memory, mourning, fear, pleasure, play, pain, fidelity,
learning, risk-taking, planning, minding secrets: all of these
we share with the birds.

And then, as always, there is sex. Most feathered creatures
copulate within two seconds. This aspect of ornithology
makes her smile. Even in the most demure publications, the
sex interest sticks out a country mile. She turns to where she
has jotted down an example. It is a passage about swifts from
Tim Dee's *The Running Sky*:

*They look joined in the air, as if one bird had four
wings, but it is hard to see whether the male actually
rests on the female or holds himself perfectly placed
fractionally above her. Then it is over, the female scoots
away, apparently breaking from beneath the male, and
he banks upwards after her, and I lose them in the
blizzard of other swifts and in my own exhilaration at
what I have just seen. All my birdwatching life seems
to be contained in those two and a half seconds of
black magic.*

On the facing page she has transcribed something from
Jeremy Mynott's *Birdscapes*, in which he includes a number
of photographic stills of naked women, in order to illustrate
an argument about the importance of movement in the
context of what attracts and fascinates us (heterosexual male
observers?) when it comes to birds:

*We are fascinated by their movements, literally
their liveliness. This encompasses all their habits of
locomotion and behaviour – how they hop, run, or
jump on the ground; how they move through bushes
and trees; how they fly in the air; how they swim,
dabble, or dive in water; how they display, court, and
threaten; how they feed, drink, and preen.*

She wonders if there isn't just a faint whiff here of what
Edgar Poe dubiously described as the most poetical topic in
the world, the corpse of a beautiful woman.

Then there's the section in *Bird Sense*, which cannot help
but betray its author's greatest excitement as he comes to
discuss the false penis of the red-billed buffalo weaver:

Holding the bird upside down in your hand, and blowing gently on its underside, reveals the full glory of this bizarre structure.

Birkhead keeps it up for several pages, before telling readers about how one of his postgraduate students, Mark Winterbottom, masturbates the creature:

After twenty-five minutes of manipulation Mark gently squeezed the phalloid organ. The result was spectacular: the wingbeats slowed to a quiver, the entire body shuddered, the feet clenched tightly on to Mark's hand and the male ejaculated. Here was as convincing evidence as one was ever going to get that birds – well, the buffalo weaver at least – have a well-developed sense of touch in their genital region.

Steadying her eyes on the page, she is for a moment in danger of laughing out loud. *Well-developed sense* in the *genital region*! Then, when she realises that the hide is in fact empty, she does. She laughs aloud. It grows into a laughter indistinguishable from a groan. She has never emitted such strange or painful laughter, such a groaning in the spirit of laughter. She stands and goes up to the glass, walking to and fro at the window of the hide, just as a gorilla or orang-utan might, having paced back and forth into insanity, gaze in from the other side. *Copulate. Copulation. Couples. Coupling.* It takes on such hollowness. Ears cupped in the cupidinous cupola of copula. That a term originally meaning grammatical or logical connection should be deemed appropriate for describing sex, as if birds were really parts of sentences... Such well-developed sense!

Everything, she's found, goes back to John Ray. He's the one who declared that *no animal at all is born spontaneously*, thus bringing Aristotle and all who followed him to their knees. It's all about Ray's eggs and how to do things with English. Modern ornithology began with the book that he wrote, based on the notes of his friend Francis Willughby, who died in 1672 at the age of 37. An extraordinary collaboration with the dead, the textual labour of mourning called the *Ornithologia* of Joannes Raius was published in Latin in 1676, and an expanded English edition appeared two years later as *The Ornithology of Francis Willughby*.

Willughby was a dashing young fellow of considerable wealth. Though only seven or eight years his senior, Ray was already teaching at Trinity, Cambridge, when Willughby arrived in 1652. Ray must have fallen in love with him more or less straight away. There would have been looks, brushings, his cape in the dusky light proceeding up the stone steps after dinner, glancing contact while poring over a vellum manuscript in the intoxicating soft candlelight, his desire to touch Willughby, a beautiful young man in his rooms, his wish to stroke the young student's face, to put his fingers to those lips, as they stand, side by side but immeasurably distant, examining the text Ray had wanted to show him, his field-jottings on the subject of local flora in Cambridgeshire. (Later Ray would write the first major history of plants in English.) The Cambridge don tingles and bristles with a longing to lie with the young man, to hang the consequences and drift his hand up inside the student's cape, let it drop down and around and touch in an irrefutable flare of improper passion the handsome boy's posterior.

— *Let me touch you, Francis.*

So, at least, she supposed, a pornographic history of ornithology might have it. No more is known about Ray's sex life than about the courting tricks of the archaeopteryx.

In a novel she might build a publishing house, Menace Books Inc, solely devoted to promoting works of erotic ornithology, flooding the market with a new kind of writing that would subsume internet porn and leave mere *human love interest* along with *human sexuality* unrecognisable, done and dusted in a singular phantasmagoric, apocalyptic birdbath. But she is not in a novel. She is in a hide.

Ray also propounds an enlightened conception of the suffering of birds and other non-human animals. She has noted a moment in *The Wisdom of God* (1691) when he counters Descartes' idea that birds, for example, are merely soulless automata:

Should it be true, that beasts are automata or machines, they could have no sense or perception of pleasure or pain, and consequently no cruelty could be exercised towards them; which is contrary to the doleful significations they make when beaten or tormented, and contrary to the common sense of mankind.

For her, the intensified feeling of borrowed time is inseparable from a new humility, a sharp sense that these waders in and around the pool beyond the window in the icy brightness of this Norfolk day have just as much weight in the world as she does. Did Phoebe Snetsinger feel something of that after discovering she had been invaded by a cancer for which she felt obliged to refuse all conventional medical treatment? And didn't birdwatching in Alaska cure her?

With such a tilt and transvaluation of the world everything might begin anew. She need not even raise her head to gaze out and confirm their enduring presence beyond the window. Closing her notebook and laying it beside her on the bench, she cups her face in her hands. A snatch of poetry occurs to her: *Imprisoned in this lonely den, obscured and buried from the sights of men...* But she cannot think where, if anywhere, it comes from.

She, too, is anonymous – she who can never be Penelope Menace or known by any other name. Her vision of another world is inspired by the kinds of disorientating, inhuman knowledge emerging from science, but it would also be a revolution of the poetic. And only now she registers something that happened earlier: it must have been when she shut the notebook and set it down on the bench. Only now does the memory emerge. A slip of paper had fallen out and fluttered to the floor. She picks it up, her senses already attuned to what it is, even though it is a couple of months since she last looked at it. It is a single folded sheet, faded in four differently sunned little rectangles, the creases at the centre mere slits from repeated consultation in years long gone. It is the one and only letter she has from her mother to her father, from the days when they were courting, more than sixty years ago. It wasn't her mother who showed it to her. She'd only discovered it after her mother's death, zipped up in a concealed flap of her father's old wallet: strangest cache. As she carefully unfolds and once again reads ('Darling... Why are you so far away? ... Did we really have two long weeks together? I miss you dreadfully, especially as I write... Have you found my little fern and given it some water? It was left in the pocket on <u>my</u> side of your car...'), the tears stream uncontrollably down her face, just as when she first opened the letter. There is no other remaining trace of her parents' love life. Alone with this faded, friable scrap of handwriting of no import to anyone else in the world, she weeps at the love that made her, at the thought of a personal conjugation as remote and eerie as that of birds.

And as her tears subside, she thinks of Ray's dictum: *Good words cool more than cold water.*

Words can be things, like soulless automata, but they can also generate new worlds, new ways of life. Alongside all the scientific breakthroughs in relation to birds, something is happening to the words. There is a spectral pedigree – no need to crane her neck for it – from Chaucer's parliament to the brainfever birds of Anna Kavan, from the Upstart Crow to jackdaw Kafka, from birds' worth in Wordsworth and redbreast Blake to all the jays Keats, Clare and Baker, from Emily D's thing with feathers to Stevens' thirteen ways of foreign song, from Thomas Browne's sparrow-camel to her beloved Cixous' ostrich, words or wounds in birds and bards in dribs and drabs slowly sublime, Norfolk broad canvas of a new earth and heaven.

Darkling I listen. In these three words she feels something of her vision, the synaesthesia of what cannot see, sweeping through the musical and melancholy song of a nightingale that is also death in a sleepy requiem of soft names, words that dissolve, disordering speech, darkling the I, not I, the bird, a common noun a proper name, adjective, present participle picking up and replaying in a warbling delirium the music of Cleopatra's *darkling world* and Helena's *O wilt thou darkling leave me?* with the sad mad Fool in *Lear* who supposes the baby cuckoo would bite off the head of a hedge-sparrow and the wakeful bird that *sings darkling* from Milton's *shadiest covert*, the voice, nestled there, suddenly visible, for the soft incense of a beloved lost one, a poetic love-making with the alien actuality of the birds, another parliament summoned, occupying new space, peopling as darkling creatures meeting times to come.

She rises and makes her way towards an exit. As she does so she finds she must manoeuvre around the foot of an imposing ladder. Someone appears to be coming down, directly overhead. She realises that it is a woman who is holding, in her left hand, a pair of old field-glasses identical to her own.

Hide 12

Thomas Hardy remembers, when he was about four years old,

> *being in the garden at Bockhampton with his father*
> *on a bitterly cold winter day. They noticed a fieldfare,*
> *half-frozen, and his father took up a stone idly and*
> *threw it at the bird, possibly not meaning to hit it.*
> *The fieldfare fell dead, and the child Thomas picked it*
> *up and it was as light as a feather, all skin and bone,*
> *practically starved. He said he had never forgotten*
> *how the body of the fieldfare felt in his hand: the*
> *memory had always haunted him.*

This is one of the last things that Hardy is thought to
have written, dictating the words to his second wife. It is a
near-death recollection of earliest childhood. What is going
on in this confession to having been haunted all one's life by
the memory of the body of a bird?

The ghost of a bird in the hand. It is perhaps to this
memory that Hardy pays oblique homage in his novel
The Hand of Ethelberta, when he describes his heroine's
response to an unpleasant practical joke:

> *Ethelberta might have fallen dead with the shock, so*
> *terrible and hideous was it. She neither shrieked nor*

fainted; but no poor January fieldfare was ever colder, no ice-house more dank with perspiration, than she was then.

But here the fieldfare has already been snapped up, subordinated within the machine-like functioning of comparative metaphor, along with the ice-house. The sense of melodrama – the stagey, dark comedy in the hyperbolic *terrible and hideous* and the anthropomorphic *perspiration* – is quite different from the tone of Hardy's childhood reminiscence about the fall of the fieldfare and the feeling of it, *as light as a feather,* in his hand, *all skin and bone.*

Such experiences may come in early years or in later life. A *hide* could also be a name for this kind of memory, a fugitive place, an experience altering with each visitation, a haunt of remembrance that watches over who we are or might become.

Hide 13

In what tone should we try to speak or write about birds? With what ear should we attend to our own ineptitude? 'Hide' would also refer to the kind of phantomatic audio-booth in which to explore such questions.

Consider the following transcript of an audio-recording, for example, bearing in mind that it was originally the product of a speech synthesiser using a text-to-speech system:

*Birds are very complex animals. Humans are very complex too. Birds have great sensitivity and grace. The same cannot always be said of humans. Birds are responsive – to one another, but also often to humans. Usually they just fly away. Humans can be responsive too – but not usually to birds. Humans have a hard time with birds. Often they kill them. They also eat them. Some birds taste better than others. Many people eat chickens. People eat many chickens. People also eat turkeys. People eat many turkeys. Americans can eat as many as 46 million turkeys in a single day. Chickens and turkeys are more or less flightless birds that people can keep and kill without any great inconvenience or difficulty. Most people are too busy or lazy to do this, however, so they buy their birds to **eat killed** by somebody else. The people who kill the birds are anonymous. When people go to buy* their freshly killed bird in order to eat it, the packaging does not advise the consumer of the identity of the killer. Before eating the freshly killed bird, it is necessary to prepare the dead body and cook it. Most people know this. Sometimes people do not, or are too hungry to care. These people can become very sick. It is not common practice to eat the entire bird, even when it is cooked. Often it is the breast or leg that is eaten. Most people know this. It is odd that it is called the breast or leg, since these are also names for **human body-parts**. Most people do not think about this. Sometimes the bird is not freshly killed but was killed some months previously. When this happens, it is called **frozen**. Some birds taste pretty bad. They taste so bad that people don't even try to eat them. Interestingly, these are also the birds that come to receive the honour of being designated a national symbol. For example, people do not eat the American bald eagle, the English robin, the kiwi of New Zealand, the orange-tufted sunbird of Palestine, the Swedish common blackbird (which is to say, the woosel cock, also known as **Turdus merula**) or the raggiana bird of paradise of Papua New Guinea. People do not eat the herring gull either, but the herring gull is not a national bird. The distinction of being designated a national bird is strange. Some people might not regard it as an **honour**. The bird is not consulted. Despite being highly responsive, a bird such as the great white pelican of Romania or the gyrfalcon of Iceland is not able to respond to enquiries about whether or not they would like to be a **national symbol**. The concepts of nationality, nationalism and national sovereignty are alien to birds. Scarcely any birds are confined to a specific national territory but even where they are, as in the case of certain island habitats far distant from other landmasses, these birds are not even mildly nationalistic. On the contrary, birds are known for their predisposition to flit abode, flying considerable distances between different countries and even different continents. When they do this, it is called **migration**. Humans also migrate. For birds and humans alike, this can result in suffering or death. Birds are not made to suffer and die for transgressing national borders as such, but humans are. It is also possible to migrate information. Cells and organs, too, can migrate or be migrated. The more the word **migrate** occurs, the less grating it may sound, but in fact it grates a lot. It grates terribly. People talk about **migration** crisis, but they do not talk about the absurdity of the concepts of nation state and national sovereignty in the context of the complexity, sensitivity and responsiveness of birds. People have a hard time with birds. Many people would rather not even acknowledge their existence. People find some birds scary. Some people find all birds scary. All birds are scary. Birds can be scary on account of the threatening nature of their beaks and claws, the way they look at people, and their capacity to startle or disturb with their sudden **inexplicable** movements. Even a chicken, carefully observed, may become as terrifying as a dinosaur. This is not altogether surprising, since chickens are closely related to those **terrible lizards**. Birds are also scary on account of their eerie superiority over humans in terms, for example, of hearing and seeing. Birdsong may provide the basic measure of human aspirations in the fields of music and poetry, but the score is only partially accessible. For birds, acoustic territories of fear and desire operate at other sonic levels, far richer and more resonant than what is available to the echolocationless cloth ears of humans. Birds observe *humans in ways that humans, at least until very recently, have scarcely begun to twig. Antique metaphors of **bird's eye view** or **eagle-eyed** need to see an optician. Human paranoia has to be reconceived. Birds watch humans with inconceivable precision. This is called **birdwatching**. The falcon's eye contains two foveas, the human only one. But this is not a characteristic peculiar to hawks or eagles. The great gray shrike, for example, a little creature despite its name, can spot a hawk literally a mile off. Just as humans lack the acuity of a second fovea, so the range and intensity of their colour-perception is **lacklustre**. With the benefits of ultraviolet vision birds see past humans, see the traces that they will have been, in lights no human's seen. All birds are scary. Nevertheless, birds have habits that attract and intrigue. They arouse **human curiosity**. Humans speak of some birds, such as the great gray shrike, as little, and others, such as the golden eagle, as big. It is all too easy to assume that there is a **pecking order** when it comes to size. Humans think of themselves as more important because they are bigger than birds. They have a hard time thinking about anything except in terms of their own size. Some humans in their dreams see giant birds. There is, for example, the giant loy, white and gray, flightless but wandering this way and that, **striding above the circular crumbling buildings** of the small Devon town, as if abandoned, crying out for a dream salvage team. Just as there are stories of giants in human form, so there are myths of giant birds, such as the simurgh and the roc. These birds may originally have been human dream-incidents. It is also possible that the stories about them derive from ancient, **unrecorded sightings** of dinosaur fossils. As in the case of the terrifying prehistoric chicken, some people are haunted by images and intuitions of* colossal birds. The **gigantic house sparrows** in Vancouver, Canada, created by Myfanwy MacLeod, illustrate this spookiness. It is the sense of scale that is disquieting. Really big birds can be tiny, and tiny birds can become frighteningly large. Some people have a hard time imagining life as a bird. Others, such as John Keats, scarcely give it a second thought: if a sparrow come before my window, I take part in its existence and pick about the gravel. All birds have feathers, collectively known as **plumage**. Sometimes they are brightly coloured. Sometimes they are not at all. There are times when being brightly coloured would be tantamount to signing one's own death warrant. Sometimes birds blend perfectly into their surroundings. When this happens, they are described as **cryptic**. Birds hatch out of eggs that the mother deposits outside her own body. When this happens, it is called **laying eggs**. In order to generate an egg, it is necessary to up one's calcium intake dramatically. So, for example, the calcium required for the creation of a robin's egg is crucially dependent on the **exoskeleton of the woodlouse**. Birds spend an enormous proportion of their waking lives consuming or looking for scran. Most of them lack the ability to keep **scran supplies** inside their bodies, as the additional cargo would make it impracticable for them to fly. [**Sounds muffled. Audio ends.**]

Hide 14

'Are you all deaf?' asks the undertaker. As if auditory space closed down and in this all-but-psychic deafness, for Beethoven the stuff of dreamier and more numerous variations than had heretofore (*six*, *eight*) tinkled in the human ear, someone might be remembered not as he was or might have been, but as he *never could have been*. For the name as misnomer came.

Let us sing and reel, reel and sing out the real, in a paean (*peent!*) to the woodcock.

And let us add a jizz to jazz, sweeten these sounds of the impossible, dreaming of a music fit for the dead and the as yet unborn, to focus not on the Eurasian, or rarer New Guinea, Javan, Moluccan, Salawesi or Bukidnon, but on the American woodcock (*Scolopax minor*). The jazz-loving undertaker never in all his days encountered such a creature. He never set foot, let alone went birding, in North America. He hadn't the remotest knowledge of it, even through TV or hearsay.

No hunting blind is needed for its observation or for its shooting, photographic or firearmed. But take your place for one last dance, here in another unique American hide for two. *Too-too-too-too!* (After this, I tell you, you're on your own.)

The history of its Eurasian counterpart (*Scolopax rusticola*) is a document in madness. In England, worse

313

than a sitting duck, its name is synonymous with folly and stupidity: for five hundred years and more, a woodcock was not only a bird, but a foolish or stupid person, someone who was duped just as easily as the bird was trapped in springe or gin. 'Now is the woodcock near the gin', to recall a line from *Twelfth Night*. Not that Shakespeare saw things in such simpleton terms. Without falling into birdolatry, the swan of Avon knew the score. It's about the gins of language. As with the old doofus Polonius warning his daughter Ophelia about Hamlet's love letters as *springes to catch woodcocks*, it has to do with the traps of writing, humans caught up reading. Always, too, there is a shadowiness about the woodcock, death in the wings. Thus elsewhere in *Twelfth Night* Feste jests that you might *fear to kill a woodcock, lest thou dispossess the soul of thy grandam*. And at the end of *Hamlet*, when Laertes in his dying words describes himself as *a woodcock* caught *in his own springe*, ornithomorphism meets its maker. Whoever imagined anything more brilliantly stupid than a woodcock devising its own death-trap?

The ignominy of 'woodcock' (= *a stupid person*) spread to North America: John Audubon remarks on the ineptness of the idiom in his essay on 'The Booby Gannet' in 1832. But for the average American hunter today it's more about the need to get over the lewd jokes the name raises, ha ha. Come in handy at some point, he could say to hisself, beautiful late afternoon early October, hunting alone in the Michigan woods, complete in regulation bright orange vest, no more observed than the implicit sexism of calling a woodcock a woodcock when only half the species could even in theory merit such a name.

Here in our last-chance American hide for two, we might observe the flickerings of feeling – between affection and belittlement – in some of its alternative appellations:

timberdoodle, bogsucker, night partridge, mudsnipe, brush snipe, hokumpoke, *bécasse*, big-eye, mudbat.

In England, the woodcock has been proverbially easy to catch and kill or keep muffled, but today in the US the emphasis is on the challenge, on how *wily* the bird is, but how *worthwhile* to kill (with or without the aid of pointer dogs).

The woodcock: always about trapping, hunting down or killing, death or the preparation for death. Never about the midst of life.

So tough, being a hunter! The woodcock is not a problem size-wise, but thanks to those elliptical wings it's quick and it breaks super-late when disturbed. Still, you can use just about any kind of shotgun: 12-gauge, 20-gauge, take your pick. And another tip: once up, it might prove slothful or zippy, but if confronted with its acrobatic marvels, relax! Just let it finish its corkscrew flight *before* you shoot!

Seek it out in the mossy regions, along the banks of rivulets and boggy bottoms!

O crepuscular and cryptic creature!

Human shadower, being of twilight, old timer in two – *Two-two-two-two!* Lover of dusklight, singing with bill and feathers of uncertain enlightenment. *Too-too-too-too!*

What words to shoot at you? What adjectival *noms de plume*?

If you are sitting on the ground and someone comes to disturb, you are not to be flushed: you *freeze*.

One more metaphor in your coffin.

They call you *game bird*. What a turd of a word for a bird. Feel the killing weight of the language lobby, where the human is the only game in town. The very term rules out any thought of games for you, the play of life in you, to you (*Too-too-too-too!*).

Ten to twelve inches long, your body, say the hunters and birders, is *stocky, plump, tubby, rotund.* They don't say *obese*: that anthropomorphism would be merely gross. Let's say a prolate spheroid: in an American twister to Lewis Carroll, you might be a football and win the Super Bowl. Played in the appropriate surroundings, none of the team-players could pick up your whereabouts. Your mottled brown-tan-black-gray-yellow disappears you in the leaf litter. But you evade detection even in forest openings and old fields, wooded riversides and wet meadows.

Cryptic isn't in it.

You, timberdoodling quietness, canonical work of leaf literature.

Short-legged, you move slowly and with care across the woodland floor. But then you dance an eerie jig. You push your front leg down on the earth and seem to rock, bob, thrust, jive, don't jive me, jazz, I love it, yes, don't give me this! Pulsation *push out*, jazz, don't jive me, thrust, *push on*, yes, follow this, my love. Perhaps, suggest some birders, the woodcock (like the herring gull) is pressing on the ground to stir its prey. Or listening with its feet.

Let's suppose that the national symbol of the United States is not the bald eagle but the woodcock. So much to be thought anew!

Your bill is remarkably long, slender and prehensile. Almost incredibly, the upper mandible of its dark tip is flexible: this enables you to open and close the tip of your bill even when it is buried in the ground. (Audubon's beautiful but garish picture of a threesome gathered close on a grassy bankside bordering mud includes one with bill buried deep in the mud, surrounded by a dozen earlier sink-holes. His painting puts the *bird* back in *buried*.) By day you hide in thickets, deploying this extraordinary bill to probe in damp soil for succulent earthworms. (Any impulse to call you an early bird should be checked: you have been around only for five or ten million years.) But you will also sink to insect larvae, ants, spiders, centipedes and millipedes, snails and beetles.

Then come your crepuscular displays. You, the male woodcock, corkscrew for or at or to the female. *To-to-to-to! Two-two-two-two!* But numbers and prepositions all lose track. During dusk in spring and summer it's your *sky dance*. In British English there is a word for this: *roding*. Like *zigzagging*, it is a verb best kept in present participle form. On the ground you emit a highly distinctive sound that has been established in birder handbooks as a *peent!*

Peent! Not pained or pined or pint or pant or peed or point or punt or pent or pinned or plaint but *peent!* For you, a paean to come: it cannot be a song of triumph, only of praise and admiration.

Peent! Some people hear or transcribe it as a loud buzzy *bzeep!* or a nasal *nzeet!* or – why not? – *pzeet!* or *pzeep!* or *bzeent!* or *pzeent!* or *zneent!* How much more richly convolved an English dictionary would be, if it sought to include all the variations on such notation and all the dusklight uncertainty that surrounds them?

Peent! Then you take to the air, high, high over the treetops, *too-too-too-too*ing upwards, two to three hundred feet in the air, before roding, spiralling, skydance-diving, sweeping, banking, lurching, veering about like the mad amateur we all are, at least sometimes, in our dreams. And so you go with bill and wing performing your electrifying body-song, sky-writing, mixing bat and owl-like, twittering, chippering, whistling, bubbling, warbling, smack-kissing before landing in silence on the ground, close to a hoped-for female.

Radically amateur, your display may very easily be for a creature long since departed, mated with another and already hatched chicks. Some might view this as confirmation of your forlorn stupidity. But male or female, queer or straight, polygamous or monogamous, isn't it also the very aim of art? Isn't that what music, painting, poetry is, trying to reach a loved one absent or dead?

Here in this American hide, in our last dance saloon, what finally allures are your round gentle darkling eyes. Set far back and high on either side of your round head, they enable you to watch for danger even or especially when your bill is buried in the earth. Their evolution has gone along with the development of an upside-down brain, something we all need in the decades ahead. *Peent!* They are unlike the eyes of any other creature. You have 360° horizontal and 180° vertical vision. How big are your eyes? On what scale should watching happen or being watched? What upside-down writing might start to respond to your watching us, big-eye? To us in the hide (*Two-two-two-two! Too-too-too-too!*), you are the closest living thing to an all-seeing narrator.

To become the national symbol of the United States, what would need to happen? An alliance of the National Rifle Association and Buddhism, the New International and the National Security Agency? Even hunters on their blogs call you *mystical* and *fantastic*. But they kill you and kill you and kill you.

In my sleep the camouflage is so intense I can't tell if I am not crunching one or more with every pulsing trepidatious step I take.

Those in the language lobby regard the woodcock as a dime a dozen, pleased or indifferent that a man might comfortably kill twenty or thirty in a day's shooting. They don't say 'kill' but 'harvest': people not only shoot to kill but shoot to kill to cook to eat. Lurking somewhere back a ways is the spectre of J. P. Morgan and a necrotic fantasy of sharing the taste, tasting the shares of his partiality – and that of other so-called gilded tycoons – for roast woodcock. Here in the hide we see more clearly. The sky-dive of extinction is quicker and truer (*too-true-too-true!*). The International Union for Conservation of Nature classifies the American woodcock as 'least concern' status. Others are not so complacent or dismissive, at least acknowledging it as 'threatened'. The Audubon Society can only say that numbers are 'probably declining'. There is wild fluctuation in estimates of the annual number shot down. Some say 350,000; others say 540,000; still others say 1,100,000.

Despite this hopeless vagueness, a clear consensus prevails: the population has been declining over the last forty years at an annual rate of 1 per cent or 1.1 per cent. *Do the math*, as people in your enormous beautiful country say. *Do* do it: the extinction of *Rusticola minor* is happening faster than anyone in a photo blind might imagine. The internet clips of *peent! peent!* and of *jive, don't jive me!* and of winging singing zipping roding already look like reanimations of a lost world. Posthumous shoots for all!

The leaves are falling in the woods. In the least perceptible breeze they fall, visible in every direction, descending through the air, wafting wafers of paper, crafted, sere, yellow bats catching, floating stilly down. They make a kind of spoken bliss, the sound of dry rain. Deep in the woods the leaves are falling without remission, yellow to brown, tan to darkening gray.

O sky-drop! O crepuscular! *Too-too-too-too!*

Hide 15

At the end of life, as the dead ones gather like leaves
already trembling in autumn wind, and Charon looks
on with eyes glowing like coals, each one is cast off
from the shore at signals, like a bird at its call.

Writing his *Inferno*, Dante has recourse to an ornithomorphism, a simile from falconry (*like a bird at its call*), in order to
evoke the movement of humans into the underworld. They
tremble like autumn leaves. But in the event of passing away,
a person may be best evoked as a bird. Dante follows Virgil
who in the *Aeneid* calls the underworld Avernus. As Virgil
says: *facilis descensus Averno; noctes atque dies patet atrr
janua Dītis*. The descent is easy because the door is open
night and day. The word *Avernus* means *birdless*. The tale-
spinning of human afterlife relies at once on the avian ('like
a bird') and on its eerie absence (Avernus).

But what if there were, beneath Avernus, a second or
new underworld, inhabited not by humans but by birds,
not in a lower place but in an opening (day and night) on to
another sky?

Imagine the world as a hide. Such would be the local
focus, the cryptic locus, the focal hocus from which birds
observe us.

Hide 16

It's got inside. A door must have been left open. Unless it found some other way. It is all grays and whites, flecked jet, soft and fluffed up in the manner of an owl to appear two or three times natural size. Except it's more like a hundred. The ladder has fallen to the floor, a makeshift perch. It is difficult to conceive how so huge a creature entered. It scarcely makes sense to imagine that it has *become* the hide. But this is not about the imagination.

Each eye is larger than a plattered human head, blazing ochreous fire. Nothing else moves.

No one likes a bird inside. It makes them uncomfortable. The more people think about the bird that is inside that shouldn't be, the more in a flap. The bystander dislikes the trapped feelings displayed, the jittering, the rising panic, the heaving breast now so visible in its anguish. It mimes a play, in the sudden image of life without an exit, flying too close for the bystander to feel a bystander, unapproachable but tormented, untethered airless force of a live burial not only flitting, skimming by your face, catching something of your breath as it flies, flicking your ear or brushing a shoulder, then hitting a wall in its feeble errancy, in your culpable bystandoffishness as it drops from banging smack into the glass, flutters once or twice, then is still, and you wonder aghast with indecent relief whether it died on impact. But then it gathers itself into life once more, to desperationally launch and lump, crash and drop again. There is nothing that you can do, you think, for, while the door may have been propped fully ajar for the purpose of letting it escape, the bird won't see, it sees only the window, and you try to compute how many times it will collide and slide, flop grounded, before its heart gives way, wings break, or head staves in.

No one likes a bird inside. People don't even like to talk about it. It so quickly puts *the interior* in a spin. It is too much in your face. It agitates and makes an airy nothing of the heart. For bird-lovers it is an affliction. For those inclined to spiritual reckonings, it is too suggestive of the flight-failure of the soul.

But this is no ordinary bird or ordinary inside.

It might have left you in peace. You might have groped your way towards an exit, discreetly hugging the walls without a word, and not been noticed. Or it might have turned its head, first sight enough to make you cry aloud, the enormous double-fovea raging wells of golden fire, and below and in between, its bulky rhamphoid prising possession, sharp as a mailsack of razors. Even then you might have managed it, racing through a blind door into dateless night. But the attention's caught, and while these massive swivellers may entertain the fleeting thought of a bit of tickle, chase and flop, even allopreen, pursuant to anything of that nature it was always going to be so deliciously simple to go the whole human hog. Peckish can't be helped: the ever implementable impulse claws, prize talon show, ripping and pelleting it up all for the sheer shredding of jizz joy. Enough of you. You is done with.

Inside is over.

Hide 17

The last fortnight of S.B. Osmer's life was, in significant respects, also the worst. It began with the party at Seaford, an occasion marked for him at the time not so much by the deadly clifftop incident as by the maddening non-occurrence of going to bed with Lily Lynch. He was already more than ready to depart when the party-smashing news started coming in. Lily couldn't just leave with him, she said, she had to stay and support Portia. This seemed to him incomprehensible and frankly enraging. Weren't there plenty of other friends and relations around to do that? But in the end, sticking to a façade of coolness, he made his own way back to London, languishing in a sort of midsummer night's miasma. It was only with Lily's candid email, tringing through to his Bloomsbury computer screen from Sydney a couple of days afterwards, that he was obliged to clarify the exact nature of that afternoon and reconstruct the dismal reality of the proceedings.

There had been a show of fate. It had happened before. Indeed this was why he had previously elected, more than once, to be the first to announce the end. He had been painfully jilted at least twice and had by now grown confident about reading the signs and seeing such things coming. The Australian email was a cataclysm out of nowhere. To a thoughtful onlooker the indications of reticence and unease on

Lily's side might have been evident for weeks or even months. Stephen's extraordinary mental gifts were vouchsafed by a kind of unconscious insouciance. In the past this had given rise to obvious upsets, such as the messy evening with Lily and Adrian Franton at the Tate. Correspondingly, he had never thought to ask himself quite why he had a pathological dislike of Tolkien, or indeed why (given Lily's feelings on the matter) he persisted in remaining such a weasel-like carnivore. Such constrictions filtered and coloured the everyday lights of Stephen's perception. He had no sense of suppression and disavowal, but could fix or switch his mental focus, substituting one thing for another, without ever feeling the need to wonder why. Thus, without reflecting, he would idiosyncratically construct his version of that fateful afternoon at Cuckmere Haven farm. For him, the unpleasant death of his host was a good deal less to the forefront of his mind than a certain elided moment of one-upmanship.

On 19 September 1850 there was a 'Great Explosion' or series of explosions at Seaford Head. Fifty-five men from the Royal Sappers and Miners, headed up by Major-General Sir John Fox Burgoyne, Inspector of Fortifications, deployed three six-hundred-pound mines to blow up the chalk cliffs and thus create an effective dam for the tidal debris coming from the east that was rendering Seaford Bay too shallow to navigate. More than ten thousand people came into the town from London, Brighton, Eastbourne and elsewhere to witness this *scientific spectacle*, as the *Illustrated London News* termed it. Spectators gathered on the beach and crowded on to boats in Seaford Bay, watched over by the war-steamer H.M.S. *Widgeon*. As things turned out, it was just one more military fiasco: winter storms rapidly washed away the 380,000 tons of chalk that the explosions had brought down. Osmer had imagined that the woodlouse would know about the 9/19 spectacular, as it were, but strongly fancied that he would *not* know that one of the crowd at Seaford that afternoon was Charles Dickens, who (under the pseudonym 'Sir Valentine Saltear') wrote up an account in *Household Words*:

> *Presently there was a low, subterranean murmur, accompanied by a trembling of the whole sea-beach – sea and all; no burst of explosion; but the stupendous cliff was seen to crack, heave outward, and separate in many places half way down; the upper part then bowed itself forward, and almost at the same instant, the cliff seemed to bend out and break at one-third of the way from the base, till, like an old giant falling upon his knees, down it sank, pitching at the same time head foremost upon the beach with a tremendous, dull, echoless roar. A dense cloud of white dust and smoke instantly rose, and obscured the whole from sight.*

At least Stephen felt sure that the highfaluting literary theorist would not have any real working knowledge of this text. Historical research was just not the professor's forte. The moment presented itself. The glimpse of a passage opened up.

— *Oi!* yells Charon.

Stephen might have heard some such strange cry, whether in admonition or welcome. He was casually face to face with the host and on the very verge of broaching his *what the dickens* (as he liked to think of it). He envisaged demeaning the old woodlouse – once it was evident that he was indeed unaware of the Dickensian connection – by quoting a couple of lines from the splendid paragraph in question. He would invoke the *low, subterranean murmur, accompanied by a trembling of the whole sea-beach,* and then the line about the cliff as *an old giant falling upon his knees,* crashing headfirst *upon the beach with a tremendous, dull, echoless roar.*

— *That,* he would go on to say with a controlled but triumphant smile, is powerful writing. And Dickens could do it in his sleep!

But the instant passed. For reasons that were never clear to Stephen, the man in his sights abruptly moved off. Osmer felt cheated. And so it was principally this missed encounter that stood in, taking pole position in his mind, when he recalled that traumatic afternoon, confronted, as he so soon was, with the oddly unmanageable fact of a man who had effectively made a cuckold of him being killed before he could even think of it.

S.B. Osmer would remain a mystery to himself to the last. The midsummer night's cloud of unknowing in which he returned alone to town was not, after all, a total blindness. The miasma, had he been minded to consider it, would have furnished figures of some dim recognition. Still the cataclysm felt complete.

He began his two-week period of leave just as planned. He spent the first day reading and rereading, assembling his notes, books and other research material. By mid-afternoon he had created the new file, inserted the title and even drafted the first paragraph, when an innocuous electronic plink announced the arrival of an email. Until then he had been ignoring all incoming messages but he saw immediately that it came from her and opened it. The business of reading it took scarcely five minutes. The time, he noticed in the top corner of his screen, was 16:07. She must have sent it in the middle of the night. After that everything went – he didn't know – he had no words for it. He was scarcely aware of his actions. He stood up. He was sweating, but felt very cold. He saved the file. He didn't remember doing this but he must have done, as it was to be sitting there waiting for him, like a dog, as if nothing had happened, very early the following day when he opened his laptop and found himself returning to it.

He walked out of the little flat, departing the mews like a somnambulist. It was an oppressively warm afternoon. The air felt heavy with dust and pollen and people and speeding traffic. He was nearly hit by a taxi as he stepped out across Guildford Street and off along the edge of Coram's Fields. Next thing he was in the British Museum. He had no idea why. Usually, coming into the Great Court, he would think to approach the Reading Room, which he always associated with his beloved Marx. But this afternoon he took the opposite direction, straight into the gallery of ancient Egyptian sculptures. It was there, through the glass that enclosed the Rosetta Stone. He couldn't account for his movements but he was standing in front of a brown quartzite figure, about seventy centimetres high, situated just a few feet further off, out of the main thoroughfare. He had no sense how long he had been there, but now a voice close to his ear was politely informing him that the museum was closing and it was time to leave.

This became his routine. He wrote in the calm of the early dawn. Usually by early afternoon he could write no more, and then he might read for a while, until he would wander out and end up, towards closing time, in front of this same statue in Gallery 4. On the third day, he took to his wheels and made for Clerkenwell. He stood for some minutes in front of the large building containing her loft apartment. Outwardly he remained rigid, silent and expressionless and yet strangely, also, he felt a desire to sing. Then he cycled back to Great Russell Street and entered the museum. He must have forgotten the padlock, in fact, for when he came out the bike was missing. A fitting addition, he told himself, to the institution itself, Britain's greatest collection of worldwide thefts and other dubious acquisitions. If this had happened a week earlier he would have been incensed. But now he merely laughed. A younger man, approaching the racks to retrieve his own machine, looked at him askance and pointedly didn't ask what was funny.

No doubt he was experiencing a kind of breakdown. He thought a great deal in the first few days about writing or trying to call her. But he saw the futility of doing so. And at the same time he didn't know what to do with what she had told him. That second day, the Tuesday, he had called his parents and told his mother, trying hard not to sound as if he was in meltdown. He made up some story about being on his way to lunch with someone. She'd called him back and offered to cover the cost of a flight down under. It's OK, he told her evenly, I just have to come to terms with it. Those were the last words he said to his mother, or to anyone else close to him.

The night of reading Lily's letter he feared he wouldn't sleep, so opted for one of the pills Brian had given him to help with a bout of insomnia a few months previously. Stephen hated any sort of personal reliance on the pharmaceutical industry, legal or otherwise, but he went to see his GP a couple of days later and got a prescription for more. Everything seemed to assume a kind of dreamlike character. Most of the time he sat at the little mahogany desk, writing, or lay on the bed, reading, in his increasingly expensive bedsit. That was another decidedly mood-enhancing development. On the Thursday of that first week he received a letter from the landlord's agent notifying him of a rent-rise. It was the third increase in as many years. It made Stephen livid, livid with the landlord, but also livid with London, with what was happening to all the ordinary non-millionaire people who were trying to live and work there. When he did venture outside, either to pick up some shopping or walk over to Great Russell Street, things seemed to be happening at incongruous speeds. At one moment everything was in slow-motion, the next he was virtually knocked to the ground by some woman frantically making her way into Great Ormond Street Hospital or pigeons, clattering up from the lower steps of the British Museum, accelerated out of his peripheral vision in a way that made no sense. Noises became disorientating too. The streets had become louder. People appeared to be shouting a lot, as if the future were already happening.

He lost interest in food, eating only in the evening. He found himself drinking heavily, draining a bottle of Famous Grouse every day or so. But he kept to the routine and he kept writing.

For the final fortnight of S.B. Osmer's life was, in significant respects, also the best. He was writing, he saw, really for the first time. It was strange. He was on course. He was writing the words that the world needed. It was the calm of the early dawn, it was the sleeping pills or the blurry combination of that and the scotch, it was Lily's letter, Lily's lies, lying with Lily, candid Lily's can do did do, it was the livid rage that drove him on. He was possessed of a sort of manic, even demonic force. It was akin, he saw, to how Dickens must have felt writing *Drood*.

It was at the beginning of the second week that he started to see the ibises. He was walking across Russell Square

Gardens. It was another very warm afternoon. The grass was yellow beneath its patchwork of loving couples, homeless individuals, groups of tourists and solitary readers lucky enough to have secured shade beneath a tree or bush. There, by the fountain, at first he assumed it was a trick of the water in the sunlight, veiled by the pleasant silvery-white churning upward of water jets, stood an ibis. But then afterwards, back at the flat, he couldn't be sure, he told himself it couldn't be, it must have been a pigeon. Not that a pigeon looked like that, but he must have been dazzled by the heat, his state of mind, the trapunto sunlight trashing the fountain, and a nearby pigeon had somehow transposed itself.

The next day he had crossed the square without incident and visited the museum as usual. But then, as he was making his way home he saw, calm as a millpond, not just one but three white ibises, standing in the entrance to the Montague on the Gardens hotel. There was no doubting what they were, with their remarkable black bald heads and necks and long decurved beaks, their bodies plumply white with black-plumed rumps.

He was writing an essay that would meet with the enthusiastic accord of the vast majority of the world's population. He was simply putting into words what billions of others thought and felt. The sense of exhilaration was becoming too much.

He turned to the source of the request and smiled. He seemed to recognise the attendant.

— Would you please now make your way towards the exit?

He was standing in Gallery 4 again. He had to be there at the end of play, in that compelling space of closure when visitors were courteously steered out across the Great Court towards the main door. These attendants were always tired. It was a wearying enough job at any time, sitting, standing, shifting from one foot to another, one seat to another, one room to another, watching over the general public, checking that no one overstepped the mark, putting a stop to any touching or clambering about on artefacts, homing in on the tripping of any alarm. They worked long hours and it was, at the end of the day, a job with very little obvious satisfaction or reward. Did anyone, whether a first-time visitor to England or a more or less permanent and devoted Londoner like himself, ever just go over and *thank* them?

He was studying once again, mesmerised, the brown

quartzite figure. It was a statue of Thoth, dating from the Eighteenth Dynasty, around 1350 BCE. A baboon on its haunches, hands on knees, in posture tilted slightly back, suggesting promise or hope, open-faced but with eyes close together. It was a stunning object, down to the finest line of a mouth that conveyed a kind of magical reserve, beyond expression, its feathers a cascade of flight etched in metamorphosed sandstone.

Scarcely anyone else gave it so much as a glance. They would swarm and jostle around the glass enclosing the world-famous stone and simply not notice the figure standing behind it. Just occasionally someone walked up and stood beside him, but they soon moved on. They saw only a crabbed, nondescript little monkey on a plinth, with a timeworn face and no message. They did not observe the curling majesty of the tail resting on the ground at his right side. They did not see the penis, a little broken, a dilapidation doubtless occurring long before the museum purchased the figure from the collection of John Barker in 1833. They wouldn't bother to walk around and peruse the figure from behind, to witness the glory of its feathers, the subtly rampant poise and overpowering serenity, with the fidgeting turmoil of tourists beyond it, swirling around the triumph of Champollion. It reminded him of Dickens's ploy in having characters positioned with their backs to the fire, like Turveydrop in *Bleak House*: a sign of not seeing, a total failure of vision.

Stephen particularly relished the end of the week, when the museum stayed open until eight-thirty in the evening. The huge interior then acquired a new kind of dusky intimacy, as if beckoning him to slip away, conceal himself and spend the night amid all the unseen ancient things.

The second Friday marked his final visit. It had rained torrentially all day and, despite being the height of summer, a strange darkness had descended. It was all over London. Like diaphanous spilt ink, he thought. He understood that he had become an object of suspicion to the staff. He was shivering. He must have been, because a voice said, *Would you like a sweater or something, a quilt?* He had been scrutinising for one last time the hieroglyphics chiselled at the base, given in translation as: *He who cuts off the face of him who cut off your face.* The attendants had been shepherding people out for a good while now. Wave by wave those visiting the museum had fallen back, receding into the Great Court enclosing the Reading Room, then on towards the exit. But, as had happened every day since his first visit the previous week, Stephen Osmer felt unable to move. And now at last he witnessed it. The feathered baboon motioned. He saw it with its own eyes, motioning him. *There's no cause to write in fetters, forget all debt.* These were the words that the kindly black man said to him, now that the rest of the building had been vacated and he was the last of them all. He was trembling with the cold, in the shadowy immensity of the empty chamber, and this attendant, doubtless exhausted himself, showed the magnanimity and beneficence of asking, *Would you like a sweater or something, a quilt?*

Actually, the man was saying:

— You have to leave now, sir, or I'm calling in security.

Not yet ready to go home, but exhausted and still shivering, Stephen avoided the busier roads as far as he could. Wandering deserted wet dark streets under the great plane trees, he knew what was to happen. He knew that he would finish writing early the next morning and that would be it. He sensed the brand of an iron-hot conviction concerning the countless numbers of people to whose feelings of justice his writing would give voice. And he also sensed the uncontainable pleasure that finishing would produce. Without thinking he began whistling softly to himself. He looked up. In a now clear sky the moon had appeared. Becoming apparent one by one, in the tops of the plane trees overhead, was a group, a crowd, a wedge, a congregation, ibis after ibis, standing about in the high branches. And then one of them took to the air. As it unfurled and curled in its huge black-tipped white wings, its flight eerily resembled the movement, but speeded up, of a giant ray in the depths of the ocean. It was practically the size of himself.

Copyright Acknowledgements

Extract from 'Anecdote of the Jar', from *Collected Poems* © Estate of Wallace Stevens and reproduced with permission of Faber & Faber Ltd.

Extract from 'Blackberrying', from *Collected Poems* © Estate of Sylvia Plath and reproduced with permission of Faber & Faber Ltd.

Thanks to Tim Birkhead for kind permission to quote from *Bird Sense: What It's Like to Be a Bird* (London: Bloomsbury, 2012).

Thanks to Kim Todd for kind permission to quote from *Sparrow* (London: Reaktion Books, 2012).

Thanks to John Marzluff for kind permission to quote from John Marzluff and Tony Angell, *Gifts of the Crow: How Perception, Emotion, and Thought Allow Smart Birds to Behave Like Humans* (New York: Simon and Schuster, 2012).

Thanks to Tim Dee for kind permission to quote from *The Running Sky: A Birdwatching Life* (London: Vintage, 2009).

Thanks to Jeremy Mynott for kind permission to quote from *Birdscapes: Birds in Our Imagination and Experience* (Princeton: Princeton University Press, 2009).

Thanks to James Trollope for kind permission to reproduce 'Rough Sea' (Splash Point) by Eric Slater (1896–1963), copyright © James Trollope. *www.ericslater.co.uk*.

myriad

Sign up to our mailing list at
www.myriadeditions.com
Follow us on Facebook and Twitter

About the author

Nicholas Royle is a Professor of English at the University of Sussex and lives in Seaford. He has written numerous books on literature and literary theory, including *Telepathy and Literature, E. M. Forster, The Uncanny, Veering: A Theory of Literature* and the influential textbook *An Introduction to Literature, Criticism and Theory* (with Andrew Bennett). His first novel, *Quilt*, was published in 2010.